KT-146-870

...won Roma...
the National Reade...
Golden Quill, and Golde...

...her husband and three ve...
Diane loves to hear from readers a...
website at: http://dianegaston.com

Regency Secrets

Regency Secrets:

The Governess
Swap

DIANE GASTON

MILLS & BOON

All rights reserved including the right of reproduction in whole or in part in any form. This edition is published by arrangement with Harlequin Enterprises ULC.

This is a work of fiction. Names, characters, places, locations and incidents are purely fictional and bear no relationship to any real life individuals, living or dead, or to any actual places, business establishments, locations, events or incidents. Any resemblance is entirely coincidental.

This book is sold subject to the condition that it shall not, by way of trade or otherwise, be lent, resold, hired out or otherwise circulated without the prior consent of the publisher in any form of binding or cover other than that in which it is published and without a similar condition including this condition being imposed on the subsequent purchaser.

® and TM are trademarks owned and used by the trademark owner and/or its licensee. Trademarks marked with ® are registered with the United Kingdom Patent Office and/or the Office for Harmonisation in the Internal Market and in other countries.

First Published in Great Britain 2022
By Mills & Boon, an imprint of HarperCollins*Publishers*
1 London Bridge Street, London, SE1 9GF

www.harpercollins.co.uk

HarperCollins*Publishers*
1st Floor, Watermarque Building,
Ringsend Road, Dublin 4, Ireland

REGENCY SECRETS: THE GOVERNESS SWAP © 2022
HARLEQUIN ENTERPRISES ULC

A Lady Becomes a Governess © 2018 Diane Perkins
Shipwrecked with the Captain © 2019 Diane Perkins

ISBN: 978-0-263-30574-6

MIX
Paper from
responsible sources
FSC
www.fsc.org
FSC™ C007454

This book is produced from independently certified FSC™ paper to ensure responsible forest management.

For more information visit: www.harpercollins.co.uk/green

Printed and Bound in Spain using 100% Renewable electricity at CPI Black Print, Barcelona

A LADY BECOMES
A GOVERNESS

To my dear friend Kristine Hughes Patrone,

with whom I've shared the delights of many
a trip to England.

Chapter One

June 1816

Lady Rebecca Pierce trailed behind the seaman carrying her portmanteau on his shoulder and the dour-faced maid who was her companion for this undesired trip sailing across the Irish Sea to England to marry a man she loathed.

The seaman led them across the deck, following other passengers, a woman with children, a gentleman, a tradesman. The seaman took them through the companionway and down the steps to the cabins below.

Rebecca inhaled the scent of brine that permeated the ship's wood. Must she be stuck breathing that sour mockery of fresh sea air for the entire journey? Would Nolan, the maid her half-brother, the Earl of Keneagle, hired to accompany her, at least allow her to spend some time on deck? She loved standing at the bow of a ship, feeling the sea breeze on her face and watching the vessel cut through the inky water.

She slowed her step, simply to annoy the woman. Nolan's duty was to make certain Rebecca fulfilled the nuptials her brother had arranged for her—forced on her—but that did not mean Nolan could control her every move.

Rebecca glanced behind her. But there was no escaping the ship, not when it was anchored in the middle of the harbour. Even if she could swim the distance to shore, her brother had also arranged it that she would have nothing unless she married Lord Stonecroft.

'Lady Rebecca!' a strident voice called. Nolan, of course. 'Hurry. Your cabin is ready.'

Her lips thinned and she simply stopped.

'Lady Rebecca!' Nolan had walked back to get her.

Reluctantly—and slowly—Rebecca followed her to the cabin.

In her cabin, Rebecca sat at the small table and chairs that were securely fastened to the floor. Through a small porthole she watched the ship leave the harbour. There was a good wind. No doubt they would reach England in the morning.

In the open sea, the water grew choppy and the ship heaved and swayed.

'Oh,' Nolan moaned, clasping her stomach. She dropped into the seat across from Rebecca. 'I'm going to be sick.'

Not in her cabin, thought Rebecca. 'Come.' She rose and helped Nolan to her feet. 'I'll take you to your cabin. You can rest there.'

Nolan had a small cabin near Rebecca's, nothing more than a berth and, luckily, a bucket. She helped Nolan into bed.

'Oh,' Nolan moaned again. The older woman had turned pale. She rolled over and faced the wall.

'Can I get you anything?' Rebecca asked. It was hard not to feel sympathy for the woman. 'Eating something will help seasickness.'

Nolan thrashed in the bed. 'No food. No food. Leave me alone.'

Rebecca placed the bucket next to the berth. 'There is a bucket, if you need it. I will check on you later.'

'No,' wailed Nolan. 'Leave me alone.'

With pleasure, thought Rebecca.

But she would check on the maid none the less. She'd never experienced seasickness herself, but in her trips across the Irish Sea during her years in school, she'd witnessed many others who had endured such misery.

She walked into the passageway and could not help feeling as if a weight had been lifted off her shoulders. She was free to do as she wished—within the confines of the ship, at least. It was worth something.

She quickly found her sea legs and easily walked to the companionway. Free of Nolan, this was the perfect time to go on deck and enjoy what she could of the voyage.

The hatch opened and a young woman descended the stairs. She wore a hooded cape that was damp and smelled of the sea.

Rebecca waited. There was only room for one on the stairs.

Head down, the woman passed Rebecca and Rebecca started up the stairs.

'Were you planning to go on deck, miss?' the woman asked. 'The midshipman sent me down.'

Rebecca turned.

The woman pulled the hood of the cloak off her head. 'Rough seas—' Her eyes widened.

Rebecca gasped.

This woman had her same pale hazel eyes, her nose and lips, her nondescript brown hair. She was of a similar height and figure and age. Her cloak was even a similar shade of grey.

Rebecca was looking in a mirror. Except her mirror

image wore her hair in a simple style and her dress was a drab brown.

When Rebecca managed to breathe again, she shook her head. 'You look like me!'

Her eyes must be deceiving her. She blinked twice, but her mirror image remained.

The other woman laughed nervously. 'I—I do not know what to say.'

'Neither do I.' What did one say to one's exact likeness?

'It is most unsettling.' The young woman straightened. 'But forgive my manners. Allow me to present myself. I am Miss Tilson. A governess. Nobody you would know.'

Rebecca extended her hand. 'Lady Rebecca Pierce. It is a pleasure to meet you.' She almost laughed. 'To meet me.'

Miss Tilson accepted her handshake.

The hatch opened and a gentleman descended.

They moved to one side so he could walk by them. Miss Tilson turned away from him.

He glanced at them as he passed. 'You ladies should stay in your cabins. The sea is rough. Do not fear. A seaman will bring your meal to you.'

Had he noticed their resemblance to each other?

Rebecca and Miss Tilson did not speak until he disappeared into one of the cabins near the end of the corridor.

'We should do as he says, I suppose.' Miss Tilson opened a door to a space as tiny as Nolan's. 'My cabin is here.'

'I would like to speak with you more,' Rebecca said hurriedly, before Miss Tilson left her. 'I am quite alone. My maid suffers the *mal de mer* and remains in her cabin.'

The young woman lowered her gaze. 'The sea has never bothered me. I suppose I have a strong constitution that way.'

As did Rebecca.

'Will you talk with me?' Rebecca's pulse quickened with excitement. 'Maybe there is some sense to make of this.' She made a vague gesture in the air between them.

Miss Tilson gazed into her cabin. 'You are welcome to come in, but there is very little room.'

'Come to my cabin, then,' Rebecca said. 'We may be comfortable there.'

The two women settled in Rebecca's cabin, seating themselves across from each other at the small table. Through the small porthole choppy waves spewed white foam.

Rebecca bit her tongue. Instead of blurting out *Why do you look like me?* she asked, 'Where are you bound, Miss Tilson?'

'To a family in the Lake District. Not a family, precisely. Two little girls whose parents were killed in an accident. They are in the care of their uncle now, the new Viscount Brookmore.'

'How sad.' Rebecca had been nearly grown when she lost her parents to illness.

'And you, Lady Rebecca? Where are you bound?' Miss Tilson spoke without the hint of an Irish brogue, Rebecca noticed. As did Rebecca. She'd lost her accent in a Reading boarding school.

'To London,' she replied.

'London!' Miss Tilson smiled. 'How exciting. I was there once. It was so…vital.'

'Vital, indeed.' Except Rebecca had no wish to go there. London would be a prison to her. With Lord Stonecroft.

Miss Tilson's eyes—so like her own—narrowed. 'You sound as if you do not wish to go.'

Rebecca met her gaze. 'I do not. I travel there to be married.'

The young woman's brows rose. 'Married?'

Rebecca waved a hand. 'It is an arranged marriage. My brother's idea.'

'And you do not wish to marry this man?'

'Not at all.' She straightened in her chair. Marrying Stonecroft was the last thing she wished to talk about. 'May I change the subject?'

Miss Tilson blinked. 'Forgive me. I did not mean to pry.'

Rebecca shrugged. 'Perhaps I will tell you the whole story later.' She leaned forward. 'For now I am bursting with questions. Why do we look alike? How can this be? Are we related somehow?'

They traded stories of parentage and lineage, but nothing seemed to connect them. Miss Tilson's family had been gentry. Her mother died giving birth to her and her overwhelmed and grieving father put her in the care of nurses and governesses and finally to school in Bristol when her father died, leaving her to fend for herself. She'd come to Ireland to be a governess and was now on her way to a new position.

Rebecca, on the other hand, was the daughter of an English earl whose estate was in Ireland, but she'd spent much of her life in England, in that boarding school in Reading.

Rebecca blew out an exasperated breath. 'We are no closer to understanding this. We are not related—'

'But we look alike,' Miss Tilson finished for her. 'An unexpected coincidence?'

There was a mirror affixed to the wall. They stood and gazed into it.

'We are not identical,' Miss Tilson observed. 'Look.'

Rebecca's two front teeth were slightly more prominent, her eyebrows more arched, her eyes a bit wider.

'No one would notice unless we were standing next to each other,' Miss Tilson added.

'Our clothes set us apart. That is for certain.' Rebecca

swung away from the mirror to face Miss Tilson instead of her image. 'If you wore my clothes, I'd wager anyone would take you for me.'

'I cannot imagine wearing fine clothes like yours.' Her likeness sighed.

'You must wear them then,' Rebecca said impulsively. 'Let us change clothes and impersonate each other for the voyage. It will be a great lark. We will see if anyone notices.'

Miss Tilson shook her head. 'Your clothes are too fine for you to give up. Mine are plain.'

'Precisely. But I believe people pay more attention to dress than to other aspects of one's appearance. Perhaps even more than one's character. In any event, I think there is nothing undesirable about wearing a simple dress.'

The other woman touched the fine vigonia wool of Rebecca's travelling dress. 'I confess, I would love to wear a gown like this.'

'Then you shall!' Rebecca turned her back to her. 'Unbutton me.'

They undressed down to their shifts and traded dresses, acting as each other's maids. Miss Tilson pulled Rebecca's hair into a simple knot at the back of her head. Rebecca placed Miss Tilson's hair—it even felt like her own—high on her head and arranged curling tendrils around her face.

They checked their images in the mirror again and laughed.

There was a rap at the door.

Rebecca grinned. 'Answer the door as me.'

Miss Tilson blanched. 'I could not.'

Rebecca gave her a little shove. 'Of course you can!'

Miss Tilson straightened into a more regal bearing and opened the door. Rebecca returned to her seat at the table.

The seaman who'd warned them to stay in their cabins

balanced a tray as the boat continued to pitch. 'Some refreshment, m'lady,' he said to Miss Tilson.

Miss Tilson lifted her chin. 'Thank you.'

Rebecca stole one quick glance at the seaman before averting her face.

Miss Tilson gestured to Rebecca. 'Miss Tilson passes the time with me. Will you bring her food here for her?'

'That I will, miss.' The crewman stepped into the cabin and placed the tray on the table. He returned a moment later with two more trays. 'Your maid, miss?'

Miss Tilson's gaze darted quickly to Rebecca, who pretended not to notice. The governess finally answered, 'My—my maid is resting. Perhaps you might leave her tray here, as well? We will tend to her.'

The seaman bowed. 'Very good, miss.' He placed both trays on the table.

When he left, Rebecca glanced up and they stared wide-eyed at each other.

'I was afraid he would notice we look alike,' Rebecca said. 'He must have glimpsed me when he left the trays.'

Miss Tilson shook her head. 'A governess is not important enough to notice, my lady.'

Their trays each held two slices of bread, some cheese and a tankard of ale with a cover on it. The two women continued to talk as they ate and Rebecca felt as if they'd known each other for ages.

As if they were sisters, although they clearly were not.

'I believe we should call each other by our given names,' Rebecca said. 'It seems silly to be formal to one's mirror image.'

Miss Tilson fluttered her lashes shyly. 'If you desire it… Rebecca. Then I am Claire to you.'

'Claire!' Rebecca felt as if she were conversing with a sister.

Miss Tilson—Claire—must have felt a similar ease. 'Might you tell me now why you do not wish to be married?' She gave Rebecca a daring look. 'Now that we are no longer formal?'

Rebecca stared into her tankard of ale which she held with both hands to keep it from spilling.

How could she explain?

'A woman gives up everything by marrying,' she said. 'Any wealth or property she might have. Any right to decide for herself what she wishes to do. If I am to give up everything, it should be to a man who loves me and respects me and will not confine me.'

Claire's brows rose. 'And this man?'

Rebecca grimaced. 'I met him only once. He merely wished to ensure himself I could produce an heir.'

Claire did not look the least dismayed by this information. 'But of course he would want an heir. Especially if he has a title and property.'

'He does.' Rebecca tapped her pewter tankard with her fingernail.

'Is the gentleman wealthy enough to provide for you?' Claire asked.

'He is said to be prosperous,' she replied. 'He must be, because he is willing to marry me with a mere pittance for a dowry.'

Claire nodded approvingly. 'Will you tell me who he is?'

Rebecca could see no reason not to. 'Lord Stonecroft.'

Claire gave her an enquiring look.

'Baron Stonecroft of Gillford.'

'Ah.' A look of understanding came over Claire's face. 'You were hoping for a higher title than baron. I mean, you said you are the daughter of an earl.'

Rebecca sniffed. 'I care nothing for that.'

Claire looked surprised. 'Did he seem like a cruel man, then? Is that your objection?'

Not cruel.

Indifferent.

Rebecca sighed. 'I do not believe there is precisely anything to object to in him. I simply do not wish to marry him.'

'Refuse, then.' Claire spoke this like a dare.

Oh, Rebecca would love to refuse. 'My brother—my half-brother—says I am too much of a burden for him to wait for me to find a husband I would like. I've refused every offer he's arranged for me. He has made certain I will be turned out without a penny if I do not marry Lord Stonecroft.' Her face heated at the memory of her brother railing at her. 'I've no doubt he means what he says.' Still, her mind whirled with ways she might avoid this marriage without being turned out into the streets.

None were viable, however.

Claire looked sympathetic. 'How sad. One would hope a brother would understand. Family should understand, should they not?'

Rebecca regarded her curiously. 'Do you have any brothers or sisters? Any family at all?'

Claire shook her head. 'I am alone in the world. Any relations are too distant to be concerned with me.'

More reason to feel a kinship towards her. 'My parents are gone,' Rebecca confided. 'And my brother might as well be dead. He said he never wishes to see me again. Ever. Even if he visits England. He made that very clear.'

Her brother had always resented her. He'd resented her mother, as well. Possibly because their father had loved her mother better than either his son or daughter.

They fell silent.

Claire finally spoke and with a resolved tone. 'I think

you are fortunate to marry, Lady Rebecca—Rebecca. You have little money or property, correct? You can only gain by marrying. You'll gain a home of your own to manage. Children of your own. Comfort and security. Even status and a respectable position in society.'

Rebecca glanced away.

All that was true. But Lord Stonecroft had only cared that she was young and healthy enough to breed and apparently tolerable to look at. He'd made no effort to *know* her. How was she to endure that sort of emotional wasteland? How was she to tolerate life with such a man?

Claire must have sensed Rebecca's desolation. Her expression turned consoling. 'Perhaps it will not be so onerous to be Lady Stonecroft.'

Rebecca managed a polite smile. 'Perhaps not.'

As if by mutual agreement she and Claire began talking of other things. Books. Plays. Art. Music. From time to time Claire, pretending to be Rebecca, checked on Nolan, who never seemed to question who she was, to Rebecca's delight.

Rebecca and Claire talked until night fell, turning the churning sea inky black.

Claire stood. 'I should return to my cabin so you might get some sleep. I'll help you out of your dress, if you help me out of this lovely gown.'

Rebecca rose and let her lookalike untie and loosen the laces at the back of the plain dress she'd worn most of the voyage. What a shame. She'd quite enjoyed not being herself, playing a woman whose life seemed so much simpler, so much within her own control.

She turned to face Claire. 'Let us see how far we can carry this masquerade. You be me tonight. Sleep in my nightclothes, in this bed. And I will continue being you.'

The young woman looked stricken. 'I cannot allow you to be closeted in that tiny berth they gave me!'

'Why not?' Rebecca countered. 'It will be an adventure for me. And you will have the comfort of this cabin as a treat. When Nolan enters in the morning, we shall discover if she still believes you are me.'

Rebecca pulled out her nightdress, made of the softest of muslin. 'Here.'

Miss Tilson fingered the fine cloth of the nightdress. 'Perhaps. If you desire this.'

'I do desire it,' Rebecca insisted, helping Miss Tilson out of her dress. 'I desire it very much.'

In the morning the sea became even more restless. The sky turned even more ominous shades of grey. Rebecca convinced Claire to continue to wear her clothes and impersonate her. Nolan, who remained abed, sick as ever, and the few seamen who attended them still did not guess that Claire masqueraded as Rebecca. Even with the two ladies together, the seamen never seemed to notice how alike they were.

The seamen were rushed and worried, however. There was a storm brewing, the seamen said. The ladies must remain below.

As the day progressed, Rebecca and Claire talked more about the weather than about their lives. They left the cabin rarely only to check on Nolan, who suffered so much she did not even react when Rebecca, dressed as the governess, attended her.

In the late afternoon, the storm broke, tossing the packet boat even more violently than before.

'We should be nearing the coast,' Rebecca said.

'If the ship can even sail in this.' Claire's face—her identical face—paled in fear.

Suddenly shouts and pounding feet sounded from above them, then a loud crack and a thud that shook the boards over their heads. The two women grasped each other's hands. Their masquerade became unimportant as the wind and sea pitched the ship so constantly that they could not change back into their own clothing.

The gentleman who'd passed them the day before opened the door without knocking. 'Come above,' he demanded in a voice they didn't dare disobey. 'We must abandon ship. Bring nothing.'

Rebecca defied him, grabbing her reticule containing all her money. When they reached the stairs, she shoved the reticule into Claire's hands. 'Here. Take this. I'll be right behind you. I'm going to get Nolan.'

Claire hung the reticule on her wrist.

'Miss!' the gentleman cried. 'We must leave now.'

'I will be right behind you,' she called over her shoulder.

Rebecca rushed to Nolan's cabin. A seaman was at Nolan's door. He turned to Rebecca. 'She refuses to come,' the man shouted. 'Hurry! We must get above.'

Rebecca pushed past him and ran to her maid. 'Nolan! Come with me.'

The older woman recoiled, rolling over and huddling against the wall. 'No. Sick. Leave me alone.'

'Come, miss!' the crewman cried. 'There is no time to waste!'

'I cannot leave her!' she cried.

He dragged her away from Nolan's door, practically carrying her to the steps of the companionway.

On deck, rain poured as if from buckets, obscuring the chaos Rebecca found above. The mast had splintered in two and lay like a fallen tree on the deck, ropes and sails tangled around it.

'To the boats!' the seaman shouted, running ahead.

She followed him, catching sight of Claire and the gentleman at the railing. The ship dipped suddenly and a wave washed over the deck. Rebecca had only a second to grab hold of a rope or be carried in its ebb. When the wave passed and she looked up, Miss Tilson and the gentleman had disappeared.

Her escort seized her arm. 'Come, miss. No time to waste.'

He pulled her along with him to the side of the ship where other passengers and crew were climbing into a rowing boat that had been lowered over the side. Claire was not among them. Rebecca glanced out to sea, but Claire had vanished. Nolan, Claire and the gentleman were lost.

There was no time for emotion. The crew lifted her over the side as the rowing boat bobbed up and down beneath her. Only with luck did her feet connect with the wood of the boat's bottom.

The boat filled quickly. Rebecca huddled next to a woman clutching her two children. Beneath their feet was at least an inch of water and more pouring from the sky. Somehow the sailors rowed the boat away from the packet. Through the darkness and rain, a shadow of coastline was visible. Rebecca kept her eyes riveted on it, watching it come slowly closer. Almost in reach.

From behind her a woman screamed.

Rebecca swivelled around to see the packet boat crash against the rocks. At that same moment the rowing boat hit something and tipped.

Rebecca plunged into icy water.

Chapter Two

Garret Brookmore, the new Viscount Brookmore, received word of the shipwreck off the coast of Moelfre while he waited in an inn in Holyhead. This was the packet he was to meet, the one on which the governess was to arrive. There were survivors of the wreck, he was told, and Garret felt obligated to travel to Moelfre to see if Miss Claire Tilson was one of them.

None of this was remotely within his experience. A year ago he'd been in Brussels with his regiment awaiting what became the Battle of Waterloo. For the past ten years he'd battled the French. Then word came that his brother and his brother's wife had been killed in a carriage accident and he needed to return to England to inherit his brother's title and all the new responsibilities that accompanied it, responsibilities over which he had no preparation. His older brother had been groomed from birth to be the Viscount. John was the family's fair-haired boy, able to do no wrong in their father's eyes, whereas not much was expected of Garret so he'd always been bound for the army.

Now the son from whom the family expected little had an estate to run, Parliament to attend and two little girls, his orphaned nieces, to tend to. Pamela and Ellen, only nine and seven, had been securely in the care of their governess, a long-time retainer of their mother's family, but fate had not finished being cruel. That woman, too, died.

How much could two little girls take? Their mother. Their father. Their governess. Left with a strange uncle whose heart remained with his regiment. Garret had witnessed thousands of deaths, but these seemed the cruellest.

When notified that his nieces' governess had died, Garret had been in London attempting to meet society's expectations of a viscount. He contacted an agency in town to hire a new governess and left his obligations there to travel back to Westmorland to the family's principal estate, to see to his nieces and await the new governess. He'd barely arrived at Brookmore when the agency sent word to expect Miss Tilson to arrive in Holyhead from Ireland.

What if Miss Tilson had drowned in this shipwreck, though? What was Garret to tell the little girls? That another person who was supposed to care for them had died?

He rode to Moelfre and enquired where the shipwreck survivors might be found. He was directed to the Pheasant Inn, a place bustling with activity.

The innkeeper greeted him. 'Welcome. Do you seek a room?'

'I am looking for a survivor of the shipwreck,' Garret responded.

The man frowned and shook his head. 'Such a tragedy. Almost forty people lost, I'm afraid. Only eleven made it through.'

That did not sound hopeful. 'I am looking for Miss Tilson. Miss Claire Tilson.'

The innkeeper broke into a smile. 'Ah, Miss Tilson! Yes. Yes. She is here.'

Relief washed through Garret. 'May I see her?'

'Of course.' The innkeeper gestured for him to follow. He followed the man up two sets of stairs. 'She's been feverish since the rescue. Some men pulled her from the water, we were told. She seemed better today, our maid said. Might not be awake.'

'I understand.'

The innkeeper knocked and a maid answered. 'Someone to see Miss Tilson.'

The woman smiled and opened the door wider. Neither she nor the innkeeper asked who he was.

He approached the bed and gazed down in surprise. He'd expected an elderly woman like the previous governess. Miss Tilson hardly looked old enough to be out of the schoolroom herself. Her skin was smooth and flawless; her features strong, not delicate. Her hair, the colour of Kentish cobnuts, fell loose over the white pillow. Would her face fulfil the promise of character shown in her repose? He was intrigued.

He looked over at the innkeeper. 'I do need a room.'

'Yes, sir, I can accommodate you,' the man answered. 'Would you like to come with me now? I will show you to the room.'

Now that he'd found Miss Tilson, he was reluctant to leave her. 'I will stay until she wakes up. So she knows I am here.'

She was bound to experience distress, waking in a strange place, after nearly drowning.

The innkeeper reached for Garret's valise. 'I'll take this to the room and come back with your key, if you like.'

Garret nodded his thanks.

The maid spoke up. 'May I leave, sir? I am very hungry. May I get food?'

The innkeeper glanced towards Garret.

'I have no objection.' Far be it from Garret to deny a hungry girl, so he wound up alone, seated at the bedside of a beauty he did not know, but for whom he was now responsible.

An hour passed, an hour spent with swirling thoughts of all he must remember to do, of all he'd learned needed his attention at the estate and even more demands in London and how much he wished he were simply marching with his men on some foreign road bound for the next battle. He missed his men. Worried about how they were faring. The war was over. Napoleon was on St Helena. Regiments were disbanding.

What was the use of wishing for what could not be? Even if his brother had not died, his army life would have changed drastically.

He had to admit he'd travelled to Holyhead mostly to give himself time away from these duties and regrets. Time to think. He could have easily sent a servant to escort her to the estate.

He rose when the innkeeper brought his key. As he settled back in the chair next to the bed, Miss Tilson's eyes—unexpectedly hazel—fluttered open.

'Where?' she managed, her voice cracking.

He poured her a glass of water from a pitcher on the bed table. 'You are safe, Miss Tilson,' he told her. 'You are at an inn in Moelfre.'

Her brow creased as if she were puzzled. 'Miss Tilson,' she whispered. 'Claire.'

He helped her to sit and held the glass as she drank. 'I am Lord Brookmore.' It still sounded strange on his tongue. In his mind Brookmore was still his brother. 'Your employer.'

She stared at him a long time and it seemed as if he

could see a range of emotions flit through her eyes. Puzzlement, horror, grief and, finally, understanding.

Rebecca's heart pounded in her chest. This was not another fever-filled vision, but a real man touching her, helping her drink. Once she quenched her considerable thirst, she became acutely aware that she wore only a thin nightdress. From where? From whom? Had even the clothes she'd worn—Claire Tilson's clothes—been lost? Her throat tightened again, but this time from grief. Claire. Nolan. All those poor people.

She shrank away from the man and he sat back in his chair, placing the glass on the side table.

He was Claire's new employer, he'd said, and he thought she was the poor governess who'd been swept away by that killing wave. He did not look like a man who would hire a governess. His rugged face and muscular frame made him look untamed. His piercing blue eyes seemed a thin shield against painful remembrances. Dark hair, longer than fashionable, was as windswept as a man who'd galloped over fields on a wild stallion. The shadow of a beard covering a strong jaw gave him a rakish air.

Her eyes darted around the room. Why was such a man alone with her? She certainly had never before been alone with a man in her bedchamber, in her night clothes.

'Why—?' Her throat closed again and she swallowed. 'Why are you here?'

His blue eyes fixed on her. 'I waited at Holyhead. News came of the shipwreck so I rode here to see if you'd… survived.'

The shipwreck. Again she watched the wave consume Claire. Again she felt the rowing boat smash against rocks and plunge her into the water.

She shivered with the memory and he rose again, this

time to wrap a blanket around her shoulders. Her skin heated at his touch.

She looked up into his face. 'How many? How many survived?'

'Eleven, the innkeeper said,' he replied.

Only ten others? What about the woman and her two children? Were they swept out to sea like Claire and the gentleman with her? Her eyes stung with tears.

'My God.' She dropped her face into her hands and sobbed.

She could feel him staring at her, even though he was still and silent. How humiliating to become so discomposed in front of this stranger. It was so unlike her.

She wrested some control, finally lifting her head and taking deep breaths.

Without speaking, he pulled a handkerchief from his breast pocket and handed it to her. She wiped her tear-soaked face.

The handkerchief was still warm from his body.

'Thank you.' She took another deep breath and started to return the now soaked handkerchief. She pulled it back, laughing drily. 'I—I will have it laundered.'

What a silly thing to say. She had no means of getting it laundered. She had no money. No clothes. Nothing.

She, of course, could identify herself. Send word to London of her predicament. To Lord Stonecroft. Who else was there to help her in London? But why would she want to ask for his help when she wanted to escape him? Being his brood mare seemed even worse than drowning.

Lord Brookmore sat back in his chair again, his face averted.

She should tell him she wasn't Claire Tilson, that she saw Claire washed overboard.

Oh, why had Claire drowned and not her? Claire had

independence. She had work for which she earned her own money and she also had the hope of finding a man to love her some day. Claire would have fared so much better than Rebecca, who had nothing to look forward to but a prison of a marriage. Why could fate not have let them trade places in death as easily as they'd worn each other's clothes?

She stole another glance at Lord Brookmore and her heart quickened.

He thought she was Claire. Perhaps she was the only one who knew she was really Lady Rebecca Pierce, doomed to marry Lord Stonecroft.

She could not die in the watery depths instead of Claire. She'd have been willing to do so. But she could trade places with Claire now. She could live Claire's life for her.

Escape her own life.

Lord Stonecroft would not mourn her; he'd merely be annoyed that he must search for another brood mare to marry. Her brother would not mourn her. He'd get to keep her dowry. She could not sacrifice her life instead of Claire's, but she could become Claire.

Guilt pricked at her. She'd be deceiving this very handsome man. What a way to repay his kindness.

He did need a governess, though, did he not? She could be a governess. How hard could that be? It would help him, would it not?

'I—I had a fever, I think,' she said. 'I don't remember much except—' Except plunging into churning, cold water and thinking she would die. 'Except the wreck.'

His eyes fixed on her again. 'I know nothing more than you were saved and you were ill.'

'Am I still to be your nieces' governess?' Will he accept her as Claire? she meant.

'If you feel up to the task, yes.' His voice was stiff and

formal and so deep she felt the timbre of it as well as hearing it. 'If you need a long recuperation—'

'I am well enough.' She sat up straighter as if to prove it. 'I am quite recuperated.'

'Good.' He stood. 'I will send for the maid and some food, if you are hungry.'

She didn't really know if she was hungry, but the mention of food made her stomach growl. 'Thank you, sir.'

He nodded. 'We can travel to Brookmore House as early as tomorrow, if you are able.'

Better to leave soon, although, out of ten other survivors, who was likely to know she was not Claire? Someone must have already identified her as such. 'I will be ready for travel tomorrow. I am certain.'

He nodded. 'Very good. Anything you need, Miss Tilson, just ask for it. I will see that it is provided to you.'

She glanced down at herself. She needed everything! Lady Rebecca would not hesitate to enumerate each necessary item, but she could not imagine Claire doing so.

'Thank you, sir,' she murmured instead.

'I will take my leave, then.' He inclined his head. 'Miss Tilson.'

'My lord,' she responded.

After he walked out the door she threw off the covers and climbed out of bed, suddenly restless. The wood floor was cold beneath her bare feet and her legs were weak. She made her way to the window and looked down upon a village street, its whitewashed buildings glowing in the waning light of early evening. Wagons and carriages rumbled by and villagers hurried here and there as if this day was like any other.

Her days would never be the same, though. A *frisson* of trepidation rushed up her spine. She was about to become a whole new person.

She rubbed her arms and smelled the faint scent of the sea on her skin. She did not want to smell the sea! She wanted to banish the memory of plunging into the water where so many others died.

There was a rap at the door and a maid entered, carrying a tray. The scent of stew and cheese and ale seemed to affirm her choice of life. A new life.

'Oh, you are up, miss,' the maid said. 'Are you feeling better? The gentleman gave me some coins and said to bring you food and whatever you need.'

Rebecca seated herself at a chair next to a small table. 'I am much better. I am afraid I was too feverish—what is your name?'

'I'm Betty, miss.' The maid put the tray of food on the table. 'What else might I bring you?'

Dare she ask? She did dare, because she needed to feel renewed. 'I would love a bath, Betty.'

The maid smiled. 'A bath you shall have then, miss.'

'And I will need some clothes.'

By the next morning, Rebecca was not only clean and well fed, but also clothed.

The maid, Betty, brought her undergarments and a dress. 'His lordship said to find you clothes and so I did,' she'd said. 'The ones you wore before were ruined.'

Claire's clothes.

Betty helped her into the simple shift, a corset that fit tolerably well and a plain dress, not unlike the one Betty herself wore. The stockings looked newly purchased and the shoes, well-worn half-boots, were only slightly too big. Included in the bundle of clothes had been a new brush and comb, as well as a set of hairpins. Betty helped pull her hair back, as Claire had done.

Rebecca looked at herself in the mirror, but in her reflection she could only see Claire Tilson. Her eyes again filled with tears.

She blinked them away.

'I'll tell his lordship you are dressed,' Betty said, hurriedly making up the bed. The maid left and a moment later Lord Brookmore entered.

'Good morning, sir.' Rebecca remembered to curtsy deferentially. This was her employer, after all. His presence made her a bit breathless, but that must be only nerves. She was lying to him, after all. It was not because he was very tall and very masculine.

'Miss Tilson.' He nodded. He handed her a bundle wrapped in paper. 'I took the liberty of purchasing items you will no doubt need on the journey to Brookmore.'

She untied the string around the bundle and unfolded the paper to reveal a paisley shawl, a silk bonnet and lavender kid gloves.

'These are lovely,' she whispered. Every bit as fine as she'd once owned.

He nodded in response. 'How are you today? We need not travel if you are not sufficiently recovered.'

'I am well!' she assured him. She was eager to start her new life.

Claire's life.

She looked up from the items. 'Thank you for these. Thank you for the clothing, as well.'

He shrugged. 'You needed something to wear.'

Everything that had belonged to Rebecca Pierce was gone.

He stood just inside the door. Her impulse was to invite him to sit, to order tea, just as she might have done at home in Ireland. How foolish! She had no means to order tea and did a governess even invite a viscount to be seated?

It would take a little work to rid herself of Lady Rebecca.

He looked uncertain, his blue eyes finding hers only fleetingly. 'I will arrange for a carriage, then. If you are certain you are ready.'

'Quite ready,' she replied.

She crossed the room to retrieve his handkerchief, which she had washed with the soap and water provided for her and dried in front of the fire. It was not pressed, but this had been the best she could do with no means to hire someone for the task.

She handed the handkerchief to him. 'It is clean, sir.'

As he reached for it, his gaze lingered on her. Their fingers brushed and she felt a flush warm her skin. She stepped back.

He cleared his throat. 'I will see to the carriage.'

He turned and left.

Chapter Three

The carriage Lord Brookmore arranged was a small two-horse landaulet with two coachmen on the box. It was comfortable enough, but if she'd had to share it with the Viscount, it would have seated them so close their bodies would have touched. Luckily he rode on horseback, so she did not have to face being in such intimate quarters with him. Unfortunately it also meant she had no company at all.

For half the day, the road skirted the sea whose sight and scent made it impossible to forget the terror and loss she'd endured from its violence. There was nothing to divert her thoughts away from those memories. With every glimpse of waves outside her window, she relived the shipwreck.

She tried to look away, out the window that did not face the sea. Occasionally Lord Brookmore rode next to the carriage and asked her how she fared. She always replied that she did very well. The truth could not be easily explained. Other than that, she was silent, even saying little during their brief contacts when they stopped only long enough to change horses and procure food which she ate in the coach.

Eventually the sea disappeared from view, replaced

by farms and fields and small villages. Rebecca's nostrils filled with the odour of growing things. Of life instead of watery death, but still, being alone, her thoughts drifted back to the sea.

Lord Brookmore, who looked even more imposing on horseback, again appeared beside the carriage. 'We are nearing Chester. We will spend the night there.'

At the inn in Chester, Garret dismounted and handed his horse off to the waiting ostler. The carriage pulled in behind him and one of the coachmen jumped down to help Miss Tilson descend the steps. Garret stood nearby, his valise in hand.

Miss Tilson carried only a small bag with those few items he had purchased for her.

In the waning sun, she looked even paler than when they'd started the journey. He'd suspected then that she was not recovered enough. Now he kicked himself for not insisting she rest in Moelfre at least one more day. He'd been impatient to return to Brookmore House, though, eager to see her settled and his nieces comfortable, and matters set to rights. Brookmore House still felt like his brother's house, not his, even though he'd grown up there. Of course, when he'd been a child he'd been constantly reminded that his brother was the heir, the eventual owner of the estate.

He needed to return to London, although he was not as eager as he ought to be. He'd been swept up in events in London. It had been like watching another person negotiating that society and its expectations. Not him. Not at all him.

But it had been what he must do. Colleagues of his brother and father guided him through the ceremony, customs and politics of the House of Lords and of what was expected of a viscount there.

He needed to secure the inheritance, they'd insisted. His family would lose everything to some distant relation if he did not beget an heir. He'd seen the logic in that and so had done his duty. Attended the marriage mart. Became betrothed.

Lady Agnes was the perfect choice, his advisors assured him. He agreed. She was the daughter of the Earl of Trowbridge. She was polished, pleasant, accomplished and beautiful. She'd be the perfect hostess. There was absolutely nothing to object to in Lady Agnes.

Except Miss Tilson pulled more emotion from him than Lady Agnes ever had.

He stepped towards the governess and reached for her small bag. 'You look fatigued. I will arrange a room for you and have a meal sent up to you.'

She gave him a stricken look that he did not understand, but he took her bag and she fell in step with him to the door of the inn.

When they entered the hall, the innkeeper's eyes darted between them. 'Welcome. A room for you, sir?' His tone was uncertain.

'Two rooms,' Garret replied. 'The lady will require a maid and a meal in her room.'

'Very good, sir.' The innkeeper bowed.

'No!' Miss Tilson broke in, her voice sharp. She immediately modified it. 'No, please. I would prefer to eat my meal in the tavern.'

The innkeeper's brows rose, as did Garret's. She wished to expose herself in a public tavern? What sort of governess was she?

Garret frowned. 'As you wish.'

The innkeeper cleared his throat. 'Let me show you to your rooms.'

Garret followed behind the man and Miss Tilson as he led them up two flights of stairs and down a long hallway.

'These two.' The innkeeper gestured to two rooms across the hallway from each other. He opened each of the rooms and handed them their keys. 'Shall I send a maid up now, ma'am?' he asked Miss Tilson.

'Not now,' she replied. 'Later. Perhaps nine or ten?'

'Very good, ma'am.' He bowed and left.

Garret placed his valise inside his room and his hat and gloves on a table, but he did not move from the doorway.

Neither did Miss Tilson.

She lifted her chin. 'Lord Brookmore, I am of a mind you disapprove of my not eating in my room. If you wish it, I will do so.'

He folded his arms across his chest. 'A public room can be a rowdy place, Miss Tilson. Not suitable for an unaccompanied woman.' Not suitable for his nieces' governess, he meant.

She lowered her gaze. 'I did not think of that. I thought only to have people around me. To not be alone.' Her voice cracked on her last word.

His insides twisted at her emotion.

She raised her eyes again. 'When I am alone, the shipwreck comes back to me.'

The shipwreck. Of course she would be reliving the shipwreck. Before yesterday she'd been too feverish to become accustomed to the memories.

'Would you accompany me to the tavern, then?' she asked. 'I would not require you to make conversation. Simply being among people—even rowdy people—would—would—distract me.'

How often after a battle did he seek the companionship of his fellow officers? To be alone with one's thoughts simply repeated the agony. Companionship, drink and carousing kept memories at bay. He ought to have realised this young woman would feel such a need, as well.

Truth be told, he was trying not to think of her that deeply.

Her lips thinned. 'Forgive me. It was wrong of me to ask.' She turned to enter her room. 'Have my dinner sent up. That will suffice.'

He crossed the hallway and seized her arm, dropping it as soon as she turned back, looking alarmed.

He straightened. 'If you do not wish to dine alone, I will not compel you to do so. I will request a private dining room and you will be my guest.'

Her expression relaxed into a relieved smile. 'Oh, thank you, my lord.'

He closed his door. 'I will arrange it immediately.'

She touched his arm this time. 'May I go with you?'

Her need for company was that strong? He nodded. 'In that case,' he said, 'allow me a few minutes to rid myself of the dust of the road and we can seek a meal right away.'

Her smile grew. 'Thank you, my lord.'

He washed his face and hands and brushed off his clothes. A glance in the mirror made him rub his chin, debating whether to take the time to shave. He decided against it. This was not a London drawing room and Miss Tilson was eager to be free of her solitude.

When he opened his door, she awaited him in the hallway. They walked together down the stairs through the hall to the tavern room.

The tavern room was everything Garret feared it would be. Loud voices, talking, laughing mingled with the clatter of dishes, tankards and cutlery. The air reeked of hops, cooked meat and male sweat. Men of all classes gulped from tankards of ale. Some enjoyed the company of the few women who shared booths with them. Serving girls threaded their way through the crowd.

Garret sought out the publican. 'We seek a private dining room,' he yelled over the din of the crowd.

The man's bald pate gleamed with perspiration. His
white apron covered a swelled girth. 'This way, sir!'

Garret held Miss Tilson's arm as he followed the publican through the room. Men definitely glanced her way,
their expressions curious, appreciative or licentious. He
pulled her a little closer, feeling protective. Had he ever
felt protective of Agnes?

Unfair comparison. He'd never walked Lady Agnes
through a rowdy tavern and he could not imagine ever
doing so.

Miss Tilson trembled beneath his touch.

He released her as soon as they reached the private
room, hoping she had not thought his actions too forward.
He'd felt protective. Nothing more.

The private dining room was simply furnished with a
table, four chairs and a sideboard. There was a window
with brown curtains and a small fireplace with a few pieces
of coal glowing on the grate. The walls were bare.

'What drink do you desire?' the publican asked as he
lit two lamps from a taper. 'I'll have the serving girl bring
them directly.'

'Ale for me,' Garret said. Not a drink for a viscount, but
he was parched. 'Miss Tilson?'

She gave him a sideways glance. 'Claret?'

He turned to the publican. 'A decanter of claret for the
lady.'

The man rubbed his hands. 'And food? We have char
fish and a mutton stew and pigeon…'

'Not fish!' Miss Tilson cried.

The publican eyed her with a surprised look.

Garret turned to her. 'Stew, then?'

She nodded.

He addressed the publican again. 'We will both have the stew. And bring some bread and cheese, as well.'

'Very good, sir.' The man bowed and left the room.

When he closed the door behind him, Miss Tilson lowered herself into a chair at the table. She expelled a nervous breath.

Garret inclined his head towards the door. 'You see why you could not come alone.'

She took another breath, pressing her hand against her chest. 'It was so odd. The voices. All the men. Walking through that room I thought I was on the deck of the ship again. I actually saw it.' She looked up at him, her forehead creased. 'Now you will think me mad.' She pressed her temples. 'I think myself mad.'

He settled in the chair adjacent to her. 'Some soldiers relive a battle after it is all done. As if they were there.'

She frowned. 'I don't understand.'

'They hear the sounds of the battle again. Even think they see the battle.'

Her puzzled eyes turned hopeful. 'Do you think it could be the same?'

'It could be.' He looked away and drummed his fingers on the table.

Seated this close, under the lamplight, her eyes—their irises thin brown rims circled in green—had captivated him, created a yearning inside him. Perhaps it was the changing emotion he saw in those eyes. Perhaps he was drawn to her because she'd suffered and she knew what it was like to survive when so many others died.

But he could not desire her. How could he desire her? She was a governess. In his employ. And he was a viscount now. A governess was beneath him.

What was he thinking? He could not desire her. He was betrothed.

He pressed his lips together, feeling as confined as if the walls were closing in on him.

She shifted in her chair. 'Have I annoyed you?'

She had no idea that annoyance was not his problem. His problem would be forgetting who he was now and thinking he was a soldier again.

'Not at all,' he responded perfunctorily.

She folded her hands in her lap and kept her gaze averted. It felt to him as if she held herself in check and he wondered what he would see if she set herself free. He laughed inwardly. Apparently they were both confined, both unable to be who they were inside.

But he did not need this sense of kinship with her, fuelling that inexplicable yearning inside him. It was not physical desire—or, more accurately, not only that.

How odd that her looks should captivate him when she did not meet society's ideal of beauty.

Lady Agnes certainly did.

Miss Tilson was too tall, too strong-featured, but somehow not plain. It was difficult for his gaze not to be riveted upon her face and her changing expressions.

She took a breath, as if trying to clear away whatever had been in her mind. 'So you were in the army?'

He shrugged. 'I was a younger son, until my brother died.' He blinked away his own intrusive memory.

The polite smile she'd pasted on her face faltered a bit. 'What regiment?'

She seemed determined to make conversation. 'The 28th.'

His father had purchased a lieutenancy for him when he turned eighteen. And why not? He'd not been suited for anything else, or so he'd always been told. As part of the 28th, he'd been in nearly every major battle of the war with Napoleon, from Egypt to Toulouse.

'Were you at Waterloo?' she asked.

He gritted his teeth for a moment. 'No.'

He could have stayed in Belgium with his regiment, when he inherited the title, but battles were unpredictable matters and he dared not risk being killed and leaving his nieces to the mercy of relatives so distant as to have no care for them.

He'd grieved not being a part of the Waterloo battle almost as much as he'd grieved his brother's death. Many of his men died at Waterloo. He should have been leading them. Protecting them.

'On the Peninsula, then?' she persisted.

'Yes. On the Peninsula. And in France.' His regiment had been a part of that bloody pursuit of the French as they retreated from the Pyrenees into France.

Her brow furrowed. 'And some soldiers relive battles afterwards, the way I relived the shipwreck?'

Apparently the shipwreck was never far from her mind. 'Yes. Many. I expect if I heard cannon right now, it would put me right back into battle.'

'It would?'

There was a rap on the door and a serving girl entered with their drinks and food. After she left, Garret took a generous gulp of ale and plunged his spoon into the stew.

Miss Tilson nibbled on a piece of bread, a pained expression on her face.

It tugged at his sympathy. 'Talk about it.'

She glanced up. 'About what?'

'About the shipwreck,' he explained. 'It helps.'

Although it might be more help to him to keep his distance from this young woman—his nieces' governess.

Rebecca glanced away. She wanted desperately to talk about the events crowding her head and overwhelming her senses, but ought she to do so?

Claire Tilson would have declined this invitation, she was sure. Indeed, Claire Tilson would not have fished for this conversation at all. She would have remained in her place. She would have gone to her room as the Viscount requested, even if spending more hours alone would have been unendurable.

Well, she would be Claire Tilson later. Right now she needed to be Rebecca Pierce, on an equal footing with this gentleman and with a great need to talk.

She faced him. 'Shortly after we woke that morning, the storm began and we were told to remain in our cabins.'

'We?' His brows rose.

She must be careful how she spoke. 'I—I befriended another young lady. We spent most of the voyage in each other's company.' And in each other's clothes.

She described how the storm grew and how their alarm escalated. And how the gentleman came to take them on deck. She told him of the wave that washed Miss Tilson and the man off the deck.

She did not tell him of being pulled away from Nolan, her poor sick maid. Could she ever forgive herself for that?

She saw an image in her head of Nolan in her bed as the water rose around her. Rebecca covered her eyes.

'Go on,' his voice demanded.

'I was dropped into a rowing boat. There was a mother and her children next to me, but then we saw the ship crash against the rocks and the rowing boat tossed us into the sea.' She remembered the cold water all around her, not knowing which way was up, not being able to breathe. 'I don't remember anything else very clearly until waking up in the inn.'

What had happened to the mother and those dear little children? She could not bear thinking of them under the water. Could not bear thinking of their dead bodies floating to shore.

She glanced at Lord Brookmore, whose gaze did not waver.

She took a breath. 'That is it. That is all.'

Did his eyes turn sceptical? She could not tell. 'A harrowing experience,' he said, more factually than sympathetically.

That was a good thing, though. Had he offered her comfort she might have broken down and turned into a watering pot the way she'd been yesterday.

He dipped his spoon into the bowl of stew, making her realise he'd refrained from eating while she told her story.

She ate a few bites, as well. 'I don't know why I was saved. Why me over so many others?'

She downed her glass of claret.

Lord Brookmore took a more leisurely sip of his ale. 'There is no making sense of those matters, you know. In battle, good men die. And yet men like me live. There is no making sense of it.'

Of course. He must know more about death than she could ever know. 'What do you mean "men like me"? Are you so bad, then?' She tried for a light-hearted tone.

He faced her, a sad smile on his face. 'There were times in my youth that my father was convinced of it.' He poured her another glass of claret.

She took a sip. 'I cannot believe it. You have been nothing but kind to me.'

He laughed drily. 'I need a governess for my nieces.'

She pursed her lips. 'I do not think a governess is so difficult to find. You could have sent for someone else and never have come looking for me.'

He met her gaze. 'And how could I have explained to my nieces that, after losing their parents and their old governess, I could not be bothered to discover if their new governess survived a shipwreck?'

She lifted her chin. 'A bad man would not have cared. I'll not hear you speak of yourself so.'

He averted his gaze.

She finished the claret left in her glass. 'Did it ever occur to you that you survived all those battles so that your nieces would still have you to care for them?'

His expression turned bleak. 'How much better it would have been for my brother and his wife to live and me die.'

His words knocked the breath from her.

Because it would have made so much more sense for Claire to have survived instead of Rebecca. Claire had everything to gain by living. Rebecca, instead, had been facing a dismal future in a loveless marriage.

At least she knew there was another good reason she had decided to live Claire's life for her. So Lord Brookmore would not have to tell his nieces that their new governess had died. He'd travelled all the way to Moelfre in the hopes that he would not have to tell them such news. She wasn't going to let his efforts be for naught.

She just needed to learn to act a little like Claire and less like Rebecca. 'Tell me about your nieces,' she asked.

He shrugged. 'They are aged seven and nine, but you probably know that.'

She knew nothing. 'Their names?'

He peered at her. 'Were you not provided their names?'

Oh, dear. She must be careful if this deception was to work.

'It was in the letter—' There must have been a letter. 'But I fear, with all that happened, I've lost my memory for the details. I do apologise.'

He seemed to accept that—to her great relief. 'Pamela is the elder. Ellen, the younger.'

Pamela and Ellen. She repeated to herself over and over.

He frowned. 'I have not been present in their lives. I can tell you little else of them.'

She returned to her stew, even though she could no longer taste it.

They fell into a silence, broken only by the clink of spoons against the bowls. Her heartbeat accelerated. How was a governess supposed to handle this?

A governess, she suspected, would sit quietly, no matter how oppressive the silence, no matter how compelling the gentleman. But Rebecca was inclined to be outspoken, even when it was better to keep her mouth shut. Silence was torture to her.

The sounds of their eating grew louder and louder in this vacuum. She'd go mad if this continued much longer.

She knew how to end this. She'd received the training. After her brother discovered that her boarding school had educated her too liberally, he'd sent her back to England to a finishing school in Bath, so she knew very well how to engage a gentleman in conversation, even though it might be quite un-governess-like to use the skill now.

'Do tell, my lord, about the house where your nieces live. Is it in a lovely part of the Lake District?'

'All parts of the Lake District are lovely.' He looked up from his stew. 'Have you not been there?'

When his gaze reached her eyes, it made her insides flutter. She glanced away. 'I never had the pleasure.'

He cocked his head as if in apology. 'Of course. Why would you?'

She forced herself to meet his gaze again. 'Tell me. What will I see?'

This time he glanced away and took a sip of ale before he spoke. 'You will see mountains. They are green this time of year, but they'll turn all shades of orange in autumn and white when winter comes. The lakes change colour, too, with the sky. From silver to blue to purple.' He looked as if he were gazing at the landscape right now. 'I have been to many places in the world, but none is as fine.'

She was moved by the suppressed emotion in his words. 'I shall be eager to see it.'

He finished his ale and his voice turned flat. 'You will not like the house.'

She felt a niggle of alarm. 'Why not?'

He shrugged. 'It is old.'

What family seat possessed a new house? She laughed softly. 'I am in no position to complain. An old house. A new house. As long as I have a roof over my head.'

He did not seem to appreciate her attempt at levity. 'I am hopeful you will find it tolerable. I do not want my nieces to lose another governess.'

And Rebecca needed a place to stay. A different life to live. Somehow she must make this work for everyone.

She'd figure it out in time.

She forced herself to smile. 'Let us not worry at the moment, my lord.' She gestured down at herself. 'As I own nothing and have nowhere else to go, let us assume I will be happy as your nieces' governess and that you will be happy with my services.'

She lifted her glass of claret as if in a toast.

Garret raised his empty tankard, more affected than he wanted to admit at the emotions flitting over her face.

He knew loss. His parents. His brother. Sister-in-law. And countless friends and fellow soldiers on the battle-field. But for him there was always something left, even if it was merely a title and property he'd never desired and never deserved. How might it be to have nothing left? Not even the clothes on one's back?

He admired her for not giving in to the raw emotions grief could cause.

He must see to replacing her wardrobe and other essentials a lady must need. There ought to be some reparation he could provide for not giving her more time to recover. He should have known that more than the body needed to heal.

He pushed the plate of bread and cheese towards her. 'Please help yourself, Miss Tilson.'

She more dutifully than hungrily cut herself a piece of bread and cheese before looking up at him. 'Shall I slice some for you?'

He nodded. 'Thank you.'

He was, perhaps, even less desirous of more food than she, but he accepted the tray, selected the bread and raised it to his mouth.

'Have you any family, Miss Tilson? I ought to have asked before now.' One more way he was remiss. 'Is there anyone you would wish to contact?'

She paused before answering. 'There is no one. No family.'

The bread tasted dry in his mouth. She *had* lost everything.

She finished the bread and cheese and folded her hands in her lap. She was thinking too much. He'd seen such a look on his soldiers' faces. Social conversation was not a skill he excelled in, but he wanted desperately to distract her from those thoughts.

'Is there anything else you desire?' he asked her.

She gave a wan smile. 'I am quite sated. The portions were generous, were they not?'

'They were indeed,' he agreed.

He did not know what else to say. Should he ask if she was ready to be alone again? How could he leave her alone after knowing how alone she truly was?

He drummed his fingers on the table. 'Have you been a governess long, Miss Tilson?'

What a foolish question. She could not be more than twenty or twenty-one, but he did not know what else to ask except about the one thing he knew about her—that she was a governess.

A look of distress flashed over her face. 'Um. No, not long, sir.'

Why the distress? He was trying to distract her.

'Then your last position was your first as a governess?' He seemed to remember that from the letters from the agency he and his housekeeper had used to fill the position.

Her eyes darted. 'Yes.' She took a breath. 'My first of any consequence, that is.'

'And…' This was not going well at all. 'Why did you leave?'

She blinked rapidly. 'Not for any bad reason, sir. I was not discharged, if that is what you are asking.'

That was not what he meant. 'No. I was merely curious.' Though it was not curiosity, just his clumsy attempt at conversation. He took another gulp of his ale. 'No other reason. I wondered what your life was like before. What the previous family was like. How many children were in your charge. That is all.'

She leaned forward with an earnest expression. 'Are you having second thoughts about hiring me? Because I would hope you would not judge me by these past two days. Or by my—my forward behaviour at this meal—'

Forward behaviour?

'Please give me the chance to show—to show what I can do,' she pleaded.

He gripped his tankard of ale. 'Miss Tilson, I am not having second thoughts. Rest easy on that matter. You remain distressed about the shipwreck. I understand that. Distraction helps at such times.'

She sat back. 'Oh.'

He attempted a smile. 'Shall we talk about something else?'

She shifted in her chair. 'Perhaps I ought to retire to my room.'

'As you wish.' He felt as if he'd driven her away, which was not at all what he'd intended.

Another reason he should have remained a soldier. Conversing with his fellow soldiers was not so fraught with peril.

He stood and helped her out of her chair.

When they walked through the tavern again, it was no less full of life. There were still men and women laughing and drinking away whatever their cares might be. He envied them. He had not imbibed nearly enough drink to drown his emotions this night.

The innkeeper greeted them when they walked back into the hall. 'I hope your meal was satisfactory.'

Miss Tilson replied before Garret opened his mouth. 'Thank you, sir. It was very satisfying.' Then she shifted her gaze to him as if he might object to her speaking.

As they approached the stairway, Garret remembered the innkeeper's offer of a maid. 'Would you like the maid to attend you now?'

'Oh, yes,' she replied. 'A maid now. Or as soon as it is convenient.' She glanced back at the innkeeper.

The man spoke up. 'I will send someone directly, miss.'

Garret followed her up the stairs and escorted her to her door. She took a key from her pocket and he opened his hand. She gave him the key and he unlocked the door. In the open doorway she turned to face him.

He was quite aware of how close he stood to her and

how the soft light of the hall lamps made her skin glow and her eyes darken.

'I'll arrange for the maid to wake you in time to leave tomorrow,' he managed to say.

Her voice turned raspy. 'Thank you, sir. For eating your meal with me.'

He lowered his voice, too. 'I hope it eased matters for you.'

Her eyes softened. 'Much better than being alone.'

That seemed faint praise.

She affected him more than he wished to admit. His arms itched to hold her.

To comfort her, that was all. Merely comfort her. He had no business acting upon any other temptation, although it struck him how easily it could be done. She could not refuse him, could she? She had nothing but the position of governess that was entirely in his control.

No. He would not touch her.

Oh. And he was betrothed. He'd forgotten about that.

He stepped back. 'My room is across the hall. Knock on the door if you need me—if you need anything. Otherwise, sleep well, Miss Tilson.'

She lowered her head and curtsied. 'You, as well, sir,' she replied dutifully.

She turned and entered the room, closing the door behind her. The key sounded in the lock.

Garret stared at the closed door for a moment before heading back to the stairway and returning to the tavern for something stronger than ale.

Chapter Four

The next day Garret rose early, ignoring the pounding in his head from too many glasses of a rather bad brandy. He sought out the innkeeper and arranged for a man to ride ahead to Preston on a specific errand.

When Miss Tilson was ready, he arranged for breakfast in the private dining parlour. The sun shone through the parlour window, lighting her face with its dark circles under the eyes. Her skin was nearly as pale as his first sight of her abed in Moelfre.

He frowned. 'I fear you did not sleep well, Miss Tilson.'

She blushed, which at least gave her some colour. 'Not very well.'

'Were you troubled by dreams?' Nightmares followed battles. Why not shipwrecks?

She glanced at him in surprise. 'I was. I dreamed of the water.'

Poor girl.

'You won't always have the dreams,' he reassured her.

She nibbled on toasted bread and jam. He ate a piece of ham and racked his throbbing brain for some way to make this trip less unpleasant for her.

'I could hire a larger carriage, if you like. Ride with you.' There was really no need for her to be alone.

Although how comfortable would it be to be so close to her for so many hours?

She looked alarmed. 'I would not so inconvenience you, my lord. I will manage well enough in the landaulet. You must not give up the pleasure of riding horseback.'

He was most comfortable on a horse, that was true. On the Peninsula, he and his horse moved as one and in battle his horse never failed him.

He glanced out the window. 'It does look to be a fine day for riding.'

Her voice turned wistful. 'A lovely day for riding.'

He heard her take another bite of her toast. He gazed out the window, but his mind was working.

Finally he turned back to her. 'Do you ride, Miss Tilson?'

To his surprise, her hazel eyes kindled with pleasure— a captivating sight.

'Once upon a time I rode every chance I could,' she said dreamily. 'So I well understand what a joy it is to view the countryside from the back of a horse.'

He nodded. 'If we can procure a riding habit for you and a ladies' saddle, would you like to ride today?'

He could pay off the coachmen. They certainly would not mind receiving the same pay for a trip they did not have to take.

Her eyes widened. 'Surely you cannot arrange such a thing.'

He lifted a shoulder. 'I can try. We shall see what can be done.'

Her eyes brightened. 'I would love to ride.'

It took some effort—and a generous output of coin—but Garret managed to provide Miss Tilson with a decent and well-fitting riding habit, riding boots, gloves, hat, riding crop and a side saddle that suited her almost as well as if made for her. He paid enough for the owner of the items to purchase three replacements and ones of finer quality, too.

But he would not tell Miss Tilson the cost. It exceeded her yearly salary, which would seem a fortune to her, but to him, now that he'd inherited wealth, it was a mere trifle.

The stable provided them both with horses, which they would change periodically at other coaching inns on the road.

The air was crisp and the sky so vivid a blue it almost hurt the eyes. Rolls of white clouds added to the day's grandeur. What finer day could there be for a ride?

In Chester the road was busy with farm wagons, mail coaches, carriages of all kinds, from the simplest gig to elegant landaus to a lumbering post chaise, but as they rode further away from the town there were times they were alone on the road and could ride side by side.

'How are you faring?' he asked. 'I can always hire a carriage if riding is too taxing.'

She was as game as he'd hoped, though. 'It is not too taxing.' She smiled at him. 'It is wonderful!'

Garret was pleased. He'd brought her some happiness after all she'd been through.

'You ride well,' he said.

She grinned. 'It is one of my favourite pastimes, I must say. When I was a little girl I rode astride and bareback on my beloved pony. When I was sent to school, my father provided a horse and I learned how to ride properly.'

'Where was your school?' he asked.

Her smile faded and she took a moment to answer. 'Bristol,' she finally said.

Whenever he asked her a question, her demeanour changed. It kept him from asking more.

But as they rode in silence for a while, he felt compelled to say something. 'You must have the use of the stables at

Brookmore. There are a couple of mares there—my sister-in-law's horses—that you would find pleasant to ride.'

Her face lit up. 'I might ride? How very wonderful!'

Changing horses at the inns gave them both a chance to stretch their muscles and ease any soreness from the time in the saddle. Garret was used to long hours on horseback, but Miss Tilson could not be as seasoned, even if she loved riding.

When they took refreshment at the inns, their conversation was more comfortable than the night before, but, then, any questions he asked her were about the inn, the food, the fresh horses they were given. Apparently questions about the present were not difficult for her to answer.

He liked being in her company. She was neither too chatty nor deadly silent.

When the sun dipped low in the sky, they reached the outskirts of Preston. Preston was a large and busy town and the traffic on the road was almost as bustling as London. Many a male rider would have found it daunting to guide a horse through such busy streets. Miss Tilson still rode confidently.

He led her to the inn. In the yard, ostlers ran up to hold the horses. Garret dismounted and turned to see Miss Tilson expertly slip off hers. Their gazes caught briefly and, for a moment, he was lost in the depths of her hazel eyes.

He quickly glanced away.

For a multitude of reasons—her position, his fiancée—he must not allow any physical attraction to her, yet at unexpected moments like this desire coursed through him.

The ostler handed him his valise and Miss Tilson gathered the small bag carrying the few items she could now call her own.

She took a step and winced.

He stepped towards her and put his arm around her. 'Are you able to walk?'

She let him support her. 'I am stiff, of course. I'm sure it will pass.'

He was more than happy to have her lean against him, although this was precisely the sort of contact he should avoid.

When they entered the inn and Garret gave the innkeeper his name, the innkeeper's eyes lit up.

'Lord Brookmore, sir. Welcome.' The man bowed. 'Let me assure you your rooms are ready and the items you requested have been placed in the lady's room.'

Miss Tilson looked at him quizzically.

He did not enlighten her.

Their rooms were on the first floor, next to each other, too close to make defying temptation easy. Better he were on the other side of the building.

The innkeeper grinned as he opened Miss Tilson's door.

Obviously the man Garret had sent ahead had managed his task very well. Across the bed were items of clothing and rolls of cloth, everything he could think of that would be of use to her.

Rebecca gasped. 'What have you done?'

The bed was laden with rolls of cloth, but there were also three dresses, shifts, petticoats, gloves and hats.

She stepped into the room as the innkeeper withdrew.

Lord Brookmore stood in the doorway, leaning against the door jamb. 'Preston is known for its cloth. I simply took advantage of this fact. I sent a man ahead.'

'The cloth is beautiful.' She gestured to the pile. 'But there is clothing here, as well.'

The innkeeper spoke up. 'My wife took up the challenge, miss. She found a dressmaker who had dresses the buyers never collected. I will send my wife to assist you whenever you wish. She has a seamstress on hand to address any alterations.'

Rebecca could not find her voice. Lord Brookmore had gone to a great deal of trouble and expense for her, so unlike how other men had treated her of late. Her brother begrudged any expense and had only arranged the marriage in order to be rid of her.

Lord Brookmore spoke. 'You must select what you like, Miss Tilson. As many pieces as you like. When we get to Brookmore House a local seamstress can make whatever you need.'

She smiled at him in wonder. 'This is so generous.'

His face stiffened. 'I am clothing my nieces' governess. You need clothing and I am well able to provide it.'

She walked back to his side. 'I am so very grateful.' She touched his arm and it seemed as if the warmth of his kindness spread all through her.

The innkeeper broke in. 'Shall I ask my wife to attend you?'

Rebecca lifted her hand away. 'Yes. Please have her come at her convenience. I will just wash off the dirt of the road.'

Lord Brookmore stepped away from the doorway. 'I will leave you now. Send word when you wish to dine.' He turned to the innkeeper. 'May we have a private room for dining?'

'I'll see to it, m'lord.' The man bowed again and left them.

Rebecca did not wish for Lord Brookmore to leave. 'What time would you wish to dine, sir?'

'Whenever you wish.' His tone softened. 'I need to clean up, as well.'

But neither of them moved. His blue eyes seemed to

pierce her, reaching parts of her that felt vulnerable and raw. Perhaps he really could see inside her. He certainly was able to anticipate her needs and discern her emotions. When had a man ever been able to do that? She'd been used to demanding what she needed.

Lord Brookmore averted his gaze and took another step back. 'I will leave you now.'

She watched him enter his room and close the door behind him. Only then did she do the same.

By the time Rebecca had stripped off her riding habit and washed off the dirt of the road, the innkeeper's wife and the seamstress knocked on her door.

'I am Mrs Bell, dear.' The woman was small and round, with a kind face and warm voice. 'This is Miss Cox. We were told of your misfortune. You poor creature!' She put her hands on her hips. 'Well, well. Let us see what we can do about providing you with some clothes to wear.'

The two women helped Rebecca out of the corset and shift she'd been given in Moelfre and into the undergarments that Mrs Bell had brought her. Two of the shifts fit her very well and one of the corsets was near perfect and so much more comfortable than the one from before. There was a nightdress that would be heaven to sleep in and two day dresses that fit her well enough.

One needed only minor alterations, which were accomplished on the spot. The other, the seamstress promised to have ready by the morning. With the help of the two women, Rebecca chose a length of wool for a winter dress and another for a cape. She picked out some plain white cotton for some aprons and caps and a print for another dress.

The ship had carried two trunks full of her clothing. She'd packed walking dresses, morning dresses, carriage dresses, dinner dresses, nightdresses and ball gowns. She had hats for all occasions and several pairs of shoes and gloves. Her undergarments had been made of soft linen. The wardrobe had been worthy of an earl's daughter and soon-to-be wife of a baron.

These makeshift clothes were—serviceable. But they were also more dear to her than all of her lost dresses. Because of the thoughtfulness behind them.

Her father had indulged her with the finest clothes and jewels—all lost now—but he'd been unable to stand the sight of his daughter after her mother died. She'd reminded him too much of his beloved wife.

When Mrs Bell and Miss Cox left her, Rebecca took the pins from her hair and brushed it out with the brush Lord Brookmore had purchased for her. She rearranged it into a simple coil at the back of her head, as Claire had done. She wore the dress that the seamstress fixed for her, a dress of plain grey.

She glanced at herself in the full-length mirror that had been provided for her.

Her breath caught.

She saw Claire Tilson.

Donning the lavender gloves Lord Brookmore had purchased for her in Moelfre and the paisley shawl, she glanced at her image again and felt a little more like herself.

She left the room and knocked on Lord Brookmore's door.

He answered it in his shirtsleeves and looked even more handsome than when wearing his well-tailored coat, waistcoat and neckcloth.

'Miss Tilson,' he said in some surprise.

Oh, dear. This was a bit improper of her. 'You said I should let you know when I was ready to dine.'

'I assumed you would send word.'

Yes, but it had seemed silly to send someone else with

the message when she was right next door. Besides, she had seen her father and brother in shirtsleeves on occasion—but they did not look at all like Lord Brookmore.

He quickly donned his waistcoat and buttoned it.

She averted her gaze. 'I can return to my room, if you would prefer to eat later.'

'No. No. I am quite ready.' He put on his coat, pulling at the lapels and the cuffs to straighten its fit. He threw a neckcloth around his neck and managed to tie it into a reasonably neat mathematical.

He paused, his eyes scanning her. 'That is one of the new dresses? It looks well on you.'

Her face flushed at the compliment. Why should she react so to such mild praise when most men's flattery left her cold? Who had ever complimented her when wearing such a plain garment?

Their dinner was a lovely relaxed affair and Rebecca marvelled that there were long moments when she did not think of the shipwreck and when she quite forgot she was supposed to be a governess.

When Lord Brookmore's eyes lit upon her, it seemed as if her insides would melt. She'd met other handsome men, but he was so much more than any man she had ever met.

How ironic that she should meet him as his lowly employee and not as a suitor. As Lady Rebecca she would have been acceptably eligible to him.

Not that he would have desired such an impulsive, wilful female, who'd defied her brother until he'd put her in a corner from which she could not escape.

Except she had escaped. All it had taken was the loss of Claire's life.

That thought brought a stab of pain.

But during the dinner with Lord Brookmore she tried very hard to push thoughts like that away and instead simply enjoyed his company.

After dinner they climbed the stairs to their rooms.

'Do you wish to ride again tomorrow?' he asked.

She glanced up at him. 'I would love to ride.' Riding had made the trip a pleasure.

'We should reach Brookmore House tomorrow.'

He walked her to her door where she would have to take on the role of governess completely and leave Lady Rebecca behind. A companionable night like this would be impossible then. A viscount simply did not become friends with a lowly governess.

Like the night before, he held his hand out for her key. She took it from her pocket and placed it in his palm, very aware of her fingers brushing his skin.

He unlocked the door and returned the key to her.

She gazed up into his face. 'My lord, this was a lovely day. How can I ever thank you for all the kindness and generosity you've shown me?'

He stared at her, not speaking. They stood close, no more than a foot apart. His scent filled her nostrils, the faint odour of horse, of lime and something very male. It was more intoxicating than the wine she'd consumed at the meal.

Once when a man stood so close to her, he had forced her into a kiss. Even Lord Stonecroft had placed his wet, pulpous lips upon hers before he'd left to return to London. She'd wanted to retch. Somehow, though, if Lord Brookmore did the same, she would not mind.

What a brazen thought!

If she were herself—Lady Rebecca—instead of pretending to be Claire, could she, this moment, invite a kiss? All she needed to do was rise up on tiptoe.

Perhaps it would not hurt to be Lady Rebecca for a few minutes longer.

Garret gazed down at her face, so close to his. His heart thundered in his chest as her words echoed.

How can I ever thank you?

A kiss would be more than thanks.

The hall lamp shone on her, making her skin glow, bathing them both in light. The darkness cocooned them. Nothing else existed but the two of them, so close.

She rose, bringing her tantalising lips a whisper closer. It was enough to undo him. Garret seized her arms and lowered his lips to hers.

She tasted of claret and raspberries, her lips whetting an appetite he'd tried hard to deny. Her mouth opened to him and she placed her palms on his cheeks, holding his kiss.

It was all the encouragement he needed. He deepened the kiss and pressed her against him, against where the need for her had escalated. Her arms wrapped around his neck and her fingers buried themselves in his hair. She returned his kisses with an ardour matching his own.

What might it be like to make love to her? Would she match his passion making love?

'Lord Brookmore,' she murmured in a voice tinged with both passion and anxiety.

It woke him up.

He was Lord Brookmore. Her employer.

He pushed her away. 'Miss Tilson, I—' Words failed. What could he say to her about what he'd done? And almost done?

He turned on his heel and strode away, back down the corridor and stairs.

Chapter Five

What had she done?

Had she risen on her toes or had he leaned down?

She'd wanted to kiss him, of that she was certain. Once his lips touched hers, she had not wanted him to stop.

She'd enticed him. How could she think otherwise? And he recoiled from her. She'd acted the hoyden and had created a disgust in him.

What her schoolteachers warned had been true—she was too forward. Too impulsive. She must take care lest she unleash the carnal impulses of a man. The man who once forced his kiss upon her blamed her for it. She had been too alluring, he'd said. But she'd been reasonably certain she'd not been too forward then and her impulse had definitely not been to kiss him.

But with Lord Brookmore? She might have enticed that kiss from Lord Brookmore. How foolish she'd been to want that kiss.

There was a knock on the door and Rebecca jumped up and rushed to the door. She hesitated. Had he returned?

She cleared her throat. 'Who is it?'

'The maid, miss.' Not Lord Brookmore.

Rebecca opened the door, unsure if she were relieved or disappointed.

The young woman helped her take off her dress and assisted her with donning her new nightdress. When the maid left, Rebecca crawled into bed and buried herself under the covers.

She had very likely ruined her respite as a governess. Brookmore would discharge her; his nieces would endure another loss and she would be forced to tell him who she really was and beg for enough money to travel to London.

Worst of all, she would have to find another way to avoid marrying Lord Stonecroft and enduring his wet, disgusting kisses.

But how could she ever kiss another man after being kissed by Lord Brookmore?

The next morning Lord Brookmore had sent her breakfast to her room to avoid her, no doubt.

After she dressed again in her riding habit, she dismissed the maid and tried to eat the cooked egg, bread and cheese Lord Brookmore provided for her. Giving up on finishing the food, she picked up her new bag packed with the new dresses and fabrics with which he'd surprised and delighted her. She left the room, fearful he might have already abandoned her.

When she entered the yard, though, he stood by his horse. An ostler held the reins of another horse wearing her side saddle. As she approached Lord Brookmore mounted his horse and avoided looking at her.

The ostler helped her into her saddle and fixed her bag behind her. Lord Brookmore handed the man a coin and started for the gate. Rebecca called a quick thank you to the ostler and hurried to catch up.

She could tell already that the horse she rode was more spirited than the horses provided for her the day before, but the enjoyment of riding such a horse was dampened by the fact that Lord Brookmore acted as if he were riding alone. He said not one word to her.

Rebecca, too, stayed silent, concentrating on keeping her horse steady and keeping up with him on the busy streets of Preston. They rode past Horrock's Mill and eventually reached the countryside.

Rebecca began this journey feeling shame about her behaviour and fear that she had lost any good opinion Lord Brookmore might have had of her. By the time the roads cleared, she felt angry. How dare he not even address what happened between them, not even acknowledge her presence? That kiss had not solely been her fault. She might have acted like a hoyden, but Lord Brookmore had not behaved as a gentleman, had he?

In any event, this silence was intolerable.

Her father might have blocked her out of his life and treated her as if she did not exist, but Rebecca would not take such treatment from anyone else.

She quickened her horse's pace until she reached his side. 'You must speak to me some time, sir.'

He darted a glance at her, but said nothing.

'I did not know you would kiss me,' she snapped.

His gaze was again fixed on the road. 'It will not happen again.'

He spoke this like an order, in a tone he might have used with his soldiers. He did not have to order her not to kiss him again. As if she would! Her anger was escalating and she was not sure if its source was his icy treatment of her or if it was her disappointment that he'd turned out to be just as thoughtless and cruel as other men in her life.

'It is unfair to blame me for it,' she retorted. 'You kissed me, after all.'

He actually looked at her. 'Blame you?'

She lifted her chin. 'I fear you are trying to discharge

me. Or perhaps you have already discharged me by giving me the cut direct.'

A day ago she would not have believed him capable of such thoughtlessness.

He gaped at her. 'I am not discharging you.'

Her voice rose again. 'Then why pretend I do not exist? Why refuse to speak to me? I am left to guess you wish me gone.' As her father had done.

He stopped his horse. His jaw flexed. 'Is that what you think?'

'What else am I to think?'

He turned his horse and came directly next to her, leaning towards her. The space between them was only a few inches more than when they'd kissed. 'Think that I behaved abominably towards you. Think that I do not know what to say to you.'

He thought he'd behaved abominably? She almost softened towards him. 'Did you also think boorishness was preferable to a simple apology?'

'A simple apology seemed inadequate.' He frowned.

He turned his horse and rode on. This time she held back a little.

He had not discharged her! She could still pretend to be Claire.

Her cheeks burned with shame. She had called him a boor and here she was, nothing but an imposter.

Garret had even more reason to chastise himself. He'd assumed she would know he regretted what he'd done to her—and what he'd almost done. He'd simply made matters worse by not speaking of it.

They stopped at an inn to change horses.

He dismounted and turned to assist her. 'Let us get some refreshment.'

She looked down at him with a haughty expression. 'As you wish.'

She slid off the saddle, landing nearly as close as when he'd kissed her the night before. He must keep more distance.

The ostlers took charge of the horses and Garret escorted Miss Tilson into the tavern. At this morning hour, the public room was nearly empty and Garret thought better of a private room. Best not to be private with her.

He chose a table some distance away from the other diners, helped her sit and chose the chair across from hers. He ordered tea and biscuits for them which came quickly, accommodating those patrons who needed to be quickly on their way.

She poured the tea for him.

He knew they must discuss what had transpired between them. He searched for a way to begin.

She spoke first. 'I want you to know that I did not intentionally entice you, sir. I have been accused of such wiles before, but, I assure you, I do not know precisely what one does to entice.'

Who was it who'd accused her? he wondered in a surge of jealousy.

Jealousy? He had not the right.

He leaned towards her and spoke quietly. 'What transpired last night was entirely my fault.'

She raised her eyes to his. 'I must have seemed too willing. That is what disgusted you, I am sure.'

She had been willing, he remembered. She'd kissed him back and resisted nothing. She'd kissed him back with a fervour matching his own.

'You did not disgust me,' he told her.

She persisted. 'But you left so angrily.'

'Anger at me, not you.' Let her be clear about that. 'It was wrong of me to kiss you.'

Her gaze did not waver. 'Then why did you?'

Why? Because she was a fascinating combination of vulnerability and strength. Because her animated features fascinated him. Because she'd been game enough to ride a whole day and never complained. He admired courage, even in small matters. She'd even been courageous enough to talk to him about the kiss when he could not think of a word to say. Because she was the first woman he'd truly wanted to kiss in a long, long time.

'You were enticing,' he admitted.

'I did not mean to be!' she cried.

He placed his hands on the table. 'I know, Miss Tilson. I placed you in an intolerable position.'

She straightened in her chair. 'I refuse to allow you to take all the blame.' She touched his hand.

It made him remember her eager response to him. The attraction was strong between them, which only made it more difficult for him.

He withdrew his hand. 'You are in my employ. A governess is at the mercy of her employer. I will not take advantage of you again.'

Something akin to self-reproach crossed her face. 'Then how are we to go along?' she asked, her voice nearly a whisper.

'I will behave correctly from now on.' He took a sip of his tea, lukewarm now. 'And I will not stay at Brookmore for very long.'

She looked more disappointed than relieved. Even more reason why he should only stay long enough to be certain his nieces accepted this enticing governess.

They finished their tea and walked out to mount fresh horses. This steed was not as spirited as Rebecca's previous one, but her mind was too preoccupied by her conversation with Lord Brookmore to care. The joy of the day before had disappeared and she was left with regret and disappointment. Regret that she'd not shown more restraint when he'd kissed her and disappointment that he did not intend to do so again. Instead he planned to leave.

They passed a house with a model of a ship above the door, reminding her that things could be so much worse for her—had been so much worse for Claire.

On the road the ease with Lord Brookmore that made the previous day so pleasurable was lacking. He kept a distance that was appropriate for a titled lord and a lowly governess.

The countryside they rode through was not unlike that around Reading where she'd attended school. Rolling hills, grazing sheep, planted fields. Gradually, though, it changed. The hills rose into mountains of brilliant green, glimpses of grey rock peeking through. In the valleys were lakes of deep blue water. The sheep that dotted the hills were a dusty brown, so unlike those in Berkshire. The houses, churches and other buildings were made of grey slate. From the mountains, no doubt. The countryside was lined with walls made with pieces of slate stacked one on the other.

The road led them up a mountain and when they were near the top, Rebecca stopped her horse and gasped.

'It is lovely,' she exclaimed, gazing down at the scene. 'The mountains and lake.' So green and blue.

He turned his horse to amble next to hers. 'We call the valleys *dales*. The mountains with grazing land are *fells* and the lakes are *waters* or *meres*. Several of our words like these are from the Vikings who once settled here.'

'It looks like a foreign land.' She made a small laugh. 'Not that I've seen any foreign lands. It looks unlike any place I've ever been.'

He moved his horse back on to the road. 'It is unlike any other place.'

It was the sort of place that could change a person, Rebecca thought. Her grim outlook lifted a bit. This land offered hope.

They stopped in a village to change horses. These buildings, too, were constructed with the grey slate, contrasted with a few that were whitewashed. The lack of colour in the buildings merely set off the green of the *fells* and the blue of the *waters*.

See? She was already speaking in this new foreign tongue.

Their road skirted a long lake.

Lord Brookmore inclined his head towards the lake. 'Windermere,' he said. 'The largest lake in England.'

It did seem to stretch for ever.

When the lake was no longer in sight they reached another village with the lovely name of Ambleside. Ambleside had the same stone buildings built on the rises, twists and turns of the land.

He pointed to a little house built on a bridge over a small river. 'See the Bridge House? It is a cobbler's house and has been here over one hundred years.'

He seemed to relax in these surroundings, places that must be as familiar to him as the landscape and villages around her father's estate and those around her school in Reading. She welcomed his ease of manner.

They left the village behind and entered a lane lined with ferns and shrubbery and trees so tall that the mountains disappeared from view. Their horses' hooves clip-clopped over a stone bridge spanning a stream, its water creating music as it tumbled over rocks.

Lord Brookmore quickened the pace. 'We are almost there.'

The wooded lane opened into fields again where cattle grazed. In the distance appeared a great house, built, of course, with the grey stone she'd seen everywhere this day. The house had a tower in front, crenelated like the castles of old, and another on the wing of the house.

'Brookmore House?' she asked as they approached, knowing it could be nothing else.

'Brookmore House,' he repeated with pride.

They passed through a wrought-iron gate and followed the road to a circular courtyard. There was no grand entrance to the house, merely a large carved wooden door. As they neared, the door opened and two footmen and a female servant emerged.

'Good day, m'lord,' the woman called. She eyed Rebecca with a puzzled expression.

'Mrs Dodd. I hope you are in good health.' Lord Brookmore dismounted.

'I am, sir,' she responded. Mrs Dodd was at least forty, a sturdy woman with a crisp apron and cap and an efficient air about her.

The footmen each took hold of a horse.

Lord Brookmore turned to Rebecca. The look he gave her set her heart to skittering.

She slid from the saddle.

Lord Brookmore addressed the footmen. 'We will need our bags. Tell Mr Lloyd to return the horses to the coaching inn.' His tone was matter of fact, even friendly. Her brother would have sneered at the men and barked out orders.

The footman holding Rebecca's horse handed the reins to the other and started unfastening her bag from the saddle.

Brookmore gestured for Rebecca to step forward, which she did.

He presented her to the female servant. 'Mrs Dodd,' he said. 'This is Miss Tilson, the new governess.'

'The governess!' Mrs Dodd exclaimed, looking her over again.

He turned to Rebecca. 'Mrs Dodd is the housekeeper.'

The woman in charge of the maids, the cook and the kitchen staff. But not the governess. A governess was not a servant, but was answerable only to who hired her.

Mrs Dodd nodded to her. 'How do you do, Miss Tilson.'

Rebecca smiled at her. 'I am a little fatigued, but quite in awe of this lovely place.'

The door opened and out dashed two little girls followed by a tall, thin, impeccably dressed man who Rebecca would wager was the butler.

'Mr Glover!' said Mrs Dodd disapprovingly.

'There was no stopping them.' The man panted.

Rebecca felt as though reality struck her full in the chest. She would be the governess to these girls. And she did not know how to be a governess!

She took in a deep breath. How hard could it be?

The two girls looked less like sisters than she and Claire had. The older girl seemed all legs and arms and was as dark-haired and serious as her uncle. The younger girl was tiny, sturdy and blonde and seemed bursting with excitement.

She remembered their names. Pamela and Ellen.

Pamela, the older girl, faced her. 'Are you our new governess?'

Why be nervous? This was a little girl.

Rebecca made herself smile. 'I am. And you must be Miss Pamela.'

The girl assessed her carefully.

The younger one bounced forward. 'I am Ellen!'

'Are you?' Rebecca squatted down to her level. 'I am— Miss Tilson.' She'd almost said Lady Rebecca.

'We saw you riding,' Ellen added.

'Where is the maid?' Mrs Dodd asked Mr Glover. 'Mary was supposed to be watching them.'

'I do not know,' the butler replied. 'The children dashed through the hall. I followed them out.' He gazed apologetically at Lord Brookmore. 'My lord.' He bowed.

'Good to see you, Glover.' Lord Brookmore nodded to the man.

Rebecca stood.

Little Pamela pulled her sister behind her as if protecting the child from her uncle.

Brookmore gestured to Rebecca. 'Mr Glover, this is Miss Tilson, the new governess.'

Mr Glover's brows rose. Undoubtedly the household expected someone different.

'How do you do, Mr Glover.' Rebecca smiled.

'Miss.' He bowed.

Lord Brookmore moved impatiently. 'Let us go in the house. Miss Tilson and I have been riding all day. I am certain she needs a rest.'

Mr Glover hurried to open the door and scooted the children inside. Rebecca followed them in to a huge oak-panelled hall. The ceiling had an ornate white plasterwork design of interlocking circles unlike anything she'd seen before. Dominating the room was a huge fireplace, like a castle might have.

A maid rushed into the room. 'Miss Pamela. Miss Ellen. You must come back to the schoolroom.' She looked fearfully at Mrs Dodd, then Lord Brookmore. 'I told them to wait. I am sorry, my lord.'

'No harm in it,' he told her. 'Perhaps you can show Miss Tilson to her room and attend her?'

'Oh, yes, sir.' The maid curtsied to Rebecca. 'This way, miss.'

As they headed for a large carved oak doorway, Rebecca heard Mrs Dodd say to Lord Brookmore, 'Mr Evans wants to see you. Something about the crops…'

The maid led them to an oak stairway, its newel post and balusters ornately carved. Little Ellen scampered up the stairs. Pamela followed, walking very correctly. They climbed to the second floor and walked down a long hall past several closed doors. At the end of the hall was another hall off to the side with more doors.

'This is the children's wing,' the maid said.

Ellen pulled on the maid's dress. 'Mary, are you sending us to the schoolroom?'

'I am,' the maid admitted.

'But I want to stay,' Ellen wailed. 'We can help Miss Tilson.'

'I don't think so, Ellen,' her sister said. 'I think we aren't allowed. It is for servants to do.'

The maid gave Ellen an affectionate hug. 'You will be with Miss Tilson soon enough.'

'Come on.' Pamela took the little girl's hand. 'I will read to you from *Aesop's Fables*.'

Reading, thought Rebecca. *I can have them do a lot of reading.*

'Miss?' the maid said. 'I will show you to your room.'

The room was a comfortable size. Its oak walls made it a bit dark, but there was a nice window overlooking other buildings. She could see one of the footmen leading the two horses to what must be the stables. Would she still be welcome to ride? she wondered. Lord Brookmore's invitation had come before he'd cooled towards her.

The maid bustled around the room, straightening things that did not look as if they needed straightening. 'I will fetch some water directly. We did not know you would arrive today. Someone will light the fire, as well.'

The other footman appeared in the doorway. 'Your bag, miss.'

The maid ran to take it from his hands and he left quickly.

Rebecca removed her gloves and her hat and placed them on a table. She felt all dusty and dirty from the ride. The maid held the bag.

'Just place it on the floor.' She stepped towards the maid and extended her hand. 'I should introduce myself properly. I am Miss Tilson, as you have already guessed.'

The maid shook her hand limply and pulled away to drop into a curtsy. 'I am Mary Beale, miss.' She backed towards the door. 'I'll run and get your water.'

When the maid was gone. Rebecca pressed her hand against her abdomen and breathed deeply. Could she truly perform this masquerade?

She'd had a governess when she was about Ellen's age. Before that her mother had taught her. She remembered her mother reading books to her and showing her numbers and letters on a slate. Her governess lasted only a year. After that she'd been sent to school in Reading.

All she remembered about her governess was that the woman never smiled and often scolded. Rebecca might know nothing about being a governess, but she would be one who would smile.

Chapter Six

Garret retreated to his room right after Miss Tilson and the children disappeared above stairs. He'd not taken over the room that had once been his father's and then his brother's. He'd not wanted the memories…the ill feelings.

He'd kept the room given to him after he'd gone to school, although even that room had never entirely felt like his. He'd only stayed there on school holidays. It was on the second floor, the same floor as the children's wing, but closer to the top of the stairway.

Inside the room was his valet, the valet who had served his father and brother and was now old enough to be pensioned off. When Garret suggested it, tears filled the elderly man's eyes. 'Where would I go, m'lord?'

Garret hadn't the heart to send him away, then, even though the job occasionally seemed too much for the man.

'Good day to you, m'lord,' the valet said.

'To you as well, Brant.'

Brant helped him off with his coat, brushing it with his hand. The footman appeared with Garret's bag and it took two hands for Brant to carry it into the small dressing room off the bedchamber.

Brant had known Garret since his boyhood. Knew everything about him. Garret could not help but wonder if the old man compared the ne'er-do-well second son with his father and sainted brother.

'So you have brought the new governess,' Brant said when he returned to the bedchamber.

'Yes.' Garret unbuttoned his waistcoat. 'I will stay long enough to make certain she is well established.' And long enough to make certain all was well on the estate. He still needed to hear why Ben Evans needed to speak with him about the crops. 'After that I might return to London.'

So not much would be required of the valet. He could rest easy.

'Indeed?' Brant took his waistcoat. 'London is hot in summer.'

Not that Brant had ever spent a summer there. He'd come to London with Garret's father and brother, but that was one accommodation Garret had insisted upon. Brant would remain at Brookmore House and Garret's old batman would act as his valet in London or elsewhere. If Garret needed him, that is. He'd happily forgone a valet on his trip to collect Miss Tilson.

Perhaps if he'd sent for his batman, Garret would not have acted so abominably towards her. Or have forgotten he was betrothed.

The memory of how Miss Tilson's lips had tasted, how she'd felt in his arms, flashed through him, more vivid than any kiss or embrace with Lady Agnes. If only he could have remained a second son. Lady Agnes would never have looked at him and he might have courted Miss Tilson.

What was the use of thinking of what could never be?

Garret stripped down, washed and donned fresh clothes, and at least felt...cleaner. Mrs Dodd had told him dinner could be ready in two hours. Garret was much too restless to sit and wait. Or to sit and consume brandy until mealtime.

It was early enough to call upon the estate manager and find out what the man wished to speak with him about. Garret left the house and strode to the manager's office and rapped on the door.

'Ben!' Garret cried. 'Are you there?'

The door opened.

'Garret. You are back.' His manager thrust out his hand to shake.

Garret accepted it warmly. Ben Evans was the son of his father's manager and he and Garret had grown up together as boys. Some of Garret's happiest memories at Brookmore House were the adventures he and Ben shared.

Garret was glad that Ben moved into the job of estate manager when his father could no longer perform it. He trusted Ben. Best of all, he could just be Garret with Ben. Not Viscount Brookmore.

'I brought the girls' governess finally.' Perhaps one day he'd tell Ben about Miss Tilson's shipwreck. He certainly would not tell him about the kiss.

Ben gestured for Garret to sit. He opened a drawer and pulled out a bottle, offering it. Garret nodded.

Ben poured a glass for Garret. 'I know you said you were not staying here long, but I want to persuade you to change your mind.'

Garret took a sip. 'Whisky?'

Ben grinned. 'Do not ask.'

Importing whisky was illegal, but smuggling the liquor was not unheard of.

Ben's expression sobered. 'Stay. Through the harvest season, at least.'

He had no intention of staying. This was his father's house, his brother's house; memories lurked around every corner. And now there was the additional temptation of Miss Tilson. 'Why?'

Ben poured a glass of whisky for himself. 'I need you here.'

'Me?' Surely not. 'You know more about managing the estate than I could ever know. Father never bothered to teach me a thing. He thought he needed only the heir, not the spare.' The spare was merely good for cannon fodder.

'I do not need you to run the estate,' Ben said. 'I need your authority.'

Garret waved his hand. 'You have it. You have my full authority.'

Ben leaned forward. 'Heed me, Garret. The workers are slacking. No matter what I say or do, they are not working as hard as they should. The farm, the quarry, it is all going to suffer because of it and, let me tell you, you cannot afford for that to happen.'

'Not afford?' Garret's brows rose. 'Are we in financial difficulty? Our men of business in London led me to believe otherwise.'

'Not yet, but it would not take much to tip the scales. A poor harvest. An outbreak of gid. Bad weather.' Ben sat back, shaking his head. 'Things have been slacking since your father died. Your brother made terrible decisions.'

'My brother?' Garret could not believe his ears. 'He was taught to run the estate like my father.'

'I know,' Ben said. 'I remember how it was, but I am telling you, John ignored all sense. His way of caring for the estate was ruinous.'

'I cannot believe this.' The fair-haired boy ruinous?

Ben downed his drink. 'He neglected the tenants and the workers. No matter what I said, he'd never authorise me to make necessary repairs to the houses or the equipment. The workers were convinced he cared nothing for

the estate and for them and they've assumed you to feel
the same. You've spent no time at all here.'

That was true. He had travelled straight to London upon
receiving word of his brother's death. He'd avoided the estate until his nieces' governess had died.

He rubbed his face. 'What's to be done?'

Ben gave him an earnest look. 'For a start, stay through
the harvest. Show yourself in the field, the stables, the
barns and the quarry. Show them you value the estate
and them.'

Garret and his brother John had known the people on
the estate their whole lives. If the estate failed, what would
become of those people? He hated thinking that they'd
be forced to leave this beautiful land to work in one of
the big factories being built near the larger towns. They
might find work, but they'd lose the mountains and lakes
and fresh air.

'You want me to act the Viscount,' he said cheerlessly.

Ben held his gaze again. 'You are the Viscount, Garret.'

He drained his glass and let the brown liquid burn down
his throat. He placed the glass loudly on the table.

'Very well, I will stay.'

Garret walked back to the house, then sat in the drawing room, sipping brandy. Glover soon announced dinner. Garret entered the dining room. His place was set at
the head of the long table in the seat that really belonged
to his father and brother. The thought of eating alone in
this cavernous room, in that seat, made his appetite flee.

He'd much prefer a simple private room in a tavern. The
last two dinners he'd shared with Miss Tilson had been
more pleasant than many he could remember.

He thought of that first night when she'd been so desperate not to be alone. Who would keep her company to-

night? The girls would eat separately. The maid would eat with the servants.

He turned to Glover. 'Do you know if Miss Tilson has dined?'

'I believe not, sir,' the butler responded. 'We would serve you first.'

'Set another place here and send word for her to join me. She should dine with me. Tell her she does not have to dress for dinner. She may come in her day clothes.'

'As you wish, m'lord.' Glover signalled to a footman to do what Garret requested.

If Garret were completely honest, she was not the only one with a dread of eating alone. At least tonight.

A few minutes later Rebecca followed a footman to the dining room, which was located off the hall.

This room had the same plasterwork ceiling as the hall, but its walls were covered in leather. All these brown walls made it feel as if she were in a box and yet the feeling was a comfortable one, warm and protected. The dining room contained a long table. Lord Brookmore sat at the far end. He rose when she walked into the room.

'Miss Tilson,' he said formally. 'Thank you for coming so promptly.'

She had not dared to refuse.

He gestured to a chair adjacent to his. Glover pulled out the chair for her and held it while she sat.

'You may serve us now,' Lord Brookmore said to the butler.

When the soup was served, Brookmore spoke to her. 'Is your room comfortable, Miss Tilson?'

He was acting as if they'd merely met an hour ago.

'It is quite comfortable,' she replied in the same tone. 'As is the schoolroom and the girls' bedroom.'

'You must let me know if you need anything.' He sounded sad, she thought, and her heart went out to him.

'I think all is sufficient,' she replied, suddenly more concerned about his mood than her own worries. She made a try at conversation. 'What did you do, my lord, before it was time for dinner?'

He took a drink of his wine. 'I visited the estate manager.'

Was that what had depressed him?

She glanced at the butler and footman, who remained in the room. Not likely he would say much in the presence of servants, but he must have invited her to dine with him for a reason. So as not to be alone? They both knew she'd understand that.

No matter the strain between them earlier in the day, Rebecca wanted to distract him from whatever thoughts plagued him, like hers had done two days before.

'Your nieces are lovely little girls,' she began. Talking of the children seemed a safe enough topic.

'Yes.' He finished his wine.

'As different as night and day, are they not?' she went on.

He nodded.

This conversation was going nowhere.

'Tell me about the estate,' she tried.

He looked up at her. 'What would you like to know?'

She took a breath. 'Well…what crops do you grow? What livestock? That sort of thing.'

'Sheep and beef,' he said.

'Those funny brown sheep we saw on the ride here?'

'Herdwick sheep. Yes, we raise them. Mostly for eating. Their wool is too coarse for weaving.'

'And crops?' she asked.

The main course was served—a lamb roast.

'Hay and oats for the livestock and what you'd expect in a kitchen garden,' he replied. 'We brew our own beer so we also grow barley and hops.'

She was impressed. Her brother's estate was not so diverse. 'It is a large estate, then.' It must be for so much industry.

He shrugged. 'I suppose.' He glanced at her sideways and a smile tugged at the corner of his mouth. 'We have a quarry, as well.'

She laughed. 'A large estate, indeed! And I will wager your quarry produces this grey slate I see everywhere.'

He nodded. 'The house was built of it. Most of this house is Elizabethan with some modernisation in the 1700s. The family has been here since the fourteenth century, though.'

That explained all the oak panelling and plasterwork. 'The hall must be Elizabethan, then. And the tower in the front of the house?'

'That remains from the original house, built in the 1300s. The matching tower on the same wing as the children's rooms is a later copy.'

She smiled. 'You've good reason to be proud of all this.'

He looked sad again. 'I never expected it to be mine.'

By the time she had finished the cake for dessert, the day finally caught up with her. Her legs ached and her arms felt like lead.

'May I have your leave to retire?' she asked him. 'I am suddenly very fatigued.'

He nodded. 'It has been a long day. Of course you may retire. I will walk up with you.'

She gave him a plaintive look. 'Are you certain that is wise?'

He averted his gaze. 'I will walk you to the top of the stairs.'

Glover pulled out her chair and Lord Brookmore rose. He followed her as she walked the length of the long room. The footman opened the door for them. When they crossed the hall, they were out of earshot of any servants.

He fell in step next to her. 'I hope you approved of my asking you to dine with me.'

Her approval was hardly necessary.

'I was surprised,' she admitted. 'But glad. I still have a dread of too much time alone and there was no one else with whom to share dinner.'

His sadness made her ache for him. A governess had no business asking him about it, but she could not help herself. 'Did something happen, my lord? Something to upset you? Besides this morning, I mean.'

A look of surprise flashed across his face. They took several steps before he finally responded. 'My estate manager requires my presence here for longer than I'd hoped. It seems I will not be returning to London as I'd planned.'

He would not leave soon? She could not help being glad.

'Is there a problem somewhere? Perhaps I could help.' She'd grown up on a farm. Not as grand as this one, but she'd learned something of farm life when home for school holidays.

He glanced directly into her eyes and seemed about to confide in her. His gaze made her remember their kiss.

Instead he said, 'Share breakfast and dinner with me. The servants should not have to serve us separately and...' he paused '...I would appreciate the company.'

See him twice a day? She should refuse. She was still too affected by the kiss. More time with him also meant more time to discover she was an imposter.

She should keep her distance.

'It would be my pleasure, my lord.' Against all good judgement, she simply wanted to spend time with him.

She could be careful.

Besides, offering her company at meals seemed a small way to repay him for the very clothes on her back.

And an escape from a marriage she could not want.

As they climbed the long stairway, he asked, 'How did you fare with my nieces?'

Rebecca certainly was not going to tell him she felt daunted by them. 'I did not see much of them. The maid took me on a tour of the children's wing. The girls tagged along. They should be in bed by now.'

The clock had struck eight as they'd finished their meal.

'You should have a tour of the house, as well,' he said. 'Tomorrow, perhaps.'

'That would be lovely.' She imagined the housekeeper would act as tour guide. She'd not made a good first impression on Mrs Dodd, she feared, and a tour would give her an opportunity to do better.

At the top of the stairs, he halted, just as he said he would. 'I will bid you goodnight here.' He stepped away from her. 'Breakfast at half-past eight? I prefer to rise early.'

She curtsied. 'As do I.'

She started down the hallway, but turned around at the children's wing and saw him walking back down the stairs.

She continued on to her room. There was a fire in the fireplace and the room was comfortably warm. Rebecca looked for her bag, but discovered the maid had unpacked it and stowed it away in a cupboard where her few dresses were neatly folded. Mary had said earlier that she would come and assist Rebecca to get ready for bed, but, for the first time in days, Rebecca just wanted to be alone.

She was able to untie the laces of her dress and pull it

over her head. She lay it carefully over a chair, intending to wear it the following day. Her stays were a bit trickier, but she managed to remove them and soon she was in the nightdress Lord Brookmore had purchased for her.

Light still shone in through the window and, tired as she was, Rebecca's mind was too full for sleep. After combing out her hair and tying it back with a ribbon, she sat cross-legged on the bed, visions of Lord Brookmore's face coming back to her. His stony expressions of the morning and the melancholy ones of this evening. What would it be like to see him each day, to share meals with him, like the equals they really were? Would he ever kiss her again?

The memory of his kiss made her senses sing.

She forced herself to think of more practical matters. How to be a governess. Should she be preparing lessons, as her teachers at school had done? What was she expected to teach? Reading and writing, certainly. Mathematics. Would she need to teach Latin? French? Or needlework, drawing, comportment?

The door opened and Rebecca jumped.

Little Pamela walked in, dressed in a long white night-dress with lace at the collar and sleeves.

'Pamela! What is it?' Rebecca cried, her heart still thumping at the surprise.

The little girl walked halfway to Rebecca's bed. 'Miss Cooper died in that bed, you know.'

A chill went through Rebecca, but she did not want this child to realise that. 'Was Miss Cooper your governess?'

Pamela nodded. 'She was always our governess.'

'And she died.' Rebecca's voice caught.

Their new governess died, too. Claire.

'She died,' another voice parroted. Ellen stood in the doorway.

Rebecca gestured for her to come closer.

Ellen scampered in and climbed on the bed. 'Mary said they brought in a new mattress, so it is not so bad, is it?' She looked uncertain.

'Not so bad.' A big difference, really.

'I liked Miss Cooper,' Pamela stated in an emphatic tone.

What to say to this child? 'So you are very sad that she died, are you not?'

Pamela did not answer, but her eyes looked huge in her little face and they glistened with tears. Rebecca's throat tightened.

Ellen nestled against her. 'I miss Miss Cooper, too!'

Rebecca put an arm around her.

Ellen looked up at her with her big brown eyes and bouncing blonde curls. 'Will you die, too, Miss Tilson?'

Oh, her heart was breaking for the little girl. 'Well, I am quite young, so I do not expect to die for a very long time.' As long as storms at sea didn't cause ships to wreck and plunge her into a watery grave.

Like Claire.

And all the others.

Pamela's voice rose. 'Sometimes people die young!'

Of course they do. These children knew that. Their parents died young.

'You are right,' Rebecca told her. 'But mostly they don't. Mostly they live for a long time.'

'Like Miss Cooper?' Ellen piped up. 'She was very old. Fifty, maybe.' She lifted her hands, but could not figure out how to show fifty.

Pamela walked to the side of the bed. 'Mrs Dodd says you are too young. She says you will be trouble.'

'Because you rode the horse!' Ellen added.

Obviously the girls had not remained in the children's

wing. And obviously Mrs Dodd disapproved of her riding a horse instead of arriving in a carriage.

'I like riding horses,' Rebecca said, jostling the little girl. She turned her gaze on Pamela. 'Do you like riding horses?'

'We were never allowed to. Miss Cooper did not like horses.' Pamela looked affronted.

'I like horses!' Ellen cried.

The clock on Rebecca's mantel chimed nine and the sky outside had darkened to a soft grey.

'Goodness! It is late. We must get some sleep, mustn't we?' Rebecca slipped off the bed and picked up Ellen, who clung to her. 'Come, girls. Let me tuck you in.'

Rebecca remembered her mother tucking her in. This was a task she was certain she could do.

Pamela ran ahead to the girls' bedchamber and she climbed into bed. Rebecca followed, carrying Ellen. She placed Ellen in the other bed in the room and covered her with the blankets, the ribbon in her hair coming undone and her hair falling around her shoulders.

'There you are, Miss Ellen. All tucked in.' She wrapped her ribbon around her hand and brushed the little girl's hair off her forehead.

She turned to Pamela, who had done a good job of tucking herself in.

'Miss Pamela, how efficient you are.' Might as well praise the child for it. 'I'll just smooth your covers a little.'

Rebecca smoothed the already smoothed covers, but stopped herself from touching Pamela. Something told her Pamela would not yet welcome it.

'There. You are both tucked in.' She straightened. 'Goodnight. I will see you in the morning.'

'Goodnight, Miss Tilson,' Ellen cried.

Pamela rolled on her side, facing away from Rebecca.

'Goodnight,' Rebecca repeated.

She closed the door behind her and walked back to her room, which was the first room on the children's wing. As she opened her door, she heard a sound. Thinking Mary might be coming from downstairs, she stepped into the hallway.

Lord Brookmore stood at a door and glanced her way, his gaze settling on her and not moving.

Rebecca was in her nightdress. And nothing else.

Her skin heated and she feared it was not from embarrassment.

'The children woke up,' she said, her voice higher than usual. 'I took them back to bed.'

Why was she explaining?

He nodded and turned to enter the room.

Was his bedchamber really so close to hers?

She groaned and ran back to her room.

Chapter Seven

Garret rose early the next morning when the golden sun was only peeking over the horizon. He'd not slept well, although he did not know if the prospect of tackling the problems of the estate was disturbing him or the fact that Miss Tilson's bedchamber was only a few steps away.

He'd known, of course, that the governess slept in that room on the children's wing. Years ago his governess had slept in the same room, but seeing Miss Tilson framed in the hallway wearing her nightclothes, her hair unbound, somewhat altered his perception.

He washed and dressed himself, trying to be quiet enough not to wake Brant, whose snores he could hear from the valet's room. Carrying his boots with him, he hurried down the stairs, stopping at the bottom to pull them on his feet. He walked to the back door and crossed the park to the stables.

His valiant horse would be there, the horse who'd brought him through battle after battle.

Garret entered the stable.

'Good morning, m'lord.' Jeb, one of the stable workers, was up early as well, tending the horses. Jeb was another worker Garret had known since boyhood. Jeb's father had worked in the stables and Jeb had grown up around the horses.

'Good morning, Jeb. Good to see you. Think I'll ride Skiddaw this morning.'

Garret had named Skiddaw after one of the nearby mountains. At Garret's voice, the horse whinnied and grew restless in his stall.

Jeb laughed. 'He'll be glad to see you. And glad for a good run.'

'As will I,' Garret said, stroking the horse's neck.

At least on the back of Skiddaw Garret could feel at home. It seemed like everywhere else he'd been these days had felt wrong. He belonged with the army. With his regiment where his skills held him in good stead. He knew how to prepare men for battle and how to lead them when the time came.

After the horse was saddled, Garret led him out of the stable and mounted him. When they reached the fields, he gave Skiddaw his head and tried to forget everything but the exhilaration of the ride.

Rebecca woke from a nightmare. She'd been under the water again until a man's hand pulled her out. In the dream it had been Lord Brookmore's hand, but he'd released her again and a wave swept her away.

It took several seconds before she realised she'd been dreaming and could remember where she was. In his house, a corridor away from him.

Even though the room only showed the barest hint of dawn, she climbed out of bed. Her bare feet touching the cool wooden floor helped reassure her the water was far, far away.

She padded over to the window and opened it, smelling the fresh mountain air. The merest hint of gold shone behind the mountains, now black in the distance. From below she spied a figure crossing the park. Lord Brookmore.

He disappeared into the stable.

What a lovely morning for a ride. So crisp and cool.

She watched until the sky grew brighter, infusing the landscape with colour. He emerged again, riding a magnificent black horse, giving it its head.

She envied him. Perhaps one morning she, too, could gallop over the green fields beneath the grandeur of the mountains.

She closed the window again, remembering she was employed to educate two little girls. A flock of butterflies seemed to flutter in her stomach. Today she would really have to be a governess.

Girding herself mentally, Rebecca turned to dress.

She'd managed to wash and was struggling with her stays when the door opened.

'Oh, miss!' It was Mary carrying a coal scuttle, broom and a bucket. 'I did not expect you to be awake so early. I am here to tend the fire.'

How early had Mary risen? 'Thank you, Mary.'

Mary swept the ashes from the fireplace and placed them in the bucket. She put some new pieces of coal on the fire and turned to Rebecca, who was still fussing with her stays.

'I'll help you with that, miss.' Mary washed and dried her hands and pulled the laces of the corset tight. She helped Rebecca put on her dress.

'In the mornings I first tend to the fires in the children's wing,' Mary said while she tied the dress's laces. 'But after that I will come and help you dress. If you know a certain time you would prefer, I will come at that time.'

'I doubt I will always be awake this early,' Rebecca assured her. 'What time do the children rise?'

'I wake them at eight, miss, but Miss Ellen is often up before then.' She rolled her eyes.

Rebecca smiled. 'I am not surprised. And Pamela always stays abed until you come, I suppose.'

'Yes, indeed!' Mary laughed. 'What else might I do for you, miss?'

'Nothing I cannot do for myself.' Rebecca could fix her own hair. 'I do not wish to disrupt your duties.'

'I am here to serve you, miss. And the little girls.' She retrieved her bucket and scuttle.

'I believe I will look at the schoolroom before Miss Ellen and Miss Pamela wake up. Prepare for the day, you know.' Try to figure out how to be a governess, she meant.

'Very good, miss.' Mary curtsied and left.

It was not half past six when Rebecca entered the schoolroom. She lit candles from the fireplace that Mary had obviously already tended.

The room was neat and tidy. Books in bookcases along the wall. Boxes stored on shelves underneath. There was a long table in the centre of the room with two slates in front of two chairs and sticks of chalk and folded cloths to wipe the slates clean.

Rebecca pulled out books, one by one. She nearly whooped in pleasure. One book was titled *The Governess or The Little Female Academy*. Surely she could discover what a governess must do from this book. She sat near a candle and read, with increasing dismay. The book was about a school where the students all tell their own stories. The teacher provides the moral to be learned, but the book was hardly a model for how to be a governess.

Unless she was to provide moral lessons for everything. She'd spent her school days and afterward bucking what she was supposed to do.

Rebecca searched through other books.

A voice startled her. 'What are you doing, Miss Tilson?'

Ellen had entered the room.

Rebecca placed a hand over her fast-beating heart. 'I wanted to see what books you have.' She peered at the girl. 'Are you not supposed to be in bed?'

Ellen sauntered closer. 'I woke up. Are you going to read one of the books to us?'

Goodness. Rebecca did not know. 'I am not certain. What did Miss Cooper do?'

Ellen made a face. 'She made us read them.'

Rebecca nodded to herself. 'What else did she do?'

'Made us do sums.'

Rebecca did not mind sums. 'Anything else?'

'Needlework.' Ellen spat out the word as if it were rancid.

Rebecca concurred. Most of the female arts held little interest to her.

Ellen stood right next to Rebecca's chair and looked up to her. 'Will you eat breakfast with us?'

She'd promised to breakfast with Lord Brookmore. 'Did Miss Cooper eat breakfast with you?'

Ellen nodded, still staring into Rebecca's eyes.

What could she say? 'Of course I will!'

She brushed the hair from Ellen's forehead.

'Now I am guessing that you should go back to bed and wait for Mary to rouse you.' Rebecca stood.

She took the little girl by the hand and walked back to her room with her. If Pamela was awake, she could not tell, but she tiptoed in and quietly tucked Ellen back in bed.

When it was nearing eight o'clock Rebecca waited for Mary in the hallway outside the children's room.

The maid looked puzzled to see her. 'Miss?'

Rebecca caught her before she reached the door. 'Did Miss Cooper eat breakfast with the girls?'

'Yes, miss,' Mary responded uncertainly. 'Why do you ask?'

'Do you know why she did so?' Was this part of being a good governess or did Miss Cooper simply want some company for the meal?

'I think she used the time to teach them manners,' Mary replied.

Manners. Was teaching manners of a priority over risking offending the man who employed her? And with whom she could not help wanting to spend time?

'Miss Cooper got them talking to her at breakfast,' Mary added. 'That was the only time I ever heard them talk about their parents. About them dying, you know.'

Talking helped, Lord Brookmore had said.

'Do you think I should eat breakfast with them?' Rebecca asked.

Mary's brows rose. 'Oh, miss. I would not presume to tell a governess what to do.'

She had no one else to ask. Except maybe little Ellen.

'Where is breakfast for them?' Rebecca asked.

'In the tower sitting room. Lots of sunlight there.' Mary started for the girls' door.

'I will eat with them,' Rebecca called after her.

She hurried to the schoolroom and found paper and ink. She wrote a note for Lord Brookmore, explaining why she would not be at breakfast. She started to fold the paper, but opened it again and added another sentence.

If you so desire, you would be very welcome to share this breakfast in the Tower Room.

He would not come, of course. What man would? Certainly not her father. Nor her brother. At least he would know that she was not avoiding his company.

She blotted the ink dry and folded the note and went downstairs. As she hoped, a footman was attending the hall.

She handed him the note. 'Would you please see that Lord Brookmore receives this note before he breakfasts?'

'Yes, miss,' the footman said.

She returned to her room and waited until Mary finished helping the girls dress.

Garret came in from his ride, feeling marginally more settled.

If Ben thought it important he help solve the problems on the estate, he'd do that. Perhaps if he kept busy, his mind would not wander to Miss Tilson so frequently.

He'd merely felt sympathy for her, because of the shipwreck, he decided. He must put her solely in the role of governess and that would be that.

He bounded up the back stairs to his bedchamber where Brant awaited him.

'Good morning, my lord.' Brant stood ready to help him with his coat.

He changed out of his riding clothes into buckskin breeches and boots and one of his more comfortable waistcoats and coats. He kept an eye on the time.

It was eight-thirty already before he descended the stairs.

When he entered the hall the footman stepped up to him. 'Beg pardon, m'lord.'

'What is it, Mason?' He tried to disguise his impatience. He'd told Miss Tilson that breakfast was at eight-thirty and now he was late.

'A note for you, m'lord.' Mason handed him the folded piece of paper. 'From the new governess.'

She was not coming. What else could it be? He unfolded the paper and read that she intended to eat breakfast with his nieces and that he was welcome to join them.

He expelled a relieved breath. A part of him feared she was writing a letter of resignation.

Breakfast with his nieces.

He could understand Miss Tilson's desire to eat with Pamela and Ellen, but why would he be included?

It would be ridiculous for him to attend, would it not? On the other hand, he would have the opportunity to see Miss Tilson with the children. Make certain all was as it should be. It would give him an opportunity to see Miss Tilson…

'May I assist you, m'lord?' the footman asked.

'Hmm?' Garret was still lost in thought. 'Oh. Yes, Mason. Tell Glover that I will have breakfast in the Tower Room with the children. Have the food brought up there.'

'The Tower Room, sir?'

It did seem unbelievable.

'Yes, Mason,' Garret repeated. 'The Tower Room.'

The Tower Room was back upstairs where the main hallway met the children's wing. Unlike the medieval tower at the front of the house, the tower that had been part of the original house, this was only eighty years old or so. Unlike the medieval tower, the rooms on each floor of the tower had large windows facing east. Sunshine poured in in the mornings.

When he'd been a boy, he and his brother breakfasted in that room with his governess. His parents often joined them. His father never tired of hearing about his brother's achievements.

So it made sense Garret had been invited. He was the children's guardian.

He opened the door.

A table was placed in the centre of the room, just as it had when he'd been a child. Miss Tilson and the children all looked over at him in surprise. The children and Miss Tilson each had bowls of porridge, just as it had been in his youth.

She rose to her feet. 'Lord Brookmore. How lovely of you to come. Are you staying to dine?'

'I am staying,' he responded. 'Glover will bring my breakfast up here.'

'How very nice!'

She sounded happy he'd come. His two nieces, though, merely gaped at him.

Miss Tilson gestured to the fourth chair. 'Do sit, my lord. I'll pour you some tea.'

He pulled the chair up to the table, but did not sit. 'I should have coffee soon.' He waited until she sat down before seating himself.

Sure enough, the footmen arrived with the food from the dining-room sideboard and a welcome pot of coffee. When they left, Garret filled his plate with ham and cheese and cold veal pie. He brought the basket of bread to the table as well as the butter, honey and blackberry jam, which he suspected the girls would like.

They went from staring at him to staring at the bread and jam.

'You may have some,' he told them. 'As much as you like.'

They seemed very hesitant.

'Show your uncle how you spread the butter and jam on the bread and do so like ladies,' Miss Tilson suggested.

Only then did they accept the treat, little Ellen taking

a gob of jam for her piece of bread. Miss Tilson gave him an amused smile over that. It was endearing, but should she not correct Ellen? It was not the best of manners to pile on so much jam.

If Miss Tilson did not scold the child, Garret certainly wouldn't.

The room felt very quiet, filled only with the sounds of chewing. Garret had supposed he would merely observe the breakfast, but now he felt as if they were all waiting for him to direct the conversation.

He addressed the girls. 'Did you fare well while I was away?' he asked. 'Did Mary take good care of you?'

'Yes, Uncle Garret,' they said in unison.

He tried again. 'Have you become acquainted with Miss Tilson? Shown her a welcome?'

'Yes, Uncle Garret,' they parroted again.

He glanced at Miss Tilson for help, but she shrugged her shoulders.

'You are so very quiet,' he remarked. 'Were you quiet when other people visited you at breakfast?'

This time they merely stared.

Finally Pamela spoke in a very quiet voice. 'No one visited, Uncle Garret.'

'Surely your parents—' he began, but stopped himself. He did not wish to remind them of their loss.

'No,' Pamela quickly cried.

Ellen piped up. 'Mama came to our classroom sometimes. And we visited her in her sitting room every afternoon.'

'And your papa?' he asked.

This time Pamela answered. 'Papa did not like us,' she said in a scathing tone. 'I heard him once. He yelled at Mama for having girls instead of boys. He wanted boys.'

Ellen's eyes grew very serious. 'He made Mama cry.'

Garret felt pain deep in his gut, an old familiar pain. This one filled him with rage, as well. His damned brother. So they were little girls. They were his children.

He glanced at Miss Tilson and saw compassion in her face.

This was more pain than he'd thought his nieces had endured.

He leaned forward. 'Your papa was my brother. He did not like me very much either.' They had that in common.

The girls gaped at him again, hungry for something besides bread and jam. He probably could not give it to them, but he'd give them something.

He turned to Miss Tilson. 'Miss Tilson, do you like boys above girls? I confess I like them both.'

Miss Tilson responded as if this point was the most important in life. 'I'm a bit partial to girls.'

He almost smiled at that. He glanced back at Pamela and Ellen. 'You may have something there. Little girls are charming.'

His nieces visibly relaxed. He had not realised how stiffly they were holding themselves, as if bracing for more hurt.

Never had he thought he had any importance to them. He'd seen them only fleetingly, spoken only two or three words to them. Now, however, he'd inserted himself into their lives and if he withdrew too soon they would conclude that his brother was right.

Another reason to stay for a while. He must compose a letter to London this day, explain the reasons for his delayed return. Surely Lady Agnes would find enough to entertain her without his presence.

The conversation did not go any more smoothly after that. After more failed attempts at engaging the children, Garret finally asked, 'What will you do after this?'

Pamela and Ellen glanced directly at Miss Tilson.

'Um.' She looked uncertain, but a light came into her eyes. 'You promised me a tour of the house. We could all do that.'

Shouldn't she have them do their lessons first? That's what his governess would have done.

She turned to the girls. 'Would you like that?'

'Yes, Miss Tilson,' they said in unison again, but at least this time they sounded a little pleased.

Chapter Eight

Rebecca followed Lord Brookmore down the stairs. Behind them both trailed the little girls, who were not nearly as thrilled at touring the house as Rebecca thought they would be.

'We will start in the hall,' Lord Brookmore said, leading them into the first room Rebecca had seen in the house.

Rebecca hesitated. He was conducting the tour? Not Mrs Dodd? She quickened her step. The children stood in the doorway to the room.

'This is the oldest part of the house,' he began. 'It used to be the central part of the house in the 1300s.' He pointed to the crest above the huge stone fireplace, so large Rebecca could have walked inside it without ducking. 'Queen Elizabeth's crest was added later, but she never visited here.'

The room was panelled in oak in parquetry squares, which indeed made it seem as old as the Middle Ages.

He proceeded to the drawing room, another oak-panelled room, but with decorative carving on the oak, especially above a smaller stone fireplace. 'This drawing room was also part of the original house.'

The chairs, tables and sofas looked at least one hundred

years old, although undoubtedly the red-damask upholstery was more recent.

Lord Brookmore gestured to a huge desk in the middle
of the room. 'The desk was my great-grandfather's, made
by Gillows of Lancaster.'

This meant nothing to Rebecca, except that the most
modern piece of furniture in the room must have been
over half a century old.

Lord Brookmore spoke of the portraits on the walls,
ancestors whose names Rebecca instantly forgot.

During this discourse, Pamela remained very still, just
inside the door, but little Ellen traversed the room, looking at whatever captured her eye, and there were certainly
several porcelain decorative items at her eye level on the
various tables. She stopped by the terrestrial globe when
Lord Brookmore pointed it out. As he went on to another
piece in the room, Ellen spun the globe.

She laughed and spun it again. The third time she swung
her arm back to give it a really hard spin and knocked over
an Oriental porcelain ginger jar. It careened off the table
and smashed on to the wooden floor.

'Ellen!' Pamela cried in a panicked voice.

Ellen burst into tears and tried to pick up the shattered
pieces.

Rebecca rushed over to the little girl, worried that she
would cut herself. She took the pieces from Ellen's hands
and took over picking up the rest while Ellen continued
to wail.

'Leave it,' boomed Lord Brookmore, crossing over to
them.

Pamela stood where she was, trembling.

'Leave it.' His voice softened. He took little Ellen's arms
and guided her away. He turned to Rebecca. 'The maids
will clean it up.'

She placed the pieces she'd collected neatly on the floor. Why had she insisted the children come on this tour? Why had she not watched them more carefully? This was not going well at all.

'No need to cry,' he said, crouching down to Ellen's level. 'Things break sometimes.'

Rebecca gaped at him. He was not angry? The jar had obviously been valuable.

Pamela continued to look shocked and Ellen's whole body still shook with her sobs. He guided Ellen over to a sofa and walked over to take Pamela by the hand to join her sister.

He sat between them and pointed to a pyramid-shaped blue and white Delft tulip vase that sat next to the fireplace.

'See that tulip vase? Two hundred years ago our ancestor collected Dutch tulips. There was no price too high for him to pay for tulip bulbs. Tulip Madness it was called later.' The two girls looked at him as if he were speaking Greek. 'Anyway,' he continued. 'when I was a boy, there were ten of those tulip vases lined up. My father's pride. He'd often tell the story of his ancestor's tulip collection. One day, I was playing chase with your father, which we were not allowed to do.' The girls' interest seemed to increase with mention of their father. 'I knocked into one of the vases and it fell against the next one and they all fell, one after the other. Only one—' he pointed '—this one—survived.'

Ellen was rapt by this time. 'Did your papa beat you?'

Her uncle nodded. 'I had a proper whipping and a scolding, as well.'

Pamela cringed.

'But I learned an important lesson that day,' he went on.

'Don't break things?' Ellen offered.

'No.' His arm around her tightened. 'I learned that no vase or any item was worth so much as to deserve a whipping or even as big a scolding as I received.' He looked from Ellen to Pamela. 'Accidents can happen, but I know I can trust both of you to be careful, now you know what can happen.'

Rebecca gazed at him in wonder. What sort of man was this who thought a little girl's feelings were more valuable than a priceless piece of porcelain? Her heart swelled.

Lord Brookmore looked up at her. 'Is there anything you wish to say to Ellen, Miss Tilson?'

She was surprised to be included, but then she remembered she was the governess. 'Yes.' She cleared her throat. 'Miss Ellen, you must be more careful.'

Lord Brookmore looked less than satisfied at her response. She was unsatisfied herself. A proper governess would have known the right way to handle this, but all she could think of was how upset Ellen had been.

The tour continued through the rest of the first floor, the library, the game room, and the bedrooms that had been the children's parents'.

Rebecca hesitated on them visiting those rooms with the girls, but she did not intervene.

It seemed like the girls had never seen their father's bedroom, but Ellen blurted out one or two memories about her mother. Pamela stood silent as a stone.

Ellen touched her mother's comb and hairbrush, still resting on the dressing table. 'Mama let me brush her hair sometimes,' the little girl said. 'Her hair was the colour of mine.'

'Would you like her brush for your very own?' her uncle asked.

Ellen's eyes grew wide. 'Am I allowed?'

Lord Brookmore smiled. 'I am the one who says and

I say you may have it.' He turned to Pamela. 'You must choose something of your mother's, as well, Pamela. Something to keep for your own.'

Rebecca's heart was melting.

Pamela stared at him for a long time. She eventually crossed the room to a chest of drawers. She opened one and pulled out a miniature.

'Ah.' Lord Brookmore nodded. 'A miniature of your mother. Good choice.'

Rebecca's throat tightened with emotion, but she managed to say, 'Perhaps you should take your treasures up to your room before we continue the tour.'

They exited the bedchamber and the girls immediately turned to their right and disappeared up a back stairway.

Garret called after the girls, 'Meet us back in the hall.' He turned to Miss Tilson. 'That stairway leads to the room where you had breakfast. You might find it more convenient at times.'

He walked with her back to the hall.

He was surprised he could keep his demeanour so matter of fact. This entire episode with the children had shaken him.

They had never been in his brother's room. Of course, what Pamela said of his brother should have made that no surprise. Their visit to their mother's room had touched him deeply. He was glad he'd let them take something from the room. Some time, before he returned to London, perhaps, he ought to tend to her other belongings. Surely there was jewellery of hers that should be kept for them. Other personal items, as well.

Then there was the broken ginger jar. He'd never entered the drawing room that he did not think of breaking the tulip vases. He'd been about Ellen's age. His father's scolding had been a thousand times worse than the welts on his buttocks. He had concluded that his father would have preferred Garret die rather than the vases be destroyed.

Garret would not have his little niece feel the same, but he'd been shocked when Miss Tilson did not chastise Ellen. Weren't governesses supposed to?

He turned to Miss Tilson. 'I was surprised you did not scold Ellen for the broken vase. My governess certainly never missed a chance to scold me.'

She looked chastised. 'I suppose I ought to have said something, but at the moment I was too afraid she'd cut herself on the pieces.' Her expression turned curious. 'For what did your governess scold you?'

He thought it a curious question. 'Well, breaking things, for one.'

The scolding did have the effect of making him careful not to be reckless around his father's possessions, but his father's reaction had the opposite effect of what he might have supposed. From that moment on Garret placed very little value on things and more in people's emotions.

Miss Tilson broke into his thoughts. 'Those poor little girls.' She sighed. 'I thought I would weep when Ellen spoke of her mother.'

At least she had compassion for the girls.

'Or when Pamela said nothing,' he added.

'You were marvellous with them, you know,' she said.

His face grew warm from her praise.

She added, 'I was quite in awe of you.'

'I'm their guardian,' he said stiffly. 'I am supposed to treat them well.'

She laughed. 'My brother was my guardian and he never treated me well.'

He stopped at the entrance to the hall. 'I thought you said you had no relations.'

She paled. 'I—I—he was my half-brother and—and—I do not credit him as a relation.'

That made sense. 'After today, I am not certain I want to credit my brother as a relation either.'

She looked relieved. Was she that worried about his opinion of her?

'It is not so unusual for a father to want sons, you know,' she said.

Not all sons, just the heir. 'I do not begrudge him the desire to have sons. God knows I wish he'd had a son, so the son could inherit.' Garret frowned. 'What I do not accept is his not wanting his daughters.'

'Well, it is obvious you value them,' she remarked as she examined a suit of armour on display.

Another compliment? He was not doing anything special that he could see.

He gazed at her as she moved from the armour to a Rubens painting. She was a puzzle, sometimes so very unlike what he expected a governess to be. When faced with a puzzle, who would not wish to solve it? The enigma she was only drew him in more.

He ought to be maintaining his distance. Instead, what had he done? He'd invited her to share dinners with him. He ate breakfast with her and, instead of giving the task to Mrs Dodd or Glover, he made himself her guide.

At least his nieces served as chaperons.

The clatter of little feet approached. The girls running. Why did Miss Tilson not tell them not to run, like any governess would? Not that Garret minded them running. Let them run through the house. He'd done so only when his father and the servants were not looking.

'We are here, Uncle!' cried Ellen.

'So I have guessed,' he quipped. 'Shall we show Miss Tilson the gardens?'

'The gardens!' Ellen took his hand and pulled him towards the door.

Pamela and Miss Tilson followed.

He led them out the front door and through an archway, the entrance to a stone-walled garden.

When Miss Tilson walked through the entrance and saw the other side, she clapped her hands. 'It is a topiary!' She ran into the garden, laughing. 'Look, Pamela and Ellen. Look at all the fanciful shapes!'

Her delight was too charming.

Ellen skipped after her and even Pamela walked briskly. Miss Tilson dashed from one sculpted bush to the other.

'Look! An archway. Very like the stone one. Look! These look like silly hats.'

She dropped to her knees when she came upon the elephant which was quite a bit smaller than many of the others. 'How clever. How very clever.'

Garret had always liked the topiary. He'd pretend some of the trees and bushes were soldiers and that the whole garden was a battlefield. That had been before he learned what a real battle was like.

'Come!' Miss Tilson took Ellen by the hand and gestured to Pamela. 'Let's run to the end of the garden!'

Ellen joined in eagerly. Pamela ran a few steps, then slowed to a walk.

Garret walked over to the gardener working in one of the squares with the cone-shaped topiary.

'Phibbs!' he called. 'Good day to you.'

The man beamed. 'Garret, my boy.' He stood and doffed his hat. 'I mean, my lord.'

Garret extended his hand. Phibbs had been tending the garden since he was a boy. 'It is good to see you. You look unchanged.'

Phibbs rubbed his hip. 'Some aches and pains, you know, but I cannot complain.'

Garret glanced towards Miss Tilson. 'Your garden has a new admirer in the new governess.'

'Governess, you say?' The older man inclined his head towards her. 'She looks a game one for the poor bab'es.'

A game one. An apt description.

'She is indeed,' Garret agreed. And very unlike what he'd expected for them.

Next Garret showed Miss Tilson the orchard, the kitchen garden and the fountain garden. On their own, without Miss Tilson's leading them, the girls ran through the gardens.

Then Garret took them to the stables. The horses were in the paddocks and, as soon as Skiddaw saw him, he cantered up to the fence.

'Oh!' he heard Pamela exclaim. Her eyes were glowing.

'Would you like to meet the horses?' Garret asked her.

She nodded enthusiastically.

Ellen was not so certain. She hid behind Miss Tilson's skirts.

Garret lifted Pamela on to the fence.

'This is Skiddaw.' Skiddaw came up to him for attention.

One of the mares approached Pamela and nudged her.

'She wants you to pet her,' Miss Tilson told the girl. She demonstrated. 'Stroke her gently on the shoulder. She will love that.'

Pamela reached over the fence and stroked the horse just as Miss Tilson showed her. 'Nice horse,' she repeated soothingly.

When it came time to leave, Pamela had to be dragged away with the promise of a biscuit and milk when they visited the kitchens. The girls ran ahead and Miss Tilson fell into step next to him.

'You need to buy them ponies,' she said.

'Ponies?'

She nodded. 'Pamela, because nothing else has turned her into a normal little girl. And Ellen so she learns not to be afraid.'

Ponies.

'We shall see,' he responded, but he liked the idea.

'They are old enough to learn to ride,' she pressed on.

He turned to her. 'Miss Tilson, you've convinced me.'

The smile she returned to him was as golden as this fine day.

By the time they reached the kitchen and Cook had given Pamela and Ellen a biscuit and milk, Rebecca was filled with energy and optimism. She knew it was because of the man beside her.

She marvelled at how he apparently attuned himself to others' feelings. He always seemed to know the right question to ask, the right support to give. Of course, he'd been a bit cruel to her that third day on the road when he would not speak to her, but that was because of the kiss and the fault had been hers as much as his.

That lovely, thrilling kiss.

Rebecca stopped that thought. She must remember she was the governess and not Lady Rebecca.

She'd made a terrible slip, mentioning her brother. She must not do that again.

Mrs Dodd appeared in the kitchen while they were waiting for the children to finish their *petit repas*.

'Good day to you, sir.' Mrs Dodd curtsied to Lord Brookmore.

He smiled at the housekeeper. 'How are you faring, Mrs

Dodd? Are things running smoothly in the house? Any problems?'

The housekeeper spoke at length about the workings of the house and the needs of the servants. While she spoke, she gave Rebecca black looks.

How was Rebecca to get on Mrs Dodd's good side? The woman had taken a severe dislike to her.

After Mrs Dodd finished and Lord Brookmore promised to look into some improvements she'd suggested, she and the kitchen servants went back to their work.

Rebecca approached Lord Brookmore. 'Do we proceed with the tour?' She hoped so. It was lovely to spend the day with him.

He darted a glance to the little girls. 'Another time, perhaps. I think your charges are too fatigued.'

Her charges.

She should have realised. The little girls could hardly keep their heads up to finish their biscuits. 'Yes, perhaps a rest is due. I suppose I should take them back to the children's wing when they've finished eating.'

'I'll not wait,' he said. 'As long as I am on this wing, I want to stop by the dairy and the brewery. See how they are faring.'

He walked over to the girls to say goodbye to them. Their faces had lost that panicked look when he came near. He'd charmed them, as he'd charmed her.

She regretted losing his company.

She approached Mrs Dodd. 'The house looks marvellously well kept, Mrs Dodd. It must take a great deal of co-ordination on your part.'

The compliment did not soften her. 'I do my job.'

Rebecca became more direct. 'Forgive me for saying so, but you seem unhappy with me. May I know why so I might make amends?'

Mrs Dodd looked her up and down. 'You don't seem like a proper governess to me. Riding next to the Viscount. Eating meals with him. He's not for the likes of you, you know. People should remain in their stations.'

Her insinuation raised Rebecca's hackles, perhaps because it was too near the truth. 'I disagree, Mrs Dodd. I believe people—men and women—should rise as high as their talent, ambition and hard work take them. I do assure you, though, that I am here as governess for Miss Pamela and Miss Ellen. No other reason.'

'Hmmph!' Mrs Dodd exclaimed. 'You'd better not have any other designs.'

'I do not,' Rebecca repeated.

Mrs Dodd turned and marched away.

Cook came up to her, drying her hands on a towel. 'Do not pay her any mind, miss,' she said. 'She's a stickler, she is.' Cook inclined her head towards the doorway by which Lord Brookmore left. 'What a fine man our Master Garret turned into. He was a rackety charver in his day, eh.'

'Charver?' she asked.

Cook seemed to search for a translation. 'A rackety boy. Full of mischief.'

Rebecca nodded, repeating the word *charver* in her head so she would remember it.

She would also remember that Mrs Dodd thought her not a proper governess.

Back in the schoolroom, Rebecca was at a loss what to ask of the children, who immediately sat at what she suspected were their usual seats.

'What would Miss Cooper have you do at this time of day?' she asked them.

'Different things,' Pamela said unhelpfully.

'Like what things?' Rebecca asked.

The little girl shrugged.

'We could play!' Ellen suggested.

Somehow Rebecca did not think that was what Miss Cooper would have done.

She found paper and pencils and put them in front of each girl. 'Why not write about what we did this morning?'

They looked at her blankly.

'Why?' Pamela asked in a suspicious tone.

'Well.' How to explain it was the only idea she'd come up with? 'To remember it. Like in a journal. You write down what you did so you remember it.'

'What is a journal?' Ellen asked.

'It is a book of blank pages that you write in about your day.' Rebecca had kept a journal, but hers were now at the bottom of the Irish Sea.

'But we do not have books with blank pages,' Pamela said.

This child was too concerned with things being just so. 'If you like doing this, I'll buy you one, so you can keep a journal.' She'd have to ask Lord Brookmore, she meant, but he would say yes.

'Why would we keep a journal?' Pamela asked.

'To remember what you did,' Rebecca replied. 'But not only what you did, but how you felt about your experiences. Because, you may not realise it, but what you do and think and feel is important.'

Pamela's eyes widened. 'May I write about the horses?'

This was progress. 'Of course you may. You may write about anything. You get to decide.'

'I didn't like the horses,' Ellen said.

'Well, then, write about something else.'

'What?' Ellen looked at Rebecca as if this was the hardest task ever asked of her.

'Anything.' Somehow Rebecca suspected Miss Cooper had never had this sort of problem when she gave the girls work.

Ellen just stared at her. Where was her imagination? At age seven, Rebecca was always making up stories.

'Write about your favourite room in the house,' Rebecca came up with. 'What you saw in there.'

'I'm not good at writing and spelling,' Ellen complained.

'I'll help you.' Rebecca pulled up a chair next to her.

Ellen wrote about her mother's room, but every word she wanted to write she had to ask how to spell, making the task tedious for Rebecca, who at least kept a semblance of good humour. At least Ellen knew her letters. What would Rebecca do if Ellen had not known her letters?

Pamela apparently had a lot to say. She'd filled one page and was starting on another.

Rebecca breathed a sigh of relief that would be short-lived. After this task, what would they do next?

'After this we'll draw pictures of what we saw,' she blurted out.

That would take up a little more time.

Chapter Nine

Later that day Garret stopped by the estate manager's office. Ben was seated behind his desk, the desk his father used before him.

'Garret.' Ben rose to his feet and gestured to a chair. 'Come in. Sit.'

'I came to tell you that I've started what you suggested.' Garret lowered himself into the chair. 'I rode the property this morning.' Because he could not sleep. 'I saw some of the workers. Spoke to them.'

Ben nodded approvingly.

'I've also talked to one of the gardeners, the stable workers, the house servants, the dairy and the brewery.'

'All that?' Ben blew out a good-humoured breath. 'I did not mean for you to accomplish everything in one day.'

'It was convenient to do so.' Because he'd given Rebecca the tour, it had pushed him to be out among those who worked on the estate.

Ben's expression turned to one of concern. 'I hope you are not trying to cram this into a few days.'

Garret held up a hand. 'I know. You want more than an appearance by me.'

'It is not what I want,' Ben stated. 'It is what the estate needs. It needs your leadership.'

'I'm not certain of that,' Garret said. 'But I want the estate to prosper. There are many people depending upon it.'

'Precisely,' Ben agreed.

Garret left Ben and returned to the house. When he climbed the stairs to his room, he had half a notion to take himself into the children's wing to see how Miss Tilson was faring.

He'd see her soon enough at dinner.

He entered his bedchamber and let Brant help him change out of the clothes he'd worn all day. A clean change of clothes for dinner made him feel presentable. In his father's and brother's days, one dressed formally for dinner, but he'd feel foolish doing so to eat alone or with Miss Tilson, who did not have enough clothes to dress for dinner.

He was eager to see her, to hear what she thought about the house, the children, the horses.

But he should not be eager to see her.

In fact, he needed to write a letter. He must do so before dinner so he could send it in tomorrow's post.

'Thank you, Brant,' he said to the valet who was brushing off his coat as if putting the finishing touches on one's creation.

'Very good, m'lord.' Brant limped away.

Garret peered at him. 'Are you in some difficulty, Brant?'

The valet looked puzzled. 'Difficulty, sir?'

Garret pointed. 'You are favouring one leg.'

Brant limped across the room to pick up Garret's discarded clothes. 'Just a touch of the rheumatism, my lord.'

'Perhaps you should rest. I can forgo your services for one night,' he offered.

Brant shook his head. 'I would not think of it, sir.'

He worried about this man. 'Very well, but you must tell me when you do need rest.'

Garret left the valet and went down to the drawing room. He took paper, pen and ink from the desk and sat to compose a letter to Lady Agnes, explaining he would be remaining at the estate for unforeseen weeks.

While he put pen to paper he tried to remember what she looked like exactly. He knew she was blonde-haired and blue-eyed and that his father's friends and advisors had enthusiastically supported a match between them, but she did not come alive in his memory.

Not like Miss Tilson.

He should limit his time with Miss Tilson. Not share breakfast with her and the children again. Rescind his invitation for her to dine with him. Keep his distance.

But if he did withdraw from her company, it would mean distancing himself from his nieces, too. He could not do that. Not now. Not when he'd made himself more important to them. Not when he learned of his brother's treatment of them.

And he did not want to eat dinner alone.

He turned back to the pen and paper, managing a short note, suggesting Lady Agnes spend the summer at Brighton as she'd planned and where he was to have joined her, although Brighton held no appeal to him.

He sealed the letter and gave it to one of the footmen to see that it reached the post by tomorrow.

Glover announced dinner.

Garret entered the dining room, wondering if there was not a smaller room in which they might dine. This was the most convenient to the kitchen, though, and he was not about to inconvenience the servants any more than he had done by breakfasting with the children.

Miss Tilson was not yet there.

'Was dinner announced to Miss Tilson?' he asked Glover.

The man opened his mouth to answer when she came rushing in the door. 'Yes, dinner was announced to me. I hope you haven't been waiting long.'

'Just arrived,' he said.

She took the seat adjacent to his, where she'd sat the night before. Garret forgot all his self-warnings and simply enjoyed her company. They talked of what they each had done after the tour and she told him about the journals. He supposed journal writing was a good day's lesson for them, but an unusual one. In any event, the time went swiftly and felt very companionable.

Dinner came to an end, and he again escorted her out of the room, but did not feel like ending the time with her.

When they were out of earshot of the footmen, she said, 'I enjoyed today so very much, my lord, and the dinner. I thank you for both.'

He should bid her goodnight.

'Come to the drawing room with me,' he said instead.

They entered the room where Ellen had broken the vase earlier that day. He walked directly to a cabinet against the wall.

'I am having brandy, if you do not mind.' Although he was unsure why he was asking the governess for permission.

'I do not mind at all.' She took a seat on one of the sofas. 'Might I have a glass, as well? It has been a long time since I've tasted brandy.'

His brows rose in surprise. Most unlike a governess.

But appealing in its boldness.

He poured her a glass and one for himself and joined her, choosing a nearby chair.

In the candlelight her skin glowed and her features soft-ened and he felt intimate with her, even though he vowed he would not touch her.

She took a sip. 'I think it so beneficial that you spend time with Pamela and Ellen. You saw what marvels you created today. You saved a little girl's pride and you sparked some life into one who dares not stray off the path of what is expected of her.' She smiled. 'And you introduced her to horses!'

'I think you make too much of nothing.' He'd done what anyone would do, surely.

Except perhaps his brother. Curse him.

'I think not.' Miss Tilson's eyes shone with admiration.

Do not look at me like that, he thought. *It is too dangerous for both of us.*

She took another sip of her brandy and appeared unrepentant for enjoying it. 'Tell me more about your tour of the estate.' He had spoken of it at dinner. 'Was all well?'

Had he betrayed his worry when speaking of it at dinner? He ought to merely say yes, all was well, but there were no servants listening and he was grateful she'd changed the subject.

'The estate manager says matters are not good. My brother apparently neglected the estate and the workers are unhappy. They are not as productive as the estate needs and my brother spent so lavishly that there are not many reserves to offset any future problems.' Saying this out loud somehow made him feel the worry more acutely.

'Your brother neglected the estate?' she responded. 'How?'

He took a sip of his brandy. 'He neglected the buildings, including the tenants' houses, which are apparently in some disrepair. I am uncertain how bad things are in that area.'

'No wonder the workers are unhappy,' she said.

'The repairs must be made, obviously, but that will take time and something must be done to encourage the men to work hard enough for the estate to produce enough revenue.' He downed the rest of his brandy and stood to pour himself another. 'That is why I must stay. At least until after harvest, Ben, the manager says.'

'Of course you must stay.' Her voice was sympathetic. 'The workers need you.'

He laughed drily. 'That is what Ben says, but I am at a loss as to what I can do. They are reluctant to talk to me.'

'Make it impossible not to.' She made it sound so simple.

'And how am I to do that?' He sat again. 'I was not bred for this. My brother was the one who was to inherit. I was merely sent to the army.'

She sipped her drink and seemed lost in thought. Finally she spoke. 'You commanded men in the army, did you not?'

'Yes, I commanded men.' And sometimes sent them to their deaths.

'There must have been something you did to make your men follow you into battle,' she went on.

'What has that to do with running an estate?' he snapped.

She finished her brandy and rose. 'Forgive me, my lord.' Her voice lost all its sparkle. 'I simply thought that commanding soldiers and commanding workers might be similar, but I see I spoke out of turn. I should retire.' She started for the door.

He caught her arm before she entered the hall, putting himself dangerously near to her, breaking his vow not to touch her.

'I did not mean to speak sharply, Miss Tilson.' Her lips were too tantalisingly close and her muscles melted in his grasp.

She held his gaze and it felt as if energy was sparking between them.

He released her. 'Yes, it is probably best you retire for the night.'

She nodded and her voice softened. 'I hope you sleep well. I am certain you can solve these problems, Lord Brookmore. I'm of a mind there is nothing you cannot do.'

She turned and left.

He walked back to his brandy and swirled the liquid in the glass, his body humming for her and his mind turning.

Was it so very different commanding workers and commanding soldiers? Was she correct? Could he do this?

Garret stayed awake half the night thinking of how he commanded his regiment in those last years and how he'd dealt with his company before his rise in rank. He'd never given it much thought, had merely done whatever he felt needed to be done, said what needed to be said. He realised finally that, before everything else, he ensured his men's needs were met. Whenever humanly possible, he made certain they had adequate food, shelter, clothing, medical care, if needed. He kept them in muskets, ammunition and powder. They rewarded him by following his orders and fighting bravely in battle.

There was no reason he could not do the same for his workers. He'd incur whatever expense necessary to repair their houses and equipment and to keep them in necessary supplies. No one on the estate should go hungry or suffer cold or endanger themselves by working with faulty equipment. This was his obligation to them, his duty, just as it had been with his soldiers.

How had his brother not seen this?

The next morning at breakfast, Pamela jabbered about horses and journals and Ellen complained about both. Ellen again asked Garret to tell the story about breaking the tulip vases. Finally as they were leaving the Tower Room, Garret had a chance to say something privately to Miss Tilson.

'I am going to speak to the workers,' he told her as they entered the corridor. 'I now know what I need to do.'

She smiled at him. 'I knew you would sort it out.'

'What you said helped,' he added.

She looked about to ask him what he meant when the children pulled her away to the schoolroom.

He'd tell her more tonight after dinner. He expected to have a lot more to tell her.

Garret hurried from the breakfast room to Ben's office, eager to put his plan into effect.

Over the next few days Rebecca was pleased to hear Lord Brookmore speak about his efforts on behalf of his workers. He'd taken command, just as she'd suggested, but the best thing of all was he'd spent time meeting with as many workers as possible, hearing their concerns and promising to address them.

He also rode into Grasmere to purchase journals for the girls and he sent a seamstress from Ambleside to sew more garments for her.

He still ate breakfast with her and his nieces, so he was practically the first person she saw each day. In the evening they ate dinner together and talked over the day's events. Her esteem of him continued to grow.

She encouraged him to do most of the talking, lest he ask her about her lessons with the children. She was an abominable governess. Oh, she managed to fill the time with the girls, but she had no idea if what she was doing was anything like what she ought to be doing. She skipped from one sort of lesson to another, usually finding some excuse to explore the gardens with the girls or visit the horses.

This morning, though, Rebecca was as restless as a

stormy sea, and no wonder. She'd dreamed of the sea, of the shipwreck, of the mother clutching her children to her. Only she was the mother and the children were Pamela and Ellen.

She'd woken in terror and could not return to sleep.

The walls confined her this day, even more so because the day was as beautiful as any she'd ever seen. The sky was vivid turquoise with puffs of white clouds as decoration. The mountains sparkled with green and the flowers in the garden danced in the breeze. The air was brisk, chillier than a normal summer, but, still, she could not bear to stay inside.

'I thought to take the girls on a walk today,' she told Lord Brookmore, although she'd merely thought of it that minute. 'Where can we go? Somewhere we can see something new or unexpected.'

He thought for a moment. 'Rydal Water is near. An easy walk from here. You can make your way around the lake and see birds and fowl. It is not difficult to find. You won't get lost.'

She turned to the girls. 'What say you, young ladies? Shall we walk to Rydal Water?'

'Yes!' Ellen shouted exuberantly.

Pamela said nothing.

Lord Brookmore gave her the direction to the lake and shortly after they finished breakfast she and the girls donned their hats, half-boots, walking dresses and jackets and started off.

Being outside in the fresh air and sunshine helped Rebecca's restlessness a bit and the children did not demand much of her. Ellen skipped ahead, stopping to examine every flower and insect, and kept up a constant narrative on what she saw. Pamela, like Rebecca, seemed lost in her own thoughts.

How much better it was to inhale the scent of elder-flower and wild garlic than the chalk dust and paper of the schoolroom.

They walked over a hill—or rather Ellen ran—and finally they could see the lake below, mimicking the blue of the sky even down to the reflections of the clouds in the water.

With a laugh, Ellen ran down the hill and Rebecca and Pamela quickened their pace. The water's edge was not accessible at the hill's bottom, but they found a path that seemed to circle the lake. Rydal Water had an island in the middle, a green spot amidst the blue water.

As they walked around the lake, it was easy to stay close to the water, although occasionally rocks or shrubbery separated them.

'What is that?' Ellen pointed to a bird that just took flight.

'A heron!' Rebecca told her. 'See its long legs and beak?'

They spied a red squirrel and an otter, and Ellen was beside herself with excitement. Pamela seemed to relax, as well, stopping to examine leaves and flowers and picking up stones to take home with her. Rebecca cleared her mind and let the peacefulness of the day calm her.

'Think of all you will be able to write in your journals,' she said to the girls. 'And to tell your uncle.'

He would listen interestedly, as if each word his nieces uttered was very important. What sort of man cared what little girls said?

A fine man.

Rebecca imagined the expression on his face as he listened attentively to her, too, when they conversed at dinner. *He'd* become important to her.

'Look! Look!' cried Ellen. 'A swan!'

The elegant creature, so white it shimmered, swam at

the water's edge, which was down the slope from the path where they walked.

Ellen raced towards it. 'A swan! A swan!'

'Slow down!' Rebecca shouted. She raced after her.

'Stop, Ellen!' her sister cried.

But the child ran too fast to stop. Ellen tripped when her feet hit the stones at the water's edge and, as she struggled to keep her balance, she stumbled into the water.

She fell in with a splash, crying out. In her effort to stand, she pushed herself further into the lake and soon was flailing into deeper and deeper water.

Pamela screamed.

Rebecca ran into the water, reaching for Ellen, who floated further away. Reeds beneath the water tangled in Rebecca's feet and she fell beneath the water's surface.

Suddenly she was back in the Irish Sea, the sounds of splintering wood and human screams muffled under the water. Her feet gained purchase on the bottom and she pushed herself out of the water, now up to her chest.

Ellen clung to a thin branch that protruded from the water. Just a step or two further into the water and Rebecca could reach her.

But Ellen's cries turned into the cries of the children in the ship's rowboat. Pamela's screams rang in her ears like those of panicked men and women facing death. The water was cold. Like that day. Cold.

'Miss Tilson! Help her! Help her!' Pamela cried.

Rebecca shook her head and the thunder of pounding horse hooves sounded in her ears. The mountains and the lake came in to focus. Ellen's hand was slipping off the branch.

Rebecca cried out and surged forward. She grabbed Ellen, but they both sank beneath the water. Ellen thrashed about, but Rebecca would not let go of her. Rebecca's feet slipped on the bottom as she struggled to lift Ellen out of the water.

Her mind's eye saw lifeless bodies of children floating under water. Her panic rose.

Suddenly she was seized from behind by strong arms that pulled her and Ellen towards the shore. Their faces broke through the water and Rebecca took gulps of air.

When she could stand again, Ellen was scooped from her arms and carried out of the water. Only then did she see their rescuer.

Lord Brookmore.

He placed the coughing and spluttering child on dry ground. Her sister ran to her and hugged her tightly.

Rebecca was afraid to move from the water, afraid of falling under again, but, no matter, Ellen was safe. Lord Brookmore charged into the lake again, took her in his arms and carried her to shore. When he released her to stand, he held her for a brief moment in a tight embrace before they both hurried to Ellen's side.

Ellen's teeth chattered and her lips were blue. Rebecca's chest hurt from the cold water and she could barely feel her legs.

Lord Brookmore's coat lay on the rocks nearby. He picked it up and wrapped it around Ellen. He lifted the child into his arms. 'We have to get her warm as quickly as possible.'

Rebecca could only nod.

He carried Ellen to his horse. 'I can't take you both. Can you walk, Miss Tilson?'

'I'll m-m-manage.' She was not at all sure she could walk, but she didn't want him to waste time with her. Ellen must be taken home immediately.

Lord Brookmore turned to Pamela. 'You must walk

Miss Tilson home. Do you understand, Pamela? Do not allow her to stop. Come all the way home.'

Pamela nodded. The girl took Rebecca's hand and pulled her until she got to her feet, still numb from the cold water.

Brookmore mounted his horse and placed Ellen before him on the saddle. He turned to Pamela again. 'Make sure you do not stop. All the way home.'

Pamela held Rebecca's hand and pulled Rebecca on. 'Come, Miss Tilson. We have to walk home.'

It was a huge responsibility Lord Brookmore had given this little girl, the responsibility of Rebecca's welfare. Rebecca could not bear it if she were to keep Pamela from completing her task.

Rebecca walked.

Rebecca heard the sounds of the shipwreck while she struggled to keep the pace little Pamela set for her. She could not always tell where she was. One minute she'd be drifting at sea and the next on a road with mountains surrounding her and a little girl telling her to keep walking.

Gradually the cold left her, but her skirts were heavy with water and her feet chafed against the wet leather of her shoes. She felt close to collapsing, but pushed on, so as not to become too big a burden for a little girl.

Just when it seemed she could not take another step, a gig appeared in the distance.

It pulled up beside them, driven by one of Lord Brookmore's coachmen. 'His lordship said to come pick you up.'

Chapter Ten

Garret's horse had made the trip to Brookmore House at great speed. He'd shouted for help and Glover and a footman ran from the house to assist him. Ellen had been swiftly placed in the arms of one of the maids who hurried her up the stairs to change her out of her wet clothes and wrap her in warm blankets.

Only then had Garret realised he was also cold and dripping water on the floor of the hall.

Brant belied his age and quickly helped Garret change out of his wet clothing and into dry ones. As soon as Garret was dressed again, he hurried to the children's room to see Ellen.

She was sitting up in bed, a shawl wrapped around her shoulders. Mary, the girls' maid, fed her some hot liquid on a spoon.

'Uncle!' Her face tensed. 'I did not mean to chase the swan! I did not mean to fall in the water!'

He hurried to her bedside and crouched down to speak to her. 'There now.' He tried to sound soothing. 'You did not know what would happen. Never worry. It was an accident.'

Tears welled up in her eyes. 'I am very sorry.'

He held her tiny hand in his. 'I know you are.' He looked her over. 'Are you hurt in any way?' She looked unharmed, except for damp hair and a pale face.

She shook her head. 'I'm cold, though.'

'That is why you must let Mary feed you—whatever it is.' He glanced at Mary.

'Camomile tea with honey,' Mary offered.

'There you go. That will warm you,' he said.

Mary offered a spoonful and Ellen dutifully swallowed it.

'Where is Pamela?' she asked. 'And Miss Tilson?'

He was asking himself the same question. As soon as he'd arrived with Ellen on the horse, he'd shouted instructions to send the gig for them. They should have been here by now.

'I am sure they will be here any minute,' he said. 'In the meantime, rest and finish your tea.'

'Yes, Uncle Garret,' she replied.

He straightened. 'I will check on you later, so don't let me hear you've given Mary any trouble.'

'Yes, Uncle Garret.'

He walked out of the room and down the back stairs, trying to decide if he should set off towards Rydal Water to find Miss Tilson and Pamela himself. He was not at all confident Miss Tilson could walk the whole distance. If the gig could not find her, she might succumb to the cold. Garret had seen soldiers die of the cold in the mountains in Spain. The men who'd kept walking stayed alive.

Garret tried to quell his worry. When had he before felt this frantic? Or cared this intensely? In the army he'd learned not to become too close to anyone; too many were killed. When a child, he'd learned not to care so much; it hurt when caring was not returned. But Pamela and

Ellen—and Miss Tilson—somehow had made their way into his heart.

He was going after the gig.

Garret was in the doorway to the hall when he heard a carriage and shouting voices. The door opened and Pamela dashed in and ran for the stairs. Miss Tilson was helped in by one of the maids. Mrs Dodd followed behind, muttering, 'You've caused a great deal of trouble.'

Garret's impulse was to snap at Mrs Dodd for her cruel remark and take Miss Tilson in his arms and carry her to her room, like he carried Ellen. He did not do either, though. Instead he held back, remaining in the doorway, watching the maid help her up the stairs.

He closed his eyes and said a prayer of thanks that he'd ridden to the lake instead of the quarry where he'd been bound. Even as he'd turned his horse on to the road to Rydal Water, he'd told himself he should go to the quarry.

Then he'd heard the screams.

He reached them seconds before seeing Miss Tilson disappear under the water trying to reach Ellen. It was easy to become tangled in the reeds and be unable to rise again, even in shallow water. But she had risen again to grab Ellen at the same moment Ellen's fingers slipped from the twig she'd grasped. Then both of them went under again.

By that time he'd jumped off his horse and torn off his coat and sprinted into the water after them.

How easy it would have been for them both to drown. What if he'd not been there to save them?

He turned away and made his way out to the garden, even though the chill still penetrated through him.

What if the water triggered another spell in her? It stood to reason she might experience visions of the shipwreck.

He'd never told anyone about the shipwreck. Had she? Even if she had, would they know how to help her if the visions returned?

Rebecca woke to a warm but darkened room. She must have slept the day away. Neglected even more of her duties.

She closed her eyes again and saw Ellen clinging to the branch, crying for her help. She rolled on her side and curled into a ball. What sort of person fails to save a child? That precious child!

There was a knock on the door. The maid or Mary come to check on her, no doubt.

She sat up and wiped her eyes. 'Come in.'

The silhouette in the opening door was not a maid.

She drew the covers over her. 'Lord Brookmore!'

He stepped inside the room and closed the door. 'I came to see how you fared.'

She turned away from him. 'Better than I ought.'

He came closer. How could he bear to even look at her?

'She cried for me and I could not move. How awful is that?' She faced him again. 'Me, who knows what drowning is like.'

He stood next to her bed. 'I did not see you hesitate.'

She blinked. 'She would have drowned!' She twisted away again. 'I am the very worst of creatures! How could I do that? She was crying for me!'

He touched her face, turning it back to look at him. 'You did not hesitate. She did not drown. She is unharmed.'

She pulled out of his grasp. 'I am supposed to take care of the children! Mrs Dodd is right. I am nothing but trouble.'

She'd been trouble for everyone. Her father. Her brother. Even at school. Now she'd almost let a child drown. Not merely any child. Ellen. Dear Ellen.

'Never mind Mrs Dodd for the moment.' His voice turned low and soothing. 'You had a vision of the ship-wreck, did you not?'

She nodded. 'But that is no excuse.'

This time when he touched her face it was like a caress. 'It was brave of you to rush into the water—'

'I was not brave. I froze,' she insisted.

'You might think you froze, but it must have only been for a second or two,' he countered.

He brushed the hair from her forehead and pulled his hand away, holding it behind his back.

She rose to her knees, forgetting to cover herself. 'It was like at the inn! I was there again. I was there and I heard the sounds. I smelled and tasted the sea. I felt the boat capsize.'

He nodded. 'Like the soldiers after a battle. You could not help the memories that came to you. But they must have lasted only seconds, because, I tell you, you didn't hesitate.'

She searched his face to see if he was telling the truth or just trying to make her feel better.

He put his arms around her and held her close. 'Do not torture yourself. You could not help but be caught in the vision. Even so, you did everything you could do.'

Her cheek pressed against his and the roughness of his beard scraped her skin. It felt so good to be held by him.

Just as quickly she pushed away. She did not deserve comfort.

They stared at each other and she did not know what to read in his eyes. Pain? Regret?

She felt angry at herself and ashamed and regretful that she could not remain encircled by his arms.

The door opened suddenly and Lord Brookmore stepped back.

'Miss Tilson!' Ellen ran in and climbed on the bed, giving her a hug. 'We heard talking. We wanted to see you.'

'Ellen wanted to see you,' Pamela clarified. 'I told her we must let you rest, like Mary said.'

Ellen turned to her sister. 'But we heard her talking, so she wasn't resting any more.' She seemed to notice Lord Brookmore. 'You were talking to her, weren't you, Uncle Garret?'

'That I was,' he said stiffly. 'Talking.'

Rebecca extended her arm. 'Come here, Pamela.'

Pamela approached the bed.

Rebecca reached over and took the girl's hand. 'This is the brave one! How can I ever thank you for bringing me home?'

Pamela reddened. 'Uncle Garret told me to.'

He touched her shoulder. 'You did a fine job, Pamela. Just as I knew you would.'

The girl glanced up at him with worshipful eyes. Rebecca knew exactly how she felt.

She hugged both girls. In these mere few days they'd become as dear to her as she could imagine her own children to be. 'I am so glad we are here safe and sound.' She released them and directed her gaze at Ellen. 'I am so sorry I did not pull you out. I am so very sorry!'

'But you caught her and Uncle Garret pulled you both out,' Pamela said.

Lord Brookmore spoke. 'Do you know why it was especially brave of Miss Tilson to go in the water after Ellen?'

Both little girls looked up at him. 'Why?' they asked in unison.

'Miss Tilson was in a shipwreck and she almost drowned. The lake water made her afraid all over again. It brought back the memories as if it was all happening again, but she still grabbed hold of Ellen.'

'A shipwreck!' cried Ellen. She glanced from Rebecca to Lord Brookmore. 'What is a shipwreck?'

'When a ship sinks in the ocean.' Pamela turned to Rebecca. 'What memories did the water make you have?'

'Of being under the water…' She paused. The children did not need to hear about the screams. About Claire and the gentleman washed overboard. About the mother and children in the rowboat. 'When I sailed from Ireland to come here, there was a storm and the ship crashed into rocks. But it was close to shore so, even though I was tossed under the water, I did not drown. Somebody saved me.'

'That is why Miss Tilson does not have more dresses,' Lord Brookmore added. 'They were all lost at sea.'

'You lost your dresses?' Pamela asked.

Rebecca nodded. 'I lost everything. What I have now is what your uncle kindly bought for me.'

'Mama had lots of dresses,' Ellen piped up. 'She even had new dresses that came after—after—you know.'

'After she died,' Pamela added helpfully.

'The dressmaker will make Miss Tilson more dresses, too,' Lord Brookmore said.

The girls knew that the dressmaker had come to measure her and collect the cloth Lord Brookmore purchased.

'But!' Rebecca pushed away this focus on her. She still must act like a governess. 'You girls should be in bed! It is late and I am sure Mary does not know you are still awake.'

'We crept out after she left us,' Ellen explained.

'Well, then, let's get you back to bed before Mary comes to check on you.' Lord Brookmore gestured for them to move out of the room.

Rebecca climbed out of bed. 'I'll tuck them in.' She wrapped herself in her shawl.

'I want Uncle Garret to tuck me in!' Ellen demanded.

'Very well.' He laughed softly. 'I'll come, too.'

Garret should have begged off, but he was charmed by his little nieces and, after the day they'd had, he did not wish to deny them anything.

Besides, he was loathe to leave Miss Tilson, although he knew he ought to.

He accompanied his nieces and Miss Tilson, wearing only her nightdress and shawl, to the girls' bedroom and tucked them both into bed and kissed them each on the forehead.

His heart filled with emotion. They were securely lodged there in his heart, all three of them. To almost lose them was taking a slice out of him. What a shock to need these three people, to need to keep them safe, healthy and happy.

Not even the woman he would marry mustered that much emotion in him.

He felt a pang of guilt.

'Now go to sleep,' Miss Tilson ordered the girls. 'Tomorrow we go back to our lessons.'

'May we start by writing about today in our journals?' Pamela asked.

'You may,' her governess said. 'If you stay in bed until morning and get some sleep.'

The girls made a show of shutting their eyes. Garret and Miss Tilson left the room and closed the door.

They walked side by side to the door of her bedchamber.

'Are you hungry, Miss Tilson?' To his knowledge, she had not eaten since breakfast.

She nodded. 'But it is of no consequence.'

'You must eat,' he insisted. 'Shall I have food sent up to you?'

'No,' she responded. 'I do not want to cause Mrs Dodd any more trouble.'

He frowned. 'Perhaps I must talk to Mrs Dodd.'

She put a hand on his arm. 'No, please do not. Let it be.' She dropped her hand. 'I will go down to the kitchen and beg for food.'

'I'll come with you,' he said.

Why ever had he said that? He ought to bid her good-night. At every turn he did the opposite of what he should. All afternoon and evening he'd told himself to stay away from her, that his servants were checking on her, that he should wait until morning when everyone was accustomed to him sharing breakfast with her and the children.

But when the sky turned dark and the house quieted, he could no longer bear the wait. He needed to see for himself that she was unharmed. He'd intended only to peek in at her, but she'd answered his knock and he'd become like a moth to a flame after that.

And he was still flying around her, unwilling to lose her light.

Rebecca wrapped her shawl around her. She ought to feel undressed around him, but it always felt right to be with him even in her nightclothes.

How scandalous was that?

Truth was, she wanted him to stay with her. He took the edge off her wretchedness. She still felt responsible for Ellen almost drowning.

Lord Brookmore stopped near the stairs. 'I have an idea. Wait for me in the breakfast room. I will go to the kitchen and tell Cook I am hungry and want to carry food up to my room. She will not question that. I'll bring the food to you.'

She shook her head. 'Have you wait on me? That cannot be right.'

'No one will complain that I am causing them trouble and you will not be seen walking with me in your night-dress.'

The truth was she did not want to encounter anyone else.

'If you insist, my lord.' She parted from him. If no one knew they were together, there would be no harm done.

And in her desolation she could not resist his kindness.

Their clandestine repast was healing for Rebecca, a moment in time where she pretended they were merely Garret and Rebecca, even though she could never call him anything but Lord Brookmore and he could only call her Miss Tilson. She did not have to think of children drowning or of pretending to be Claire. She could simply enjoy being in his company.

She could enjoy loving him.

But now the candles were wearing to nubs and the clock had passed midnight.

'We should retire,' she said.

'It is late,' he agreed. She stacked the dishes, but he put a stilling hand on hers. 'I will take them to my room later.'

And keep the secret of their lovely meal. Bread, cheese, wine and blueberry tarts.

He stood and extended his hand to help her up. His hand so strong and warm in hers. She remembered his arms around her pulling her out of the water. She remembered the feel of his body against hers when she wrapped her arms around him in that grateful embrace.

She threaded her arm through his as they sauntered down the hallway, slowing the walk to her bedroom as much as possible.

Once there she leaned against the door, looking up at him, at the face that had become so dear to her. 'How am I to thank you, my lord? I seem to ask this once again.'

She remembered the last time she asked this of him. In the inn. When he kissed her. That night had also been an idyll, but then she did not know the half of how wonderful he was. Surely it would do no harm to kiss again. Just once more, to keep the fantasy of this night a bit longer, that it was right to love him, just this once.

He looked down at her, his eyes darkening, his features softening. He placed his hands against the door, caging her between them. That time at the inn, she could not be certain if she or he initiated the kiss. This time there would be no question.

She rose on her tiptoes, slid her arms around his neck and reached for his lips.

Desire exploded inside Garret when her lips touched his. He lifted her in his arms to deepen the kiss and feel the soft curves of her body against his.

He'd longed to hold her again, to taste of her, to share with her the passion that simmered between them from that first moment when she'd opened her eyes to him after the shipwreck. He needed her forthrightness, her daring, her admiration of him. He needed her lips against his, a joining, that, forbidden as it was between them, he could not resist.

He yearned for more, however. His passion flamed, urging him to ask for more. God help him, he wanted more from her. He wanted that completeness between man and woman, that shared ecstasy that would bind them as one.

She moaned beneath his lips and opened her mouth to him. He lifted her higher, wrapping her legs around him. He opened the door and carried her through, closing it behind him with his foot. He brought her to the bed, kicking his shoes off as he went. Her shawl fell to the floor. Once he placed her on the bed she pulled him with her. He rose over her, rubbing his hands over her breasts, sliding his hands down until he could reach beneath her skirt.

'Garret,' she murmured, her voice as urgent as his senses. 'Yes. Yes.'

She pulled him down for another kiss.

This was the sort of drowning from which he wanted no rescue, drowning in the pleasure of her warmth, her skin, their shared need.

The clock on her mantel chimed once and jolted him awake from his reverie.

'No,' he said more to himself than to her. 'We cannot do this.'

He pushed himself off her and off the bed.

She covered herself with her nightdress and sat up, her expression panicked. 'Sir?'

He turned back to her and stroked her hair. 'Do not fear. I am not angry with you and I do not blame you. I put us in this position of intimacy.'

'You have to know I wanted it,' she said quietly.

He did know, but had he not nurtured that desire in her? Had he not brought her to this very place where she would want to make love so urgently that she would abandon all good sense?

'I knew how to make you want it,' he admitted.

She slid off the bed, stood and faced him. 'I am not experienced in these matters, but I do know that you have been unlike any man I've known, certainly unlike any man in my family, and I wanted more than anything else to be that close to you.'

'We cannot,' he said again.

'Why not, if I am willing?' she countered.

Because she was not experienced she would not know why not.

'Are you willing to give up your reputation?' he asked. 'We cannot keep this a secret. There are no secrets in a house like this. You would be giving up any chance to make a respectable marriage.'

'The chances of my marrying are slim, are they not? Besides, I wanted this with you.' She held on to the bed-post as if she had trouble standing.

He'd be making her his mistress. Because he was marrying Lady Agnes, there was no other choice. But he cared too much for her to make her his mistress. And there was nothing else she could be, not with him promised to another.

'Would it make a difference if I were not a governess?' she asked.

What an odd question.

'But you are a governess.' He searched for another argument. The obvious one. 'You would risk conceiving a baby. What would you do then?'

Rebecca lifted her chin. 'Raise the child. Love it.'

'How would you live?' He put on one shoe then the other. 'No one would hire a governess with an out-of-wedlock child.'

She averted her gaze for a moment, then faced him again. 'You would support me and the child. You are that sort of gentleman.'

She knew with every fibre of her being that she could trust Lord Brookmore to take care of her and a baby. He did not abandon those who needed him. He was indeed that sort of gentleman.

He faced her and looked her directly in the eye. 'There is something else, Miss Tilson—'

She longed for him to call her Rebecca.

'Something I should have told you before.' His eyes

held hers and it seemed an age before he spoke. 'I am betrothed. I am to marry the daughter of the Earl of Trowbridge. Lady Agnes. It is a good match.'

Rebecca felt as if all the blood drained from her body. He was betrothed. He was to marry. An earl's daughter. Like her.

'I cannot cry off,' he went on. 'It would be assumed that I found something objectionable in her. It would ruin her for other suitors.' He frowned. 'I cannot make love to you, Miss Tilson. It would dishonour you and her.'

Rebecca closed her eyes against the pain of her foolishness. To weave this fantasy of sharing carnal love with him for one night. To convince herself it would have no consequences. To believe she could be content with one night.

All along he'd belonged to another woman, her social equal. It stung.

'I should return to London. To—her. Not remain here.' His brow furrowed. 'You will stay, will you not? You will stay with Pamela and Ellen?'

She crossed her arms over her chest. 'I will stay.'

Would he be honourable enough to give her a good reference if she wished to leave? What would he think if she told him who she really was?

She could not leave, though, or tell him the truth. Because she wanted to stay with Pamela and Ellen. Losing them would truly be like losing everything dear to her. Pamela and Ellen.

And him.

'I will stay.' She calmed herself. 'And so must you. You have been telling me for days how you must help your tenants and workers and give them a reason to work harder for the estate. You would be neglecting them if you left. How honourable would that be, my lord? I will not allow you to leave them because of me.'

His voice turned low. 'How can I remain with what passes between us?'

But even if he were not betrothed to Lady Agnes, there would still be a barrier between them. She'd given up her social status equal to Lady Agnes's and if she revealed herself to be Lady Rebecca, she'd lose Pamela and Ellen and they would lose her along with the other losses they'd endured.

'Then go,' she said, keeping her voice carefully even lest she reveal the confusion of emotions swirling inside her. 'Leave this house. Leave your nieces. Leave all these people who work for you and esteem you. Leave this room, too. I suddenly wish to be alone.'

He straightened, almost as if receiving a blow. With one long gaze at her, he turned and walked away.

Rebecca stood, grasping the bed post, watching him until the door closed behind him.

Chapter Eleven

Rebecca rose early the next morning, having slept little, fired by the emotions within her. About herself. About Lord Brookmore.

She'd been too impulsive once again, a fault her teachers told her would be the death of her. Perhaps Lady Rebecca, with all her illusions and fantasies, ought to pass away.

She needed to be Claire. A governess who knew her place. She'd made a choice to be Claire impulsively, but it could not be undone without hurting Pamela and Ellen and that she would never do.

If she had not pretended to be Claire, Lord Brookmore would have disappeared from her life, nevermore to be seen. She was glad to have made that impulsive choice, glad she'd had this time with him.

She was even glad to have been kissed by him. And refused to feel guilty for wanting to make love with him. After a day so harrowing, so filled with life and death, she'd needed him. That had been one impulsive choice she did not regret. She only regretted that he'd stopped. It had been her only chance to experience that sort of love and she'd only wanted that sort of love with him.

There was something between them, that elusive element for which she'd yearned, but had been absent in any other suitor. What she felt for Lord Brookmore bound her to him, even if he married another.

Still, he'd been right to stop. At that moment, she'd been wild with disappointment and still was, really, but he'd been right.

It was not right of him to leave his nieces and his estate because of her. That she could not allow.

One of the lower maids entered the room to tend the fireplace. She jumped when she noticed Rebecca seated in the chair by the window. 'Oh, miss!' the maid exclaimed. 'You startled me.'

'I am up early, I know.' Rebecca smiled at the young woman. 'Please tend to your task as if I were not awake.'

The maid swept the ashes into her bucket and placed new coals on the few that still glowed. She refilled the coal bin and wiped the hearth with a damp cloth.

She gathered up her things and started for the door. 'I'll be going, miss.'

Rebecca stopped her. 'May I beg a favour? You are Meg, are you not?'

'Yes, miss,' the maid said.

'Will you help me into my riding habit?'

The maid put down her things and wiped her hands. 'Yes, miss.'

A few minutes later Rebecca made her way down the back stairs, out of the house and across the park to the stables, determined to ride, as Lord Brookmore had once invited her.

She would ride until these emotions blew off her, like leaves off a tree, and hopefully she would be calm in time for breakfast with the girls.

And Lord Brookmore.

The stable door was open and she walked in.

'Is anyone here?' she called.

A stable worker emerged from one of the stalls. 'Miss?'

She lifted her chin. 'Lord Brookmore said I might ride. Is there a horse you could saddle for me?'

He wiped his hands on a cloth as if considering her request.

'I assure you, I am an experienced rider,' she added. 'The more spirited the horse, the better.'

'Yes, miss.' His voice was sceptical.

She walked through the stable until reaching the tack room. She pointed to her saddle, one of two side saddles that hung there. 'That one is mine.'

He took the saddle and walked by two or three stalls, whose horses eagerly reached for him with their muzzles. He finally chose a lovely bay mare.

'This is Lily,' he told her.

While he saddled the horse, Rebecca introduced herself to the animal, stroking its neck and getting it used to the sound of her voice.

'You know horses, miss.' The stableman nodded approvingly.

'I love horses.' She pressed her cheek against the horse's neck.

The stable worker checked the saddle and led the horse to a mounting block. Rebecca was soon in the saddle and out in the crisp morning air.

The stable worker had chosen well. Lily was steady, but eager. When Rebecca accustomed herself to the feel of the horse, she lengthened the reins and gave Lily her head.

Galloping over the fields and jumping fences with the green mountains shrouded in fog gave Rebecca exactly what she'd craved. The pleasure of the ride. Freedom from thought and emotion.

Lily slowed and Rebecca turned back towards Brookmore House. They kept a sedate pace. Inhaling the clear morning air, Rebecca felt cleansed.

The day before, so filled with drama, was over and she could move past it, just as she'd moved past the shipwreck and entered Claire's life. Time would make everything better. She'd get used to being a governess. She'd get used to Lord Brookmore marrying an earl's daughter.

Rebecca would keep her distance from him, as she'd learned to do with her father whenever they were in the house together. Lord Brookmore would not have to leave because of her.

She patted Lily and drank in the beauty all around her.

As the house and stable came in to view, so did another lone rider making his way back, as well.

Lord Brookmore.

He saw her and stopped to wait for her to reach him.

'I heard you took a horse out,' he said when she came near.

He had invited her to ride, had he not? She felt her emotions bubbling to the surface. She pushed them down.

'I needed a good run.' She leaned forward to pat the horse. 'Lily is a wonderful horse.'

He rode beside her, not speaking, like that last day on the road, the day they'd arrived at Brookmore House.

Like that day she broke the silence. 'I suggest we leave yesterday in the past,' she began. 'I plan to devote myself to Pamela and Ellen, nothing more.'

She darted a glance towards him. Did he realise what she meant? No more kisses. No lovemaking.

He frowned. 'Very well, Miss Tilson.'

She bit her lip to keep from saying more and managed to accept his silence for the rest of the way to the stable.

They walked back to the house together, still not speaking. Rebecca still felt the same towards him, as if they were tethered together, but she could not indulge such a feeling.

They walked up the back stairs to the second floor and emerged into the hallway near the breakfast room. Would he eat with them this morning, Rebecca wanted to ask, but she held her tongue.

He started to walk away from her, towards his room, but he turned. 'I will see you and the children at breakfast.'

At least she had not spoiled that for Pamela and Ellen.

Garret expected great difficulty being in Miss Tilson's company, but over the next week she made it easy, never getting close, never turning the conversation to anything personal between them. How was she able to do that? he wondered. He still felt the physical yearning for her, but because she kept herself at an emotional distance, he managed to do the same. On the outside, anyway.

That he'd been busy helped, as well. He'd joined his tenants and workers in the fields, the stables, or wherever they toiled, and he'd asked them to tell him of their needs, their complaints, their ideas for improvement. He'd kept a log of everything they'd said and worked with Ben to begin with the most important repairs. He abandoned his plan to leave right away. He'd stay as long as he could.

He continued to eat dinner with Miss Tilson—he could not bear to give that up—but they limited their conversation to his work with the tenants and hers with the children, even though he longed to ask if she still had visions of the shipwreck, if her new dresses pleased her, if she were happy.

She rode almost every morning, as did he. Twice they'd ended their runs riding next to each other and all he could think of was of riding next to her on the trip from Moelfre, how his admiration of her grew on the trip, how he had kissed her.

Would another moment eventually come when he—
or she—would weaken and they'd again be caught in a
whirlpool of desire? He hoped for her sake he could resist.

This day was to be another busy one, busier than most,
in fact. Today the sheep shearing was to begin. Garret was
surprised how much he looked forward to this. It had been
many years since he'd thought of the delights of the sheep
shearing. He'd loved it when he'd been a boy.

That morning at breakfast he'd invited his nieces to
watch the shearing, which meant, of course, that Miss Tilson would also come.

Garret walked with Ben to the pen set up for the shearing. Already they could hear the bleating of sheep.

'It sounds like the clipping has begun,' Garret said.

Ben responded, 'I am glad you are staying for the clipping. The sheep are everything to the workers and the
sheep are everything to the farm.'

Garret nodded. 'I confess, I am itching to be down there
with them.'

Ben grinned. 'Like when we were boys.' He turned serious. 'The workers like to see you out there with them, doing
the work. That is something even your father did not do.'

Garret smiled. 'I remember my father standing with
my brother, instructing him on the shearing. They never
noticed me in the midst of the sheep.'

Garret had herded the sheep to the shearers or rolled
the sheared wool into bales. In those days he'd do whatever the workers let him do, which was mostly the dirti-
est jobs. Garret hadn't minded. The dirtier the better, he'd
thought at the time.

The sheep had been brought down from the fells into a
pen that funnelled them one by one to the shearers, several
who were itinerant, making a living by going from farm to
farm in July when the Herdwick sheep were typically shorn.

Miss Tilson and the girls were already at the wooden fence watching the operation. Pamela and Ellen had climbed on the slats of the fence so they could see over the top. Miss Tilson leaned on the top slat, her face alight with interest. Her eyes seemed involuntarily drawn to him for an instant, but she immediately turned her attention back to the sheep.

Garret greeted the men and joined the work, some of the older men joking with him that they'd give him the same dirty jobs they'd given him when a boy. The Herdwick wool did not bring in much money; it was too coarse for most clothing, but the sheep were valued for their meat and the shearing protected them from blowflies and bluebottles laying eggs in their wool.

Garret loved it all, loved the bleating of the sheep, the scraping of the shears and the voices of the workers as they toiled. He walked among them, helping when he could. There was no slacking off on this job as far as he could tell. Everyone worked with efficiency and skill. Ben said it was because Garret was among them.

Throughout the morning, though, Garret was aware of Miss Tilson. He felt her gaze as if it were an actual touch.

The afternoon wore on and eventually the numbers of sheep shorn exceeded those in the pen preparing for the clippers. Garret's skin softened with wool oil. His back was damp with sweat.

He was picking up stray bits of wool when Ben tapped him on the shoulder. 'A carriage is coming towards the house.'

Garret glanced to the road. A large black coach, an aristocrat's carriage drawn by four horses, approached, but was too far away for him to see the crest on the side.

'Who the devil could that be?' he said aloud.

He wiped his hands on a towel and made his way out of the sheep pen, striding towards the house.

'Where is Uncle Garret going?' Ellen asked, twisting around to watch him.

Rebecca, of course, had seen him leave the pen and cross the paddock. Her gaze had followed him wherever he'd been. Helping pull sheep into the shearing area. Holding sheep until the shearer had the animal well in his grasp. Rolling the wool and gathering the stray bits that scattered on the floor.

She turned to see. 'A coach is coming.'

'A coach!' Ellen cried. 'A big coach!' She jumped down from the fence. 'I am going to see who it is!'

'No, Ellen!' Pamela cried. 'Uncle won't like it.'

But Ellen paid her sister no heed.

'Ellen!' Rebecca called after her. 'Come back!'

Both she and Pamela left the fence and chased after Ellen.

'She should know better,' Pamela exclaimed to Rebecca. Pamela had become her ally in trying to rein in Ellen.

'Stay away from the coach's horses!' Rebecca cried after the little girl.

Lord Brookmore had already reached the front door. Two footmen emerged from the house as the carriage pulled up.

Rebecca and Pamela caught up to Ellen several feet away from the carriage. Rebecca caught the little girl by the nape of her jacket just in time to see a fashionably dressed young lady emerge from the carriage.

'Let us go see who it is!' Ellen tried to pull away.

'Not like little hoydens,' Rebecca said. 'We will walk like ladies and when I say stop, you must stop. No running up to your uncle. He will tell you who it is if you are to know.'

'Yes, Ellen.' Pamela mimicked Rebecca's tone. 'Do not act like a little hoyden.'

Pamela took her sister's hand to guard against another impulsive run, Rebecca thought.

An older woman and a maid also disembarked from the coach.

Rebecca allowed the little girls to approach a little closer, close enough to hear, but not to be in the way.

'You weren't able to send a message?' Lord Brookmore asked the young lady.

'Brookmore, darling. I wanted to surprise you,' she replied.

Rebecca had a sinking feeling she knew who this was.

The young lady was petite enough to make Rebecca feel like an Amazon. Pale blonde hair peeked out from beneath her exquisite silk bonnet, the same deep blue as her perfectly tailored travelling dress. The hue complemented her blue eyes, their colour visible even from this distance.

Lord Brookmore wore the expression of someone punched in the stomach.

'Oh, are these sweet little girls your nieces?' the lady asked while her maid carried in a large piece of luggage.

Ellen skipped towards her and curtsied.

'Yes,' Brookmore said stiffly. 'May I present Miss Pamela and Miss Ellen.'

The young woman laughed, a musical sound. She smiled at the girls. 'Your uncle forgets to say who I am. I am Lady Agnes. His fiancée.'

Rebecca took in a gulp of air. As she'd guessed.

'What's a fiancée?' Ellen asked.

Pamela answered, 'It means that Uncle Garret is going to marry her.'

Both girls glanced back at Rebecca with unhappy expressions. Lord Brookmore's face remained stiff.

The fashionably dressed, beautiful, petite, blonde, blue-eyed fiancée then seemed to notice Rebecca. 'And you are the governess, I presume.'

Rebecca met the woman's gaze and executed an obligatory curtsy. 'Miss Tilson, my lady.'

'Not in the schoolroom, I see?' Lady Agnes said, ever so disapprovingly.

Rebecca smiled. 'On such a fine day? We were watching the sheep shearing.'

Lady Agnes wrinkled her nose. 'You do not say!'

'Lady Agnes,' Lord Brookmore finally spoke. 'Come in the house.'

Rebecca curtsied again and the girls mimicked her.

'May we go back to the sheep?' Pamela asked. The once too-correct child had become enamoured of animals. The horses were still her favourites.

'I want to go inside with the lady,' Ellen insisted.

Rebecca scooted them away. 'We are not going inside to bother her. We will watch the sheep some more.'

Ellen was full of questions on the walk back to the shearing station. 'Where did she come from?'

'From London, I suppose,' Rebecca answered.

'Will she stay in the house?'

'I expect so,' Rebecca said.

'What room will she sleep in?'

Would Ellen's questions never stop? 'I do not know.'

'When will they be married?'

This question was the most painful. 'We will have to ask Uncle Garret.' Although Rebecca had no intention of asking that question.

They watched the sheep for another hour before returning to the house, but Rebecca could not tell what they had seen or what they'd spoken to each other. It had taken her a long time to even remember to breathe. She brought the girls into the house through the back entrance and up the back stairs to the children's wing where they washed their faces and hands and changed their clothes. Cook sent up a meal of soup and bread with blueberry tarts for dessert.

Afterwards the girls wrote in their journals and somehow Rebecca read to them from *The Shepherd Boy*, a book that seemed to suit the day—at least the sheep-shearing part of the day.

Mary helped the girls get ready for sleep and Rebecca kissed them both goodnight. So dear and sweet they were, she thought. Her efforts at being a governess might fall short, but she loved these little girls. She could not imagine having a stronger love, even for children of her own.

Not that she would ever have children of her own.

She left their bedchamber and sought refuge in her own room. On an ordinary night she would ready herself for dinner with Lord Brookmore, but this night she simply sat in the chair and stared out the window at the waning light. In mid-July it would be more than an hour before the sky turned dark.

She watched the setting sun paint the fells in shades of purple and wondered how to bear spending another day in this house. With *him*. With *her*. She imagined them together in the dining room, Lady Agnes dressed formally for dinner, seated in the chair near him. Rebecca's chair.

Lady Agnes was dazzling in a way Rebecca could never be, even if dressed in her finest gowns and jewellery, the ones lost at sea. Lady Agnes also had charm, although Rebecca detected a bite to it, hidden behind a smile. A governess was nothing in comparison.

She remembered what Claire had said—*'A governess is not important enough to notice.'*

Chapter Twelve

Garret felt like another person walked in his skin. From the moment Lady Agnes stepped from the carriage, he'd felt like an automaton, going through the motions. He'd walked Lady Agnes and her companion, an adoring aunt, into the house and called for Mrs Dodd to make rooms ready for them and serve them tea in the drawing room. All the while, his spirit was with Miss Tilson, wanting to explain that he hadn't known Lady Agnes was coming, that he would have warned her had he known.

Lady Agnes kept up enough chatter that he needed only to nod or speak one or two words.

Mrs Dodd readied Garret's sister-in-law's room. He trusted the housekeeper would remove Maryanne's personal items, items he must save for his nieces.

When the room was ready, he parted from Agnes and went to his room to change for dinner. He'd still had the mud from the shearing on his boots and bits of sheep's wool clung to his buckskin breeches. No doubt she'd been appalled.

As Brant dressed him, his mind whirled. Why had Lady Agnes come? The trip from London was a journey of at least five days in a private coach. She'd made it clear she disliked travel. He'd never expected she would make such a journey.

Garret hurried down the stairs and knocked at his sister-in-law's bedchamber door.

Lady Agnes's maid answered.

'Come in, Brookmore, dear,' Lady Agnes trilled. 'I am almost ready.'

She sat at the dressing table putting sapphire earrings in her ears. She wore a blue-silk gown and looked as if she'd be gracing a London dining room.

He remained standing.

'This room is charming,' she went on. 'All this oak wainscoting quite transports me to an earlier era.'

'Most of the house is panelled in oak,' he said.

'It is quaint, is it not?' She rose from her chair. 'Aunt Theodora will not be joining us. She is very fatigued.' She took his arm. 'So it is just you and me.'

His insides plummeted. What about Miss Tilson?

When he and Lady Agnes reached the dining room, Miss Tilson was not there and the table was set only for two. But for which two? For him and Lady Agnes? Or him and Miss Tilson?

Agnes surveyed the room. 'Now I do feel transported. Spanish leather wall covering!'

The wall covering had been on these walls since the sixteenth century.

Lady Agnes managed to keep conversation flowing throughout dinner, even though he could offer few words and his eyes kept wandering to the door wondering if Miss Tilson would appear, wondering why she had not.

She finally asked something about him. 'Tell me, Brookmore, what has been occupying you here?'

It took him a moment to focus his thoughts enough to answer. 'Estate business.'

She pressed for more. Why not answer her? If he were to share his life with her, why not tell her how he'd spent his time. At least some of his time.

'I've been meeting with the tenants and the workers, asking their needs, taking their complaints and planning to address them.'

'Goodness!' She blinked. 'That is what an estate manager is for. If you like I will write to Papa. He can certainly recommend someone who is up to the job.'

He took a long sip of wine. 'I have an estate manager.'

She laughed softly. 'I meant a good one.'

He averted his gaze. 'That is not necessary.' Miss Tilson had admired his efforts with the workers.

After dinner they retired to the drawing room. In the midst of her commentary, he gazed at her, perfect in every way a viscount's wife should be. It would be a good partnership, so why did his mood plummet to the depths?

What had changed inside him? Or, rather, who had changed him?

When he finally suggested they retire and she agreed, he escorted her back to her room.

On the way he said, 'I take breakfast with my nieces at eight-thirty in the morning.' *And Miss Tilson.* 'You are welcome to join us.' *But please don't.* 'Or you may have breakfast in the dining room, if you prefer.'

'How sweet.' She smiled. 'And a little absurd, too, is it not? The lord of the estate eating with children? I am certain I would be excessively entertained, but I believe I will sleep in and ask for breakfast in my room.'

'As you wish.' They reached her door.

She put a hand behind his neck and urged him to lean

over. She kissed him on the lips, a lingering kiss, but one as cool as the evening air.

'Goodnight, Brookmore,' she murmured before slipping into the room.

Garret strode away and climbed the stairs to his room, putting his hand on the door handle, but he did not open the door. Instead he walked down the hallway to the children's wing.

And knocked on Miss Tilson's door.

Rebecca answered the door in her nightgown, expecting Mary coming to offer her food one more time.

'Lord Brookmore.' Her heart leapt at the sight of him, but she quickly steeled herself.

He stared at her with his intense blue eyes and she remembered that, once again, he'd encountered her in her nightgown.

Finally he spoke. 'You did not come to dinner.'

'Surely you did not expect me?' She almost laughed.

'I did not know whether to expect you or not.'

She lowered her gaze. 'I would not intrude.'

His brows knitted and again he paused before speaking. 'Did you eat?'

He should not trouble himself of whether or not she ate. 'I ate,' she lied. She started to close the door.

He stopped her with a hand on the door. 'May I speak with you?'

She should say no. She should close the door and turn the key in the lock.

But she opened it the rest of the way and stepped aside so he could enter. The last time he'd entered her room was·after a passionate kiss that sent them both to her bed—something he regretted, but even now she could not regret.

She waited for him to speak, her arms folded across her chest.

He walked over to the window and looked out into the night, as she had done before his knock.

Finally he turned. 'I did not know Lady Agnes would come.'

'I see.' Claire would not have expected to be informed of invited or uninvited guests. Rebecca must not either.

He pressed his lips together. 'I would not have invited her.'

Why did he believe it mattered? Merely because the governess developed romantic notions about him?

'But had I known of her visit, I would have told you,' he added.

She lifted a shoulder. 'It is of no consequence.'

He took a step towards her. 'I want to explain. When I inherited the title, I took my duty very seriously, including the duty to make a good marriage and ensure the line of succession. I was not prepared—'

She stopped him. 'You do not have to tell me this.'

He shook his head. 'I do need to tell you. I need you to understand.'

He was making it difficult for her to build a cage around her emotions. 'I do understand,' she murmured. 'You are trying very hard to do all that is required of a viscount.'

'It is not what I wanted,' he shot back. 'And I have not done well. I've made mistakes. Big mistakes.' He sounded pained. 'I tried to do as my brother would have done, but then I discover he was a terrible model.'

She looked directly into his eyes. 'You are nothing like your brother.'

'How could you know that?' he snapped.

'For one thing, you care about other people, even your

tenants and workers.' She added, 'You care about his little girls, which certainly he did not.'

He turned his face away. 'You give me too much credit.'

It struck Rebecca like a bolt from the heavens that she, too, had often thought only of herself and not others. Perhaps she ought to have considered her father's grief over losing her mother with more sympathy, rather than be hurt at being ostracised by him. Perhaps she could have seen that her brother had been the most unloved of them all. After marrying her mother, her father had not cared a fig about his son. Perhaps she even should have understood Lord Stonecroft's desire for an heir.

This was new territory for her. Lord Brookmore had been the cause of it. She'd watched him being kind to her, being loving to his nieces and concerned about his workers. She'd opened her heart to Pamela and Ellen, because she'd seen them through his compassionate eyes.

She could not tell this to him, though. They could no longer share confidences. He could never be her lover, nor could he be her friend. She must remain in her place as governess.

Rebecca lowered her arms and softened her voice. 'I will tend to Pamela and Ellen,' she told him. 'But I'll have no expectations of dining with you or otherwise placing myself in your way. You can rest easy on that score.' She paused. 'But I would like to continue to ride in the mornings.' Without that release she feared she'd go mad, because, although she was acting strong and noble, inside she felt as if every organ was shredded.

She knew how to keep her distance; she'd perfected the skill with her father.

'Of course you may ride. You must go on as you were,' he insisted.

'No.' Sadness filled her voice. 'That is what I must not do.

I will act the governess from now on.' She forced herself to smile. 'And a governess must not entertain the Viscount in her bedchamber.' She walked to the door, which he'd kept open. 'I bid you goodnight, sir.'

He crossed the room, but slowed as he passed her. His hand rose and she thought he might touch her, but he dropped it again. 'Goodnight, Miss Tilson.'

The next morning Lady Agnes did not sleep as late as she'd told Brookmore she would. She rose early, sent her maid down to the kitchen to get her a pot of chocolate and something sweet to eat.

Her Aunt Theodora sat in the ancient upholstered chair that must have been a century old, while Lady Agnes stood at the window overlooking the park and the outbuildings, one of which showed signs of activity. More sheep shearing, no doubt.

'It is very rural here, is it not?' Agnes remarked, her lip curling.

'Indeed,' her aunt agreed. 'Quite rural.'

She gazed at the far hill, dotted with grazing sheep. Lord Brookmore had smelled of the vile creatures the day before. She hardly could stand it until he washed and changed for dinner. This was not something she would tolerate.

But she knew that was a battle to be engaged in at a later time. No husband of hers would smell like a farm labourer.

He was less elegant than she would have liked, possibly from all those years in the army, but she intended to give him polish and working with farm animals, alongside unwashed underlings, would not do it. The previous day he'd seemed preoccupied with these farm people. Well, after their marriage he'd discover she had no intention of spending her days on a farm.

But first she had to get him to the altar.

His delay at returning to London and accompanying her to Brighton had worried her. Something was afoot and she'd come all the way to this…wilderness…to discover what it was.

She moved the curtain—how old was that piece of cloth? she wondered.

Two riders approached the outbuildings and it took only a moment's observation to recognise Brookmore and that governess. They were not riding side by side, but they were both riding early in the morning and returning to the stables at the same time.

Agnes felt her neck tense the way it always did when she sensed trouble.

She'd noticed the way he'd looked at the governess the day before. And this nonsense about breakfasting with the children every morning. Undoubtedly the governess was present. Now both he and the governess were riding?

The night before, he'd avoided any discussion of a wedding date. Or of a time he would be ready to leave this rustic area. Was it because of this governess?

Her maid entered the room with a tray bearing the pot of chocolate, two mugs and a plate of sweet breads filled with currants.

Agnes turned to her maid. 'Holly, put the tray on the table and go find Mrs Dodd, the housekeeper. Ask if she might come speak with me.'

Holly curtsied. 'Yes, m'lady.'

'And bring another chocolate cup when you return,' Agnes added.

Aunt Theodora sat at the table, but waited for Agnes before eating or pouring the chocolate.

Agnes joined her.

A few minutes later Holly brought the chocolate cup. 'M'lady, Mrs Dodd said she would call on you directly.'

'Excellent!' Agnes turned to her companion. 'Aunt, would you mind taking your breakfast in your room? I should like to speak with the housekeeper privately.'

Aunt Theodora immediately stood. 'Of course, dear.'

Agnes signalled to Holly. 'Help her.'

When Mrs Dodd knocked on the door, Agnes was quite alone.

'You wished to see me, Lady Agnes?'

The housekeeper appeared cordial enough and well she ought. Lord Brookmore had introduced Agnes as his fiancée. Mrs Dodd would eventually answer to Agnes when she became Lady Brookmore. Assuming Agnes would ever set foot in this antiquated house again.

'Thank you so much for interrupting your busy day to speak with me.' Agnes smiled her sweet smile. 'Please do come in.'

Mrs Dodd entered and Agnes gestured for her to sit. 'Please have a cup of chocolate with me.' These upper servants sometimes liked such niceties.

'Thank you, my lady.' Mrs Dodd sat.

Agnes started the conversation with polite enquiries as to Mrs Dodd's health and her satisfaction with her position and her staff, complimenting her lavishly as she went on. She finally reached the point of her request to see the housekeeper.

She poured Mrs Dodd more chocolate. 'And what of this governess? I understand she is new.'

Mrs Dodd pursed her lips before answering. 'She is an odd one. I will say that for her.'

Agnes's brows rose. 'Odd one? How so.'

The housekeeper leaned forward. 'When she arrived

with Lord Brookmore, she rode on horseback with him. Most unseemly!'

'Oh, I agree. Most unseemly. Can you imagine?' Agnes readily agreed.

The housekeeper went on. 'She had only a very small bag with her. Almost no clothing. No personal items at all. The children's maid said she'd been in a shipwreck, which would explain it, but...' She trailed off, clearly sceptical.

'Do go on,' Agnes encouraged.

Mrs Dodd took a sip of chocolate. 'She takes the children outdoors most of the day. They hardly ever are inside the schoolroom. Not like the dear governess who came before.'

'What can they be doing out of doors all day?' Agnes asked.

'Well.' She took another sip. 'One day she almost got Miss Ellen drowned. His lordship had to rescue Miss Ellen and Miss Tilson.'

'You do not say!' Agnes put on a shocked expression. 'How did such a person become a governess?'

The housekeeper seemed eager to impart information. 'She came with an excellent reference from the lady of the house whose children she cared for. And she was registered with a reputable agency, but there is something havey-cavey about her.'

Agnes suspected as much!

'I cannot abide this!' Agnes said. 'Those poor dear children.' She put a hand to her chest. 'I must make certain that dear Brookmore was not deceived. Perhaps I could write to the agency. Or to her previous employer. Only I would like to do this without Brookmore knowing.' She smiled conspiratorially. 'I do not wish to worry him, of course.'

'I have the letters from the agency and the reference,'

Mrs Dodd said. 'I will show them to you so you have the proper address.'

Agnes stood. 'Thank you. You may spare these children from irreparable harm.'

Mrs Dodd also rose. 'I will bring the letters to you right away.'

After the housekeeper left, Agnes paced the room. Her instincts were never wrong. She was certain there was something to discover about this governess that would sour Lord Brookmore on the young woman.

Yes. Mrs Dodd confirmed Agnes's suspicions. The governess was the problem and Agnes excelled at eliminating problems.

Chapter Thirteen

Garret managed to endure the day in a tolerable fashion. Breakfast with the children and Miss Tilson that morning had been difficult, but he and Miss Tilson had already become practised in remaining remote while still engaging the children. Afterwards he invited Lady Agnes and her aunt on a tour of the house and garden, which served only to remind him of when he'd done the same for Miss Tilson and the children. He'd next seen Lady Agnes and her aunt at dinner. By then he'd endeavoured to be more civil than the previous night. Lady Agnes's aunt excused herself after dinner and Garret spent the rest of the evening alone with his fiancée.

He'd had one piece of happy news that day. In an effort to please the children, as well as Miss Tilson, he'd asked his stable master to scour the countryside for suitable ponies to purchase for Pamela and Ellen. The man found two perfect fell ponies just the right size and temperament for the girls. They'd arrived that afternoon and Garret planned to surprise the girls the next day.

In an attempt to be convivial, he'd spoken of it to Lady Agnes.

'Ponies?' Her brows rose. 'Are not they a bit young for riding?'

'I was younger than Pamela when I started,' he said. 'And she is pining to learn.'

'But you are a man,' she exclaimed. 'Riding is a necessity for a man.'

Necessity or not, no one could have kept him off a horse in those days. Pamela had that same passion for horses—as did Miss Tilson.

'These are gentle animals,' he said. 'The girls will be safe.'

'I was not thinking of safety, although that is important, of course,' she countered. 'There is a risk of indulging a child's every whim, especially little girls. One does not wish them to grow up horse-mad, does one? They will have to make a good match some day and that means embracing feminine pursuits.'

Garret frowned. 'I intend to indulge whatever whims give my nieces pleasure. They have lost their mother and father and the governess they'd known since birth. They deserve to be indulged. I will do what makes them happy.'

Her expression turned sympathetic. 'Of course you are right, my dearest. The poor darlings. How are they getting along?'

He nodded. 'They are doing well now.' Because of Miss Tilson.

The next morning at breakfast Garret told Pamela and Ellen—and Miss Tilson—that he had a surprise for them in the stables. He told them to meet him at the stables at ten o'clock. He was rushing to get there before them when he encountered Lady Agnes on the stairs.

'Brookmore!' She smiled. 'How are you this morning? How was your little breakfast with the children?'

'Pleasant, as always,' he responded. Not counting the ache he felt whenever he was with Miss Tilson.

She gave an amused look. 'I was about to take a turn in the garden. Will you join me?'

He shook his head. 'I cannot. I am on my way to the stables. The children are to meet me there soon, but I want to make it there before them. I am surprising them with the ponies.'

'The ponies.' Her face fell, although she quickly smiled. 'How very sweet of you to make it a surprise.'

He hesitated, sensing her disappointment and feeling guilty for having an excuse to avoid her company. 'You may come, too, if you wish.'

'To the stables?' She wrinkled her nose, but again put on a smile. 'I would love to, but I must change my shoes, I fear.'

She lifted her skirts to show she wore dainty slippers that would be ruined in any bit of mud or muck. The glimpse of her ankle should have been alluring, but Garret was unmoved.

'I must hurry there now,' he said. 'Come as soon as you are ready. Any footman can show you the way.'

Her smile lit her beautiful features. 'I will hurry, as well.'

His guilt rose again for feeling his surprise gift to the children would be a bit spoiled if she came.

Rebecca and the girls hurried down the back stairs, the fastest way to leave the house and reach the stables.

'What is the surprise, Miss Tilson?' Ellen asked for the hundredth time.

'I still do not know, Ellen,' Rebecca replied, laughing.

Pamela piped up, 'Stop asking!' But her eyes, too, were filled with excitement.

Rebecca thought she knew the surprise, though, and she, too, could hardly wait to see if she was correct.

When they reached the door, Lady Agnes was there, about to leave with a footman.

'Good morning, children,' she chirped.

'Good morning, Lady Agnes,' they responded, both their voices dampened.

'May I walk with you?' she asked. 'I believe you are off to the stables for the big surprise.'

She knew of it?

'Are you going, too?' Ellen's enthusiasm quieted somewhat.

'Yes,' Lady Agnes replied. 'But I do not know the way to the stables.'

Rebecca's insides clenched. 'You may walk with us.'

What right would she have had to refuse, even though the lady had not acknowledged her, only the children?

Lady Agnes turned to the footman. 'Thank you so much, Mason, but I will not need you now.'

The footman looked pleased that she'd addressed him. 'M'lady.' He bowed and held the door for them.

Pamela and Ellen ran ahead, leaving Lady Agnes to walk with Rebecca.

Lady Agnes wrapped her shawl around her. 'It is cold for a summer day, is it not, Miss Tilson?'

'Yes, my lady.' Rebecca kept repeating to herself that her status was now lower than this earl's daughter.

'The children are quite excited, are they not? Running like that.'

There it was again, Rebecca noticed. That sweet tone that held a bite.

'Indeed,' she responded.

'Well they might be,' Lady Agnes said with a little laugh.

'You know the surprise?' Rebecca could not help feeling hurt that Lord Brookmore had apparently confided in her.

'Yes, of course.' Lady Agnes looked pleased. 'But I will not spoil it for you.'

Rebecca felt a pang of jealousy, but what right had she to feel such an emotion? They were not rivals. He would share confidences with this lady that he would never do with her.

Lord Brookmore stood outside the stables and Rebecca's heart lurched when he scooped up Ellen into one arm and put the other around Pamela's shoulder.

'We must wait for Miss Tilson,' she heard him say.

He glanced her way and his smile faltered for a moment when he saw her walking with Lady Agnes.

When they came closer, he acknowledged his fiancée. 'Lady Agnes.'

Her smile turned more dazzling. 'See? I did not need an escort after all.'

'I do see.' His gaze slipped to Rebecca for an instant, before he turned again to the children. 'Well, shall we see the surprise?'

'Yes! Yes!' cried Ellen.

He carried Ellen, but held Pamela's hand as he entered the stables. Lady Agnes followed. Rebecca waited to be last.

The stables were dark compared to the sunny day outside and it took a moment for her eyes to adjust. There, held by two of the grooms, were two ponies, one light, one dark, one larger than the other, but the perfect sizes for Pamela and Ellen.

'Oh!' exclaimed Pamela, her tone awed. 'Oh.'

Lord Brookmore put Ellen down. 'The larger one is yours, Pamela. Go say hello.'

Rebecca could tell Pamela wished to run to the pony, but she forced herself to approach slowly.

She turned back to Lord Brookmore. 'Mine, Uncle Garret?'

'Yours,' he repeated, his voice soft.

Pamela stroked the pony the way Rebecca and Lord Brookmore had taught her. The little horse nuzzled her and Pamela threw her arms around its neck.

'What is her name?' she asked.

'Biscuit,' the groom told her.

The pony was a dappled grey, a pretty creature any little girl would fall in love with. Already the horse was delighting in Pamela's affection.

'Biscuit is a perfect name!' Pamela placed her cheek against the horse's neck.

Tears stung Rebecca's eyes. She exchanged a glance with Lord Brookmore and saw he understood. Pamela was truly happy.

Ellen, still a bit wary of horses, held back. 'The other one is mine?'

'Yes, yours,' Lord Brookmore assured her. 'Her name is Pixie.'

Pixie was a bay mare, a rich reddish brown with a black mane.

'Will she bite?' Ellen asked.

He squatted down to her level. 'She won't bite. She likes little girls. She'll like to be petted the way Miss Tilson and I showed you.' He gave her a gentle push. 'Go to her.'

Ellen crept forward. 'Hello, Pixie,' she said in a slightly anxious voice.

The pony did not wait, but stepped towards her, already nudging her with her muzzle. Ellen drew back, but soon laughed and patted the pony's neck.

Lord Brookmore again shared a glance with Rebecca.

His tenderness to the girls nearly undid her. She gulped to keep from becoming a complete watering pot.

'May I ride, Uncle Garret?' Pamela asked. Rebecca thought she would leap on the pony at any moment.

'You will have your first lesson right now, if you like,' he responded.

'Yes!' cried Pamela.

A few moments later both girls were on the ponies' backs, being led around the paddock. Lord Brookmore walked beside Ellen, reassuring her all the way. Pamela spent the time either talking to her Biscuit or exclaiming that she could not wait to ride on her own.

Rebecca watched the scene with her heart full of happiness for the girls.

Lady Agnes sidled up to her. 'They look so sweet, do they not?'

'Yes, indeed,' Rebecca responded, not inclined to do anything to further the conversation.

'I must confess,' Lady Agnes went on. 'I told Brookmore I was concerned about Pamela and Ellen riding at such an early age.'

Early? Pamela and Ellen were latecomers. 'Where I come from children begin riding as soon as they can walk.'

'And where is that, Miss Tilson?' Lady Agnes asked sweetly.

Rebecca had said too much, but she'd cause more suspicion if she did not answer. 'Ireland.'

Lady Agnes smiled as if amused. 'Oh. Ireland.'

Rebecca caught the implied aspersion.

'I do worry about Pamela.' Lady Agnes sighed.

'Why?' Rebecca asked.

'I suspect she is the driving force behind acquiring these ponies.' Lady Agnes shook her head in disapproval. 'I believe it is dangerous to let children dictate what they must have and what they must do.'

Rebecca was appalled. It was such a profound misunderstanding of how reticent Pamela had been to ask for anything.

'I do not believe it is dangerous for young girls to tell us what they need,' Rebecca said, trying to keep her voice calm. 'I believe girls need to learn to think for themselves and speak their minds. They should feel free to pursue what interests them, to do what makes them happy.'

She'd hate to think of Pamela or Ellen forced into thinking they must please others and do what others say. Or marry whomever they were told to marry.

'Oh, dear,' said Lady Agnes in a humorous tone. 'Have you been reading Wollstonecraft?'

Rebecca had, indeed, read *A Vindication of the Rights of Woman* when she'd attended her very progressive school, but she declined to respond to Lady Agnes.

She watched Lord Brookmore walk around the paddock with Ellen and wished that his fiancée was someone she could like. Lady Agnes definitely was not.

The next three weeks gave Garret no pleasure at all, at least not in the company of Lady Agnes. If only she would see how wrong their marriage would be and cry off, there would be no harm to her reputation. Surely her time at Brookmore House showed her how ill-suited they were.

She detested common labour, but he was happiest when fully immersed in the farm and the quarry. He loved to be in the thick of things, with the people he counted upon and who counted upon him. It was close to riding into battle, but without the risk. She disliked horses, but he, like Miss Tilson, felt the need to ride every day. He needed the release of a fine gallop across the fields.

Garret still enjoyed sharing breakfast with his nieces, who seemed happier and more relaxed as his days became unhappier and more tense. Breakfast gave him his only opportunity to see how Miss Tilson was faring. She'd been resolute in keeping her distance from him. He thought she looked more strained.

Like him.

Garret spent part of his day teaching his nieces to ride, a task in which Miss Tilson enthusiastically participated and about which Lady Agnes complained.

Her complaints were couched in words of concern, of course. Might the children be harmed by being out so much in the sun? Would they be falling behind on their lessons? Would it be prudent to engage a piano teacher or a dancing master as well for some balance?

He realised Lady Agnes must be going mad from boredom. There was very little for her to do but write letters, do needlework, play the pianoforte and read ladies' magazines he brought her from Grasmere, since she disliked the books in his library.

How many letters could she write, though? How much needlework could she finish? How did her poor aunt stand it, as well? The older lady seemed to nap most of the day, probably from lack of anything more interesting to do.

In this past week, Lady Agnes had begun to press him to make her acquainted with other good families in the area, meaning other land owners with titles, if possible. Garret had neglected to call upon his neighbours. He'd always meant to, but he wanted to see to the estate's needs first.

At Lady Agnes's request he sent a servant to Ambleside every day for the mail. She received more letters than everyone else in the household combined and he franked all the letters she sent in return. He did not care enough to notice to whom they were addressed.

This afternoon he carried some ledgers into the house, planning to go over some figures he and Ben had discussed. Agnes encountered him in the drawing room.

'Brookmore! How lovely to see you,' she chirped. 'I was about to take a turn in the garden. Would you join me?'

To deny such a little request seemed churlish. 'Certainly.' He put the ledgers in a desk drawer. 'Which gardens?'

Brookmore House had, of course, more than one garden. He'd toured them all with her when she first arrived. As he had toured with Miss Tilson and the children.

Lady Agnes took his arm. 'The topiary. It is so quaint.'

Quaint was a common word she used when talking about the house and its gardens.

Garret walked with her out the front entrance and through the gate to the topiary. This day she did not remark at all about the whimsical shrubbery. She talked of the unseasonably cool weather and lamented that Garret had been working too hard which could not possibly be good for him.

Suddenly a screech came from behind the shrubbery and two laughing little girls ran straight for them.

Lady Agnes cried out in surprise.

'Uncle Garret! Uncle Garret!' Ellen ran up to him. 'We are pretending we are afraid of a snake, but we aren't really, because the snake is a garden snake and only does good by eating bad things.' She paused. 'At least that is what Phibbs tells us.'

'You gave me such a fright!' Lady Agnes fanned herself.

Pamela eyed Lady Agnes and spoke mechanically. 'Sorry, Lady Agnes.'

Lady Agnes took a step backwards. 'Is there truly a snake?'

'A very long one,' Pamela said.

'A garden snake is harmless,' Garret told her.

'But we were pretending it was a viper,' Ellen explained. 'Phibbs said there are vipers in the gardens, too.'

Lady Agnes trembled. 'Do not say so!'

Garret reassured her, 'Vipers prefer to hide. You have nothing to fear. Even the gardens in London have them.'

'We saw a big garden snake, though,' Ellen said. 'Want to see it?'

Lady Agnes smiled stiffly at the little girl. 'Are you two unsupervised?'

'No, Lady Agnes.' Miss Tilson appeared from behind the shrubbery. 'I am here.'

Miss Tilson looked lovely in the wide-brimmed hat she wore for excursions like this one, her colour heightened by the summer air. The little girls looked like miniatures of her, in similar hats and a healthy glow to their faces.

'Goodness!' Lady Agnes laughed. 'Do you stay out of doors all day? Riding all the morning and now playing in the garden? When do the girls do their lessons?'

Miss Tilson lifted her chin. 'Their lesson is about the flora and fauna found here. Phibbs has shown the girls plants of all varieties and insects and this lovely snake.'

'Phibbs?' Lady Agnes looked quizzically towards Garret.

'The gardener,' he responded.

Lady Agnes's lip curled. 'The gardener!'

'He is a fine man,' Garret said.

'I am certain he is,' laughed Lady Agnes. 'And apparently a suitable playmate, as well.'

'Not a playmate,' Miss Tilson broke in. 'I could think of no one more knowledgeable about plants and insects and the like.'

When he'd been a boy, Garret learned much from Phibbs, but he'd escaped his governess to do so. He had to admit he sometimes wondered if his nieces received any lessons in the schoolroom. Miss Tilson certainly did not teach as he had been taught, but the little girls had blossomed under her care and that was enough for him.

'If you will pardon us,' Miss Tilson went on, 'we will return to our lesson. Come, girls.'

Garret watched her walk away, holding the hand of each of the girls who skipped at her side. It was a sight he wanted to embed in his memory.

'Such an interesting person.' Lady Agnes took his arm again. 'Do you not agree?'

He did agree. And that was what made life so difficult at the moment.

Chapter Fourteen

Lady Agnes seemed to dismiss Miss Tilson more easily than Garret could. She took his arm again and turned down a path away from where Miss Tilson and the children had disappeared.

She spoke. 'I have a surprise for you, Brookmore, dear.'

'A surprise?' Garret suspected he would not like a surprise from Lady Agnes.

Her expression was that of a mischievous child. 'You know how often I have mentioned to you that it would be a courtesy to call upon your neighbours?'

He nodded.

'I decided you have been much too busy, so I took matters into my own hands so to speak.'

'What did you do?' His voice turned cold.

She grinned. 'I have planned a dinner party.'

'A dinner party?' She planned a dinner party without his knowledge?

'Do not concern yourself,' she said quickly. 'I consulted with Mrs Dodd and Glover regarding the guest list. I will show it to you when we are in the house, but I know you will approve it.'

'I am not certain this is a wise idea,' he said carefully.

'Of course it is a wise idea!' She laughed.

'You should have consulted me, not Mrs Dodd and Glover.' *You are not my wife and hostess yet,* he wanted to say.

'It has been a lovely diversion for me, Brookmore,' she went on. 'Surely you can see how much pleasure it gives me to do this for you.'

Not for him. For her. Because she wanted it.

'Please, Brookmore?' She blinked up at him. 'Please let me show you how skilled I am at giving a party like this?'

Having her so publicly act as his hostess felt like another link in the chain of a marriage he no longer desired.

A marriage that was inevitable, though.

'Show me the guest list.' He had no intention of approving this dinner party without knowing who would be invited. 'Then I will decide.'

'I am very happy to show you the guest list,' she retorted. 'But it is too late for you to decide.'

His anger kindled. 'What do you mean too late?'

She smiled her sweet smile. 'The invitations have already been sent.'

'You sent out the invitations?' His voice rose.

She faced him, nonplussed. 'You know you've neglected your duty to your neighbours. This dinner party will remedy that. You have a standing in this area. You must assert your importance.'

He did not mind dining with neighbours and hearing of local matters. What he did not like was Lady Agnes manoeuvring to get what she wanted in an underhanded way.

'You have made it impossible for me to refuse, have you not?' he snapped.

She laughed and put her arm through his again. 'Of course I have! But know I have done it all for you, my dearest one.'

That did nothing to appease him. 'When is this dinner to be?'

She squeezed his arm. 'In a week's time.'

'A week's time?' How long had she been working on this in secret?

'You will love it, I promise you,' she insisted. 'It will be the loveliest dinner party!'

He'd get through it, he was certain. He'd got through many a dinner party, ball and other entertainments in London.

He must accept some of the blame for this, as well. He'd not troubled himself to know how she occupied her days. He'd left her too much to her own devices.

'Next time, no secrets, Lady Agnes.' He much preferred plain speaking. Like Miss Tilson engaged in.

'I shall never hide anything from you, Brookmore.' She sounded sincere for a woman who'd kept this secret for some length of time.

She pulled him towards the garden gate. 'Come inside with me! I will show you the guest list and the menu. I am sure you will be more than satisfied.'

He let her lead him back inside the house. As soon as they entered through the front door, the butler approached him.

'What is it, Glover?' he asked.

'A caller,' Glover replied. 'A gentleman who wishes to see Miss Tilson.'

Lady Agnes dropped his arm.

'Miss Tilson?' he asked. Who would call upon Miss Tilson? Who would she know? 'Did the gentleman give his name?'

'Sir Orin Foley, m'lord,' the butler replied. 'He is seated in the hall.'

Lady Agnes started for the door of the hall. 'Let us see what the gentleman wants.'

Garret followed her.

A man who looked to be in his thirties stood at their entrance. He was not as tall as Garret and was fair, with red hair that was starting to recede from his forehead.

He stepped forward with an ingratiating smile. 'Lord Brookmore, I presume? I am Sir Orin Foley.' He bowed.

Garret looked at him suspiciously. Where had this fellow come from? 'And you are here to see Miss Tilson?'

'If she will receive me.' Foley smiled again.

'Is she acquainted with you?' Garret asked.

He laughed softly. 'Indeed. I am her former employer.'

'And your business with Miss Tilson?' Garret pressed.

Lady Agnes broke in. 'Brookmore, maybe the business is private.'

Garret did not care.

'I have no secrets, I assure you,' Foley said. 'I am her former employer and, to be frank with you, I am here to ask her to return with me.'

Take her back to Ireland?

Lady Agnes spoke again. 'You must let her speak to the man, Brookmore. It is her affair, certainly.'

He supposed he must, although every piece of him wanted to toss the man out before Miss Tilson knew he was here.

'Very well,' he said. 'I will send someone to find her.'

Lady Agnes watched Brookmore stride out of the hall. She approached Sir Orin.

'I am Lady Agnes, sir. I wrote to your wife to enquire about Miss Tilson, but I would prefer you not tell Lord Brookmore that. He likes to believe he must do everything.'

Sir Orin's expression turned mournful. 'I regret to say my dear wife passed away shortly after Miss Tilson left us. I am here to entice her back. We need her desperately.'

Lady Agnes touched his arm. 'My condolences, sir. How very sad for you and the children.'

'Yes.' He sighed. 'The children need Miss Tilson to return to them.'

'I do understand,' she assured him. 'You found her services satisfactory?'

He smiled again. 'She was an angel!'

That would not be Agnes's description of her. Obviously the men who hired her saw her much differently. In Sir Orin's case, though, this might be the answer she'd been hoping for.

'Until your letter, I did not know where Miss Tilson had gone,' he said. 'I am very indebted to you.'

'I confess, I wished to know more about her,' Agnes told him. 'For the children's sake. I was not involved in hiring her—' She broke off. 'But I should tell you I am betrothed to Lord Brookmore, so soon it will be my duty to take care of such matters.'

Agnes asked him more questions, keeping an eye on the doorway for Brookmore's return.

'I am so sympathetic to your plight, sir,' she said. 'To have no one. At least Brookmore's nieces have me. I will do what I can for you, but you must let no one know that I sent that letter.'

He gave her a shrewd look. 'It is a bargain, Lady Agnes.'

Rebecca and the children knelt by a bed of sweet alyssum, watching a bumblebee dart from one tiny white flower to another. She looked up at the sound of footsteps.

A footman hurried up to them. 'Miss Tilson, you have a caller.'

'A caller! For Miss Tilson!' Ellen parroted excitedly. She jumped to her feet. 'Let us go see who it is!'

Rebecca rose as well, her heart pounding. Who would call upon her? She knew no one here.

'The caller is for Miss Tilson, not you,' Pamela chided her little sister.

'I want to see who it is!' Ellen cried.

Rebecca brushed off her skirt. 'I had better go alone. You children stay in the garden. I'll be back in a few minutes.'

She could not imagine this taking long. It must be a mistake.

She followed the footman back to the house. When she entered the front door, Lord Brookmore waited there for her.

'Who is it calling upon me?' she asked him.

He did not look happy about this visitor. 'Your former employer.'

'My employer?' Claire's employer, he meant. A man? A woman? She did not know who to expect. What to expect. Would her masquerade be exposed?

'He is in the hall,' Lord Brookmore told her.

He. A man. That answered one question. But she did not even know his name.

She pulled off her hat and walked into the hall, legs trembling.

A red-haired man, talking with Lady Agnes, glanced over at her and broke into a smile. 'Claire!' he cried.

Lady Agnes gave Rebecca a knowing look. 'I will leave you two.' She nodded to the man. 'A pleasure to speak with you, Sir Orin.'

Sir Orin. Sir Orin was his name.

Rebecca remained where she was as Lady Agnes swept by her. Sir Orin strode over to her.

'Claire, it is so good to see you.' He reached out to touch her, but she stepped back.

She came directly to the point. 'Why do you call upon me?'

'You must know why.' His eyes scanned her from head to toe in a manner that made her skin crawl.

'I do not. I wish you to tell me,' she demanded.

Goodness. She was not acting like Claire, was she? Claire would not have demanded anything. Rebecca needed to be direct, though. The less time he was with her, the better the chance of him not seeing she was not Claire.

'When I just discovered your whereabouts, I came right away.' He moved closer to her.

She stepped back again.

'My wife is dead, Claire,' he told her excitedly. 'You must come home with me now.'

A *frisson* of alarm crawled up her spine. He sounded almost happy about his wife dying.

Oh, why had she not asked Claire about her employment in Ireland? She'd certainly filled Claire's ear about her situation. She'd never thought to ask Claire anything about hers.

Rebecca tried to remain calm. 'I am employed here now, Sir Orin. I am content here.'

His eyes flashed with anger, but he quickly altered his demeanour and lowered his voice. 'The children need you. *I* need you. You must come.'

Rebecca looked him in the eye. 'I choose to stay here. You must find another governess for the children.' She had no idea how many children he had. Boys? Girls? Their names? She knew nothing.

'Let me persuade you.' He looked at her entreatingly.

'No.' She stepped back again. 'I am very sorry you travelled all this way, but you should not have come. I am not going back to Ireland.'

'It does not have to be Ireland, my dear,' he purred. 'I can move the children to England. Anywhere you desire.'

My dear? This intimate tone unnerved her. So did his use of Claire's Christian name. *Claire, what happened to you there? With this man?* she asked silently.

'I have given you my answer.'

'How may I change that answer, my dear?' he murmured. 'I must change your mind.'

This man looked harmless enough, but his words and manner made the hairs on Rebecca's neck rise.

She raised her voice. 'My position is here now. I do not wish to discuss this further.'

'Claire, you must let me persuade you!' he pleaded, extending his hand.

She turned away. 'Please leave now.'

'But—' he began.

A voice from the doorway broke in. 'She has asked you to leave, sir.'

Lord Brookmore must have been standing there. Rebecca's shoulders relaxed in relief.

Sir Orin did not move, however.

Lord Brookmore repeated, 'You must leave. Now.'

Lady Agnes stepped into the hall, walking up to Sir Orin. 'Come. I will walk you out.' She took his arm and he left with her.

Lord Brookmore turned and watched them leave before speaking to Rebecca. 'I could not hear your conversation, if you are wondering. Something about him… I did not think you should see him alone.'

She was grateful to him. Excessively. 'It was nothing. He came for nothing.'

'He upset you,' Brookmore said.

She wanted so badly to ask for his comfort. She wanted him to hold her and tell her Sir Orin would never bother her again and she would never have to worry about her deception being exposed.

But she could not ask him for comfort. Lady Agnes was here now.

Rebecca waved a hand. 'He wants me to be his children's governess again.'

'And what do you want?' he asked.

She met his gaze. 'I wish to remain here.'

Lady Agnes walked Sir Orin all the way out the front door where no one could hear them.

'Best you not press her now,' she told the dejected man.

'I am determined to have her back.' He put on his hat and pulled his gloves over his fingers.

'Then you must try another day.' Agnes certainly was not ready to give up. 'Where are you staying, sir?'

'Ambleside. The Unicorn Inn,' he said.

She nodded. 'Enjoy your stay there. I will contact you soon, I promise. Do not lose hope.'

He smiled charmingly. 'I am so very grateful to you, Lady Agnes. I am obviously in need of an ally.'

'As am I.' She returned his smile. 'I should tell you she rides early every morning, but do not make use of that information tomorrow. Give her a day or so.'

'She rides?' He looked puzzled. 'I had no inkling she was a horsewoman.'

'She is quite enamoured of the out of doors, actually.' Anything to do with the farm.

'Is she?' His brows rose. 'That is a change. I can see there is more to discover about Claire Tilson.'

'She did not spend her time out of doors with your children?' Agnes asked.

'Not at all,' he responded. 'Oh, she took the occasional walk, but most days she closeted herself in the schoolroom with the children.'

This was curious indeed, Agnes thought. Of course, she could favour the out of doors because that was where Brookmore was likely to be, working on the farm like a common labourer.

Sir Orin brightened. 'Perhaps I can entice her back with some prime horseflesh!'

'An excellent idea.' Extravagant gifts never hurt.

'I will work on that.' He tipped his hat to her. 'You have been very helpful, Lady Agnes. I will remember all you have told me.'

He headed down the lane leading to the gate. How gauche to have walked from Ambleside.

She went back into the house and joined Brookmore and Miss Tilson in the hall. 'I've sent him on his way,' she told them.

Miss Tilson actually looked grateful. 'Thank you, Lady Agnes.' She released a breath. 'I am much relieved.' She slid a glance to Brookmore before turning back to Agnes. 'I really should get back to the children. Will you both excuse me?'

'Of course,' Agnes said in her sweetest voice. 'The children.'

Miss Tilson curtsied and left the room.

'Well, that was certainly dramatic,' Agnes remarked to Brookmore.

'The whole matter is odd, if you ask me.' Brookmore's words were more spontaneous than usual when he spoke to her. 'Why did he show up in the first place?'

'I attempted to discover his reasons while you sent someone to find Miss Tilson.' She might as well have him think she was trying to be helpful to him. 'He told me his wife died and he needed Miss Tilson to return to care for his children. They are all alone now, you see.'

'They are alone, so he travels all the way here?' Brookmore huffed. 'He might have stayed with his children and written a letter.'

It was pathetic, really, these two gentlemen fawning over that plain spinster of a governess. She was too tall. Too…robust. And lacking in refinement.

She shook her head. 'A letter would not do, you see. A personal contact like this is much more convincing.'

He darted a fiery glance at her. 'You sound as if you are taking up his cause.'

'Do I?' She laughed. 'I do not mean to sound that way. I do have some sympathy for Sir Orin, losing his wife. And his little children, losing their mother. If Miss Tilson returned to him, his children would regain some stability.'

'I want stability for my nieces,' Brookmore stated. 'They lost both their parents.'

She slid her arm through his, brushing her breast against him. 'Don't get in high dudgeon, Brookmore, dear. I am excessively proud of the way you have taken care of your nieces. Those dear little girls. But, I must say, Miss Tilson is not like any governess I ever knew.'

'Nor I,' he said absently.

She seized on this. 'She seems to take them outside all day. Is she ever in the classroom? Do you know if they are learning French? Italian? Or doing needlework? Or learning the social graces?'

'I have not discussed the details of Miss Tilson's lessons with her,' he admitted.

What did he discuss with her, then?

They walked into the drawing room. He went over to a cabinet and took out a decanter.

'Some claret?' he offered.

'Please.' She smiled.

While he poured, she draped herself gracefully on one of the sofas. He handed her a glass.

She took a ladylike sip. 'Would you like me to involve myself with the nursery? I could visit the schoolroom and see what exactly Miss Tilson is teaching your sweet nieces.'

'No,' he shot back. 'Leave it. Ellen and Pamela are starting to be happy again.'

She took another sip. 'As you wish.'

Chapter Fifteen

It took Rebecca three days to calm down from Sir Orin Foley's visit. The day of his visit, she'd gone into Lord Brookmore's library and looked up Sir Orin in *Debrett's*. She'd had to comb through all the listings, which were by title and not given name, but she'd found it finally. Orin Foley of Newpark, Second Baronet. As of 1814, that issue's publication date, Sir Orin had been married to Anne Walsh, daughter of the Earl of Branard and had issue, one son, Charles, and three daughters, Mary, Margaret and Bridget.

She wished she could discover what had happened to Lady Foley and what had happened to Claire to make her leave her position.

But the days settled into their usual order and her thoughts about Claire and Sir Orin became more fleeting. Her feelings regarding Lord Brookmore settled into a quiet ache and she sometimes could see him without feeling like the wound had been reopened to bleed all over again. Lady Agnes more and more took over the house as if it were hers, which, of course, it was destined to be.

Rebecca's teaching had settled into a routine, as well, if one could call her haphazard lessons a routine. Sometimes she remembered to teach them sums and French, but mostly she read to them from Lord Brookmore's extensive library or they went outside and looked at everything. How the plants grew, how the animals behaved, both those on the farm and in the wild, how the weather changed, although it didn't change much. It remained unseasonably cold.

Every morning the girls had riding lessons on their ponies. Pamela was taking to riding as though she was born on a horse, but Ellen, the typically intrepid one, was slow to giving up her fear. Her pony was the sweetest creature, though, and was steadily winning her over.

She encouraged them to talk to her about their thoughts and feelings or to write them down in their journals. If nothing else, she was determined they know their own minds.

This morning, as the sun merely peeked over the mountains, Rebecca mounted Lily, the horse that was hers in her heart, although she'd never again own a horse. Galloping on the fields, she and Lily seemed to have one mind. She loved her morning rides. For a few minutes every day, Rebecca could feel free as the wind whipping through the fells.

On her way back, in the distance a man on horseback appeared on the next hill. Rebecca's heart thrilled, as it always did when she saw Brookmore unexpectedly, but a second later she realised it was not Brookmore. She rarely saw anyone else on her early morning runs, except workers beginning their day's toil.

The figure rode down the hill out of her sight and she put him out of her mind. The ride back was when she talked herself into being grateful for what she had. Life, for one. So many others on the ship lost theirs. She again thanked Claire for the chance to live Claire's life, even though nothing turned out like she thought.

She made herself think of Pamela and Ellen, of how they were blossoming under her care. Inept as she was as a governess, something she was doing made these little girls happier. She and Lord Brookmore, of course. He daily showed he cared about them.

Lily climbed the far hill where Rebecca had seen the man. She started to plan her lessons for the day. They always seemed so organised in her mind. In practice, though, it never worked out so neatly.

She rode over the hill and was startled to see the rider waiting there.

Sir Orin.

'What a surprise to see you riding, Claire!' He spoke to her as if continuing an ongoing conversation. 'I did not know you rode.'

'There is much you do not know about me.' Like the fact that she was not Claire.

He started riding beside her. 'Yes, indeed. You are so changed. I find it exciting.'

Anxiety crept up her spine. 'Why are you still here, Sir Orin? I told you that I am happy in my position here. I'm not returning to your employ.'

'Can I not tour the Lake District? It is becoming fashionable to do so, I understand.' He smiled at her.

'You should go home to your children,' she admonished.

'Not without you,' he said.

'You must not speak to me that way.' Can Lily gallop home? she wondered. She didn't wish to try for fear of overworking the horse.

'Why did you leave, Claire?' He acted as if she'd not spoken. 'I told you I would find a way for everything to work out.'

Had he romanced Claire? It certainly seemed as if he had, but he wasn't precisely stating so. She did not want to say the wrong thing.

'I am quite content here, sir. There is nothing more to discuss. I am riding back to Brookmore House and I do not want you to follow me there.' She signalled Lily to canter and she did not look back, but she could hear no hoofbeats behind her.

Later that day Lady Agnes asked to be taken to Ambleside for shopping. Her aunt did not accompany her. Ordinarily Agnes preferred riding in her carriage, but, since the ride to Ambleside was only three miles, she allowed herself to be taken in the gig. One horse instead of four. Her coachman drove instead of one of Brookmore's stablemen.

'Take me to the Unicorn Inn,' Agnes said as they neared the village. 'I have an errand there before shopping.'

'Yes, m'lady.' Her coachman would spend the time in the inn's tavern, she guessed. And he lacked any curiosity as to her business.

Agnes entered the inn.

A man, obviously the innkeeper, attended the hall.

'Good day to you, my fine lady,' he said in the jovial manner so common to these sorts.

She gave him one of her charming smiles. 'Good day to you, sir. I am looking for a gentleman of my acquaintance. Sir Orin. I wish to speak with him. Is he here, do you know?'

'Sir Orin.' He nodded. 'I believe he is in the parlour reading the newspaper. Shall I get him for you?'

Silly question. 'Either that or show me to the parlour.'

He extended his arm. 'This way, madam.'

She was not a madam yet, not until she got Brookmore

to the altar. This plan of hers would get the deed done, though, she was certain of it.

Sir Orin fortunately sat alone in the parlour.

'A lady to see you, sir,' the innkeeper announced.

Sir Orin looked up and smiled. He stood and walked over to her. 'Lady Agnes. How good to see you.'

When the innkeeper closed the door, Agnes spoke. 'I told you I would come.'

He gestured for her to sit.

She brushed off the upholstery of a chair and lowered herself on to it.

'I hope you are well,' he said as he chose a chair facing hers. He leaned forward as if eager to hear what she had to say.

'I am glad you have not given up,' she said.

His expression turned serious. 'I shall never give up. Do you come to offer me some hope?'

She turned serious, as well. 'I wish you to be very honest with me.'

A slight smile lit his lips. 'I am the soul of honesty, my lady.'

Then he was a fool. Everyone needed to tell a falsehood now and then.

She refrained from rolling her eyes. 'Tell me truthfully. Do you wish Miss Tilson back as your children's governess or is there another reason?'

He clamped his mouth shut as if considering whether to answer her question or not. Or to lie or not.

Finally he spoke. 'I am determined to make Miss Tilson my wife. I wish this above all things.'

She leaned back. 'I suspected as much.' How convenient that his wife had died. 'And does she return your regard?'

He glanced away. 'How could she have done? She was too honourable. And she was loyal to my wife.'

Who now was conveniently out of the way.

Agnes straightened her spine. 'Well, I have contrived another opportunity for you.'

'Excellent,' he said. 'I rode this morning and intercepted her, to no avail. I did not recall her being so stubborn.'

'I think there are other factors at play here.' She was not going to divulge them to him, though. He was a man, after all, and men could so easily ruin things. 'In any event, you are invited to my dinner party this Saturday next. Five other couples, all I could find who would be suitable. I will insist she be a member of the party, as well, and that you have an opportunity to speak with her privately.'

'A dinner party?' He did not look convinced.

'Let her see you with other good people.' Or at least the best she could find in this remote area of England. 'Put on the charm.'

He gave her an earnest look. 'Do you believe I have seemed too eager?'

'Absolutely.' She believed he'd played this all wrong. 'Be a gentleman. Make the others like you. Let her see you through their eyes.'

He sat back and grinned. 'I dare say I can do that.'

'I am certain you can.' She stood. 'Come at eight o'clock. Come by carriage. Do you have proper attire?'

He rose, as well. 'I do indeed.'

He extended his hand. She put her gloved hand in his and accepted the handshake.

'Until Saturday, then, Sir Orin,' she said.

When Agnes returned to Brookmore House she changed out of her walking dress and went in search of Miss Tilson. She climbed the stairs to the second floor and passed what she supposed was Brookmore's bedchamber. At least, it was the room his valet exited as she walked by.

'Good day, m'lady,' the old man said.

'Good day,' she said brightly.

The valet shuffled off and Agnes wondered why Brookmore did not pension off such an ancient servant. Surely the man had no sense of men's fashions today. It could not be pleasant to have such a wrinkled creature touch him or his clothes.

But, never mind. That was a task for another day.

She continued down the hallway until coming to what she supposed was the children's wing. She heard a voice and listened through the door.

The voice was Miss Tilson's, sounding as if she was reading from a book:

"The elk is twice as big as a hart and bigger than a horse in Norway and Sweden. It is tamed and put into a coach, chariot or sledge to draw men through great snows and upon the ice. It is said to be more swift and to run more miles in one day than a horse..."

Agnes opened the door without knocking.

'Lady Agnes!' Miss Tilson closed the book.

The little girls were seated at the table, their backs to the door. They whirled around to the doorway.

'Stand and curtsy to Lady Agnes, girls,' Miss Tilson said.

They scrambled off their chairs and did as she said.

'How darling!' Agnes let her gaze encompass the three of them. 'What were you reading?'

Pamela answered. *'A Description of Three Hundred Animals.'*

'Beasts, Birds, Fishes, Serpents and Insects,' Ellen added.

'Animals,' Agnes repeated. 'How delightful.' She turned to the governess. 'May I speak to you alone for a moment, Miss Tilson?'

As Miss Tilson made her way to the doorway, she

handed the book to Pamela. 'Read some of this to Ellen while I speak with Lady Agnes.'

Agnes stepped back out to the hallway. Miss Tilson joined her and closed the door behind her. She did not speak, but merely gazed at Agnes.

Agnes smiled. 'Do not fear, Miss Tilson. I bring you very pleasant news.'

The governess looked sceptical, but still did not speak.

Agnes took a breath. 'I am inviting you to our dinner party on Saturday night. I have invited some of the area's important people and it would be so kind of you to join us.'

It took Miss Tilson several seconds to finally speak. 'I must respectfully decline, my lady. I do not have suitable clothes to wear.'

Agnes waved a dismissive hand. 'Simply wear your best dress. It will do, I am sure.'

'I do not think so,' Miss Tilson said.

Agnes gave her a steely smile. 'I must insist. I need you at the table, otherwise the numbers will not be even. Come to the drawing room at seven-thirty.' She nodded a dismissal, turned on her heel and left.

Rebecca watched Lady Agnes walk away. The tension from the encounter came in a rush and she tried to quiet her breathing.

Refusing to attend this dinner would likely cause more drama than enduring it. She'd have to attend.

She wished she were a man so she could curse!

Her fists clenched and unclenched.

Finally when she felt like she could act with some semblance of normalcy, she opened the classroom door.

Pamela and Ellen both jumped back with guilty looks on their faces.

'Were you two listening at the door?' Rebecca asked, although she knew very well they were.

'Yes, Miss Tilson,' Pamela admitted.

Ellen's eyes grew big. 'Are you really going to a dinner party?'

'I don't know, Ellen.' Rebecca sat in her chair and the two girls came to her side.

Ellen's brow furrowed. 'What is a dinner party?'

Pamela looked exasperated. 'It is when you invite people to eat dinner with you and they come dressed in pretty clothes. Do you not remember Mama and Papa having dinner parties?'

Ellen shook her head.

Pamela turned to Rebecca. 'You do not have pretty clothes, though, do you, Miss Tilson? Your pretty dresses are all at the bottom of the sea.'

'I am afraid so.' Rebecca looked down at herself. 'I'll have to wear this.'

'You cannot wear that,' Pamela insisted. 'The other ladies will be in silks and laces and such.'

Ellen jumped up and down. 'I have an idea!' She pulled Pamela some distance away and whispered in her ear.

Pamela's face brightened and she whispered something back. Ellen jumped up and down again. This time Pamela pulled her back to Rebecca.

Pamela took Rebecca's hand. 'Come with us, Miss Tilson.'

Ellen grabbed her other hand and they pulled her out of her seat.

'We'll need a lamp,' Pamela said.

Rebecca picked up one from the schoolroom and followed them into the hallway. They led her to another staircase, one she had not seen before.

'This is the attic,' Pamela said.

They climbed the stairs up to a third floor and opened the door to a cavernous area dotted with trunks, wooden boxes, furniture covered with cloth. The girls walked over to a trunk stashed near the entrance. It was made of the same carved oak wood that panelled most of the rooms in the house.

It took the two girls to lift the lid.

'Come see, Miss Tilson!' Ellen cried.

She carried the lamp closer and placed it on the lid of a nearby wooden box. She peered inside the trunk. There appeared to be women's clothes carefully folded.

'What are these?' Rebecca asked.

'Mama's dresses,' Ellen said. 'You could wear one to the dinner party.'

Rebecca stepped back. 'Oh, no. Not your mother's clothes.'

The girls could not possibly know how it would feel to see their mother's clothes on someone else.

'It is all right, Miss Tilson,' Pamela said. 'Mama never wore these. They were delivered after…after the accident. Nobody has ever worn these.'

'But I could not…'

Pamela put her hands on her hips. 'Did not Uncle say that our mother's things belong to Ellen and me now?'

He'd told them that at breakfast many times.

'Then we can say who wears these dresses,' Pamela added.

'Miss Ellen! Miss Pamela!' Mary's voice reached them.

Ellen ran to the doorway. 'Up here, Mary!'

Mary's footsteps sounded on the stairs. 'You girls know you are not supposed to play up here.' She reached the top. 'Oh, Miss Tilson.'

Ellen looked up at her. 'Miss Tilson is going to the dinner party and she doesn't have a pretty dress and Pamela and I want her to wear one of Mama's—the ones Mama never wore.'

'You've been invited to the dinner party?' Mary looked surprised.

'I am afraid so,' admitted Rebecca. 'Lady Agnes has demanded I attend.'

Mary rolled her eyes. 'The dinner party. She has everyone below stairs at sixes and sevens over it. Except Mrs Dodd. Mrs Dodd is over the moon that there will be a party.'

'The children want me to wear one of these dresses.' Rebecca gestured to the trunk.

'Oh, the dresses that came after.' Mary knew instantly which dresses she meant. 'We did not know what to do with them so we simply put them in this trunk in the attic.'

'Otherwise she'll have to wear an ugly dress,' Ellen explained.

The children's maid laughed. 'We cannot have that. Not if Miss Tilson is invited to the *dinner party*.' She put an exaggerated emphasis on *dinner party*. 'Let's have a look.' Mary knelt next to the trunk and lifted one dress out. 'It is too dark here. Let's look at the dresses in Miss Tilson's bedchamber.'

Mary pulled out three dresses and draped them over Rebecca's arms. Mary carried three more. 'Miss Pamela, you carry the lamp.'

'What can I do?' Ellen whined.

'You must close the door,' the maid said.

They made their way to Rebecca's room and spread the dresses over the bed. There was one dress Rebecca could not help but love. A deep green patterned silk with a flounce at the hem and a gold ribbon tied under her breasts. It was plain, but elegant. She knew instantly that it would complement her colouring and make her eyes turn green.

It was just the sort of dress Rebecca would have worn in her real life.

'Which one?' she asked, thinking the girls would like to choose for her, since it had been their idea.

'The green one,' Mary, Pamela and Ellen said together.

Rebecca laughed. 'That is the one I like the best.'

Ellen came over and hugged her. 'We will dress you up and you will be as pretty as Mama.'

That night at dinner Lady Agnes seemed especially cheerful. No doubt it was due to the impending dinner party. She hardly talked of anything else.

Garret wished it would never take place, but not because guests were invited. He'd known these people most of his life. He objected because Lady Agnes manipulated the whole event and he disliked being manipulated. More reason to dread marrying her.

'How was your day?' he asked Lady Agnes out of politeness.

'It was lovely!' Her colour was heightened, which made her even more beautiful. 'I went to Ambleside to do some shopping and you will never guess who I encountered there.'

He detested guessing. 'Who?'

'Sir Orin.' She took a sip of her wine.

'Sir Orin, yes.' Her aunt who sat across from her nodded approvingly. 'You told me about him. A baronet, you said.'

Sir Orin? Garret remembered him. Miss Tilson's former employer. 'He is still here?'

'He is indeed,' Agnes responded. 'I invited him to the dinner party.'

'How very nice, dear,' her aunt said.

Garret put down his fork. 'You did what?'

'I invited Sir Orin to the dinner party,' she repeated.

This was too much. 'Un-invite him, then. He is nothing to me.'

She spoke calmly. 'Now, Brookmore, another couple is needed to balance out the table. And he is a baronet. This area is quite thin of aristocracy. A baronet will improve the company.'

Sir Orin Foley had pressed Miss Tilson to return to his employ. He'd used her Christian name. 'This dinner was supposed to fulfil a social obligation to my neighbours. Sir Orin is not a neighbour. I do not want him here.'

Her eyes twinkled. 'There is another reason,' she said, but did not immediately elaborate.

'What other reason?' he asked finally. Why the devil did she not simply tell everything instead of feeding it to him piecemeal?

'He confided in me.' She leaned towards Garret. 'He is sweet on Miss Tilson.' She laughed as if that idea was amusing. 'He wishes to convince her to marry him. That is why he has remained in the area.'

'Marry him?' Garret felt his skin turn cold.

'How nice,' her aunt broke in.

It was not nice. It was decidedly not nice. 'How can you think she will welcome his suit? She sent him away when he called here.'

'Yes, but that was when she thought Sir Orin merely wanted her as governess.' Lady Agnes speared a piece of roast fowl with her fork. 'It is quite another matter to be a baronet's wife.'

Garret's appetite fled. 'I fail to see how inviting him to the dinner party furthers his aim to marry Miss Tilson.'

Lady Agnes swallowed and took another sip of wine. 'Oh, I invited her, too, of course. She evens out the numbers.'

Garret frowned into his plate. Miss Tilson would not desire this. 'I dislike these machinations, Lady Agnes.'

Her aunt wiped her mouth with her napkin. 'Agnes, dear, I am feeling a bit ill. I believe I will retire.' She turned nervously to Garret. 'With your permission, sir?'

He nodded.

Lady Agnes avoided looking at him until her aunt left the room. Then she turned to him with a wounded expression. 'These are not machinations, Brookmore dear. I did need one more couple for the dinner party. And more elevated company. And I can only see this as a favour for Miss Tilson. You must admit, her life would more vastly be improved by marriage. She would have a household of her own to manage. She would have wealth and security.'

Everyone knew the life of a governess was a dismal one. Long hours. Little chance of meeting a respectable suitor. A victim of those on whose employment she was dependent. Was he right in wanting nothing to take her away from here? From his nieces, he meant.

'Am I not correct?' Lady Agnes pressed.

He faced her. 'Does she know all this?'

Lady Agnes glanced away and back. 'Well, she does not know he seeks her hand in marriage. To tell her seemed like too much interference.'

It all seemed like too much interference to Garret.

'And she is willing to attend the dinner?' he asked.

'Certainly she is,' Agnes said brightly.

He didn't believe her. He hoped he could contrive an opportunity to ask Miss Tilson if she wished to attend this cursed dinner party.

They finished the meal with little conversation.

Lady Agnes took his arm to be escorted from the room. 'Do not fear, Brookmore, dear. This dinner party will be a success, I assure you. I know precisely what I am doing.'

Chapter Sixteen

The night of the dinner party came quickly. Mary and the little girls were so excited for Rebecca she couldn't help feeling a bit of their enthusiasm herself. The only detail she knew about the party was that she was expected to show up in the drawing room at seven-thirty. Mary and the girls insisted they devote the whole afternoon to preparing for it.

Rebecca had successfully avoided being alone with Lord Brookmore the last three days. He'd spoken of the dinner party at breakfast, letting her know she was free to decline.

But she wasn't really free. To decline only brought more attention on her. She would attend and be precisely what Lady Agnes wished—a person in a chair so the party had symmetry.

After the girls ate their midday meal, they would join Rebecca in her bedchamber. Lady Agnes did not know—no one knew—that Rebecca knew exactly how to prepare for a party, although she did not have any tools to do so. She would do the best she could with what she possessed.

'Look what we found,' Ellen cried from the hallway.

Rebecca stepped out of the room.

Pamela and Ellen carried a big wooden box, so large it took the two of them to manage it.

What had they got into now? Rebecca took it off their hands before they dropped it and did themselves an injury.

'What is it?' she asked.

Ellen jumped up and down in excitement. 'Bring it to your room! You will see.'

She carried it into the bedchamber, the two girls following at her heels. She placed it on a table. Ellen immediately pulled up a chair and knelt on it. Pamela was tall enough to open the box.

'Oh, my!' Rebecca picked through the contents.

'This is everything I need. Where did you find it?' There were curling papers, pomade, rouge, ribbons and hair pins.

'It is Mama's things,' Pamela said solemnly.

The girls somehow discovered the box in which their mother's dressing table had been packed away.

Rebecca closed the box again. 'Oh, no. I cannot use your mother's things.' The items were too personal, too intimate.

'You must,' Pamela pleaded. 'We used to watch Mama make herself ready for parties. We want to see you do it, too.'

'She looked very pretty.' Ellen's bottom lip trembled.

'We want you to look pretty, too,' Pamela said.

'Prettier than Lady Agnes!' Ellen added.

Rebecca opened the box again. Was she to live this part of Lady Brookmore's life, as well as living Claire's? Perhaps she could use Lady Brookmore's things so her little girls could once more watch her dress up.

She could make it a lesson, as well. Some day the girls would be dressing up for some social event. They needed to learn.

'Shall we start with my hair?' Since she'd become Claire, she'd not arranged her hair in any way more decorative than Claire's plain hairstyle.

Rebecca took out the curling papers, triangle-shaped tissue paper. She searched through the box and found what else she needed at the bottom.

'Here it is!' Rebecca pulled out an iron instrument similar to a small coal tongs, but with disc shapes on the ends.

'What is that?' Ellen asked, reaching for it.

Rebecca let her hold it. 'It is a *papillote*. We will use it to curl my hair.'

There was a quick knock on the door and Mary entered, carrying the green-silk dress. 'I've cleared away the girls' meal and have everything else done, so I am at liberty to assist you.' She saw the box. 'Lady Brookmore's things. I packed them up from her dressing table when Lady Agnes arrived.'

'The girls brought them in,' Rebecca explained.

'Miss Tilson is going to curl her hair.' Ellen held up the *papillote*.

Mary put one hot coal from the fireplace into the coal scuttle and brought it over to Rebecca's dressing table. She placed the *papillote* in it. 'Now you girls must not touch it. It will become quite hot.'

Rebecca took the pins from her hair and brushed out the tangles. She separated her hair into sections. 'Now I will show you how to make *papillote* curls, Pamela, Ellen. Watch carefully.'

Explaining each step as she performed it, Rebecca placed a tiny amount of pomade on to a strand of hair and wound it around her finger, so that it was the size of a coin. She wrapped it in the curling paper and Mary carefully pressed the curl with the heated *papillote*. She continued until every strand on her head was wrapped in paper.

'Now I let it cool and you will see what comes next,' she told the girls.

'I remember!' Pamela cried abruptly. 'Mama's head was all full of curls.'

'That's right,' Rebecca told her.

The girls' eyes had been large as saucers as they watched her wrap her curls. They were eager and happy observers. At least this measure of fun, sharing her preparations with the girls, would make this event worth it.

'Would you girls like curls, too?' she asked impulsively.

'Yes! Yes!' they both cried.

She and Mary carefully curled the girls' hair, then the girls insisted Mary have some curls, too, and the four of them laughed at how silly they looked with paper stuck all through their hair.

Mary had Rebecca try on the dress which needed more minor alterations. Mary had lengthened it by letting out the hem and sewing the flounce at the very bottom. With another tuck or two, the gown would fit Rebecca perfectly.

While waiting for the dress to be finished, Rebecca went through every item in the box of Lady Brookmore's things, making the girls guess at items they should know and giving the names and purpose of items they did not.

They all stopped for tea as the afternoon headed into evening and soon it was time for her to complete her *toilette*. Rebecca enhanced the colour and shape of her eyebrows with burnt cloves. She dabbed her cheeks and lips with a faint tint of rouge and she dusted her face with a tiny bit of powder.

'Is it too much?' she asked Mary.

'No!' the girls replied.

Mary surveyed her carefully. 'It looks very natural to me.'

She took a deep breath and looked into the mirror. 'Time for the hair.'

She pulled out the curling papers and her head was a mass of curls. She pulled her hair on top of her head, secured it with ribbons and pins and let the curls cascade wherever they wished. The shorter hair curled around her face in a nice frame.

She turned to see what her audience thought.

Ellen threw her arms around her. 'You look so pretty!'

After fixing the girls' hair in a similar style and Mary's into some curls that would not cause her trouble with Mrs Dodd, it was already seven-thirty and she would be late.

As if she cared to be on time.

Mary helped her into the dress and she donned a pair of slippers and gloves they'd found in the attic. Mary gasped. 'You need to see yourself! Come with me.'

Mary picked up a lamp and took Rebecca's hand. She led Rebecca and the girls to one of the bedchambers on the hallway near Lord Brookmore's room. She stood Rebecca in front of a full-length mirror.

Rebecca took in a quick breath. Her legs trembled.

The reflection in the mirror looked nothing like Claire Tilson, the governess. In the mirror stood Lady Rebecca Pierce.

She'd almost forgotten about her.

This evening would be a social engagement much like those Lady Rebecca would have attended. The company would be like the company with whom she would have conversed. Lady Rebecca was the social equal of Lady Agnes. She might even have precedence over her.

Lady Rebecca was also the social equal of Lord Brookmore.

Tonight, just this one night, she would be Lady Rebecca again, she decided.

She turned to Mary and the girls with a grin. 'Will I do?'

The girls ran to her and she hugged them close, not even

thinking about how her dress might get a wrinkle. When she released them, she kissed them goodnight and promised to tell them all about the party the next day.

They walked her back to the hallway where she hugged the girls again and hugged Mary. 'Thank you, Mary. Thank you, Pamela and Ellen.' She swept her arms from her head to her toe. 'This is all due to you.'

Rebecca hurried to the stairway, turning to wave at the girls one more time. When she descended to the first floor and entered the hall, she straightened her spine and lifted her head and again became Lady Rebecca.

All the guests had arrived and had been served glasses of claret, but Garret kept glancing towards the door.

Had Miss Tilson decided not to come?

Lady Agnes approached him when others were not close by. 'I do hope your governess has the courtesy to show up. I shall be excessively peeved if she ruins the numbers in my dinner party.'

He said nothing, knowing he'd given Miss Tilson permission to stay away. He refilled Lady Agnes's wineglass and poured another to hand to Mr Henson, Reverend Elliman's curate.

Sir Orin walked up to him and handed him an empty glass. 'It was kind of you to include me in your party, sir. I have been missing good company.'

Garret filled his glass. 'You must thank Lady Agnes. She tendered the invitations.'

Sir Orin smiled charmingly. 'I do thank her, then.' He lifted his glass to Garret and glanced at the door.

He's waiting for her, too, Garret thought. He looked at the clock. Ten minutes to eight. Lady Agnes had been clear that Glover should announce dinner precisely at eight.

Glover stepped inside the drawing room. 'Miss Tilson,' he announced.

All eyes went to the door. Garret worried on her behalf. She would not expect this attention.

She appeared and Garret felt the air leave his lungs.

Here stood a different person, tall and regal, wearing a fine green dress that perfectly complemented her colouring and her statuesque figure. Her features, always striking, could only be described as beautiful.

'Who is she?' gasped the curate.

'My nieces' governess.' Garret stifled an urge to laugh in appreciation of her triumph. She outshone every woman in the room. Especially Lady Agnes.

Sir Orin took a step towards her and Lady Agnes put a stilling hand on his arm, showing more consideration than Garret gave her credit for.

Miss Tilson directed her gaze to Garret and started to walk towards him, but Lady Agnes intercepted her.

'Everyone,' Lady Agnes said, 'this is the girls' governess. She has kindly offered to even our numbers at dinner.' She took Miss Tilson's arm and guided her to the guests, starting with Sir Orin.

Miss Tilson turned white at the sight of him.

'Sir Orin you already know,' Lady Agnes chirped.

He bowed. 'Claire.'

Her eyes flashed. 'Sir,' she said curtly, turning her head away.

Agnes, following precedence, introduced her to Mr and Mrs Howard of Levens Hall, Squire Lloyd, Mrs Lloyd, Reverend Elliman and his wife, the curate, and Mr and Mrs Wordsworth.

Her eyes brightened. 'Mr Wordsworth! This is a pleasure! *"I wandered lonely as a cloud, That floats on high o'er vales and hills, When all at once I saw a crowd, A host, of golden daffodils.'''*

He beamed with pleasure. 'You read poetry, Miss Tilson?'

She smiled at him. 'I read your poetry, Mr Wordsworth.'

Agnes guided her away.

Garret spoke up. 'Would you care for a glass of claret, Miss Tilson?'

Her gaze turned to him again. 'Thank you. I would.'

She stepped away from Lady Agnes and walked up to him, her back to the rest of the room.

He handed her the glass. 'You did not know Sir Orin was invited, did you?'

'No,' she snapped. 'You might have warned me.'

'I was told you knew.'

She turned away from him and walked over to Mrs Howard and Mrs Wordsworth.

Glover entered the drawing room again. 'Dinner is served.'

Garret clasped Lady Agnes's arm and spoke through gritted teeth. 'You told me she knew of Sir Orin's invitation.'

Lady Agnes gave him an innocent look. 'I am sure I never did say that.' She glanced towards Miss Tilson. 'Where did she find that gown? Did it conveniently survive the shipwreck?'

'Ask her,' he shot back. '*She* will tell the truth.'

Lady Agnes had been cruel to not tell Miss Tilson that Sir Orin would be among the guests. Worse, she'd lied about it.

Cruelty and lies. Two things Garret could not abide. He'd seen enough cruelty and was told enough lies while in the army. And now Lady Agnes seemed to have a strong capacity for both.

* * *

Garret's anger persisted throughout dinner. At least Lady Agnes was at the other end of the table, too far for him to converse with her. He talked politics and the army with Mr Howard, who was a Member of Parliament and had been a lieutenant colonel in the Irish 9th Garrison. He'd lost an eye in the Helder Expedition. He also spoke with Reverend and Mrs Elliman. Elliman had been the vicar when Garret was a boy and the man cared passionately for his parishioners. He and Squire Lloyd knew all the news and gossip in the local area.

In the middle of the table Sir Orin was busy entertaining the ladies, making conquests of Mrs Wordsworth, Mrs Lloyd, Mrs Elliman, even Lady Agnes's aunt Theodora. Mrs Howard looked at him with some scepticism.

Squire Lloyd leaned over to Garret. 'Who is this Sir Orin?'

He frowned. 'Someone Lady Agnes wished to invite.'

Garret watched Miss Tilson, who seemed to converse comfortably with Mr Wordsworth and the curate, who was clearly smitten. She held herself regally and confidently.

She was full of surprises and that intrigued and captivated him. He wished he could get her aside and tell her how beautiful she looked.

But he could not speak to her that way.

If it were not for Sir Orin and Lady Agnes, Rebecca might have enjoyed herself. She was beyond thrilled to actually meet the poet Wordsworth and his dear wife who so clearly worshipped him. Mrs Howard was another interesting person. Shrewd, but kind, the sort of lady who would make a formidable friend.

Rebecca was very aware of Sir Orin's eyes upon her and aware of a seething animosity underneath Lady Agnes's sugary exterior. It was painful to think of Lord Brookmore being fooled by her sweet facade. Rebecca was certain Lady Agnes's aim had been to hurt her. She'd succeeded, but Rebecca had no intention of letting her know.

'Miss Tilson,' Lady Agnes asked in her sweet tone. 'Wherever did you get that dress? It is so lovely.'

Rebecca smiled at her. 'Did you ever read "Cinderella"?' It was one of the tales in the book by the Brothers Grimm that she found in the schoolroom.

'Is that a novel?' Lady Agnes smirked. 'I am not overly fond of novels. I prefer reading something more edifying.'

'Very true,' agreed her companion, her aunt Theodora.

'Not a novel,' Rebecca retorted. 'A tale for children. Edifying, in that it instructs how kindness is eventually rewarded. Cinderella received her gown for a ball from some helpful doves.'

'Your dress came from doves?' Lady Agnes laughed derisively.

'Two little doves,' Rebecca responded, daring a quick glance towards Lord Brookmore.

'A tale for children,' Lady Agnes repeated. 'Was that one of your lessons?'

'A lesson about kindness, yes,' Rebecca retorted.

Lady Agnes addressed the dinner guests, 'Miss Tilson has a unique way of teaching. One wonders if she ever attended school.' She turned to Rebecca. 'Where did you attend school, Miss Tilson?'

Such a question risked exposure. She knew very little about Claire's schooling. 'A boarding school in Bristol.'

'Its name?' Lady Agnes pushed.

'You would not have heard of it,' Rebecca said. 'It was a school for gentry and merchants' daughters and the like.'

Lady Agnes glanced at the other ladies. 'Her lessons are conducted mostly out of doors.'

Rebecca cringed inside, but she refused to let Lady Agnes see her discomfort.

'Rousseau,' Mrs Howard piped up. 'She is following Rousseau. Are you not, Miss Tilson?'

Rebecca remembered learning about Rousseau at school, but all she could recall was that he was a French philosopher who had something to do with the French Revolution.

'It is odd,' Sir Orin broke in. 'When Miss Tilson was in my employ, she kept my children in the schoolroom most of the day.'

'Miss Tilson worked for you?' Mrs Elliman asked, giving Sir Orin an opportunity to wax poetic over her excellence as a governess.

Lord Brookmore looked grim during this discourse.

Rebecca wanted the attention off her. She turned to the curate, who was perhaps as young as she, and asked him questions. Where he was from. Where he attended university. When he became ordained. She asked him if he read poetry in university and whether he had read any of Mr Wordsworth's poems. This led to a discussion with Wordsworth about the inspiration of his poems, which started him talking about his love for the Lake District, a topic that was joined by the rest of the table, barring Sir Orin, Lady Agnes and Aunt Theodora.

Soon the dinner was over and the ladies retired to the drawing room again. Lady Agnes gathered all the women around her and poured tea for them. Rebecca remained on the periphery, by Lady Agnes's design, she supposed, although Mrs Howard and Mrs Wordsworth sent friendly smiles her way.

After a time, Lady Agnes shivered. 'It is chilly in here, is it not?'

The other ladies professed to be comfortable.

Lady Agnes persisted, though. 'Aunt, are you chilly? Do you need your shawl?'

Her aunt looked uncertain at first at how to respond. 'I am a bit chilly,' she finally said.

Lady Agnes turned to Rebecca. 'Miss Tilson, be a dear and fetch Aunt Theodora's shawl from her room, would you please?'

Rebecca's cheeks burned. This certainly was a pointed insult, no matter the sugary language in which it was made. There was a footman in the room—a servant—whose job it was to see to such tasks.

But she was not going to nip at Lady Agnes's bait. 'Certainly, my lady.' She stood and walked out of the room, passing the footman who gave her a surprised look.

There was another footman attending the hall. She could have asked him to do the task, but it seemed easier merely to do as Lady Agnes asked. She'd already brought more attention towards herself than she'd desired by her Cinderella story. Lady Agnes had not been pleased.

Rebecca entered the corridor to the first-floor bedchambers and a man's hand seized her arm. Sir Orin.

'Claire,' he murmured, close to her ear.

She pulled away. 'Unhand me, sir.'

He moved closer to her, his eyes sweeping her body. 'You look so different, Claire. Even more beautiful than before. I am quite enamoured.'

She raised a hand to fend him off. 'Do not speak to me.'

He made a quick move and pinned her against the wall, holding her shoulders. 'Do you not see, Claire, my darling. Do you not see what I want? What I yearned for? What I can finally possess?'

Claire, I know now what you fled, Rebecca said silently.

She glared at him. 'Take your hands off me.'

He dropped his hands, but her back was still against the wall. She could not move away from him. 'If you think this is the way to hire a governess, you are very mistaken, sir.'

'A governess?' His eyes grew dark as he perused her again. 'I do not want you back as a governess. I want you for my wife.'

'No!' It was unthinkable. 'How can you ask? Your wife is hardly cold in her grave.'

His eyes flickered with a cold emotion. 'She was the one thing in our way.'

At that moment he looked dangerous enough to have caused his wife's death.

She took a careful breath. 'I will never marry you, sir. Now, allow me to continue on my errand for Lady Agnes. She will be wondering where I am.'

'Lady Agnes will understand,' he said with a knowing smile.

She understood why Lady Agnes had sent her on an errand. Lady Agnes had arranged this meeting.

'Release me now!' Rebecca demanded.

He put his hands on her again.

The door opened and he backed away from her.

Lord Brookmore stepped into the hall. 'Miss Tilson? Lady Agnes's aunt needs her shawl.'

Lord Brookmore rescued her. 'Yes, my lord.'

Sir Orin moved out of her way. She hurried to the elderly woman's room, trusting in the fact that Lord Brookmore would make certain Sir Orin would not accost her again.

Chapter Seventeen

Sir Orin gave Garret an angry look. 'That was a private conversation, Lord Brookmore. You interrupted it.'

Garret returned a steely gaze. 'When Miss Tilson returns I will ask her if she wishes a private conversation with you. If she does, I will summon you. Until then return to the drawing room or take your leave.'

Sir Orin huffed, but he turned on his heel and walked through the doorway to the hall. Garret waited and a few minutes later Miss Tilson appeared carrying the shawl Lady Agnes's aunt did not need.

'Thank you,' she said when she reached him. 'I could not get away from him.'

'I take it you did not desire that encounter?' Lady Agnes had insisted she would welcome it.

'Indeed not!' she exclaimed. 'He asked me to marry him. His wife could not be dead more than a few weeks and he asked me to marry him.'

'His suit is unwelcome?' Garret asked.

'How can you ask me that, Lord Brookmore?' she said crisply. 'Of course his suit is unwelcome. I do not want anything to do with him.'

Garret felt relieved. He wanted her to stay. For his nieces.

'I am sorry. I fear Lady Agnes arranged that encounter.'

Their gazed locked. He felt that pull of attraction he always felt when near her. He had nothing but admiration for her this night. From her appearance to her deft handling of the dinner-table conversation to her quiet dignity in the face of Agnes's mistreatment. Agnes had tried to cow her, but Miss Tilson had kept her head high.

She glanced away and lifted the shawl in her arms. 'I should bring this to Lady Agnes's aunt.'

He smiled wryly. 'I should return, as well. I am supposed to be the host of this party.'

They walked side by side to the door.

Garret put his hand on the door handle. 'I suppose the two doves who brought you the dress were named Pamela and Ellen.'

She grinned. 'They just happen to be.' Her expression sobered. 'They were very sweet to me.'

He softened his voice. 'You look lovely, Miss Tilson.'

Two spots of pink tinged her cheeks. 'Thank you,' she murmured.

He began to open the door, but turned to ask her one more question. 'I do not suppose those two doves arranged your hair, as well?'

She lowered her gaze, but smiled. 'No, that was my doing. With Mary's help, of course.'

He nodded. 'You did well. It is very becoming.'

As he opened the door, she shot him a glance. 'I believe you will see plenty of curls tomorrow morning at breakfast, my lord.'

He stepped aside and held the door for her. She walked briskly to the drawing room. He followed more slowly.

He reached the door to the drawing room as she handed the shawl to Lady Agnes's aunt.

'I am sorry I took so long,' she told the elderly woman. 'I was detained.'

The poised, well-spoken woman she had become returned as she conversed with Mr and Mrs Howard.

Garret walked over to Lady Agnes who was momentarily alone. 'That was not well done of you, Lady Agnes.' He turned away from her to converse with the Ellimans and the Wordsworths. Sir Orin stood in a corner of the room, consuming a brandy and alternately glaring at Garret and watching Miss Tilson.

After what seemed like an interminable period of time, the guests began to say goodnight. The Howards were the first to leave, having a carriage ride of at least two hours before they reached Levens Hall. Miss Tilson slipped away when they were saying their goodbyes, as did Lady Agnes's aunt.

Garret had made his carriages available for the other guests—except for Sir Orin, that was. He did not care how the devil the man made it back to Ambleside.

When they were finally all in their carriages and riding away, the lamps on the carriages danced down the lane to the gate.

Garret turned to Lady Agnes, who gave him a bright smile. 'That was a success, do you not think?'

'In spite of your machinations, do you mean?' He spoke severely.

Her eyes widened in all innocence. 'I do not know what you mean.'

'Manipulating that meeting between Sir Orin and Miss Tilson.'

She looked wounded. 'I told you, I merely was trying to help them. Sir Orin managed to tell me it did not go well. I do hope that was not because of you interrupting them.'

'Stop any assistance to Sir Orin. Miss Tilson does not welcome his suit. I expect you to respect that.'

'She doesn't?' Lady Agnes sounded surprised, but at this point Garret did not believe anything she said. 'I am astonished. It is a better match than a governess could expect. She is a fool not to secure him while she can.'

'You are to respect her decision and stop your interference. I mean that.' He added, 'And I will not have you belittle those who are lower status than you. Not in this house.'

Her mouth dropped. 'When did I ever do that?'

He looked her in the eye. 'You called attention to Miss Tilson's position, not once but twice in a manner that was belittling.'

She blinked. 'I would never do that. Never. If she took it that way, I am very sorry.' She stepped closer to him and threaded her arm through his, clasping his arm so that her body touched his. 'I will apologise to her tomorrow. I promise.'

'No,' he said. 'Leave it. Leave her to her duties.'

'Are you sure?' She batted her eyelashes at him. 'I am desolated that she believes I belittled her.'

'She has not said so. I say so.' He stared into her fluttering eyelashes. 'Leave her alone.'

She squeezed his arm. 'Whatever you wish, Brookmore, dear.'

Agnes knew Brookmore did not want to walk her to her bedchamber, but by taking his arm, she ensured he would. At the door, though, she was forced to let go of him.

He stepped away quickly, saying only a curt, 'Goodnight.'

She entered the room, kicked off her shoes and threw them against the wall with a cry of frustration.

Her maid appeared from the dressing room. 'Shall I help you prepare for bed, m'lady?' the maid asked.

'Yes. Be quick about it,' she snapped. 'I am very tired.'

When she was finally ready for bed, though, she could not settle down. She threw things around the room. Nothing that would break. Her clothing mostly. Things her maid would have to tidy up in the morning. She let herself have a proper tantrum until she flung herself on the bed.

Everything had gone wrong. Lord Brookmore was angry with her and if she did not do something to fix it, he might cry off. Think of the shame of that!

She sat up. It would never happen. She would cry off first and tell some horrible tale of how wicked he was. Or worse, how very provincial.

She pounded the pillow. No! She would not give up so easily. He needed her. She was the perfect wife for him. Everyone said so.

That governess was the problem. Agnes knew it from the moment Miss Tilson entered the drawing room and Brookmore could not stop looking at her.

If Agnes had thought Miss Tilson could dress like she had vouchers for Almack's, she might never have included her in the dinner party. She'd hoped only that the dinner would give Sir Orin an opportunity to propose to the governess. How could Agnes know that Miss Tilson would refuse?

She was a fool. Sir Orin was a baronet. She was a nobody.

Unless she was holding out for a viscount. Which, of course, she was.

Brookmore would not be so foolish to consider marriage to a governess with no name and no position in society. A dalliance with her, perhaps, but not marriage.

At this point, though, if he fancied himself besotted with the creature, he might very well call off the wedding.

Agnes certainly would not stand for that.

The next morning when Garret entered the Tower Room to share breakfast with Miss Tilson and his nieces, he was greeted with two smiling faces framed with bouncing curls. Even Miss Tilson's curls remained.

When the children's maid walked in for a moment, Garret laughed out loud. She also sported some curls.

'All four of you?' He grinned. 'I've never seen so many pretty curls in all my life.'

Pamela and Ellen giggled.

'Miss Tilson says there is another way to make curls without using the *papillote*.' Ellen frowned. 'I didn't like the *papillote*.'

'So we might come to breakfast with curls every morning,' Pamela added.

He pulled on one of Pamela's curls and watched it bounce back into a spiral. 'You are very pretty with or without them.'

He loved these little girls and was as proud of them as if he'd sired them. They'd emerged from a cloud of grief and found their way back to the sun.

Thanks to Miss Tilson.

They all sat down to bowls of porridge and cups of tea. It was a breakfast Garret relished, only realising during this time how it evoked those more carefree days of childhood. In a way he'd thrived on his father's neglect. He'd been free to explore every part of the estate, learning of the work by doing it and learning of the people by working beside them.

'Was your dinner party enjoyable, Uncle?' Pamela asked, sounding like a young lady making conversation.

He glanced towards Miss Tilson who had raised her teacup to her lips.

'There were many fine moments,' he said. 'Although I am certain your mother and father had parties that were much more successful.'

'Mama loved parties.' Pamela sighed.

'Did you like the party, Miss Tilson?' Ellen asked.

'Much of it,' she said, brushing her hand through Ellen's curls. 'I was asked about my dress and I told them it was like Cinderella—do you remember us reading "Cinderella" in the fairy tale book?'

Ellen nodded.

'I told them two doves brought me the dress!' She grinned at the girls.

Pamela's eyes grew wide. 'Did they believe you?'

She darted a glance towards Ellen and winked at Pamela. 'I dare say they did. And did you know there was a famous poet who came to the party? William Wordsworth. He lives near Ambleside in a fine house called Rydal Mount.'

Pamela appeared very impressed. 'May we read the poems he wrote?'

Garret spoke. 'I believe there are some volumes of his poems in the library. You are welcome to them.' He looked directly at Miss Tilson. 'You are welcome to use the library as freely as you wish. I hope you knew that.'

She glanced at both the girls. 'Thank your uncle.'

'Thank you, Uncle Garret,' they said in unison.

Ellen wiggled in her seat. 'Tell us more about the party.'

Miss Tilson told the girls about the other ladies' dresses and how they wore their hair. She told them what food was served and described the cakes and tarts and fruit that were eaten at dessert. She made no mention of how mistreated she'd been by Lady Agnes, how trapped she'd been by

Sir Orin, but, of course, she wouldn't mention such things to the children.

Garret saw so clearly how his nieces adored her and how caring she was of them, making them a part of the dinner party, fussing over them by curling their hair, making an exciting story out of a rather dismal gathering. She seemed more like a loving mother than a governess, cuddling them and making them feel important and special. He was glad of it.

When they finished eating Mary came in to stack up the dishes and place them on a tray for one of the kitchen maids to collect. She left again.

'What now, Miss Tilson?' Ellen asked.

'May we go see the ponies?' Pamela asked. 'May we ride?' Pamela was riding on her own, but only in the paddock.

Before Miss Tilson could answer, Garret said, 'Wait in the schoolroom for Miss Tilson. I wish to speak with her a moment.'

The girls ran out of the room and their footsteps clattered down the hallway to the schoolroom.

Now that he was alone with Miss Tilson, Garret did not know what to say.

She waited, a wary look on her face.

He finally asked her, 'How do you fare?'

She paused for a moment before answering. 'I am well enough.'

'I mean after last night,' he clarified.

She answered in a careful tone. 'I was unharmed.'

She stood in a ray of sunlight streaming through the Tower Room windows, making the curls in her hair gleam and her hazel eyes sparkle. He did not dare take a step closer to her for fear he'd not be able to keep from wrapping his arms around her.

'I apologise for it.' He added, 'For Lady Agnes. She disappointed me greatly last night.'

Miss Tilson lowered her eyes. 'Please do not discuss Lady Agnes with me.'

Garret went on, though. 'I fear I have made a grave error.'

She lifted a hand. 'Say no more, Lord Brookmore.'

But he wanted to explain. To her, of all people. 'I was convinced she was the sort of woman my brother would have chosen and in many ways she was the perfect wife for a viscount.'

She looked into his eyes, then. 'From what the children say to me, their mother was nothing at all like Lady Agnes and you are twice the Viscount your brother could be.' She glanced down quickly. 'I really should see to the children.'

She turned and left.

Garret made his way down the stairs. His morning ride had not settled the restlessness inside him, but he could think of nothing at the farm to engage him this day. Perhaps he should go to the quarry and see how the workers fared there. Or he could walk to the workers' cottages and see how the repairs were coming along. Check on the crops.

He entered the hall.

From a corner, Lady Agnes rose from a sofa. 'Brookmore! There you are. I waited in hopes of seeing you.'

He nodded curtly. 'Lady Agnes. You are up early.' The last person he wished to see this morning.

'I could not sleep a wink.' She walked towards him. 'I was desolated that you felt I had been…demeaning last night. I want to make it up to you and especially to Miss Tilson. What can I do? Shall I ask her to share dinner with us? Some governesses do eat with the family, you know.'

And further expose Miss Tilson to her sugary venom? Never.

'Leave it. Do nothing. I told you this last night.' He walked towards the door. The footman attending the hall brought his hat, gloves and topcoat. 'Was there anything else? I have much to do.' He just was not certain what it was.

She lowered her head. 'You are still angry with me and I cannot blame you. This is not the time to ask you…' Her voice trailed off.

The footman helped him on with his topcoat. 'Ask me what?'

'If we should announce the banns here.' She quickly added, 'I would not mention this, but Mr Elliman did ask me last night.' She smiled wanly. 'It is a lovely idea, is it not? Announcing the banns in the church of your childhood.'

Not a lovely idea at all. Announcing the banns felt like hammering another nail in his coffin. 'No banns,' he said before walking out the door.

Lady Agnes fumed as she watched Brookmore stride out of the house. All her careful plans were fraying into useless strings. She spun on her heel and crossed the hall to the stairs.

Aunt Theodora was in her room eating her breakfast. 'Do eat, Agnes,' the elderly lady said. 'You need your nourishment.'

Agnes slumped into a chair. 'He will barely speak to me.'

'Now, dear, is it that bad?' Her aunt patted her hand.

Agnes pulled her hand away and threw the napkin on to the floor. 'It is that bad. I need a plan, something to turn his affections back to me.' She crossed her arms over her chest. 'I need to be rid of that governess.'

'Yes, dear,' her aunt said meekly.

Chapter Eighteen

Three days went by and Brookmore House seemed to settle into its former routine. Garret no longer attempted to speak about Lady Agnes to Miss Tilson, and, since she was only in his company at breakfast and rarely otherwise, he hardly spoke to her at all.

He'd spent much of his time trying to consider what to do about Lady Agnes. She'd reverted to the sweet, charming woman he'd known in London, never setting a foot out of place, correct and considerate.

He no longer believed any of it.

One evening he'd stared at her while she played the pianoforte, wondering what it would be like to have children with her. Good God, he feared they would turn out as manoeuvring and manipulating and cruel as she was.

She carefully avoided any mention of banns or marriage, which was good, although he'd soon have to have a frank talk with her. Each day more convinced him he could never marry her.

This morning Garret rode as usual, hoping, as usual, that he would encounter Miss Tilson. He knew she was riding because her favourite horse, Lily, was not in the stable. He scanned the countryside, hoping to catch sight of her.

To his right, he saw movement and stopped to see if it was her. It was a horse, but a riderless one. He rode towards the animal and, when close enough, saw it was Lily, Miss Tilson's horse. He managed to grab the horse's reins and calm the animal.

'Where is she, Lily? Lead me to her?' Garret feared she'd been thrown from the horse and lay injured.

He'd scour every inch of this land to find her, if necessary.

Lily turned and retraced her tracks. When they reached the crest of a hill, he spotted another riderless horse, a striking white steed, and quickened his pace. Both his horse Skiddaw and hers nickered anxiously. Lily pawed the ground.

Garret scanned the area and found her. Sir Orin pinned her against a tree.

'Damned man,' he said beneath his breath.

He galloped towards them, slowing enough to jump off and seize Sir Orin by his collar and pull him off her. Sir Orin cried out and swung around to strike him, but Garret blocked his fist and threw him to the ground. Sir Orin leapt up at Garret and both men fell, rolling on the ground. Sir Orin fought like a man possessed, but Garret had battled far worse. He rose to his feet, backed off and waited for Sir Orin's next attack.

Sir Orin stood and readied himself to rush at Garret again, but suddenly Miss Tilson appeared from behind him. She swung a large stick at Sir Orin and struck him across the back. He staggered and Garret seized the opportunity to grab him in a choke hold, immobilising him.

'Shall I finish you?' Garret could easily snap his neck. 'I've killed before.'

'No!' rasped Sir Orin. 'No.'

'Wait!' Miss Tilson cried.

Garret did not heed her.

'Go away,' he growled to Sir Orin, in his most fero-
cious soldier voice. 'Go back to Ireland. Never show your
face here again. Or else.' He squeezed harder. 'Do I make
myself clear?'

Sir Orin made choking sounds.

'Lord Brookmore, do not kill him,' Miss Tilson said
in an even tone.

But Garret knew what he was about.

'Do I make myself clear?' Garret raised his voice and
tightened his grip.

Sir Orin's legs buckled under him.

Garret loosened his hold.

'Yes. Yes,' Sir Orin managed to gasp. 'Give my word.'

Garret released him and the man fell down on his knees,
taking in loud gulps of air. Garret pulled him to his feet
and shoved him towards the white horse he assumed Sir
Orin had ridden.

Garret turned to Miss Tilson, wanting to touch her.
'Did he hurt you?' Garret thought he might kill Sir Orin
if he had.

'No.' She rubbed her upper arms. 'At least nothing to
signify.'

Her horse came up and nuzzled her.

'Lily!' She pressed her forehead against the horse's
neck.

Garret walked towards Sir Orin, who was trying to
mount his horse. The horse edged away from him.

Garret held the horse's head. 'I meant what I said, Sir
Orin. Leave this area and never contact Miss Tilson again.
Or I'll finish what I started.'

Sir Orin finally reached the saddle. 'You do not understand.' His voice rasped. 'She was not like this in Ireland.'

'No matter. She has told you to go away. That is all you

need to know.' Garret turned the horse in the opposite direction of his farm and tapped its rump.

The horse bounded away, Sir Orin hanging on.

Garret returned to Miss Tilson. 'Are you feeling ready to ride back? We can wait, if you are not.'

'I need a minute.' Her whole body trembled.

Garret enfolded her in his arms. 'You are safe now. He will not bother you again.'

He was in no hurry to release her. To hold her again filled an emptiness he'd possessed since the night he'd told her about his betrothal, the night he'd almost made love to her.

'He was waiting for me,' she said, her voice shaking. 'The horse was supposed to be a gift. He wanted me to ride to Holyhead with him.' She took a breath. 'When I refused, he pulled me off Lily and—and pinned me against that tree. I—I was afraid he would—'

She couldn't finish, but Garret knew what she would have said. Had he known this, he might have indeed killed the man.

'He won't hurt you now, I promise,' Garret murmured.

He'd warn the estate workers and servants about Sir Orin and make certain he never again came near her. He'd check in the village and ensure Sir Orin left.

Garret felt her relax. She took in a deep breath and he released her.

He walked her over to Lily and boosted her into the saddle. Touching her had heightened his senses. If only he could hold on to her for ever...

Garret whistled for Skiddaw, who trotted over immediately. He mounted and he and Miss Tilson started towards the farm.

Garret gestured towards her horse. 'Lily led me to you, you know.'

'She did?' She leaned forward and gave the horse an affectionate pat. She turned back to Garret. 'I wondered how you found me. You have rescued me over and over, Lord Brookmore. How can I ever thank you?'

Those words again. Did she remember those were the words she spoke before they kissed that first time? And nearly the same words before he'd almost ravished her? And all he wanted now was to keep her safe and never allow any harm to come to her.

Had Lady Agnes sensed his attraction to Miss Tilson? He'd certainly tried very hard not to act upon his feelings, nor show them to anyone else. But had Lady Agnes somehow seen through these efforts? It would explain why she'd gone out of her way to assist Sir Orin in his pursuit of Miss Tilson. But nothing excused Lady Agnes's belittling Miss Tilson in front of guests.

Lady Agnes had certainly hidden her true character when he'd met her. In a way he was fortunate to have discovered this mean spiritedness before marrying her.

Rebecca was grateful that Lord Brookmore said little on their ride back to the stables. She needed the time to sort out this experience and to shed it from her once and for all. Brookmore's strength and violence had alarmed and thrilled her. He was the only man of her acquaintance who would have been willing to fight to protect her, to even kill to protect her.

The thing was, he would have been equally as willing to protect, to kill, for any person on his estate, for any person in jeopardy from one more powerful.

She glanced at him, so tall and comfortable in the saddle. She tried to imagine him in his red coat and shako, charging into a battle, slashing with his sabre, firing his pistol, fighting with fists like he'd done with Sir Orin. Her insides fluttered at the thought.

A flash of memory intruded, a memory of Sir Orin pressing his hand against her breast, of him jutting his leg between hers and rubbing it against her most private place. She shuddered. Sir Orin had been about to take what Rebecca so freely wished to give to Lord Brookmore. Rebecca was so very grateful to Lord Brookmore for arriving when he did.

Her heart filled with love for him.

And filled with pain.

He could not be hers. The most she could hope for was that he would not be Lady Agnes's.

As they neared the stables, they passed some of his workers ready to start a day of toil. Each worker doffed his hat and greeted Lord Brookmore with a cheerful voice. Even the stablemen, to whom Lord Brookmore and Rebecca handed over their horses, looked pleased to see him and eager to tend to his horse.

They walked out of the stable together.

'G'morning, m'lord.' Another worker tipped his hat. 'Miss.'

She wondered how his list of repairs and improvements was faring. What a caring thing it was to ask what his workers and his tenants needed from him. When had she ever heard of a gentleman so mindful?

Another reason to love him.

They neared the house.

'Please tell no one what happened today,' she asked him. She could not bear to speak of it to anyone or even to endure their sympathetic looks.

'Lady Agnes needs to know.' He glanced at her. 'She needs to know what sort of man she foisted on you. I would like to tell her.'

'Very well,' Rebecca conceded. 'But only Lady Agnes.' She frowned. 'You might tell her that Sir Orin may be even more dangerous than he showed today. His wife died so conveniently I cannot help but be suspicious.'

He paused, still holding her gaze. 'When did she die?'

It must have been after Claire left Ireland. Sir Orin gave it as new information that Claire did not know.

'I do not know precisely, but very recently or so Sir Orin says,' she responded. 'The timing of it seems very convenient for him and he is not at all sad about her death.'

'A dangerous man indeed.'

They walked across the lawn behind the house.

A wave of fear washed over her. 'Will he leave here like you asked?'

His expression turned dark and fierce. 'I will make certain he leaves.'

Her fear receded as quickly as it had come. Lord Brookmore would protect her.

'What a stupid man Sir Orin is.' She shook her head.

'In what way?' he asked.

She'd meant it rhetorically, but she tried to piece together her thoughts. 'He could not have behaved more abominably. How did he think that would appeal?' Why had Sir Orin not believed her when she spurned him the night of the dinner party? Why had he thought assaulting her would further his cause?

They reached the garden gate that led to the back entrance to the house.

'Indeed,' Lord Brookmore responded. 'Surely he knew that was not the way to gain your affections.'

That feeling of connection with him returned, but Rebecca steeled herself against such feelings. She'd become accustomed to staying distant from him, just as she'd done with her father, but since he'd acted as her protector that night of the dinner party, her resolve had broken and she yearned for that closeness they'd briefly shared.

He went on. 'For Sir Orin to come all the way from Ireland claiming a wish to marry you, then behaving like this… It makes little sense.'

It made no sense to Rebecca.

Lord Brookmore opened the gate. 'What happened in Ireland before you left?'

She went cold. 'What do you mean?'

'I mean, there must have been something that happened between you and Sir Orin, something that led to this. His behaviour must have risen from something.' He touched her arm, stopping her from proceeding through the gate. 'Did he assault you there?'

She glanced up into his concerned eyes. Her heart pounded. How was she to answer such a direct question? Should she make up a story? Lie to him directly, lie to this man who had just rescued her once again?'

She could not do it.

'Did he assault you when you were in his employ?' he asked again, his voice more insistent.

She held her gaze steady. 'I do not know.'

He released her arm and stepped back. 'What do you mean you do not know?'

She passed through the gate, but turned to face him again. 'I mean, I do not know what happened in Ireland.'

His expression turned sceptical. 'Miss Tilson, you must know what happened. You were there.'

Rebecca released a pent-up breath. 'Come with me.'

She led him to a secluded spot near the willow labyrinth. There was a bench there, but she had no wish to be seated.

'Well?' He crossed his arms over his chest, waiting for her explanation.

She averted her gaze. 'It is a long story. One, I suspect, you will not like hearing.' She drew in a deep breath. 'I was never there.'

'Never where?' He looked confused.

'I was never in Sir Orin's house. I never cared for his children. I never knew his wife.' She breathed again and made herself look him in the eye. 'I am an imposter, Lord Brookmore. I am not Claire Tilson.'

'Not Claire Tilson?' His confusion turned to a flinty anticipation. 'You had better explain.'

'I met Claire on the packet boat. We looked exactly alike—' She swallowed. 'Like twins, but we have no family in common—'

'Say no more.' He held up a hand. 'You expect me to believe you happened to meet a woman, unrelated to you, who looked exactly like you?'

'Yes. That is it,' she responded. 'Claire Tilson looked exactly like me. So much so even the maid sent with me could not tell us apart.'

Nolan! Rebecca had not thought of the maid for weeks. Now she again saw the woman rolling over in her bed, refusing to leave the ship with her.

'Miss Tilson was lost in the shipwreck?' His voice brought her back to the present.

Rebecca's throat became raw as the events of the shipwreck rushed back to her. 'When the storm came, she was washed into the sea. She—she died, but I survived. But everyone thought it was me who died and that I was Claire—' She swallowed. 'Then you came and thought I was Claire. So I decided to be her.'

'You decided to deceive me, you mean.' Colour rose in his face. 'Who are you, then?'

Her hands trembled. 'I am Lady Rebecca Pierce. My brother is the Earl of Keneagle.'

He looked sceptical. 'Are you? Why would the sister of an earl change places with a governess?'

'I was headed for London and an unwanted marriage.' She again felt Lord Stonecroft's appraising eye and his wet, dough-like lips. 'My brother made it impossible for me to refuse this marriage. I decided being a governess would be preferable.'

'Being a governess was preferable to marrying?' He scoffed. 'Who was the man? Some kind of monster?'

'Lord Stonecroft,' she said.

'Stonecroft?' he cried. 'I have met Stonecroft. Being a governess was preferable to marriage with him?'

She averted her gaze. 'It was. It still is. And you can probably guess that I know nothing of being a governess.'

His voice turned cold. 'Did you not consider that two children would be victims of that ignorance?'

She felt a shaft of pain pierce her heart. 'No, I did not consider it. When I chose to be Claire, I thought only of myself. But I did not know Pamela and Ellen then. How dear they would become—' She paused to fight back tears. 'I have tried my best for Pamela and Ellen. I would never do anything to deliberately hurt them.'

But he would not believe that.

'Depriving them of a real governess was not hurting them?'

She felt the shaft stab deeper. 'I admit they have not had proper lessons—'

He waved a hand. 'Never mind that. You are playing us all for fools, pretending to be what you are not. Making yourself into someone you are not. Using a dead woman's life because it was convenient for you.' He paced in front of her.

She lifted her chin. 'I did not perceive it as using Claire, but as living life for her.'

He stopped and leaned into her face. 'Do not try to vindicate yourself by pretending you did this for her. You did this for you.'

He might as well have slapped her, but she swallowed the pain—and her shame—and boldly met his eye. 'At the beginning, yes, I did it for me. But I did not celebrate Claire's death. She deserved to live so much more than I did.'

He kept on. 'Why? Did she have integrity? Would she have refused to masquerade as someone she was not?'

'Certainly.' Could he not see? Rebecca meant no one any harm, even if her decisions were self-serving. It wounded her that this man she so admired—loved—would think the worst of her. 'While we are speaking of pretending to be someone one is not, what about you, Lord Brookmore?'

He blew out a breath. 'I am not pretending to be someone I am not.'

'Are you not?' she shot back. 'You've tried to be your brother or your father. You thought you had to be them to be a viscount. Where has that idea taken you, Lord Brookmore?' She did not give him a chance to respond. 'I will tell you where it has taken you. To a betrothal with Lady Agnes.'

His eyes flashed. 'See here, Miss T—!' He shook his head. 'What am I to call you? I do not even know.'

She held her head regally. 'Call me Lady Rebecca.'

'Lady Rebecca,' he spat out.

Her anger rose higher. 'At least I have always acted like myself. I have used Claire's name, but I have acted like Lady Rebecca. You must have acted like a shell of who you are when you pretended to be your brother, the Viscount. When you are you, you are a better viscount than your brother ever could have been.'

He glared at her. 'You did not know my brother.'

She glared back at him. 'I have learned of him from your nieces and have overheard your workers talking about him. They admire you, not him. Because you listened to them and acted on their behalf.'

He held up a hand again. 'Stop. Do not turn this discussion on to me. This is about your lies, your deception.'

She shot back. 'Yes. I have deceived you, but I have not lied to you.' What did it matter now? This time she told the truth and look what happened.

His eyes looked wounded. 'I am sick of people who are not what they seem. I thought you were different.'

She lowered her gaze. He was about to send her packing. Her pain returned. 'You will wish me to leave, I know, but may I beg for a little time? The children are just now coming out of their grief. It would be another loss for them, would it not?'

'You use them as an excuse,' he accused.

Was she? Perhaps he was right, but she felt shattered at the idea of losing Pamela and Ellen, as well as him.

His voice remained hard. 'You will stay. I'll not have my nieces suffer another loss so soon. You will stay until I say it is time to find them another governess.'

Her spirits lifted, but only slightly.

'I will leave,' he said. 'I'll go back to London. Or go to Brighton. I dare say Lady Agnes will be happy to leave here.'

'No, don't leave!' she cried, then bit her lip. He belonged to this place. He did not belong with Lady Agnes.

'No more discussion,' he said. 'I am going to the house. You do what you wish.'

What she wished? When had she ever received what she wished?

Chapter Nineteen

Garret strode away, a kaleidoscope of emotions spinning inside him.

Was no one honest? Did no one reveal their true character or was everyone hiding who they were?

He was furious at being deceived by her, by being played for a fool. He'd been attracted to a fiction, not a real person. She was no better than Lady Agnes. Or even Sir Orin.

Or even himself.

It angered him, what she'd said about him.

Because it was true.

He had tried to be a viscount like his father and brother, until he discovered that his brother had been a terrible viscount and a worse father. Then he'd tried to make it up to everyone. To his workers, his servants, his nieces. He couldn't leave. Not with everything half-done.

Pamela and Ellen were what mattered most and, after them, the estate and its people. Not his wounded feelings. Not even Miss Tilson's—Lady Rebecca's—deception. Both he and Lady Rebecca must stay and he must endure it.

He entered the house and climbed the back stairs. As he reached the first-floor landing, Lady Agnes appeared. He stopped on the stairs, two steps below her.

'Brookmore!' she said brightly. 'I had hoped to catch you.'

'Lady Agnes.' He had no wish to speak to her. 'You are awake early.'

'With purpose, sir!' She smiled. 'I rose early so I might join you at breakfast with your nieces. I wish for them to know me, you see, and I simply can never catch them at another time of day. They are always outside, it seems. Who knows where?' She laughed.

She just could not resist a dig at...the governess...could she? Angry as Garret was at *Lady Rebecca*, he would not be so cruel as to inflict Lady Agnes on her. Not after what happened this morning. With Sir Orin. With him.

'Not today, Lady Agnes.' He put a foot on the step to rise past her.

She moved in front of him, her face nearly level with his. 'Is something amiss, Brookmore? You look so preoccupied. I do worry about you.'

He kept his foot on the step. 'This day has already been...disturbing. Now if you will pardon me...'

She did not move. 'I was watching for you from the window, so I would know when you were back in the house. I saw you enter the garden with Miss Tilson. Is she the source of your disturbance? Perhaps I can help.'

He'd already seen what her efforts to help could do. She'd brought Sir Orin back into his house. She'd encouraged his pursuit of... Lady Rebecca.

'I will tell you what happened, Lady Agnes.' He faced her on the landing, elbows akimbo. 'Your friend, Sir Orin, forced himself on Miss...Tilson while she was riding. Fortunately I was able to stop the assault before he did worse to her.'

'No.' She looked genuinely shocked. 'Sir Orin? But he was so besotted! Believe me, Brookmore, I had no idea he was such a man. He fooled me completely!'

She did not ask about Lady Rebecca's well-being, Garret noted.

'I have sent the man packing. I expect him gone, but if he shows up here, he is not to be admitted to the house and he is not to come near Miss Tilson.'

'Oh, my goodness, of course not,' she agreed.

He rose to the landing and she did not stop him this time.

He started to pass her, then turned. 'Do not speak of the assault to anyone. Miss Tilson does not wish it to be known.' He looked her directly in the eye. 'Do you understand? Speak of it to no one. I mean this, Lady Agnes.'

'Why, Brookmore, I would never pass on such gossip.' She blinked in all innocence.

Not unless it suited her, he thought.

Garret continued up the stairs.

Garret's valet had the good sense to remain quiet as he helped him change into other clothes. He would be only a few minutes late for breakfast with his nieces.

He thought about skipping breakfast, not wishing to see the lady imposter so soon.

Lady Rebecca.

The name suited her, did it not? She was more of a lady than a governess, more outspoken, more independent, more…regal. She was never a governess employing the ideas of Rousseau, as Mrs Howard had suggested; she was the daughter of an earl playing at being a governess.

He left his room, determined to stop thinking of her. To wipe his mind of all that had happened and behave as his nieces would have been accustomed. As unsettled as he was, he did not wish for anything to disturb Pamela and Ellen.

Lady Rebecca had better feel the same.

He walked down the hallway and entered the Tower Room.

'You are late!' Ellen cried.

The two girls were seated at the table, but were alone in the room. The bowls of porridge were at each place at the table and the tea, milk and some other fare were set in the middle.

Would Lady Rebecca not show?

'Pamela showed me on the clock,' Ellen went on. 'You are late and so is Miss Tilson.'

He walked over to each of them and kissed them on their heads. 'Some mornings are like that.' He took his usual seat. 'Shall we begin eating before the porridge gets cold?'

Pamela shook her head. 'We should be polite and wait for Miss Tilson.'

But she might not come.

'You are right.' He pointed to the clock. 'We will wait five more minutes, but then we must start eating.'

Ellen got out of her chair and pulled it over to the mantel, climbing atop it so she could see the clock. 'When is five minutes?'

Pamela answered her. 'When the big hand is on the nine.'

Ellen climbed down and pulled her chair back to the table.

The door opened and Lady Rebecca entered. Her face looked strained, but her bearing was tall. Unbowed.

'Miss Tilson!' Ellen cried happily. She bounded over to her governess and was enfolded in a hug.

Pamela was included in the embrace.

'Good morning, my little ladies,' Lady Rebecca said, although Garret could tell her cheerful tone was forced. 'I am so happy to see you this morning. And I am sorry I am late.'

Garret stood.

Lady Rebecca released the girls and shooed them towards their chairs. The girls sat adjacent to each other, which meant that Lady Rebecca was adjacent to Garret. At least they were not forced to face each other.

As Lady Rebecca took her chair, she glanced at Garret. 'Good morning, Lord Brookmore,' she said formally.

He inclined his head.

'What made you late?' Ellen asked her.

Lady Rebecca paused, probably to invent an excuse. She looked from one girl to the other. 'Remember how I go riding most mornings?'

They both nodded.

'I was detained, so I came back a little late.'

That was the truth, although with no details.

'Uncle Garret was late, too,' Ellen said.

He made himself smile at the child. 'I was detained, too.'

Pamela regarded them. 'You were detained together.'

He exchanged a glance with Lady Rebecca. 'That would make us both late, wouldn't it?'

She averted her gaze and poured the tea and spoke of the food while the children ate their porridge. Garret noticed that she ate only a few bites of hers. When the children were not looking her way, her smile faded.

He refused to feel compassion for her. She'd created this situation for herself. It was none of his doing. She'd deceived him and the girls. That was despicable, was it not?

He watched her hide the tension in the room—the tension between him and her—from Pamela and Ellen, by focusing on their thoughts, their wishes, their desired plans for the day. Her behaviour towards the children was completely kind and unchanged.

He remembered their first days eating breakfast together and those first evenings when he'd shared dinner with her. He remembered how they'd managed an ease between them, even after that emotional night when he'd nearly seduced her. By God, he was only a little more contemptible than Sir Orin, was he not?

He wished those early days could have lasted. He wished they would have been real.

'What would you like to do today?' she asked the girls.

Now he knew why she did not do the things he expected a governess to do. She was never one in the first place. What governess would ask the children what to do?

'May we ride our ponies?' Pamela asked.

Ellen looked less excited about this prospect, but she nodded her agreement.

'Very well,' Lady Rebecca said.

Her love of horses. That was genuine, Garret supposed. One could not disguise such skill and enthusiasm.

Ellen turned to him. 'Uncle Garret, will you come, too?'

He'd enjoyed the time he'd spent helping them learn to ride, but he could not be with her, not even with the children there. This breakfast was difficult enough.

'Not today, Ellen,' he said. 'I have estate business.'

She jumped out of her chair to come and hug him. 'We will miss you, Uncle Garret.'

He would miss this, too, even though some of it was not real.

Later that morning when Lady Agnes was certain Brookmore was otherwise occupied, she had her coachman drive her to Ambleside, to the Unicorn Inn.

She marched into the hall and demanded of the innkeeper, 'Find Sir Orin. I wish to speak with him privately in the drawing room.'

The innkeeper pulled on his forelock and bustled off to do her bidding. Lady Agnes swept into the drawing room, which was empty. A good thing because she would have sent anyone there packing. She was too agitated to sit. She paced the room.

Finally Sir Orin appeared, with a cut on his cheek, a large bruise forming under his eye and pouting lips.

'Lady Agnes,' he said unenthusiastically.

She walked right up to him, glaring. 'What an idiot you are, Sir Orin. You forced yourself on Miss Tilson? How could you be so stupid?'

'I was tired of her spurning me.' He rubbed his jaw. 'I purchased a beautiful horse for her. She would not even look at it. I tell you, she is so changed.' He glanced away. 'Had to sell the horse, too. Lost a bundle on him.'

She faced him. 'I only speak to you because I want to be rid of her and you are still my best chance. Do you still want her or not?'

'I want her,' he responded earnestly. 'But she will have nothing to do with me. I do not have the luxury of time to change her mind. Your fiancé made it clear I was to leave the area. I only await the mail coach which is expected in a couple of hours.'

She waved her fingers. 'We can work around Brookmore's edict.' She stared into his face. 'Are you willing to force her to leave with you? How far are you willing to go to achieve this desire of yours.'

'There is nothing I would not do.' The look in his eyes turned malevolent. 'I have already gone quite far.'

She liked a man who went after what he wanted, even if this one was not smart enough to achieve it on his own. 'We need a plan. We need some way to force her to come to you.'

He gestured for her to sit down. Her restlessness had abated now that she could focus on her desire—to have Miss Tilson gone. She lowered herself into one of the chairs and he sat across from her.

'What of Brookmore?' He touched the cut on his face. 'I suspect he will check to see I've gone.'

This part was easy. 'Ride the coach as far as Outgate, then disembark there. Then find a secluded cottage to rent. Somewhere apart from other people. Send me word of where you are.' She could not receive mail from him at Brookmore House. 'Send word here. I will arrange for my coachman to pick it up.'

'How am I to entice Claire there?' he asked. 'She will not want to come.'

Lady Agnes's mouth stretched into a smile. 'We must provide her with incentive.'

Lady Agnes's plan came to her quickly, but it was foolproof. Miss Tilson would come running to Sir Orin and Lady Agnes would be rid of her at last.

Then, she was convinced, Brookmore would turn to her once again and the marriage could take place very quickly.

The next few days brought disruption to the routine which had so recently made Rebecca restless. She rarely saw Lord Brookmore. He'd stopped sharing breakfast with her and the children, but not because of Rebecca. She'd heard through Mary that the crops were suffering from the unusual cold and that Lord Brookmore spent most of his time with the tenant farmers and his estate manager trying to figure out how to keep the people and livestock fed throughout the winter. They'd decided to purchase stores now in anticipation of hardship later. He and the manager would be gone for a couple of days to accomplish this task.

It was the first time he would be away from Rebecca since she woke to see him standing over her in Moelfre, after the shipwreck. He'd made a point to inform her that Sir Orin had left Ambleside in a mail coach bound for Liverpool, but still she felt rudderless without him.

When he'd spoken to her about Sir Orin's departure, he had been cold. She could not blame him. She'd deceived him and now she could see the real harm that came from that decision.

At least she could relax in her role as governess. It did not matter if she performed like a real governess or not. He knew she was not. She and the girls simply did whatever came into their minds. They learned writing and spelling by keeping their journals. They read the books in the schoolroom and Rebecca read to them books she found in Lord Brookmore's library. On a rainy day they explored the attic, finding many of the children's mother's things and some of their governess's things, prompting the girls to talk about both of them. Rebecca even started them on needlework, a skill at which she was only passable, but she knew enough to teach a nine- and seven-year-old.

And they rode the ponies.

Pamela and Ellen finally did ride enough to venture out of the paddock. Rebecca led them on Lily and the girls followed. One of the stablemen rode along for a little more security. Though it was unusually cold, it felt delightful to ride amongst the fells and waters, the mountains and lakes.

This day Rebecca and the girls were in the schoolroom practising their needlework. To Rebecca's surprise Lady Agnes came to the door.

'May I join you?' Lady Agnes asked, walking in before her question could be answered. She looked at what the girls were doing. 'Oh, needlework! I adore needlework.'

'Say good day to Lady Agnes, girls,' Rebecca told them. 'As I taught you.'

Pamela and Ellen got out of their chairs, faced Lady Agnes and curtsied. 'Good day, Lady Agnes,' they parroted.

'How charming!' Lady Agnes clapped her hands. 'Now show me your needlework. Are you making samplers?'

'We are merely practising stitches,' Rebecca said. 'Pamela is practising ten basic stitches and Ellen is practising the running stitch and the backstitch.'

Ellen lifted her embroidery hoop so that Lady Agnes could see her efforts.

Lady Agnes sat next to the little girl. 'Shall I show you how to do it?'

Ellen politely allowed Lady Agnes to criticise her childish efforts, making her start over again. Rebecca watched this performance and tried to guess why the woman had come to the schoolroom, when she'd never shown an interest in doing so.

When Ellen had her hoop and needle in hand again, Rebecca asked, 'Is there some purpose to your visit with us, Lady Agnes?'

Lady Agnes sighed. 'I am afraid I am missing dear Brookmore. My aunt naps and I am feeling quite lonely. I decided to see if I can make myself useful and become more acquainted with Brookmore's nieces.' She smiled at Rebecca. 'You do not mind?'

To be in her company, especially after all she'd said and done at the dinner party? 'Of course we do not mind,' Rebecca said.

Pamela, who sat so only Rebecca could see, rolled her eyes. Rebecca winked back.

What she could not figure was Lady Agnes's true reason for this visit.

Lady Agnes came back to the schoolroom the next day and the next and she invited Rebecca to join her and her aunt for dinner. Rebecca might have seen this behaviour as an attempt at friendliness, perhaps even some empathy for the assault Rebecca endured from Sir Orin, but often enough Lady Agnes said something unkind to or about someone, revealing her true nature. Her words were always spoken in the most amiable tone and her barbs were subtle, but Rebecca heard them. Lord Brookmore had not yet returned and perhaps Lady Agnes's cordiality was simply so she could tell him how good she'd been while he was away.

In any event, Rebecca suspected it would cease when Lord Brookmore returned.

This morning, Lady Agnes stopped Rebecca in the hallway outside the schoolroom where the girls were waiting after they all finished breakfast.

Lady Agnes pressed her fingers to her temple. 'May I ask a favour of you, Miss Tilson?'

'Very well.' Rebecca held her breath.

Lady Agnes attempted a pained smile. 'Would you ride into Ambleside and purchase a headache remedy from the apothecary? My head is pounding so I cannot go myself.'

'I have to attend to the children,' Rebecca responded.

'I will stay with them,' Lady Agnes said. 'If I sit my headache is not so bad.'

'Could your maid not go?' Errands for guests of the household were not the responsibility of the governess. What was Lady Agnes's true motive?

'She's attending to my aunt, who is feeling unwell today.' Agnes looked at her with slitted eyes. 'Please, Miss Tilson? I do so need your help. There is no one else I can ask. My coachman will drive you.'

'Then send your coachman on the errand!' Rebecca said.

Lady Agnes produced tears. 'I cannot ask him! The man is illiterate. I need someone who can discuss things with the apothecary. How do I know he will have the right powders? If he doesn't, I need someone with judgement to make a decision what to buy! Please, Miss Tilson!'

Rebecca was either being manipulated by an excellent

actress or Lady Agnes truly had a terrible headache. In any event, the argument over whether she should go or not was likely to take longer than the errand itself. She could be back in an hour or so.

'Ambleside is not far. I can walk it faster than the horses could be hitched to a coach.'

'Then you will do it?' Lady Agnes's smile turned grateful. 'He could take you in the gig.'

Rebecca was still uncertain about this. 'I will walk. What do I ask for from the apothecary?'

Lady Agnes handed her a folded piece of paper and a purse full of coin. 'I have written it down.'

'Very well. Let me tell the children and I will go.' Rebecca entered the schoolroom and Lady Agnes followed.

'I have an errand in Ambleside,' she told the girls. 'Lady Agnes will sit with you.' She turned to Lady Agnes. 'Really, teach them anything you like.'

Lady Agnes nodded. 'I will.'

Rebecca returned to her room to collect her bonnet, gloves and the shawl Lord Brookmore had given to her that first day on the road. She told the footman attending the hall where she was going and stepped out into the morning air, which was a bit warmer than when she rode Lily earlier. A brisk walk would warm her.

She might even enjoy the exercise and the solitude.

Chapter Twenty

Lady Agnes made the girls practise their needlework and while they did so, she leafed through the latest issue of *La Belle Assemblée*.

After a half-hour, she glanced at the clock and stood.

She clapped her hands. 'Pamela! Ellen! I have the most fabulous idea.'

The girls looked up at her.

'Do you know how Miss Tilson had to do an errand for me in Ambleside?'

They nodded.

She went on. 'Well, she said she would walk there.' How lucky Lady Agnes was that Miss Tilson decided to walk. It made matters so much easier. 'Would it not be the loveliest surprise if I asked my coachman to drive the two of you to Ambleside to meet her so she will not have to walk home? Would that not be the very best surprise?' She could see she'd kindled their interest. She intended to make it impossible for them to refuse. 'I will give you coins so you may purchase some gingerbread. Would you like that?'

'I would,' cried Ellen, bursting with excitement. She turned to her sister. 'Pamela, you would, too, would you not?'

'I suppose.' Pamela was obviously a little wary.

No matter. Agnes was not about to allow a nine-year-old child to stop her.

'Wait here a moment.' She hurried to the door. 'I will see to my coachman.'

Agnes descended the back stairs and left the house through the back entrance, careful that no one saw her. She walked through the garden and across the park until she could see a village cart waiting on the road, obscured from view by a group of trees. She waved to Sir Orin and he waved back.

When she returned for the girls, she made herself animated again. 'We are so lucky! I caught him already driving a village cart. Would you like to ride on a village cart?'

'Yes!' cried Ellen.

'Then you shall. I have another idea!' Agnes went on. 'Let's tell nobody what we are doing. Let us leave them a note.' She took a piece of paper and opened an inkwell. She wrote on the paper and folded it, leaving it on the table.

In no time they were walking through the garden and out the back gate.

'He will meet us on the road.'

It did not matter that the children could tell Brookmore or anyone else that Agnes arranged their little wagon ride. She would just say they were making it up. Who would believe children?

'Hello there!' The driver of the cart jumped down and helped the girls over the stone fence.

After he put both girls on the seat and climbed up next to them, Pamela cried, 'Wait, Lady Agnes. Are you not accompanying us?'

She laughed. 'Of course not! There is not enough room. As it is, one of you will have to ride on Miss Tilson's lap coming home.' She reached in her pocket and handed Pamela several coins. 'This is for your gingerbread. Do not lose it.'

Pamela closed her small hand around the money and glanced up at the sky. 'It is all grey today. Maybe it will rain.'

'It will not rain,' Agnes assured her. And if it did, a little rain would not hurt them.

'I do not think we should do this,' Pamela said as Sir Orin pulled away. 'It might rain and we might become ill with a fever.'

'Nonsense,' Agnes said, waving them off.

Agnes heard Sir Orin say in a jovial voice, 'Do not worry, little lady. It will be an adventure.'

Agnes grinned to herself as she watched the cart drive away. It was a masterful plan she'd created. She'd wait a half-hour before sounding the alarm that the children were missing. Sir Orin would be well on the road by then. He would take the girls to a rented cottage on Lake Windermere, where he would entertain them until Miss Tilson arrived to secure their release. She would be handed a letter while she was in Ambleside saying that the children had been abducted and her acceptance of Sir Orin's suit was the ransom she must pay.

Of course, the abduction was merely a ruse. The children would be returned later with a dramatic tale to tell, but Agnes had already invented a much more plausible explanation that surely would be believed. The best part was Miss Tilson would have already left with Sir Orin.

'When wanting someone to do your bidding, find their weakness,' she said aloud.

The children were Miss Tilson's weakness.

Agnes turned towards the house and started walking back.

Rebecca left the apothecary with a vial containing the headache remedy Lady Agnes had requested. She no sooner stepped out into the street when a boy approached her.

'Are you Miss Tilson, miss?' he asked.

'I am.' She was puzzled he would ask.

He handed her a folded piece of paper that bore a plain seal, bowed and left.

She broke the seal and read.

Dearest Claire,

I cannot live without you. I must have you. I am desperate. I have abducted Lord Brookmore's nieces. If you value their lives, you will come to me.

Go to the Unicorn Inn. There is a carriage waiting for you that will take you to Far Sawrey. From there you will walk two miles along the coast of Lake Windermere. I will find you and bring you to the children.

Tell no one. Leave immediately. If you do not follow my instructions to the letter, I cannot vouch for the well-being of the children.

Yours, etc.

You know who I am.

She folded the paper, her heart pounding.

She should tell Lord Brookmore! But he would not return until tomorrow. She could not wait. The children's lives depended on her. There was no choice but to do what Sir Orin said.

How could he have known she would be here?

Rebecca felt the blood drain from her face. Lady Agnes.

This was why Lady Agnes befriended her. This was why she sent her on this errand. Surely she was not so depraved she would risk the lives of the children?

Sir Orin was that depraved, however.

She stopped a man on the street. 'Please direct me to the Unicorn Inn.'

* * *

It was almost two hours before she alighted at Far Sawrey and began walking. The coastline of the lake was heavily wooded and the breeze through the trees chilled her to the bone. She could not think of her comfort now. She thought only of the children.

She half-expected Sir Orin to jump out from behind a tree, accost her like he'd done on her morning rides. She half-hoped there would be other people on the road, someone who might help her, but she was very much alone.

She walked on. Surely she'd walked two miles already? Finally she spied a cottage, far from the road at the edge of the lake. Her senses heightened. Was this where he would be? She slowed her pace, carefully surveying her surroundings. There was the cottage and one outbuilding, both difficult to see from the road.

Sir Orin stepped from a path that she assumed led to the cottage. He smiled.

'Claire, you are finally here.' He approached with arms outstretched. 'I knew you would come.'

She stepped back. 'Where are the children?'

His smile faltered, but remained on his face. 'They are in the cottage.' He gestured for her to follow. 'Follow me.'

The path was bordered with scrubby brush and jagged rocks.

Sir Orin swept his arm over them. 'One way in to this cottage.' In an open area, a village cart stood. He pointed to it. 'Our transportation.'

'Are the children unharmed?' she demanded.

He turned back to her. 'I have no wish to harm them.' He grinned. 'That is, unless you do not co-operate with me.'

A chill went up her spine.

The path led to the outbuilding, which was a stable. Rebecca could see the horse inside. Fat raindrops started to fall, kicking up the dirt of the path.

Sir Orin stopped and looked up at the sky. 'Rain. I had not anticipated rain.'

The raindrops fell faster.

They finally reached the door of the cottage. Sir Orin took a key from his pocket and unlocked it.

When he opened the door, Rebecca rushed through. 'Pamela! Ellen! Are you here!'

Footsteps sounded from a back room. The children appeared, running towards her. She knelt down and scooped them into a hug. They looked unharmed. They felt unharmed.

She examined them more closely.

'See! I told Pamela you would meet us here,' Ellen cried. 'Just like John Coachman said.'

'John Coachman?' Was there another man here?

'That is what he told us to call him.' Ellen pointed to Sir Orin. 'He said all coachmen are called John Coachman.'

'I am here now and all will be well,' she said, hugging them again. 'Have you had something to eat?'

'Sweetmeats and tea,' Ellen said. 'And we've played games. But Pamela was worried you would not come.'

Pamela nodded. 'It is a diversion to Ellen.' She spoke this in a way that showed she thought it anything but a diversion.

Pamela looked sad. 'I hope we will be home soon.'

Rain pattered the roof of the cottage, louder and louder, until it sounded like one constant din.

Sir Orin went to the window and looked out. 'It appears we are here until tomorrow unless this rain lets up.' He shooed the girls towards the back room. 'Leave us now. I need to talk to Miss Tilson.'

The girls looked reluctant to leave her.

'Go,' she told them. 'I will be with you in a moment.'

Pamela took Ellen's hand and pulled her into the room.

Sir Orin closed the door and turned the key in the lock. 'Do not worry. They have cards to play with. And spillikins.'

'You do not need them now. I am here. Take them back to Brookmore House.' She needed them to be safe.

He gestured to the window. 'In the rain?'

In rain, snow, anything as long as they were away from him. He was more dangerous than being caught in the rain.

He came closer. She backed away.

'Do not fear, Claire, dear, I am not going to force myself on you. Not like before. I do apologise.'

'What do you want from me, then?' she asked.

He became serious. 'I still want you to marry me. Marry me and come back to Ireland with me.'

'Or?'

His eyes turned cold. 'Or you will be very unhappy.'

'You cannot want me,' she insisted. 'You know I despise you.'

His forehead creased. 'You do say the most frightful things to me now. In Ireland you protested only that I was married and that you had no wish to betray my wife. Now you simply refuse me.'

'Never mind about me. Please let the children go. Take them to Far Sawrey, at least. It is only two miles.' She could think of nothing else.

He walked to the window, turned and smiled. 'I would not wish them to get wet. That was not in the plan.'

'The plan.' Of course, this abduction was planned. 'You planned this with Lady Agnes, did you not?'

'She has proved to be a valuable ally,' he responded.

'What was supposed to happen, if not for the rain?' she asked.

He laughed. 'According to Lady Agnes, the children were to be returned once I secured your...*affections*, shall we call it, then you and I were to be in a carriage on our way to Gretna Green before the sky turned dark.'

What did he mean *according to Lady Agnes*? 'And according to you?'

He lowered himself into a chair and looked up at her. 'I was thinking, what would make you stay if the children were returned safely? Lady Agnes did not consider that, did she? So they will come with us to Gretna Green, after which I will not need them any more, because you will finally be mine.'

Rebecca trembled inside. Did he mean he would return the children safely or not? A man who most likely killed his wife would be equally as capable of doing away with children. Rebecca could not take the chance. They must escape him.

He continued. 'You have left a note, asking for money in exchange for the children, with elaborate instructions for its delivery. That is all a humbug, you see. Some poor fool will find the money and be thought to be your accomplice. No one will suspect me, of course, because I left Ambleside the day after Lord Brookmore threatened me.'

Sir Orin and Lady Agnes had no idea exactly how plausible this scheme would be to Lord Brookmore. It was the sort of thing an imposter with no money might do rather than risk being kicked out without a reference or pay.

If that imposter had no love for the children and their uncle, that was.

Her heart raced wildly, but she needed to remain calm.

She sat in a chair near him. 'It seems you and Lady Agnes have thought of everything.'

He turned pensive. 'I did need her, at least before this. I've no doubt that I might have devised a workable plan on my own, but—' He gave her a meaningful look. 'I was in the throes of passion. My head is clear now, though. I will not make any future mistakes.'

If he did not make another mistake, the children were doomed. No matter what, she must not make any mistakes either. No more defiance. She must make herself as much like Claire as she could be until a way to escape offered itself.

He gestured to a kettle on the fire in the fireplace. 'Make me some tea, Claire. Have some yourself, if you like.'

At one end of the room there was a scullery with dirty cups, saucers and plates piled in it and a pantry where she found a tea caddy, some sugar, a large jug of milk and a tin of biscuits.

'Is this all there is to eat?' she asked.

He shrugged. 'That is all I bought. That and some sweetmeats for the children, which they have eaten already.' He waved an arm. 'Bring me some biscuits, as well.'

She put some tea in the pot and poured water from the kettle into it. 'May I offer some tea to the children?' she asked.

'The children.' He laughed. 'I quite forgot about them. You may serve them after you serve me. I prefer they stay in that room.'

She did as he bid as deferentially as she could manage, although she had considered throwing boiling water on him and making a run for it. She didn't think she could release the girls from their prison fast enough, though.

When she'd finished serving him, she picked up the tea tray. 'May I spend some time with the children? I fear if I do not, they may become alarmed and hysterical.'

'Excellent point, Claire.' He rose and unlocked the door. He even opened it for her so that she could carry the tea to the children.

He left the door open.

Pamela and Ellen rose from their seats and came to her.

'I brought us some tea.' She set the tray on the table and set out the tea cups as if they were in the Tower Room at Brookmore House.

'When will we go home?' Pamela asked.

Ellen stood next to her chair and leaned against her. 'I want to go home, too.'

She did not want to alarm them. 'Our adventure is going to last a bit longer than expected.'

She glanced out the window. The cottage overlooked Lake Windermere. Wind whipped the trees that grew at the lake's edge and the water's waves washed over a stone jetty. Tied to a post by the jetty was a rowing boat bobbing in the water like a bucking horse.

Rebecca's stomach roiled and she felt as if she were in another rowing boat being tossed by waves. She closed her eyes and turned back to the girls.

'Do not worry,' she told them. 'I will not leave you.'

Chapter Twenty-One

The rain fell in sheets, but Garret and his estate manager decided to push through the bad weather and make it back to Brookmore House before dark rather than stay in one more uncomfortable inn.

Being away had been good for Garret. He'd at least solved one of his problems, securing enough stores to get them through a bad harvest. His more domestic problems remained unresolved, but the distance from them had done him some good. That and spending his days on Skiddaw's back like in the army. Garret felt more himself than he'd felt since his brother died. He was not certain what that meant ultimately, but it felt much better to be in his own skin again.

He'd missed Pamela and Ellen. He'd even missed Lady Rebecca.

The roads had turned muddy and the horses made slower progress, but eventually Garret saw the Brookmore gates and knew they'd soon be warm and in dry clothes.

As they approached, a woman emerged from the house and ran towards them, hatless and coatless and unheeding the pouring rain.

'Lord Brookmore! Lord Brookmore!' It was Mary Beale, the girls' maid.

'Mary?' He halted his horse.

She grabbed on to a stirrup. 'Sir! The children are missing! They are missing! And Miss Tilson.'

His calmness fled. 'What? When?'

'We found them gone late this morning. They haven't returned!' she cried.

'Have you searched for them?' Ben asked.

'Yes!' She took a breath. 'Mr Glover sent several men out, all over the countryside. No one found any sign of them.'

Visions of Ellen and Lady Rebecca in the lake assaulted him. They wouldn't be so foolish a second time, would they?

'Here.' He extended his hand to her and pulled her up on to his horse.

They hurried to the house. When they reached the door, Garret helped Mary down and dismounted himself.

'I'll take the horses,' Ben said. 'When they're settled I'll come back. See how I can help.'

Garret rushed inside.

Glover, Mrs Dodd and several of the other servants were in the hall. A footman came over and helped peel off his wet clothes.

He wasted no time. 'Tell me what happened.'

Mary, shivering from dashing out into the rain, spoke. 'I was coming to the schoolroom to see if Miss Pamela and Miss Ellen wanted nuncheon when Lady Agnes ran out, saying the girls and Miss Tilson were gone.'

'Lady Agnes?' Garret's suspicions rose.

'She'd been spending time in the schoolroom the last couple of days,' Mary explained.

'In the schoolroom?'

Mary nodded. 'We sent up an alarm in the house, but no one had seen them and no one had heard them go out, but we knew they did, because their hats, gloves and jackets were gone.'

'I saw Miss Tilson,' one of the footmen said. 'She left to do an errand in the village, but she never came back.'

Glover spoke up. 'We sent men to search the estate and the countryside, but we didn't find them. A villager saw a cart and driver with what might have been two little girls, but he was not certain.'

Brant made his arthritic way down the stairs. 'I found this!' He waved a letter in his hand, but halted when he saw Garret. 'My lord! You are back. Thank God.'

Garret bounded up the stairs to his valet, who handed him the letter. Still on the stairs he broke the seal and saw it was written in a careful hand.

He read it.

> *Dear Lord Brookmore,*
> *I have taken your nieces to a place where you will not find them. Follow these instructions carefully or you will never see them again.*
> *I want five hundred pounds for their safe return...*

There followed instructions on when and where to leave the ransom.

Garret skipped to the end of the letter.

> *Yours,*
> *C. Tilson*

Claire Tilson.

He crushed the paper in his hand. 'Where is Lady Agnes? I wish to see her immediately.'

'The poor dear is in her room with her aunt,' Mrs Dodd responded. 'She is quite shaken by this, as well we all are.'

Garret continued up the stairs to Lady Agnes's room. He opened the door, not bothering to knock. 'Lady Agnes.'

She sat on the sofa, leaning against her aunt, patting her hand. At his abrupt entrance both ladies jumped.

Lady Agnes emitted a cry. 'Brookmore! You are here.'

Was that shock on her face? He was not expected until tomorrow.

He looked pointedly at her aunt. 'Leave us.'

He must have appeared fearsome, because the aunt's eyes widened in fright.

'I should st-stay,' she stammered. 'Not proper.'

'Leave,' he said again.

Lady Agnes wiped her eyes with a lace-edged hand-kerchief. 'Oh, leave us, Aunt Theodora. These are special times. Brookmore needs me now, I am certain.'

Her aunt needed no more encouragement.

When she'd gone, Lady Agnes flung herself against the sofa. 'You've heard! They are gone. I am certain something terrible has happened to them.'

He walked through the room, stopping by the writing desk, opening its drawers.

'Are you looking for something, Brookmore, dear?' she asked sweetly.

He was looking for something with her handwriting on it.

'Tell me what you know.' His clothing was still wet and dripped on the carpet.

She acted as if she were stifling a sob. 'I do not know much. I spent some time with Miss Tilson and the dear children—I thought I must do something to make up for the night of the dinner party—I had been with them earlier. When I came back, they were gone and no one knew where they were.' She wiped her eyes again. 'That is all I know.'

'What of this?' He shoved the letter in her face.

She took it from his hand and smoothed out the paper.

'Oh, my goodness!' she cried as she read the letter. 'I do not believe it.'

'I do not believe it either.'

She shook her head. 'I had no idea Miss Tilson was capable of such treachery! I mean, she was odd, not like a governess at all, but...this?'

'You spent time with her,' he said.

She sighed. 'I treasured the time I spent—not with her, but with Pamela and Ellen. Those little girls are so sweet.' She looked him in the eye. 'I could not have guessed Miss Tilson would ever threaten to harm them.'

He seized her by the shoulders and pulled her to a standing position. 'Tell me what you did.' The letter fluttered to the floor.

She wriggled beneath his grasp. 'Stop being brutish!' Her despairing tone fled. 'You are cold and wet.'

He released her. 'You wrote this.' He picked up the letter.

'Me?' She made a nervous laugh. 'Do not be absurd!'

'Who else wanted her gone?' He glared at her. 'Now tell me where she and the children are.'

'How would I know that?' She twisted her face into a wounded expression. 'I am desolated that you would think such a thing of me.' She took a shuddering breath. 'You simply do not wish to believe she wrote that.' She blinked as if fighting back tears. 'She must have written it. I know it is painful to think of her doing it. After all, you trusted her with your nieces. But it makes no sense for anyone else to write it.'

She was trying too hard to convince him.

'I know she did not write it.' He shoved the paper at her again.

She perused it once more, as if examining it carefully.

'I am so sorry, Brookmore.' Her voice turned a sugary sympathetic. 'But how well did you know her, really? Did you know her writing?'

He did. She'd written a note to him. He could not remember her handwriting specifically, but this was not hers. He knew it.

He pointed to the letter. 'I know this is not her writing.'

She put a hand on his arm as if in consolation. 'Dear Brookmore. You waste time. You must do as the letter says, for the children's sake. She is missing and the children are missing and she left you a letter explaining it all. You cannot know this is from anyone but her.'

He removed her hand. 'I do know.' He knew because she would not have signed her name Claire Tilson. He was not about to divulge her secret to Lady Agnes.

He took Lady Agnes by the arm and sat her back on the sofa. 'Let me tell you what I think you have done. You have colluded with Sir Orin who has kidnapped the three of them. Tell me where I am to find them before it is too late.'

She brushed off where he'd touched her. 'Did not Sir Orin leave here after you brutalised him?'

He leaned over her. 'Did he tell you I brutalised him?' She'd just confirmed his suspicion that she was involved.

She flushed. 'I do not know what you mean.'

'If I send someone to Ambleside, will they find an innkeeper who remembers a meeting or two between Sir Orin and a lady?'

'It is too rainy to go to Ambleside.' She glanced away and back. 'Besides, perhaps the lady could be Miss Tilson.'

He turned her head back. 'Blonde hair. Blue eyes. Fine clothing?'

She jerked away.

He turned her back again. 'Now tell me everything. Tell me where they are.'

'You are making a fuss over nothing!' she protested. 'The children will be home tomorrow and your precious governess will be gone. All will be well.'

'You are a fool, Lady Agnes. A man like Sir Orin is not going to release the children.' He was likely a murderer already. What would be one or two more?

'Tell me.'

She sighed. 'Oh, very well. But I assure you no one would come to harm. Your nieces will have had a lark and that woman would have another chance to accept a marriage proposal.'

She explained the plan.

When she was finished, Garret stepped back, his hands flexing into fists. 'You remain here. If they are unharmed, you will leave. You will tell everyone you broke our engagement. You will tell them you simply changed your mind. If you say otherwise, this story will be told with you as the villain.'

She glared at him.

'If they are harmed in any way, I will call in the magistrate and you will pay for your petty treachery.'

He turned on his heel and left the room.

Sir Orin allowed Rebecca to stay in the room with the children for over an hour. She played simple card games with them and spillikins, but all the time she was aware he watched them from the other room.

The sky turned dark but the sounds of the wind, rain and waves reached Rebecca's ears, pricking at her memory of another storm, another time of danger. She needed to stay in the present, even though the past tugged her backwards.

'Claire, my love,' Sir Orin called to her. 'Come sit with me now.'

'One moment, Sir Orin.' Rebecca hugged both girls. 'I'll just be in the other room.' There was a sofa in that room, right beneath the window. 'Lie down on the sofa and try to sleep.'

The girls climbed on the sofa and she covered them both with her shawl. She kissed them on their heads, blew out the lamp and walked out of the room, closing the door behind her.

'I am here,' she told Sir Orin.

He patted a chair next to his. She obediently sat next to him.

He turned his chair a little so that he looked directly at her. 'You are so good with children, Claire. That is one of the first things I loved about you.'

Her entire experience with children had taken place in these last few weeks.

'You have not asked about the children. Do you not wonder how they fare?'

She did not know them. 'How could they fare? Their mother died and their father left them.'

He scowled. 'I must curb that biting tongue of yours.'

Better she curb it. She had no wish to agitate him.

She glanced around the room. There was just the one door and windows facing the front.

'The children were inconsolable when you left, you know,' he said.

'Were they?' She could see how they might be. She'd become instantly fond of Claire. 'But do you not think they miss their mother more acutely?'

He shrugged. 'I suppose. She did dote on them.' He waved a hand as if wiping that thought away. 'I thought you would have more to say about the children. You must have cared for them deeply. They said you cried when you said goodbye.' He wagged a finger at her. 'You sneaked away without me knowing. I would not have let you go, you know.'

Had Claire realised what this man was capable of? Was that why she left? She'd run away, obviously.

He smiled. 'Guess which one of the girls cried the most after you left?'

Rebecca felt panicked inside. She struggled to remember the names she'd read in *Debrett's*. 'Margaret?' she guessed.

He frowned. 'Margaret, you say?'

She struggled to remember the others. 'Was it Mary? Not Bridget, certainly.'

He peered at her. 'Why do you call them Margaret and Bridget?'

She remembered correctly, she was certain. 'Those are their names.'

'We have always called them Meg and Biddy. You should know that.' His eyes turned suspicious.

Her muscles tensed.

He leaned a bit closer. 'Tell me the name of my estate.'

Had it been in *Debrett's*? She could not remember.

His voice rose. 'Tell me the name of the village. The county.'

She was discovered.

Rebecca straightened. 'I cannot tell you those things.'

His expression turned dark. 'Why not?'

She lifted her chin. 'Because I am not Claire Tilson.'

He made a sound like the low growl of a wild dog.

She taunted him. 'I look like her. A lot like her, but not exactly. I wonder that a man so besotted with Claire would not see the difference.'

'You are deliberately toying with me,' he said, his voice low.

She went on. 'You said so yourself. That I was not like myself. Of course I was not. I was never Claire.'

'How can this be?' His voice turned smaller.

'By chance. We met on the packet boat. We instantly saw the resemblance and we formed a friendship over it. We even fooled my maid into thinking Claire was me.'

He shook his head. 'Who are you, then?'

She gave him a regal look. 'I am Lady Rebecca Pierce. I am of the aristocracy and I am well connected with men of power.' Of course, all her connections were gone. Lady Rebecca was thought to be dead.

'Why are you pretending to be Claire?' he asked.

She was not about to confide in him. 'My reasons were private ones. You need not know them.'

He swung away from her. 'No. No. You are playing with me. You are Claire.'

'I am not. I do not know where you live. I do not know your pet names for people. I know nothing of your life. I can only imagine what a nightmare it was to be married to you. Not so horrid to lose one's life over.' She should stop herself, but her words came out like a tidal wave.

He stood and paced in front of her. 'Where is Claire, then? Where is she? I demand to know.'

She did not know how he would take this news. 'Sir Orin, Claire is dead. Our packet boat was caught in a terrible storm. She drowned.'

'No.' He groaned. 'No.'

He paced away from her and twisted back. 'This changes everything, you know.'

She hoped so. 'You do not really want me. I'm not Claire. There is no reason why you cannot simply walk away from us.' She spoke soothingly, as she might to a spooked horse. 'You could leave now. You would get wet, of course, but you would be long gone before anyone would know.'

'No.' He spoke more to himself than to Rebecca. 'No. You'd tell. You'd tell.'

Her hands shook. 'I won't tell. I—I do not want attention called to myself. All I wish is for you to be gone and for the children to return home safely. I must disappear, too, you know.'

'No,' he said again.

There was a loud crack and a crash that put Rebecca back on the packet boat, when the mast had broken above their heads. The room grew dark and images of the angry sea overwhelmed her.

'Blast.' He walked to the window and peered out. 'A tree. It looks like it hit the stable. He walked to a hook on the wall where his topcoat hung. He put it on and grabbed a lantern.

He opened the door and turned to her. 'Do not try to escape. I will see you. There is only this one door and one path to the road and one road. Do not do anything foolish.' He walked out the door.

She immediately ran to the room where the children were. When she opened the door, they jumped back.

'We were listening,' Ellen said. 'Are you really not Miss Tilson?'

'Never mind that. We have to get out of here.' She ran to the window.

She pushed on the window and it finally opened wide enough for them to climb through. The distance to the ground was one storey high.

She had to think fast. 'Put your jackets on.' She helped them. 'I am going to climb out the window and hang over the side. Pamela, you climb down on me and drop to the ground. Then wait to help Ellen down.'

Rebecca climbed out into the rain. The window sill was slippery, but she hung on.

'Pamela! Come out now.'

Pamela scrambled out and climbed down Rebecca, holding on to Rebecca's dress as she lowered herself, finally letting go. Rebecca heard her hit the ground.

'I'm ready for Ellen,' she said in a loud whisper.

Rebecca's arms were aching. 'Hurry, Ellen. You can do this.'

Ellen climbed out like her sister and scurried down quickly like a little monkey.

'I'll catch you,' Pamela said.

Ellen let go and Rebecca heard her land.

'Now move away.' Rebecca's fall would be farther than the girls. She said a prayer that she not injure herself.

She landed in a bramble bush, the thorns piercing her skin and ripping her dress, but she was able to get to her feet. The rain pelted them like icy shards.

'Where do we go?' Pamela asked. She held her little sister's hand.

There was only one way to go.

If they tried to run for the road, Sir Orin would see them. Even if they managed to slip past him, he'd likely find them eventually. They needed an escape route he could not follow.

'We're going to the lake,' Rebecca said. 'There is a boat there. Hold on to me and to each other.'

It was so dark, Rebecca could only see inches in front of her. She found the path to the lake by trial and error and by listening to the slapping of the waves against the shore. They slipped and slid down the path, but they reached the jetty. There was enough light to see white caps on the lake and the bobbing of the rowing boat.

Rebecca pulled on the rope that tethered the boat to the

post, bringing it close enough to the jetty to grab hold of it. As she reached for it, it dipped away and the memory of being dropped into the rowing boat from the sinking ship made her freeze. She again felt herself seated next to the mother huddled with her two children.

She shook her head.

These two children were her responsibility now. She would not allow them to die like the others.

She caught the boat and held it against the stone jetty. 'Climb in.'

The girls did not hesitate, but they did not know what rough water could do. They climbed in because they trusted her. She climbed in after them and freed the boat from its moorings. She pushed hard against the jetty and the boat floated on to the lake.

The water was rough and the rocking of the boat jabbed Rebecca with memories, but she stayed focused on whatever she must do next. The boat was filled with rain water and they busied themselves bailing out the water with jugs they found in the boat. There were oars, but Rebecca was too weary to try to use them. The wind and the water floated them further and further from shore. They were safe. From Sir Orin, at least.

'Let's huddle together to keep warm,' she said to the girls, wrapping them in an embrace, holding them as close to her body as she could.

'Are we safe?' asked Pamela.

'Yes,' she assured her. 'He cannot reach us on the water.'

'He was a bad man, wasn't he?' Pamela said.

'Yes,' Rebecca agreed. 'A very bad and dangerous man.'

'But Lady Agnes sent us off with him,' Ellen said. 'She said we were going to surprise you.'

'She lied to us.' Pamela huddled closer.

Ellen whimpered.

They clung to each other and Rebecca tried not to think about the rocking of the boat or of how cold it was or of how and when and where they would reach the shore. If they would reach the shore.

Finally Ellen quieted and Rebecca hoped she'd fallen asleep, but her little voice popped up. 'What are we to call you, Miss Tilson?'

She kissed the child's head. 'Call me Rebecca.'

Chapter Twenty-Two

Garret made his way up the road along Lake Windermere from Far Sawrey, looking for the cottage Sir Orin had rented. The rain had stopped at last, but Ben and two of the stablemen who started out with him had been slowed by the mud and rain. Skiddaw, seasoned by years of army life, plodded on and Garret soon was ahead of the others.

There was something about danger that drove away the non-essential clutter of life, leaving a stark clarity of what was important. In the time-consuming effort it took to get this far, Garret became very clear about one thing. Lady Rebecca, Pamela and Ellen were the most important people in his life. He would die to protect them. He did not care what anyone in society or Parliament or even on the throne thought of him. He wanted to share his life with Lady Rebecca and to rear his nieces as if they were his own children.

He'd been this way in battle. Able to see what he and his soldiers must do to win. And survive. His men had esteemed him and, because he saw himself reflected in their eyes, he'd been secure in believing he was a competent officer.

Now he realised from those first days, he'd seen admiration reflected in Lady Rebecca's eyes. He realised her steadfast support of him helped give him confidence to manage the estate's problems his way. She'd enabled him to put himself back in touch with the people who'd helped forge him as a boy. His workers were his soldiers now and he knew he could bring them through any adversity.

Lady Rebecca had seen him clearly when he'd been unable to see himself. He no longer cared that she'd deceived him as to her name. He, too, had seen her true self clearly.

And now, when he feared losing her, he knew he loved her.

It had taken Garret and his men a long time to reach this road. Lady Agnes did not know all the details, like which cottage Orin had rented. It took time to discover that in Far Sawrey. The darkness thwarted Garret. He feared the cottage would be so obscured by the thick trees and shrubs that he could pass the cottage by.

Up ahead, though, he thought he saw a light through the trees. A lantern? He urged Skiddaw forward. Yes. There was definitely a light.

Garret came upon a path leading down towards the lake. He dismounted, leaving Skiddaw there, and followed the path. He passed a village cart in a clearing—a villager had seen a man in a village cart. He walked farther and could dimly see the outline of a cottage. Light shone through the windows, but faintly, as if only a candle burned inside. A brighter light was visible in the outbuilding, its roof smashed by a fallen tree. Garret stealthily moved towards it. He peered through a gap in the wall and saw a man trying to free a horse blocked in by rocks and timber. He could not see if it was Sir Orin, but he made his way to the cottage and went inside.

'Lady Rebecca?' he called quietly. 'Pamela? Ellen?'

There was no answer, but he found two teacups and saucers. More than one person had been there.

He entered a second room and found more dishes, a deck of cards and a game of spillikins. On the sofa was the shawl he had purchased for her in Moelfre.

She had been here! The children, too, unless Sir Orin had a fondness for spillikins.

Where were they now? Was he too late?

Garret strode out of the cottage and back to the out-building.

He stood in the doorway. 'Sir Orin!'

The man turned and froze for a moment. The light from the lantern shone on his face. It was indeed Sir Orin.

Sir Orin charged at Garret, who deftly stepped aside and caught him by the arm, sending him sprawling. Sir Orin picked up a piece of splintered wood and swung it at Garret, who ducked and seized him from behind.

'Where are they?' Garret snarled.

'I do not know what you are talking about.' Sir Orin struggled to free himself.

'Do not lie to me. I found her shawl in the cottage.'

Sir Orin froze. 'They are gone?'

'Where are they?' Garret roared.

'I rid myself of them!' Sir Orin struggled again, twisting and turning until both men were outside the building.

Garret's foot slipped in the mud, loosening his hold enough for Sir Orin to break free. They scuffled in the mud, but Sir Orin managed to scramble away and run into the trees, quickly disappearing from view.

Garret's heart pounded in fear. Which was true? Sir Orin's surprise they were gone? Or saying he got rid of them?

He picked up the lantern and returned to the cottage.

He searched the first room, but there was nowhere they could be hidden. He looked in the second room where he'd found her shawl.

It looked as if they'd just stepped away, but where?

The window was open. Garret walked over to it and leaned out, holding the lantern for light. Could they have climbed out the window? He carried the lantern outside and examined the ground underneath the back window. He found footprints in the mud that led to a jetty.

He walked to the end of it and lifted the lantern high.

The water was choppy, but the wind was blowing the storm clouds away. The moon suddenly shone down on the lake. Garret spied a rowing boat on the water and it looked like someone was in the boat.

Had she escaped with them in a boat? How much courage had that taken?

His heart skittered. 'Rebecca!' he called. 'Rebecca!'

He saw the figure divide into three. There were three of them!

'Rebecca!' he called again. 'It is Garret Brookmore!'

'Garret!' she called back. Using his given name warmed him.

'Uncle Garret! Uncle Garret!' two young voices cried.

He waved the lantern. 'Come in. It is safe. He is gone.'

He watched while she positioned herself with the oars and rowed. Her progress was slow, but she came closer and closer until he finally could reach the boat and pull it to him. He secured the boat to its moorings and held it steady so they could climb out.

Rebecca lifted each girl and handed them to him and finally he reached for her, lifting her out of the boat and into his arms.

He held her against him. 'Thank God you are safe. Thank God you are all safe.'

* * *

An hour later Rebecca and the children were in dry clothes and comfortably warm in an inn in Far Sawrey. Rebecca, Garret and the girls were in one room, cosy on one bed. There was no separating them, not after the frightful night they'd had.

Garret's men had reached the cottage by the time they were out of the boat and they wasted no time in finding blankets to warm them. They hitched the horse to the village cart and drove back to the village, to the inn. Garret's men rode on to Brookmore House to inform them that Rebecca and the children were safe and would return the next day.

Rebecca lay in Garret's arms while Pamela and Ellen slept like little angels next to them.

'I am sure we will be the subject of gossip in Far Sawrey tomorrow,' Rebecca murmured.

'I am sure I do not care a whit,' Garret answered. He glanced at Pamela and Ellen. 'Besides, we are well chaperoned.'

'That is not likely to stop talk.'

'Very well.' He placed his lips on the top of her head. 'You will have to marry me then or you will be thought a fallen woman.'

She sat up and looked at him. 'Marry you?'

His mouth widened into a slow smile. 'Marry me.' His expression sobered. 'Marry me.'

Rebecca was afraid to trust in such happiness. 'Are you certain?'

'I am very certain.' He held her gaze.

She looked away. 'I do not know. I have made such a mess of things. I cannot marry you as Claire Tilson. I am not Claire Tilson. But I am not certain I want to be Lady Rebecca either. That brings more trouble, I am afraid.'

He sat up as well and gently moved her face so that she looked at him again. 'I need to know only one thing. Do you love me? Because I now know I have loved you since that first glimpse of you, before you even opened your eyes.'

'You couldn't possibly—' She started to argue with him, but stopped herself.

'Do you love me?' he asked again.

She loved him so much the words would not form in her mouth, but she nodded.

He embraced her again.

'You are the finest man I have ever known.' Her voice worked again. 'I once hoped for a man I could love, but I never imagined there could be a man as principled, kind and generous as you are.'

He hugged her tighter. 'I am not certain I deserve such praise.'

'You do,' she murmured against his chest, relishing the beat of his heart and the warmth of his body. 'But perhaps love does not solve our problems.'

'If you love me,' he said, 'none of the other problems matter.'

She just could not figure it, though. She couldn't have banns read as Claire Tilson and she was not eager for anyone to know Lady Rebecca was still alive. There was no way around it.

'I have an idea,' Garret said.

'Mmm,' she responded.

'We'll go to Gretna Green and marry over the anvil. You marry me with your true name. Then we come back and to everyone you will be Lady Brookmore. To me you will be Rebecca, but we can say that is your middle name or something.'

She sat up again. 'But it is scandalous to elope to Gretna Green.'

He pulled her back into an embrace. 'Pick your scandal, Lady Brookmore.'

She revelled in the comfort of his arms again. 'Did you know that was Sir Orin's plan? To marry me at Gretna Green. As if that would have made me stay with him.'

'Will it make you stay with me?' he asked.

'Absolutely,' she said.

Epilogue

Two weeks later Rebecca and Garret lounged in bed in an inn in Carlisle on their way back from Gretna Green. They were thoroughly man and wife in every way possible. Their breakfast had been sent up to their room and they'd managed to eat it in bed, being loathe to leave its comforts and each other and continue on the road back to Brookmore House. To be close, to be touching each other, was the perfect way to prolong the languid pleasure that came after lovemaking.

The innkeeper sent up newspapers with the meal, the latest local newspaper from Carlisle and a recent paper from London.

Rebecca read the London paper.

'Oh, no!' she cried, bolting out of bed.

'What is it?' Garret put down his paper.

'Listen to this. *"Rescue at sea. Two survivors of the tragic shipwreck of the packet* Dun Aengus *were rescued at sea days after the ship ran aground at Moelfre. Miraculously Lady Rebecca Pierce, sister of the Earl of Keneagle, survived by clinging to debris, along with another passenger, Lucien Roper of Kent. Lady Rebecca convalesced in Dublin until arriving in London one week ago."'* She looked up at him. 'Claire is alive.'

'Alive?' He left the bed and faced her.

'Who else could it be? That is my name. She didn't use her own, so she must have taken on my identity, as I took on hers.' She covered her face with her hands. 'She is alive. Claire is alive.'

He put an arm around her. 'Then this is good news, is it not?'

'Yes! Wonderful news.' She felt as if she would weep.

'Then why look so distressed? Be happy.' He gently shook her.

She turned and let him enfold her in an embrace. 'Do you not see? I stole her life. She should have met you. She should have been Pamela and Ellen's governess.'

He kissed the top of her head. 'But it is you I love. You must never forget that. I love your courage and independence and forthrightness—everything about you. Claire might look like you, but she could not *be* you, could she? Any more than you could be her. Besides...' he hugged her closer '...she would not have been at that inn to meet me, so you couldn't have taken a life she never would have had.'

'That is confusing,' she murmured.

He laughed. 'That whole situation is confusing. At least I am sure about one thing.'

'What are you sure of?' When he held her like this, all problems seemed solvable, all obstacles, surmountable, all mistakes, forgiven.

'That I love you.' He leaned down and kissed her.

She wrapped her arms around his neck and lost herself in his kiss.

When he stopped for air, he leaned his forehead against hers. 'I am sure of one other thing.'

She sighed. 'And that is?'

'I would be married to Lady Agnes, if you had not come into my life.'

She smiled. 'Thank God for that shipwreck.'

She'd come to see the shipwreck not as a trauma to be feared, but as a rebirth. The shipwreck had given her a new life, one with everything she'd dreamed of—and more. On the rare occasions the memories returned, she embraced them and promised all those lost that she would appreciate every day of her new life.

'Thank God for that shipwreck,' Garret murmured, capturing her lips once again.

She broke away abruptly. 'Garret, what if Sir Orin reads this newspaper? He will guess Claire is alive, as well. I told him who I am. He will guess that the Lady Rebecca in the newspaper is her.'

Garret looked directly into her eyes. 'We must warn her.'

* * * * *

SHIPWRECKED WITH THE CAPTAIN

To Jane Austen,

who briefly lived in Bath and in whose footsteps
I was honoured to walk.

Chapter One

June 1816

Lucien Roper stood at the rail of the packet ship, watching the Dublin harbour recede into the distance. He inhaled the salty breeze and felt the bracing wind on his face. Voices of the sailors tending to their tasks rang in his ears.

Only a few more days, then, with luck, he'd be back on the deck of a ship of his own, with his old crew, and back to the life from which he'd received so much. A fortune in prize money. Recognition and respect. A place he belonged.

A woman's laugh sounded over his shoulder, its sound so joyous, so unlike his restless mood that he turned, startled. She wore a grey cloak, shrouding her face.

What pleased her so? he wondered.

This was the sacrifice the navy life demanded of him. He was not free to court a young woman with a joyous laugh. Not for him to marry a woman and leave her for his mistress, the sea. He'd seen what happened when a navy man married and he and his wife spent most of their days apart.

As his own parents had done.

It had been a long time since he'd suffered the effects of having an absent naval father. Lucien himself had been at sea for more than twenty years now, since the age of twelve. This was his life and before it, a mere memory.

He was eager to get back to it. His beloved *Foxfire* had been sold for breaking up, no longer needed now the war was over, and the Admiralty had promised him a new ship. Of course, there were dozens of captains like him, clamouring for a ship, but he'd earned a spot near the top of the list. At least with the wind this brisk they could count on making it to Holyhead by the next afternoon and he'd be in London a few days later.

He studied the sky and frowned. This crossing would be rough. Maybe too rough. Likely their departure should have been delayed a day, but the sooner he reached England, the better.

Still…

He sauntered over to where the packet captain stood.

'We're in for a patch of bad weather,' Lucien remarked.

The Captain knew who Lucien was—a decorated navy captain, a hero of the Adriatic Sea and Mediterranean.

'What?' The Captain looked surprised Lucien had spoken to him. 'Oh. Bad weather. Yes. Must sail through it.'

Lucien had made it through many a storm. He'd make it through this one. He'd prefer, though, that the Captain seem less preoccupied and better able to attend to the weather and what was happening on his deck.

Like noticing the young grey-cloaked woman back away from sea spray and stumble a little.

'Would it not be a good idea to order passengers to stay below?' Lucien asked him in a tone more demanding than questioning.

'Hmm?' This Captain was as sharp as a slop bucket.

Pay attention, man.

'The passengers,' Lucien snapped, gesturing to the young woman, 'should stay below.'

'Oh?' The Captain's brows rose. 'Of course. Was about to make that order.' He called one of his men over. 'Tell the passengers to remain below.'

Lucien shook his head in dismay and strode away. He traversed the deck and, out of habit, took notice of the seamen preparing for the storm. He scanned the sails and the ropes. All seemed well enough. Shipshape. He glanced back at the Captain who held a hand to his chest and seemed to be studying his coat buttons.

Lucien expelled a frustrated breath. He'd better get below himself before he began barking orders.

He walked to the companionway and opened the hatch. At the bottom of the stairs stood two women, both in grey cloaks. Which was the woman with the captivating laugh? He could not see the face of one, but the other was a beauty. An expensively dressed beauty. He might have spoken to them and hoped to finally see who had uttered such a lovely laugh, but it was clear he'd intruded on them. They stepped aside.

He nodded and passed them, but turned back. 'You ladies should stay in your cabins. The sea is rough. Do not fear. A seaman will bring your meal to you.'

At least he hoped such an arrangement would be made—if the Captain thought to order it.

Lucien continued to his cabin.

Claire Tilson had quickly averted her face when the tall, dark-haired, broad-shouldered gentleman opened the hatch and descended the stairs. Her heart was already beating fast; this encounter—this lady—had been disturbance enough, but she'd glimpsed the man on deck and he was every bit as handsome as she'd suspected, with thick brows and eyes as light brown and as alert as a fox's.

What was wrong with her? Taking notice of any man. She'd just fled from the country house where she'd been governess to three lovely little girls, because their father had tried to seduce her—practically under the nose of his sweet wife. He'd sworn his undying love. As if she could trust a man who so ill-used his wife.

Claire shook herself. She need not be distracted. She needed, instead, to address this lady standing next to her, this lady she'd met a moment ago.

This lady who looked exactly like her.

Same brown hair. Same hazel eyes. Same face.

What do you say to a stranger who looked like your twin?

Lady Rebecca Pierce was her name, she'd said.

Claire waited until the handsome gentleman disappeared into one of the cabins near the end of the corridor, but she debated whether it was her place to ask for explanations.

'We should do as he says, I suppose,' she said instead. She went to a nearby door and opened it. 'My cabin is here.'

What she wanted to say was, *Wait. Talk to me. Why do you look like me? Where are you from? Are you a relation?*

Claire would love to have some family relation to claim her.

She ought not to push herself on a lady, though. She took a step across the threshold.

Lady Rebecca called her back. 'I would like to speak with you more. I am quite alone. My maid suffers the *mal de mer* and remains in her cabin.'

Claire glanced down. 'The sea has never bothered me. I suppose I have a strong constitution that way.'

'Will you talk with me?' Lady Rebecca asked. 'Maybe there is some sense to make of this.' Her hand gestured between them.

Claire gazed into her cabin, perfect for a poor governess, but unsuitable for a lady. 'You are welcome to come in, but there is very little room.'

'Come to my cabin, then,' the lady said. 'We may be comfortable there.'

Claire followed Lady Rebecca to her cabin, which included a berth larger than the one in her cabin and a table and chairs that provided a view of the sea through a porthole. As the gentleman had said, the sea was rough, with choppy waves and white foam.

Lady Rebecca waved towards a chair, inviting her to sit. When they were both settled across from each other at the table, Lady Rebecca asked, 'Where are you bound, Miss Tilson?'

Claire would have thought she'd ask the obvious question, the one that burned inside her—*why do we look alike*?

'To a family in the Lake District,' she responded. 'Not a family, precisely. Two little girls whose parents were killed in an accident. They are in the care of their uncle now, the new Viscount Brookmore.' And with any luck at all, the Viscount wouldn't often be in residence.

'How sad.' The lady frowned sympathetically.

Yes. The little girls were alone in the world. Claire knew how that felt.

But she did not wish to dwell on gloomy feelings, not when her life might improve. 'And you, Lady Rebecca? Where are you bound?'

'To London,' she replied.

'London!' Claire smiled. A city of shops, palaces, theatres and town houses in picturesque squares. The Tower. Westminster Abbey. Hyde Park. 'How exciting. I was there once. It was so…vital.'

'Vital, indeed.' Lady Rebecca, looking like Claire herself, appeared scornful.

Claire peered at her. 'You sound as if you do not wish to go.'

The lady met her gaze. 'I do not. I travel there to be married.'

Claire's brows rose. 'Married?'

Lady Rebecca waved a hand. 'It is an arranged marriage. My brother's idea.'

There were worse things than an arranged marriage. 'And you do not wish to marry this man?'

'Not at all.' Lady Rebecca straightened in her chair. 'May I change the subject?'

Claire blinked. She'd forgotten herself and had spoken out of turn, as if they were equals. 'Forgive me. I did not mean to pry.'

Lady Rebecca shrugged. 'Perhaps I will tell you the whole story later.' She leaned forward. 'For now I am bursting with questions. Why do we look alike? How can this be? Are we related somehow?'

The same questions Claire longed to ask.

They discussed possible family connections, but came up with none that connected them.

It would have been more of a surprise if they had been relations. Lady Rebecca was the daughter of an English earl whose estate was in Ireland and Claire was the daughter of an English vicar who'd rarely travelled out of his county.

They had both grown up in English boarding schools, however, although Lady Rebecca's was a rather progressive school in Reading and Claire's Bristol school had catered to girls like her, who would eventually have to make their own way in the world. It was through her boarding school that Claire had procured the governess position in Ireland.

Lady Rebecca blew out an exasperated breath. 'We are no closer to understanding this. We are not related—'

'But we look alike,' Claire finished for her. 'An unexpected coincidence?'

Lady Rebecca stood and pulled Claire towards a mirror affixed to the wall.

'We are not identical.' Claire was almost relieved to find some differences. 'Look.'

Claire's two front teeth were not quite as prominent and her eyebrows did not have Lady Rebecca's lovely arch, and

Claire's eyes were closer together. Still, the differences were so minor as to be easily overlooked.

'No one would notice unless we were standing next to each other,' she admitted.

'Our clothes set us apart. That is for certain.' Lady Rebecca turned from the mirror and faced Claire. 'If you wore my clothes, I'd wager anyone would take you for me.'

Claire admired the travelling dress Lady Rebecca wore, a vigonia-wool confection with ribbon trim at the hem. She'd also admired Lady Rebecca's cloak, grey, like hers, but of a much finer wool. 'I cannot imagine wearing fine clothes like yours.' She sighed.

'You must wear them, then.' Lady Rebecca's eyes—so like Claire's eyes in colour and shape—brightened. 'Let us change clothes and impersonate each other for the voyage. It will be a great lark. We will see if anyone notices.'

Claire was horrified. 'Your clothes are too fine for you to give up. Mine are plain.'

'Precisely.' Lady Rebecca crossed her arms. 'But I believe people pay more attention to dress than to other aspects of one's appearance. Perhaps even more than one's character. In any event, I think there is nothing undesirable about wearing a simple dress.'

Claire's dress was certainly simple. A plain brown poplin.

She touched the fine wool of Rebecca's travelling dress. 'I confess, I would love to wear a gown like this.'

'Then you shall!' Rebecca turned her back to her. 'Unbutton me.'

They undressed down to their shifts and swapped dresses, acting as each other's maids.

'Fix my hair like yours,' Lady Rebecca said.

Claire pulled Lady Rebecca's hair in a simple knot at the back of her head, feeling inexplicably sad to make Lady Rebecca as plain as she.

'Let me do yours now.' Lady Rebecca removed Claire's hairpins and her hair fell on to her shoulders. She brushed Claire's hair high on her head and, with a little pomade, twisted curling tendrils around her face.

Claire and her likeness gazed in the mirror again and laughed. They had indeed traded images.

There was a rap at the door.

'Answer the door as me.' Lady Rebecca grinned.

Impersonate a lady? 'I could not.'

Lady Rebecca gave her a little push towards the door. 'Of course you can!'

Claire straightened her spine as Lady Rebecca sat back down at the table.

Taking a deep breath, Claire opened the door.

It was a seaman deftly balancing a tray as the boat continued to pitch. 'Some refreshment, m'lady.' He took her to be Lady Rebecca!

The lovely clothes made Claire feel like a lady. 'Thank you.'

Would he also assume Lady Rebecca was the governess? Claire gestured to her. 'Miss Tilson passes the time with me. Will you bring her food here for her?'

'That I will, miss.' The crewman stepped into the cabin and placed the tray on the table right in front of Lady Rebecca. He returned a moment later with two more trays. 'Your maid, miss?'

Claire looked to Lady Rebecca for guidance, but the lady turned away.

Claire finally answered, 'My—my maid is resting. Perhaps you might leave her tray here, as well? We will tend to her.'

The seaman bowed. 'Very good, miss.' He placed both trays on the table.

When he left, Claire put her hand on her chest to still her rapidly beating heart.

'Especially if he has a title and property.' Gentlemen, especially peers, needed an heir.

'He does.' Rebecca tapped her pewter tankard with her fingernail.

'Is the gentleman wealthy enough to provide for you?' Claire asked.

'He is said to be prosperous,' Rebecca replied. 'He must be, because he is willing to marry me with a mere pittance for a dowry.'

She certainly did not look as if she had a mere pittance for a dowry.

'Will you tell me who he is?' Claire asked.

Rebecca shrugged. 'Lord Stonecroft.'

This was not a name Claire knew, but, then, why would she?

'Baron Stonecroft of Gillford.' Rebecca said the name as if biting into rancid meat.

'Ah.' Now Claire understood. 'You were hoping for a higher title than baron. I mean, you said you are the daughter of an earl.'

Rebecca sniffed. 'I care nothing for that.'

Then, what? 'Did he seem like a cruel man, then? Is that your objection?'

Rebecca sighed. 'I do not believe there is precisely anything to object to in him. I simply do not wish to marry him.'

'Refuse, then.' Surely this lady had choices.

Rebecca rolled her eyes. 'My brother—my half-brother—says I am too much of a burden for him to wait for me to find a husband I would like. I've refused every offer he's arranged for me. This time he made certain. I will be turned out without a penny if I do not marry Lord Stonecroft.' Her face turned red. 'I've no doubt he means what he says.'

Claire knew how it felt to have no choices. Her heart wrenched in sympathy. 'How sad. One would hope a brother would understand. Family should understand, should they not?'

Rebecca gave her a curious look. 'Do you have any brothers or sisters? Any family at all?'

Claire's throat tightened with emotion. 'I am alone in the world. Any relations are too distant to be concerned with me.'

'My parents are gone,' Rebecca responded in a like tone. 'And my brother might as well be dead. He said he never wishes to see me again. Ever. Even if he visits England. He made that very clear.'

Another way they were alike. Both alone. Both without parents. Lady Rebecca went on to say her father died two years before, her mother, a decade ago.

At least she'd known her mother. Claire's mother had died giving birth to her; her father, over five years ago.

But Rebecca had one choice Claire would probably never have. The chance to make a good marriage. 'I think you are fortunate to marry, Lady Rebecca—Rebecca,' she finally said. 'You have little money or property, correct? You can only gain by marrying. You'll gain a home of your own to manage. Children of your own. Comfort and security. Even status and a respectable position in society.'

It sounded like a wonderful choice to Claire. She yearned to have a man to love her—that is, the right man, one she was free to love in return. She suspected she would even enjoy the pleasures of the marital bed, because sometimes when seeing a handsome man—like the man who'd spoken to them in the hallway—she'd wonder how it would be for him to kiss her or hold her.

Could men sense such impulses in her? It often seemed the wrong men paid her attention.

How much easier it would be to simply be married. To have such security.

She opened her mouth to speak of this to Lady Rebecca, but the lady's expression had turned desolate.

Claire wanted only to comfort her now. 'Perhaps it will not be so onerous to be Lady Stonecroft.'

Rebecca gave a polite smile. 'Perhaps not.'

Claire changed the subject, to save Rebecca more discomfort. They talked about their interests. What books they'd read. What plays they'd seen. Their favourite pieces of music. From time to time, Rebecca convinced Claire to impersonate her and check up on her maid, Nolan. The woman accepted her as Rebecca, each time.

They talked until night turned the angry sea dark. It felt lovely to Claire. She'd not had such a friend in a long time.

But Rebecca's eyes, so like Claire's, grew heavy and, as they talked, she tried to stifle yawns.

Claire, feeling guilty for claiming her company for so long, stood. 'I should return to my cabin so you might get some sleep. I'll help you out of your dress, if you help me out of this lovely gown.'

Rebecca rose and turned her back so Claire could untie the laces at the back of the plain dress she had owned for years. It had been such a pleasure to wear something a bit decadent, if one could call wool decadent. Ladies who frequently purchased new dresses did not realise how it felt to wear the same drab garments, day after day.

As Claire loosened the laces of the dress, Rebecca turned to her. 'Let us see how far we can carry this masquerade. You be me tonight. Sleep in my nightclothes, in this bed. And I will continue being you.'

Claire blanched. 'I cannot allow you to be closeted in that tiny berth they gave me!'

'Why not?' Rebecca looked defiant. 'It will be an adventure for me. And you will have the comfort of this cabin as a treat. When Nolan enters in the morning, we shall discover if she still believes you are me.'

She pulled out her nightdress, made of the softest of muslin. 'Here.'

Claire fingered the fine cloth of the nightdress. 'Perhaps. If you desire this.'

'I do desire it,' her likeness insisted. She helped Claire out of her dress. 'I desire it very much.'

By morning, though, the weather had worsened and the boat pitched and rose even more fiercely than the night before. Claire was awoken by Rebecca knocking on the door of her own cabin. She rose and had difficulty crossing the room to answer the door to admit her new friend. They looked even more alike, both in their nightclothes, their hair loose about their shoulders.

'I checked on Nolan,' Rebecca said. 'She is even more ill today. I also saw the seaman who brings our food. He said we must stay below.' She lifted her arm. 'I brought your bag.'

Claire had packed a clean shift, her brush and comb, and a small bar of soap for the boat trip. The small trunk that held the rest of her clothing was stowed away. The dress she'd wear again today was draped over one of the chairs.

'We can help each other dress,' Rebecca said.

Dressing was a challenge, though. They had difficulty staying on their feet and the pitcher of water for washing had mostly spilled on to the floor. They managed to get into their shifts and corsets, and Claire reached for her dress.

Rebecca stopped her. 'Oh, do let us continue our masquerade. It was such a lark.'

Claire did not need much convincing. She'd relish wearing Rebecca's lovely dress again and having her hair in curls.

As the day crept on, though, their impersonation of each

other was forgotten. It was clear the ship was in very rough waters. A seaman did attend them, bringing food and drink, but his face seemed pinched in worry.

'A bad storm brewing,' he told them.

Lucien had spent most of the day on deck, though he had no control over the lack of decision by the Captain. Curse naval discipline! It was clear to him that the ship could founder at any moment. The time was past to do anything to prevent it.

He ran over to the Captain. 'Give the order to abandon ship! Get these passengers into the boats while there is still time.' They were near the coast. The boats might make it to shore.

'Yes, yes.' The man's face was ashen. He suddenly clutched his arm and his face contorted in pain. He collapsed on the deck.

'Blast,' Lucien cried. He grabbed one of the men to attend to the Captain and another to see that the order to abandon ship was given. He ran to the cabins to get the passengers to safety.

Suddenly there was a loud crack and Lucien watched lightning travel down the main mast. It split in two and crashed on to the deck.

Time was running out. He dashed back to the cabins and burst into the next one.

He found the lady and her companion. He'd learned the lady was Lady Rebecca Pierce, sister to the Earl of Keneagle. Certainly that had been a surprise. The other woman was a governess. But he had no time to lose.

'Come above,' he commanded. 'We must abandon ship. Bring nothing.'

Lady Rebecca jumped to her feet, but the governess defied his order and pulled a reticule from her satchel. He'd still not seen her face.

'Come on!' he ordered.

When they reached the stairs, the governess shoved the reticule into the lady's hands. 'Here. Take this,' she said. 'I'll be right behind you. I'm going to get Nolan.'

'Miss!' Lucien yelled to her. 'We must leave now.'

'I will be right behind you,' she called over her shoulder.

'Blast!' He pushed the lady up the stairs and seized her arm when they climbed on deck.

The deck was in shambles. Ropes and sails and smashed wood everywhere. The main mast lay like a fallen soldier in the midst of it all.

'To the boats!' he ordered, still gripping her arm.

He pulled her over the debris to the railing, but as they reached it, the ship dipped. A huge wave, as tall as a mountain rose above them.

God help them. Lucien wrapped his arms around her.

The wave engulfed them and swept them into the swirling sea.

Chapter Two

Lucien held on to her as the roiling water pushed them into its depths along with pieces of the broken mast, barrels and other rubble.

Nearly twenty years at sea in all kinds of weather, all kinds of battle, he'd be damned if he'd perish from crossing the Irish Sea in a packet boat.

A large piece of wood smashed into them, hitting her on the head. She went limp, but Lucien hung on to her. He let the sea do its will, pulling them deeper and deeper. With luck it would release them. His lungs ached, but he forced himself to wait. He hoped she was not breathing in too much water.

After an eternity, the sea let go. He kicked them to the surface. When his face broke through, he gulped in air. Lady Rebecca remained limp.

Was he too late?

Lucien resisted panic. Their lives depended upon him remaining calm.

Part of the mast floated nearby. Still keeping hold of her, he swam to it and laid her over it. He blew into her mouth, a trick an old sailor taught him years ago. She coughed and spewed water and mumbled something unintelligible.

He expelled a relieved breath. She was alive.

It was fortunate the debris that had hit them had knocked

her unconscious. She might have struggled otherwise. He might not have been able to keep hold of her.

A piece of rope floated nearby. Lucien grabbed it and tied her to the mast, doing his best to keep her face above the water.

A bolt of lightning lit the sky and he could see the ship a distance away heading towards the rocky shore. The sea pulled them further from it, but into calmer waters. He looked around him for anything that might be useful. A small floating barrel. A large piece of canvas sail. More rope. A hatch door appeared, a piece large enough to hold them both. He took a chance she'd be secure enough on the mast and swam to the door, pulling it back to her. He strained to place her on the door. He gathered the other items he'd collected before climbing on to the door himself.

The storm had cleared, but the shoreline narrowed into no more than a thin line against the sky. He wrapped them both in the canvas sail and held her against his body to keep her as warm as possible. They'd be on the water all night, he guessed.

Lucien doubted anyone would search for them, but perhaps some vessel would sail near enough to find them.

He gazed down at her, still unconscious, but breathing. She had a lovely, refined face.

How ironic that, of all people, he should have saved the granddaughter of the Earl of Keneagle, the Earl who'd cheated his mother's family of their fortune, impoverishing them and changing the course of their lives. His mother's life.

But what of the governess? Had she survived?

Lucien hoped so.

Morning dawned to clear skies. Lucien's arms ached from holding Lady Rebecca the whole night. She'd struggled against him, but never gained full consciousness. The night had been dangerously cold, but soon the sun would warm them.

Before it, too, became an enemy.

At least he had the piece of sail to shade her.

She seemed to be merely sleeping now. She'd been lovely enough in her travelling finery when he'd encountered her in the companionway, but she looked more appealing to him now, with curls gone and her expression vulnerable. Was she the lady with the lovely laugh? It could have been the woman with her, the governess. He hoped her running back to find someone else had saved her. He could not have held on to them both.

He glanced away. He'd never been tempted by aristocratic ladies, those few he'd encountered. They seemed shallow and silly, too eager for pleasure and too ignorant of how the rest of the world lived. He'd seen privation and could never forget how wretched life could be. As a boy, he'd heard the story over and over, how the Earl of Keneagle had impoverished his mother's family. How his mother had lost the chance to marry a title. How she'd had to settle instead for his father, a mere captain in the navy, like Lucien was now. Even though his father had risen in rank and had provided well enough for her, his mother preferred the company of the local Viscount when his father was away at sea—which he'd been for months, even years, at a time.

Lucien had grown up feeling a responsibility to his Irish relatives. They had been the reason he'd sailed to Ireland, to provide financial help to his uncles, who struggled to make ends meet. Lucien could afford to help them. He'd squirrelled away almost all of his prize money over the last twenty years. Thank God it was safe in Coutts Bank in London and not at the bottom of the Irish Sea.

Like he and Lady Rebecca might be if the sea claimed them.

His lids grew heavy and the rocking of their makeshift raft lulled him.

'No!' Lady Rebecca pushed against him. 'No!'

Fully awake now, he tightened his grip on her. 'Be still,' he ordered. 'Do not move.'

Her lovely eyes flew open. 'What? Where am I?'

'You are safe, my lady.' She would panic, certainly. He kept her restrained. 'But we are on the open sea.'

'On the sea?' Her voice rose in confusion and she struggled. 'No! Let me go!'

'I cannot. Not until you are still.' He forced his voice to sound calm. 'You are safe if you remain still.'

The waves bobbed them up and down and slapped water on to the raft. The canvas covering them fell away and Lucien blinked against the blazing sun.

Her head swivelled around and her voice became more alarmed. 'No! Why am I here?'

'Do you remember?' he asked. 'We were on the packet from Dublin to Holyhead. There was a storm—'

She raised a hand to her head. 'I was on a packet ship? Where is it now?'

He didn't want to tell her it had probably crashed into the rocks and that some people would not have survived. 'We were swept away from it.'

'But someone will find us, won't they?' she asked. 'Someone will be looking for us?'

More likely they'd think they'd perished. 'Many ships cross the Irish Sea. Chances are good we'll be rescued.' Chances were at least as good as finding a needle in a haystack.

She scanned the horizon again as if a ship might magically appear.

'I don't remember being on a ship,' she finally said accusingly.

Perhaps that was a godsend. 'Best not to remember.'

She looked at him with hysteria in her eyes. 'You do not understand. I don't remember the ship. I don't remember anything.'

'You suffered a blow to the head. It happens some-times to have difficulty remembering.' Or perhaps it was the trauma itself, of the storm, of being swept into the sea. He'd heard stories of soldiers in battle forgetting where they were. No one had suffered a similar affliction on his ship, though, and they'd been through plenty of trauma. 'Try not to worry over it, my lady,' he reassured.

She peered at him. 'Why do you keep calling me "my lady"?'

He gaped at her. 'I was told you are Lady Rebecca Pierce. Was I misinformed?'

'Lady Rebecca Pierce,' she repeated in a whisper. Her voice rose. 'Is that who I am?'

He searched her face. Her distress seemed genuine. 'You do not remember your name?'

'I do not remember anything!' she cried. 'My name. Why I am here. Why I was on a ship. Why you are here.'

None of that mattered at the moment. They were in a battle with the elements. If the wind stirred the sea again, they might be tossed off this makeshift raft. If they could not shield themselves, the sun could burn their skin. And if they survived today, would they survive another cold night? They had no food, no water. How long could they last without water?

But he did not tell her any of that. He held her closer. 'Try not to fret. It will not help. It is important to stay as calm as you can.'

She leaned against him and turned quiet again. He knew she must be cold so held her closely.

After a time she spoke. 'Do I know you?'

'We met briefly on the ship. I am Captain Lucien Roper. No reason for you to know me.' Except that her family had ruined his mother's family, but what use was it to tell her that? 'I am bound for London.' Or will be if they survive.

She stirred a little. 'I wonder where I am bound.'

* * *

Claire pressed her cheek against his warm chest. She was cold and her head ached and her situation terrified her. She was adrift on the sea with a stranger, a man who stirred some unsettled emotion inside her, an emotion she could not name.

Was she to die in the arms of a man she did not know, without even knowing her own name? Her past?

Was she Lady Rebecca Pierce, as he'd said? The name meant nothing to her, but then, her mind was a blank when she tried to think of something, anything, about herself.

There was only this man. His chest was firm and warm and his manner confident and able. He'd covered their heads with the canvas again, but she could glimpse the sea from beneath it. The vast empty sea.

The sun's reflection on the water hurt her eyes, but when she closed them the rocking of their raft seemed even more pronounced.

Would they die here? she wanted to ask him. But that was one question the answer of which she feared the most.

Had other people died? Had there been someone on the ship she knew? Someone dear to her? She tried to conjure up a feeling of attachment to someone, anyone, but there was only this man. Only he seemed real.

Maybe he knew. 'Was I with anyone on this ship?'

He hesitated before answering. 'I saw you with another woman. She was in the cabin with you.'

'Who was she?' A mother? A sister? Did she belong to anyone? If so, had they survived?

'I did not learn her name.' He sounded regretful about that.

'Was she related to me?' She wanted to belong somewhere, to someone.

'I do not think so,' he replied. 'She was dressed plainly

and I was told she was a governess. I never saw more than a glimpse of her.'

A governess? Was she connected to this governess in some way?

Was there anyone who cared for her? Who would search for her? All she could conjure up was a feeling of being alone. She lifted her arms, wanting to press her fingers against her temples. On one of her arms dangled a lovely but sodden red-velvet reticule.

She stared at it. 'Is this mine?'

'I remember now,' he said. 'The woman with you handed it to you as we left the ship.'

Who had she been? Why would she hand her a reticule?

Claire strained to remember, but nothing came.

She shook her head. 'What happened to her?'

'I do not know,' he replied. 'She hurried off to find someone else and we never saw her after that. We climbed up on deck.' He paused. 'Then the wave came.'

The wave that swept them into the sea? How could one forget such an event? How could she not know who'd sailed with her?

How could she not remember her own name?

She shivered and stared at the water. How easy it would be to slip beneath its surface and join the void, so like the void in her mind.

Lucien Roper tightened his arms around her again, stilling her trembling, reminding her that she *was* someone, even if she could not remember who.

And, no matter what, she wanted to live.

'Do you know anything about me?' she asked him.

He paused before answering. 'Very little. That you sailed from Dublin. Your name. That you are sister to the Earl of Keneagle.' His voice stiffened.

She did belong to someone! 'Do you know the Earl of Keneagle?'

He shifted his body a little. 'He is an Irish earl, that is all I know.'

'Then someone will look for me.' She relaxed against him again.

'These waters are well travelled,' he said.

He did not sound convincing.

The waves beneath them rocked them like a bumpy carriage ride and the air smelled of brine. Her skin itched from the salt. They'd lapsed into silence. Only the slapping of the water against their raft made a sound.

The emptiness was driving her mad. She needed memories, any memories.

Even his would do. 'Will you tell me about you, Lucien Roper?'

He stirred a little. 'I am in the navy.'

'The navy?' Keep talking, she wanted to beg. He was her only reality at the moment. He and some brother she could not remember. A governess who'd been her companion.

And probable death. 'What do you do in the navy?'

He shrugged. 'I am a captain.'

'Do you have a ship?' Captains had ships, she somehow knew.

His ship, his home, was likely scrap by now. 'Not at the moment. I'm bound for the Admiralty to be given a new ship.'

How could she know what the navy was and nothing about herself?

Maybe if he kept talking…

'Are—are you on half pay?' she asked.

Half pay, Lucien thought. She obviously knew what half pay was.

He nodded. 'Until I'm given a new ship.'

'You had a ship? What happened to it?' she asked.

'The war is over. The navy does not need so many ships.

It was sold.' He could not bear to tell her the *Foxfire* would be broken up. The ship had more life in her.

'How sad for you.' Her voice sounded genuinely sympathetic. 'What was the name of your ship?'

'The *Foxfire*.'

'A lovely name,' she remarked. 'What kind of ship was it?'

'She was a Banterer-class post ship with twenty-two guns.'

'How impressive sounding,' she said. 'I know nothing of ships—at least nothing I can remember—but I know of the war somehow. I know it is over. Is that not strange?'

Strange that she remembered some things and not others? 'I suppose it is.'

'I—I cannot remember anything to do with me.' She said this quietly, but he heard the pain of it in her words. She moved enough to look him in the face. 'Would you tell me more about you? About being in the navy, perhaps? I need to know that there is more than us drifting on this water. I need to know someone has memories.'

His heart resonated with her pain. The fact that they were drifting on these boards in the middle of the sea would be terrifying enough without amnesia on top of it. She might be a spoiled aristocratic lady, but at the moment she did not know even this. And, although he would not say it to her, she must realise they faced probable death.

If talking about himself would ease her anguish, he would talk about himself.

'My father is an admiral,' Lucien said. 'My grandfather was an admiral. I was always meant for the navy, as well. It is in my blood. And I've done well in it.'

'How long have you been in the navy?' she asked.

'Twenty-one years. Since age twelve. At fifteen I was in the Battle of the Nile. At twenty-two I was at Trafalgar and, since then, countless encounters with French, American and Danish ships. Mostly in the Adriatic Sea and the Mediterranean.'

'You did well in the war, then.' Her sympathy seemed genuine.

He gazed out to the horizon. 'I also sent good men to their deaths.' He closed his eyes and saw the carnage of battle. He saw his quartermaster blown apart. His midshipman, a mere youth, set afire. Why had these memories come and not the glory of capturing enemy vessels?

'Did you earn prize money.'

There it was. He should have known she would ask about his money. A man's monetary worth was of prime importance to aristocrats.

'I did well enough.' Good enough for him to retire, if he chose to—if they ever made it to shore again. Good enough for him to pay his uncles' debts and set them up more securely. They should have no financial worries now.

'And you will be given a new ship?'

'So I have been told.'

If they survived, that was.

As the day wore on, the sun warmed them as he'd expected. It dried the canvas and most of their clothes. Lucien scanned the horizon for ships, to no avail. Lady Rebecca remained calm, eerily calm, as if detached from the danger they were in and the suffering they would endure if rescue did not come soon. She must be as hungry and as powerfully thirsty as he was, but, unexpectedly, she did not complain. Instead, she asked more questions about his life and Lucien found himself telling her things he'd never shared with anyone.

Like being left to his own devices as a young boy in a village outside Liverpool. How his mother, in her loneliness when his father was at sea—which was most of the time—sought amusement elsewhere by pursuing the local

Viscount, who took his pleasure from her when the fancy took him. His mother was always too preoccupied by this love affair to bother much with a little boy or to make certain his nurses attended him. Lucien told her about how he'd been left to his own devices, sometimes to cope with situations he was too young to understand. His mother seemed happy when he was sent to sea.

He told her how his life changed after that. He'd loved the structure of rank and the discipline the navy required. Every man had his place and his duty and together they conquered the enemy and the sea itself. The sea, which so often was beautiful. A beautiful, if often treacherous, mistress.

Lucien shared with this woman what he'd never spoken of with anyone else. How he loved the sea.

He didn't tell her that he'd be happy to die at sea and be sent to his rest beneath its depths.

Not yet, though. He wanted to live. He wanted her to live.

The sky darkened as the sun dipped closer to the horizon. Lucien continued talking, recounting his experiences at sea and his ship's victories. He left off the close calls of horrific storms and the carnage of battle.

She listened and asked questions that showed some knowledge of naval matters, not entirely without memory of facts, at least.

He'd thought about telling her of the connection between their families, of how her grandfather had cheated his grandfather out of his property and fortune, but what good would that do? She had enough agony without him adding to it.

Her predicament almost made him forget his thirst, his hunger and the dire consequence of spending another night floating to nowhere.

He kept his eye on the horizon as he talked. His years at sea had given him sharp vision for which he was grateful.

Suddenly he saw a shape form in the distance. It sailed closer, but still too far to notice them, a mere speck in the vastness. He watched it, saying nothing to Lady Rebecca. Why spark an expectation that likely would never come to fruition?

He eventually could tell it was a two-masted ketch, a fishing boat, likely. And it looked as though it was sailing straight for them.

Lucien waited as the ketch sailed closer. Odds were still greatest that it would pass them by, but his heart beat faster.

He quickly tied the rope to the latch on the door that was their raft. 'Hold on to this,' he told her. 'And be still. There is a ship. I'm going to stand and try to signal it.'

'A ship?' Her voice rose.

In hope, he supposed. 'With luck they will see us.'

When she'd secured herself he carefully rose to his feet and waved the piece of sail that had sheltered them. He waved the canvas until his arms ached with the effort. From time to time the waves threatened to knock him off balance.

The ship came closer and closer. It still could miss them, though. Lucien knew how easily their small raft could be a mere speck, but he continued to wave the canvas.

When he could faintly hear voices from the ship, he shouted to them, 'Ahoy! Ahoy!'

Lady Rebecca added her voice to his.

Finally a voice from the ketch returned their call. 'Ahoy! Ahoy! We are coming.'

Lucien sat down and again put his arms around Lady Rebecca. 'They see us, my lady. We are rescued.'

Chapter Three

It took another hour for the ship to approach and lower a boat to row out to them, but Claire did not mind the wait. They were rescued.

Soon enough they were safe on board the ketch and greeted by a man who introduced himself as Captain Molloy.

Lucien immediately told the Captain, 'The lady needs water and food.'

Claire had not realised the strength of her thirst until Lucien mentioned it.

Lucien.

She could not think of him in more formal terms than his given name. He'd saved her life and he was the only person she had in her memory.

He kept an arm around her, though she thought she could walk on her own.

'We'll get you both below.' The Captain ushered them towards a hatch. 'What vessel are you from?'

'The *Dun Aengus*,' Lucien replied. 'Packet from Dublin to Holyhead.'

Captain Molloy walked them to his cabin, a tiny space, but one with a table, four chairs and a berth. Anything else in the room must have been stored behind the cabinet doors which lined the walls.

One of the men brought water. Claire nearly pulled the tin cup from the man's hands.

'Take small sips,' Lucien warned her. 'You'll want to keep it down.'

She nodded.

He watched her drink before taking any water himself.

'Can we find the lady some dry clothes?' Lucien asked the Captain.

Captain Molloy signalled to his man, who nodded and left. 'We've been out only a few days, so there should be enough clean clothes to be found.' He nodded to Lucien. 'For you as well?'

'I would be grateful.' He took another small sip of water. 'You are fishermen?'

'That we are,' the Captain said. 'We're after cod and haddock.'

Claire saw concern flash on to Lucien's face.

'I am afraid you will be with us for a bit.' The captain looked apologetic. 'We'll be at sea for three weeks at least.'

'Three weeks?' She gasped. It seemed so long a time.

But why was she concerned? She knew of no other place she must go, no other place she belonged. She might as well be at sea.

'My lady, you will have the use of my cabin.' Captain Molloy glanced over at Lucien. 'We'll find a place for you, as well.' He looked away and muttered, 'Although I cannot imagine where.'

Claire spoke up. 'I do not wish to trouble you so. Is there not room for Lucien here with me?'

She was not entirely selfless. She dreaded being alone with the emptiness in her mind. He was her one link to her previous life, the life she could not remember.

'I cannot stay here,' Lucien protested. 'Your reputation—'

'My reputation cannot matter here.' She turned to Captain Molloy. 'Can it, Captain? No one will speak of this, will they?'

The Captain answered eagerly. 'I'll see they don't.'

A muscle in Lucien's cheek tensed. 'As you wish.'

'Well, that is settled.' The Captain clapped his hands together. 'I need to return to my duties. Food and clothing will be brought to you shortly.'

'Thank you, Captain,' Claire said.

He bowed to her, a gesture of respect that seemed foreign to her.

After he left, she lifted her cup to sip more water, holding back from gulping the whole contents at once.

Lucien frowned. 'Are you certain about sharing the cabin, my lady?'

'They saved us, Lucien.' Was it not the least they could do in return? 'I cannot repay them by causing more discomfort.'

He nodded. Grudgingly, she thought.

The reticule still hung from her wrist. She untwisted its strings and slipped it off.

'Look inside,' he said. 'Its contents might tell you more about yourself. Spark a memory, perhaps.'

It looked as alien to her as this fishing boat cabin, but she loosened its strings and reached inside to pull out the contents.

A small purse filled with coin. A tortoiseshell comb. A white enamel etui painted with exquisite flowers and containing a tiny scissors, needles, pins and hairpins. A linen handkerchief with an embroidered edge and a monogram—R.P. Rebecca Pierce. The name that didn't seem like her name. The items that didn't seem like her possessions.

'Nothing looks like mine.' She trembled. 'It is as though I have never seen these things before.'

He moved closer.

If only he would hold her. She'd become accustomed to his arms around her.

Instead he crossed his arms over his chest. 'Too much has happened. Your memory will return in time.'

At the moment, he was her memory.

A few minutes later, one of the fishermen brought two tankards of ale and bread and cheese, which she ate slowly, as Lucien directed. When another man brought clothes, Claire looked down at herself. The lovely travelling dress she wore seemed as unfamiliar as the fishing boat. It had laces at the back.

She glanced over at Lucien. 'I fear I must ask for your help.' She turned her back to him.

He stood. 'You could not have undone this by yourself. Might you have been travelling with a maid?'

She turned her head to look at him over her shoulder. Her insides twisted in pain. 'Do you suppose I was?' She turned back. 'Did she die?'

Did someone who tended to her needs die and she did not even remember them?

His hand flattened against her shoulder and his voice softened. 'We survived. Others would have, too.'

'I cannot remember.' She also could not remember if another man had ever touched her so—so gently.

He loosened her laces and stepped back. 'You'll want me to leave. Give you some privacy.'

'No!' she cried, then felt guilty for it, but she had a dread of being alone. 'Just—just turn your back.'

He did as she asked and she slipped off the dress. But there were her stays. They tied in front, but she could not undo the knot.

'Lucien, I need more help.' She drew a ragged breath. 'My stays. The knot is too tight.'

He turned again and stepped towards her. His gaze was

downcast as he worked the knot, his gentle hands touching her even more intimately.

His touch was more quenching than the cup of water.

Her breath quickened and her breasts rose and fell. He was only inches from her.

He made quick work of her stays, though, and stepped back once more. 'I'll turn around again.'

She slipped out of her stays and removed the rest of her underclothes, aware she stood naked in the presence of a man.

Lucien clenched a fist, letting his fingers press into his flesh. Being so close to her in her undressed state had stirred him. The sounds of her removing her underclothes aroused his senses even more. He was only too aware of the vision she must present in her nakedness.

And of how it felt to touch her.

In the past twenty-four hours he'd rarely not been touching her, but his fingers brushing against her skin stirred him as a man, not a rescuer. It had been a long time since he'd been with a woman, true, but this situation certainly did not warrant such a response.

And she was the last sort of woman he needed to be aroused by—the aristocratic daughter of the family he'd been raised to despise. Besides, she was much too vulnerable for a gentleman to take advantage.

'I am dressed,' she said. 'You may turn around now.'

He turned. She'd donned the loose shirt and breeches the fishermen wore and held the rough knitted stockings that covered their legs and feet.

'I must remove my half-boots, but I'm well covered now.' She sat in one of the chairs.

For the first time he noticed her half-boots. Something about them… They looked worn, not at all what he would have expected her to wear.

She removed one and held it up. 'I have no memory of these.' She shrugged and set the shoe aside. 'You must change now, as well. I promise not to look.'

He smiled. 'Will you help me if I cannot undo my buttons?'

She coloured. The flush on her cheeks only made her more lovely.

Lowering her gaze, she said, 'Of course I will, if you need me.'

He coughed. 'It was a jest, my lady.'

She turned her chair away from him and quickly donned the stockings. He continued to watch as she then busied herself taking pins from her hair, most of which had already fallen to her shoulders in tangles. It was remarkable that any pins remained. She took the comb from her reticule and started working on her hair, one strand at a time.

Lucien forced his eyes away and changed into the clothes the fishermen provided.

He hung their old clothing and her reticule on pegs on the wall and joined her at the table.

She looked over at him and smiled. 'These clothes are remarkably comfortable, although I feel a bit as if I am in my nightdress.' Her face fell. 'How is it I remember how a nightdress feels and I do not remember owning one?'

He had no answers for her. 'When we are back on land you can consult a physician.'

Her eyes widened. 'I would fear he'd send me to Bedlam.'

Such a worry was not unfounded, but surely her family would not allow such a thing. *He'd* not allow it.

'We are likely to be on this boat for three weeks,' she said after a time. 'Is that not what the Captain said?'

'It is,' he responded. 'We must make the best of it.'

Her expression turned determined. 'I am glad of it. I am certain I can manage such a small world.'

'And, who knows?' he added. 'Perhaps your memory will return by then.'

She detangled her hair strand by strand and it calmed Lucien to watch her. When done, she put her hair in a plait.

She held the end of her plait in her fingers. 'I suppose it will only come loose again without a ribbon.'

Lucien rose and picked up the neckcloth he'd taken off. He cut the edge with the knife they'd used to slice the cheese and ripped a long strip.

He handed it to her. 'This should work.'

'But you've ruined your neckcloth.' She reached for it.

He laughed. 'I'd say the sea ruined it already.'

She wound it around the end of her plait and tied the ends with a bow.

They finished the rest of the bread and cheese and soon Lady Rebecca's eyelids closed and her chin dipped on to her chest.

She jolted awake.

'You must go to bed.' Lucien rose and helped her to the Captain's berth.

She curled up beneath the blanket, her eyes blinking in an effort to stay awake.

'Sleep now,' he murmured.

She seized his hand. 'Where will you sleep, Lucien? There is only one berth.'

He tried again. 'I should not sleep in this cabin with you, my lady. It is not proper.'

'I do not care.' She gripped harder. 'To tell the truth, I am a little afraid to be alone.'

She looked very afraid.

'Very well,' he said. 'I'll make a bed for myself on the floor.'

Lucien waited until she was sound asleep before gathering their dishes and slipping out the door. He found the galley and the Captain, who again said how pleased he was that he did not have to squeeze his men any more than merely finding another berth for himself. The fishermen managed to give Lucien another blanket and he returned to the Captain's cabin.

She still slept.

Dead tired himself, Lucien formed a hammock of sorts with the blanket. As soon as he was settled in it, he, too, fell asleep.

He was awoken by Lady Rebecca's cries. The room was pitch black.

'No! No! Stay away! Stay away!' She thrashed around in the berth.

He made his way to her in the darkness and held her arms to still her. 'Wake up. You are having a dream.'

Her thrashing stopped and she threw her arms around his neck. 'Lucien! I was being chased and then I was in the water and you were too far away to reach me.'

He unwrapped her arms from around his neck. 'Only a dream.'

She kept hold of his hand. 'Yes. A dream. I am awake now.'

'Who chased you?' Someone from her past? This was hardly the sort of memory he wished returned to her.

'I do not know. It was as if the blackness pursued me.' She trembled. 'I am quite recovered now.'

He remained at her side. 'Are you certain?'

'Oh, yes,' she said, but her hand trembled.

The nightmare was still with her then. 'I'll sit beside you for a while,' he told her.

Her hand seemed small and vulnerable in his larger one.

In the darkness he heard her murmur, 'Everything was black, then all I could see was you.'

He sat with her until her hand relaxed and her breathing came soft and rhythmic.

* * *

When Claire woke the next morning, Lucien was gone. She sat up quickly, her heart pounding.

She was alone!

But she remembered where she was—on a fishing boat—and she remembered Lucien.

She remembered, too, that he'd woken her from that terrible nightmare and remained beside her in the narrow berth. She also remembered how she'd thrown her arms around him.

Her cheeks burned.

Although she could not remember who she was or anything about her past, she knew with certainty that it was shameful of her to embrace a man like that. Even if he had been a perfect gentleman.

Perhaps she was wanton. Could that be? Could it be she'd already compromised herself and that was why she'd felt no hesitation to insist he share the room with her? She might be a lady, but was it possible she was anything but ladylike?

She glanced down at herself and realised the fisherman's clothes she wore had come loose of her makeshift belt. Standing, she straightened her clothing, but the breeches seemed ready to fall down at any moment. She remembered the etui from the reticule—she could not think of it as *her* etui or *her* reticule. She found it hanging from a peg. She took the pins from the etui and used them to fit the breeches to her body.

The door opened.

It was Lucien. 'I have brought you some breakfast.'

He'd brought a steaming bowl of porridge and a mug of warm cider. How kind of him.

'Thank you, Lucien.'

Her appetite was hardy. Was she always a big eater? Scenting the porridge, she remembered how it tasted—but she could not remember a time she ate porridge.

She felt Lucien's gaze upon her as she ate.

She swallowed a spoonful and looked up at him. 'I am sorry I woke you last night.'

He paused before speaking. 'How do you fare this morning?'

She laughed lightly. 'I wish I could say I feel quite myself this morning, but I do not know who myself is. I do feel rested, though.'

He nodded.

'And you, Lucien,' she asked. 'Are you well?'

He waved off her question. 'Very well.' He leaned forward. 'Rest today, if you need to, but I want to assist the fishermen. There are only five of them, including Captain Molloy. I am certain they can make use of me.'

She had not expected him to help catch fish, not a captain in the navy. How good of him. Did he always consider others, perhaps even over himself? How could she be selfish enough to insist he stay with her?

Just because she was afraid to be alone.

'I do understand.' She took a nervous breath. 'I will amuse myself somehow.' She managed a smile.

His eyes pierced into hers. 'I will check on you, my lady. Or make certain someone else does.'

She lifted her chin and nodded, hoping she looked braver than she felt.

Lucien had expected her to complain and demand he remain with her. It was clear that she did not want to be alone. But she had not. And why had she insisted he stay in the cabin with her? If it became known, it would certainly ruin her in her aristocratic circles. Was it her memory loss? Did she not remember how important reputation was for an earl's daughter?

Spending the night in the same room posed a different problem for Lucien. The intimacy of sleeping near her fuelled fantasies of sharing her bed, of tasting her lips, of feeling her naked skin next to his. He would never seduce her, though, would he? It would be taking advantage of her in the most reprehensible way.

Over the years he'd met many high-born men who'd boasted about conquests, usually leaving the lives of lower-born, but respectable, young women in tatters. Even Lucien's mother had been an easy conquest for Viscount Waverland.

Not that she'd been anything less than willing.

In any event, Lucien had no patience for aristocrats who called themselves gentlemen and behaved like rutting animals around any woman dazzled by their status.

And he refused to sink to their level.

He watched her finish her porridge. He could at least keep her company that long.

'Do you know about fishing, Lucien?' she asked between spoonsful.

He gave a dry laugh. 'Very little. But there must be something I can do.'

She blinked up at him. Her eyes were a remarkable mix of brown circled by green. 'You could captain the ship, could you not?'

'I could, but this boat has a captain.' Although if he had taken over from the Captain of the *Dun Aengus*, perhaps the ship would not have foundered.

There was no reason to doubt the Captain of this vessel, though. He and his crew depended upon the sea for their livelihood.

'I know nothing of fishing,' Lady Rebecca said. 'They use nets, do they not?'

He smiled. 'Yes, they do, so you do know something of fishing.'

She lowered her gaze to her bowl and carefully scooped out another spoonful. She lifted it to her mouth.

Lucien looked away. Her lips had become a distraction, one he could not resist for long. He glanced back.

Her expression sobered. 'I cannot understand why I know so many things, but I do not know anything about me.'

'Take heart in that,' Lucien replied. 'If you remember those things, then surely your memory of yourself will return.'

She took another spoonful of porridge. He looked away again.

'I am becoming accustomed to not knowing.' She averted her head for a moment before turning and looking directly into his eyes. 'It is as if my life started on the raft when I woke.'

He reached over and put his hand on hers. 'I believe you will recover your memory.'

She merely continued to stare into his face.

He withdrew his hand and stood. 'I should go on deck.'

A look of panic flitted across her face, but she quickly forced a smile. 'Yes. I believe I will see if our old clothing needs mending. I think I remember how to use a needle and thread.'

Lucien was surprised that her first idea was to do something so useful. 'I will come back to check on you, as I said.'

He turned to leave, but Lady Rebecca stopped him. 'Wait a moment, Lucien.'

Just when he thought she would not become demanding.

She gave him a determined look. 'I—I wish you would not call me "my lady" or "Lady Rebecca." It simply does not feel right to me.'

He stood at the door. 'That is who you are.'

'What I mean is, I am not formal with you. I call you Lucien. I realise I never asked if I could call you Lucien. Is it offensive to you? Should I call you Captain Roper?'

Her use of his given name could be meant as condescending, but, if truth be told, he rather liked the sound of his name on her lips.

'Call me what you wish,' he responded.

'Then will you call me something less formal as well?'

His brow furrowed. 'I think not.'

Her head turned as if she were flinching from a blow. 'I see.'

'Lady Rebecca.' The name did not rest easy on his tongue. 'It is better if I preserve the formalities.' It helped him keep his distance. And keep his hands off her.

She seemed to force another smile. 'Of course. If that is what you want.'

Chapter Four

That first day Lucien did indeed check on her when he could and he was surprised that she worked so diligently at mending their clothes. She even found a brush and tried to brush away the salt and seaweed that clung to the cloth.

When finished she held up her dress and his coat to show him. 'They still look like they've been in a ship-wreck.' She sighed.

'At least they can be worn,' he responded.

She'd done an excellent job.

On the second day Lucien felt badly about leaving her with nothing to do.

'I will find something,' she assured him.

At mid-morning he looked up from his toil to see she'd ventured on to the deck.

She sought out Captain Molloy. 'What might I do to help?' she asked him.

'You wish to help, m'lady?' The Captain laughed. 'We will find you something.'

He soon had her carrying water to the men and serving food in the galley.

But at the end of the day when she had swabbed the deck, cleaning off the fish parts that littered the boards,

Lucien approached her. 'You are not required to work.' He frowned. What lady swabbed up fish guts? 'Especially tasks like this one.'

She stopped mopping and faced him. 'I like helping. I like being a part of it all.'

And she quickly became a part of it all, as if she were another crew member, not a lady. The others began to depend on her. Seeing her on deck became familiar. At night they both slept soundly, fatigued from the labour of the day.

Claire relished the days at work. The ship became her world, a world that remained in her memory as did the men's faces and names. It was as if her world—and her mind—was complete.

At the centre was always Lucien. It was his presence that made her secure, like an anchor secured a boat. As the days wore on, his face became shadowed with a beard making him look as swarthy as a pirate. The Captain and the other men wore beards as well, though none as dark and dashing as Lucien's.

She watched him help haul in the nets and load the fish into the hold. She silently prayed for his safety when he climbed the tall mast to untangle the rigging.

At night the blackness of the cabin reminded her, though, that most of her life she could not remember. It helped that Lucien was near. He stirred within her a yearning she did not quite understand, a desire to feel the strength of his arms around her, the warmth of his breath, the beating of his heart, as she had on the raft.

Some of her dreams were of him, of his bare skin against her bare skin and his lips against hers. What did it mean that she dreamt so? It made her blush to think of it.

Of being so intimate with him.

Other dreams were no more than jumbled images that

slipped from her mind by morning. She much preferred the days of toil and people she recalled from day to day.

By the third week, the boat's hold was filled with fish and the Captain set sail to Ireland, a place she knew about, but of which she had no memory. The wind would carry them to port this very day.

She donned her mended dress with Lucien's help and folded the clothes the fishermen had lent her. 'I will miss these,' she said to Lucien. 'They are ever so much more comfortable than wearing this dress and stays.'

He smiled. 'I'm glad to be out of mine.'

His were soiled and smelled of fish and sweat.

She took his borrowed clothes from his hand and folded them with the others. No doubt some fisherman's wife would be laundering them soon.

She tied the ribbon around her plait and remembered how he'd torn it from his neckcloth for her. How nice it was to have memories.

She felt tears sting her eyes. 'I will miss this boat.' She blinked them away. 'I suppose because it is so familiar now. I do not know what happens next.'

He gazed at her, sympathy in his eyes. 'You've endured a shipwreck and three weeks on a fishing boat; you will be up to whatever comes next.'

She was not so certain. 'You are right. I must buck up, mustn't I?'

She would not tell him what she feared even more than the unknown was losing him, but she'd been enough of a burden to him already. He had a life to pursue, a new ship, plans he'd talked about with her, this next phase in his life.

From above them they heard a voice cry, 'Land, ho!'

His face appeared strained. 'We should go up on deck.'

She nodded and picked up the reticule that seemed to be her only possession.

They made their way to the deck and stood at the railing. A narrow line on the horizon slowly formed into land.

'Where will we sail into?' Claire's heart beat faster. Would she remember anything once they landed?

'Bray,' he responded.

'A fishing village, is it not?'

'You know it?' His brows rose.

She gazed at the land, now rising green. 'I know of it, but I do not know why.'

She had asked him many things about his life over the last three weeks, because, of course, she knew nothing of her own life, but she'd never asked him what would happen when they reached shore. That was as black to her as the night, as black as her past. As long as they were on the boat she'd been content to avoid the topic.

'You will travel to London, I expect. For your new ship.' She watched the shore coming ever closer, not daring to look at him for fear she'd crumble. 'Will you catch another packet from Dublin?'

He would leave her and be as distant and unattainable as her past.

He paused before answering. 'I will see you safe to your brother, first.'

She swallowed. 'No, Lucien. I have troubled you enough. I am certain I can manage.' Somehow.

'I will see you safe to your brother,' Lucien repeated. 'I'll not leave you on your own.'

Lucien had no desire to meet the present Earl of Keneagle, but he could not simply leave Lady Rebecca to fend for herself. True, she could mail her own letter to her brother and arrange her own transportation to his estate, but how difficult would it be for her to not even know if a man standing before her was her brother or someone else?

'We will travel together to Dublin and contact your brother from there,' he said to her. 'I will be able to draw funds from the bank there as well.' He'd dealt with a Dublin bank to transfer funds to his uncles. 'We should be able to purchase whatever we need, as well.'

She lifted her reticule. 'I have some money. Perhaps I have other funds to repay you.'

He shook his head. 'I am well able to afford whatever we need.' What else did he need his money for?

He leaned his arms on the railing.

'We are getting closer to land,' she said in a shaky voice.

Soon enough the ketch was moored at a dock and they were saying goodbye to Captain Molloy and his men. To Lucien's surprise, Lady Rebecca hugged each man who, after three weeks, like him, was rather reeking of sweat and fish.

Captain Molloy pointed. 'Walk to the top of that street and you'll find the inn. My cousin runs the place, Niall Molloy, so give him my name and he will see to your needs.'

Lucien shook the Captain's hand. 'We owe you a great debt of gratitude.'

The man looked abashed. 'Aw, 'twas nothing. You more than earned your keep. The lady, too, poor *bhean*.'

Still, Captain Molloy and his men would each receive a generous gift from Lucien as soon as it could be arranged.

He climbed off the boat and on to the dock, turning back to help Rebecca disembark. She jumped the gap and landed in his arms. She felt too good in his arms.

She found her footing and turned back to say a final goodbye.

He offered his arm. 'Your legs may take time to get used to land.'

'I will miss the crew.' She allowed him to steady her as they walked away from the dock up the street.

On the small boat, they were rarely not in someone's company.

'At least you will have a room of your own in the inn,' Lucien reassured her.

She sighed. 'It will seem strange after the fishing boat.'

They found the inn and entered its public rooms, seeking out the innkeeper who was serving ale to several men seated at tables.

'Niall Molloy?' Lucien asked.

'That I am,' he answered.

'We are off your cousin's boat,' Lucien told him. 'Rescued at sea from the wreck of the *Dun Aengus*.'

The man's bushy red eyebrows rose. 'From the *Dun Aengus*? We heard news of it. Finn picked you up? Is that not a jest? My cousin. Imagine. How long before Finn rescued you?'

'The second day,' Lucien replied.

'I imagine that was time enough.' He wiped his hands.

Lady Rebecca broke in. 'Can you tell us about the shipwreck. Did—did many die?'

The innkeeper lowered his head. 'All but a handful, reports say. Maybe a dozen survived, as I recall it.' He smiled. 'A dozen plus the two of you.'

Her face pinched in pain.

'Well, sad it is, but the sea giveth and the sea taketh away.' He clapped his hands together. 'You need a room? What else may I do for you?'

'Two rooms,' Lucien said. 'But, for now, a good meal.'

The man laughed. 'Finn's food not the best, eh? I guarantee we will show him up.'

He gestured for them to sit at a table separate from the

other diners and quickly served them large tankards of ale and mutton stew.

The other men seated there did not hide their curious glances.

'Am I not presentable?' Rebecca asked. 'They keep looking at me.'

Lucien turned and glared at the other patrons and they quickly averted their gazes. 'Presentable enough. They probably are not accustomed to seeing a lady here.'

She looked up, her eyes questioning. 'Should I not be here, then? If I do not belong here?'

He must remember that much would be new to her. 'You can certainly be here.'

'Good,' she said. 'Because I am happy to be eating so well.'

So well? Compared to the last three weeks, perhaps, but surely this food was as beneath her as the simple fare on the fishing boat.

She dipped her spoon into her stew and lowered her eyes. 'They are staring again.'

He shrugged. 'More likely, then, it is your beauty that attracts them.'

Her eyes flew up and were filled with anxiety. 'My beauty?'

'You are a beauty,' he said. 'Did you not know that?'

She blushed. 'I—I have not seen a mirror since—since the shipwreck. I do not know what I look like.' She dropped her spoon and lifted her hands to her face.

The innkeeper entered the room. 'Stop acting the maggot, fellas. Leave the lady alone.'

'No harm in lookin',' one of the men grumbled.

'Yeah?' the innkeeper said. 'I'll give ye a knuckle supper if ye do not stop.'

Rebecca lowered her gaze again. 'I am causing commotion.'

Her distress disarmed him. 'It is mere banter. Do not pay it any mind.'

Lucien tore off a piece of bread and dipped it in the stew. She took careful spoonfuls, as if made self-conscious for being an object of attention.

It had never occurred to him that she would not know what she looked like. Was it possible she had no memory of her appearance?

She placed her spoon on the table and folded her hands in her lap.

He put down his piece of bread. 'Would you like to see your room now?'

She'd want to be away from the staring eyes. Or where she could look in a mirror.

She set her chin determinedly. 'Yes.'

He called the innkeeper over.

'My wife will take you to the rooms,' the innkeeper said.

A kindly faced woman with hair as red as her husband's met them in the hall. 'I am Mrs Molloy, I am. My husband told me you were in a shipwreck and Finn saved you. Finn is a good man.'

'A very good man, ma'am,' Lucien agreed.

She took them up a flight of stairs to two rooms side by side. She opened the doors to both of them and gave them the keys.

Claire noticed right away there was a mirror above a bureau.

'Shall I come and help you undress when the time comes?' Mrs Molloy asked.

Claire forced her gaze away from the mirror. 'That would be very kind.'

'Anything else we can do for you?' the woman asked.

Claire responded. 'I can think of nothing—'

Lucien interrupted her. 'Baths? May we arrange baths?'

Mrs Molloy smiled. 'To be sure you'll be wanting baths after what you've been through. Would you want your clothes laundered, as well?'

'I am not certain they are salvageable,' Lucien said.

'We'll just have to find you something else to wear, won't we?' She patted his arm and left.

Claire could not take her eyes off the mirror, but she hesitated.

Lucien took her by the arm. 'Delay never helps.' He walked her over to the mirror and stood her directly in front of it.

His grip gave her courage. She lifted her head and looked in the mirror.

'What do you see?' he asked.

She laughed in relief. 'I see me! I feared I would see a stranger, but I look like me. Same brown hair, same eyes, same nose that is unfashionable, same lips. I look like me.'

Was she a beauty? If so, she disliked the stares of men.

Except for Lucien. That he thought her beautiful made her feel warm all over.

His reflection was behind hers, his expression unreadable. He was so very handsome. Tall, broad-shouldered, hair and beard dark as the night, eyes as brown and alert as a fox's.

Alert as a fox's. Where had that thought come from? She inhaled a quick breath. Had she remembered him?

She opened her mouth to tell him she might have had a memory, but shut it again. How could she explain it was all about him?

Instead she turned to face him. 'Brilliant of you to ask for baths, Lucien. A bath will seem like heaven.'

She remembered how pleasant it was to lie in a warm bath, to rub soap against her skin and to feel clean again.

She just could not remember a time or place before this when she'd taken a bath.

* * *

The bath was in a room close to the kitchen, so the hauling of water would not be too onerous for the maids and the water would remain hot. Lucien allowed Lady Rebecca to go first and he went in search of Mr Molloy, mostly to distract himself from thinking of her naked in the tub, stroking her skin with soap.

'Molloy,' he said, finding him back in the public rooms. 'I need your assistance. We have nothing. Where can I purchase necessities?' He had some coins that had remained in his pockets, sufficient to buy what they needed.

'You'll be wanting Brady's store.' The innkeeper directed him to the place.

He purchased a razor and comb for himself, toothbrushes for them both, a hairbrush and hairpins for Rebecca. And ribbons.

Mrs Molloy made good her promise to find them clothes.

By the time the sun had set, the last vestiges of the sea were washed away and clean clothes replaced ones ruined by salt water.

'It feels wonderful,' Rebecca said. 'I wonder if I have ever had a bath that felt as glorious or clothes that felt as good against my skin.'

He could agree. He was glad to be rid of his beard and the only clothes that would feel more right to him would be his uniform.

They returned to the public rooms to dine. The rooms were more crowded than before, with both men and women sharing food and drink, but the people were warm and welcoming. Their story of surviving the shipwreck had spread and they spent the meal answering questions about the event.

Lady Rebecca, so at ease among these simple villagers,

surprised him at every turn. When had he known any aristocratic lady like her? Even his mother, who merely aspired to the aristocracy, looked down her nose at those she perceived as inferior. Of course, Lady Rebecca did not remember being of high birth. That must explain it.

They were treated to endless tankards of ale and the inn's brew was particularly hoppy and refreshing. All the voices in the room grew louder as the night wore on, but Lucien could hear Rebecca's laugh above the din.

A lovely sound, one he remembered from the packet. So she had been the lady with the captivating laugh. She swayed and caught herself by leaning against a table.

Lucien came to her side. 'It is time to retire, my lady.'

She nodded with a grateful look and coloured with the hum of approval that followed in their wake.

'I feel so unsteady,' she said as they entered the hall and started up the stairs.

'It is the ale.' He kept a firm hold on her.

'It was quite delicious ale, was it not?' She reached for the banister. 'I wonder if I liked ale before, because I quite like it now.'

'I noticed, my lady.'

She stopped on the stairs. 'It feels so odd for you to call me "my lady."'

'Because you do not remember,' he said.

'I do not like it.' She leaned against him and tipped her head up to look him in the face. 'It makes me different from everyone else.'

'That is not so bad a thing,' he reassured.

'I suppose I am different.' She kept staring into his eyes. 'I have no memory.'

'Even so, you have done well in every situation you've encountered,' he told her.

'Have I?' She smiled and swayed closer to him, tantalisingly close.

He took a bracing breath and eased her away. 'It is time you were abed.'

Her eyes widened and her lips parted.

God help him.

He clasped her arm. 'Come.'

After a few steps, she leaned against him again, but he managed to walk her to her room without taking her in his arms and pressing his lips against hers.

He took her key and opened the door. 'I'll send Mrs Molloy to assist you.'

She put her arms around him and pulled him inside the room. 'You could assist me, Lucien. Like before.'

His head dipped down and she reached up and brushed her lips against his.

God help him.

Before he lost all control, he gripped her upper arms and eased her away. 'No.'

She put her hands to her temples. 'Did I just kiss you? Forgive me, Lucien. I cannot imagine why I acted that way. I am not so scandalous, I would hope.'

'You merely had too much ale.' That did not explain his desire, though.

'Perhaps I *am* scandalous.' She sat on the bed. 'Then it would do no harm for me to kiss you again, would it?' She half-reclined on the bed, resting on her elbows.

Was she trifling with him now? He'd once been propositioned by a countess looking for a new plaything. He'd easily turned down that woman. It was proving more difficult to resist Lady Rebecca.

'Perhaps you are virtuous,' he countered, 'and need to preserve your reputation.'

She sat up. 'You are correct, of course.' Her enticing hazel eyes looked up at him, shining like exotic jewels.

He turned and walked to the doorway. 'I will send for Mrs Molloy.'

'Goodnight, Lucien.' Her voice was low and soft, stirring him even more.

He managed only a nod before closing the door. He needed a barrier between them this night.

Chapter Five

When Claire woke the next day her head ached and she wished there was one memory she could banish from her mind. She'd acted like a brazen trollop with Lucien. Goodness! She'd wanted him to kiss her and hold her and spend the whole night in her bed. She still could feel his breath against her lips and the warmth of his touch.

Surely that was brazen? Was she truly such a woman?

She tried again to remember something about herself that could answer that question.

There was nothing.

Lucien hired a carriage to take them to Dublin. Claire felt almost as grief-stricken saying goodbye to the Molloys as she'd felt leaving the fishermen. Captain Molloy, his cousin, Mrs Molloy, the fishermen and the others at the inn were the people in her life, the only ones, except for Lucien. Now she was headed to a city she did not remember to eventually reunite with a brother who was a complete stranger to her.

After the buildings of Bray receded into the distance and she'd wrestled her emotions into some sort of order, she became aware of how close Lucien was seated next to her and of how comfortable it was for her to be beside him. She did not want to face saying goodbye to him, but that would come soon enough.

Lucien was everything to her. She, on the other hand, was merely an obstacle to his returning to London and back to the life at sea he so loved.

She must take care and never let it slip that she wanted him to stay with her longer.

She looked out the window at the countryside rolling past. Had she seen it before?

She did not know.

Their journey would take half the day and so far Lucien had said little to her. Of course, she, as well, only spoke to him when absolutely necessary. What could she say? That she regretted trying to seduce him? Or that she regretted not succeeding? Perhaps she should say she was sorry to be such a burden.

After changing horses one last time and taking some refreshment at the coaching inn, they finally reached the bustling streets of Dublin.

'I wonder if I will remember anything here,' she murmured, more to herself than to him.

'Perhaps something will spark a memory,' he responded.

She studied the scenes passing by her window. 'Nothing I see is a surprise.' Not the wagons or carriages or riders or people walking. 'I simply cannot remember another time I saw such things.'

His eyes looked sympathetic and she felt a pang of guilt.

'I do not mean to sound as if I am complaining,' she explained. 'What is important is that I am alive. I owe that to you.'

He averted his gaze. 'And the fishing boat.'

'And the fishing boat,' she agreed.

The carriage pulled up to a large red-brick town house. 'We are here,' Lucien said.

A footman emerged from the building and opened the carriage door. Lucien climbed out and turned to help her disembark, then he reached in and picked up the two small parcels that contained their meagre belongings.

They wore the clothes that the Molloys had found for them. The clothes they wore in the shipwreck were gone. The footman looked them up and down with haughty contempt, no doubt due to those plain clothes of a simple fishing villager.

'Your luggage?' the footman said with a sneer.

'We have none.' Lucien turned to the coachman and paid him out of some coins he took from his pocket.

The man grinned. 'I thank you, sir!'

Lucien then straightened and glared at the footman with an expression that would make any man quake. 'We require two rooms and I am well able to pay.'

The footman nodded curtly. 'Follow me.'

They entered a large hall with marble floors covered in part with a brightly hued floral carpet that looked like it came from the looms at Axminster.

Axminster? Somehow she knew such carpets were made at Axminster. That was not a memory, though. It was knowledge.

Along the walls were pale green sofas and tables with brass embellishments. It was all quite opulent and Claire had the sense she'd never seen anything go grand.

But that was not a memory, was it? More like an absence of memory.

There also was an impressive mahogany desk and a finely dressed man rising from its chair.

Lucien strode over to him. 'Mr Castle.'

The man peered at him for a moment before gasping. 'Captain Roper? You are returned.' He continued to look puzzled.

'Unexpectedly,' Lucien replied. 'Forgive our simple clothing.' He turned to Claire. 'Lady Rebecca, let me present Mr Castle, the hotel owner. I stayed here when previously in Dublin.'

Before the shipwreck, he meant.

'Mr Castle.' Claire curtsied.

Lucien turned back to Mr Castle. 'This is Lady Rebecca Pierce, the Earl of Keneagle's sister. We will need two rooms, Mr Castle. And a great deal more.'

Mr Castle's gaze darted between them. 'Your luggage?'

Lucien was quick to reply. 'We have none. Our ship to England foundered. We survived, but lost everything.'

'Foundered?' Mr Castle turned to her, an expression of sympathy on his face. 'Oh, my. Were you on the *Dun Aengus*? We heard it wrecked. What a terrible ordeal. The hotel will assist you in any way we are able.'

'We are most in need of clothing.' Lucien gestured to the plain brown, ill-fitting coat he wore.

'I will make enquiries as to how we might attire you quickly.' Mr Castle took keys from a drawer in his desk.

'That would be so kind of you,' Claire said.

Mr Castle smiled and signalled to the footman to escort them to their rooms on the second floor.

Their rooms were again next to each other. Lucien would not be so far away.

He stood in her doorway. 'I will leave you here to rest. There is time for me to visit the bank.'

Her stomach fluttered.

How silly to have nerves simply because he was leaving her alone. This was not some wilderness—or the open sea—but a respectable hotel.

She could try to do something useful. 'Perhaps I should write to my brother. There is bound to be pen and ink somewhere.' She began opening drawers until finding the one with paper, pen and ink. 'What should I say? I don't have his direction.' She gave a dry laugh. 'Or his given name. He will think me odd to call him Lord Keneagle.'

He remained in the doorway.

She turned to him and made herself smile. 'But you must go.'

He hesitated longer before finally speaking. 'I will write to your brother, if you like.'

'Would you?' Her muscles relaxed. And she hadn't realised she'd been tense. She caught herself, though. 'I cannot ask you to do so much for me.'

'I offered.' He shrugged. 'I will write it before I go to the bank and have it sent by messenger.'

Lucien returned to his room and opened the desk there, removing a pen, ink and paper.

It made sense for him to write the letter, even if it was to the descendent of the man who'd created the genesis of his mother's unhappiness.

Perhaps his own, as well.

Neither he nor Lady Rebecca had anything to do with that event, however. They'd not even been born. It was his mother who'd kept the angry fires burning all these years.

He uncapped the ink and dipped the quill into it. As concisely as he could, he described the shipwreck, Lady Rebecca's amnesia and their whereabouts in the weeks since.

The Earl would send for her, Lucien was certain. Would he send someone to accompany her? Without a memory it would be hard for her to travel alone. Perhaps Lucien would be compelled to go with her and see the estate that had reaped the benefits of his family's financial demise.

He finished the letter and wrote its direction on the envelope.

Leaving his room, he made his way back to Mr Castle's desk. 'There is something you can do for me, Mr Castle.'

'I am at your service.' The man smiled.

He handed Castle the letter. 'Send this by messenger. To the Earl of Keneagle. Make certain it reaches his hands.'

Mr Castle took the letter. 'It will be done.'

Lucien left the hotel and walked the two miles to Number Two College Green, the Bank of Ireland.

The clerk he had dealt with before greeted him with the same level of surprise Mr Castle had shown. 'Captain Roper? I thought you were already in England.'

Lucien repeated the story of the shipwreck, explaining his duty to see the Earl of Keneagle's sister back safely to her family. He did not mention her amnesia.

'I need access to funds,' Lucien explained. 'All was lost in the shipwreck.'

As well as seeking funds for his own use, he arranged for generous rewards to be sent to Captain Molloy and his fishermen. And to Molloy's cousin and his wife as well. When everything was settled, he returned to the hotel.

When he entered the hall, Mr Castle called him over.

'I hired a messenger for you. He has started the journey.' He handed Lucien a piece of paper. 'And I procured the name and direction of a second-hand shop that sells clothing that should meet your standards. I can arrange a hackney coach to take you there today, if you like.'

They desperately needed clothes. What Lady Rebecca wore now was serviceable, but certainly inappropriate for an earl's daughter.

'I am very grateful, Mr Castle,' Lucien responded. 'I will ask the lady what she wishes and have your answer directly.'

He hurried up the stairs and knocked on her door.

She opened it. 'Lucien. You are back.'

Had she expected he would leave her alone all day? 'Mr Castle has found a shop where we might purchase clothing second-hand. We can go there right now, if you desire it.'

* * *

Claire did not mind the clothing she wore. The dress fit her well enough, even though it was nothing like the dress she had worn during the shipwreck. That dress must have once been very elegant. It would be expected of her to wear fine clothing, she suspected.

'I will get my hat.'

Claire donned the bonnet Mrs Molloy had given her and returned to the hall with Lucien.

'I sent a messenger with the letter to your brother,' he told her as they waited for the hackney coach. 'He should receive it tomorrow.'

That gave her a whirlwind of nerves and no pleasure. Meeting her brother and losing Lucien.

'I do appreciate that, Lucien.' Although she felt disingenuous saying so.

'And I have arranged ample funds,' he added. 'We can purchase whatever we need.'

She lowered her gaze. 'You must let me repay you.'

He shook his head. 'I said before. No need.'

But there must be some way to repay him.

When they entered the shop, a male clerk greeted Lucien by name. 'Captain Roper? Mr Castle said to expect you today or tomorrow. What may we show you?' Obviously Mr Castle had provided his name when he arranged the visit.

'We need everything,' Lucien said.

A female clerk took Claire in hand, while Lucien went with the man.

'You were in a shipwreck, we were told, my lady,' the woman said. 'How very frightening for you.'

Perhaps she was lucky not to remember it. 'Yes. But we were saved.'

'Well.' The clerk pressed her hands together. 'We shall

have to find you a new wardrobe. You will see, of course, that all our garments are clean and mended.'

The items were, indeed, almost like new, but Claire had no idea what to select. She feared the cost as well. These appeared to have been very expensive dresses.

The clerk suggested she at least purchase two of everything. Two shifts. Petticoats. Stays. Stockings. Another pair of walking boots and two pairs of slippers. Another nightdress to add to the one Mrs Molloy had given her. A robe to wear over it. A shawl. A cloak. The list seemed staggering.

After nearly an hour she'd selected the other necessities, but still had not settled on dresses or hats. She loved the finest dresses, much like the one she'd been wearing when she woke up on the raft, but her eye kept being drawn to more sensible, simple, nondescript designs.

She chose one to try on and stood before a mirror.

Her image looked as she expected. It also made her sad, but why she could not say. There was nothing wrong with the dress. It was very…serviceable.

'My lady, are you certain you want such a dress? It is so drab.' The clerk pointed to two other gowns draped over a chair. 'There are so many other prettier ones.'

'I am trying to be practical.' But the other dresses were lovely.

'I will ask your gentleman what he thinks.' The clerk left the room before Claire could stop her and explain that Lucien was not *her gentleman*.

Claire turned to the mirror again and frowned. The dress *was* drab.

Lucien entered through the curtain behind her. 'You need me?'

He was attired in a tolerably well-fitting deep blue coat with a matching waistcoat, grey trousers that hugged his thighs and brown leather Hessian boots that covered his calves. His neckcloth was as bright white as the shirt beneath.

He took away her breath.

She swallowed and finally could speak. 'I am uncertain what to choose.'

His gaze swept over her. 'Not that one, certainly.'

She felt her cheeks flush.

The clerk stepped forward. 'I would suggest these.'

She showed him the dresses draped over the chair and brought out some others.

Claire tried on dress after dress, watching the admiration in Lucien's eyes when she donned the prettiest ones. His opinion as to what she was to select was the most important criteria. All the dresses were beautiful to her.

She twirled around in an evening dress of pink silk with an overdress of white gauze trimmed in lace.

'This seems too extravagant, Lucien,' she said, although she yearned to wear such a lovely gown.

'We do not know how much of your wardrobe was on the ship,' he responded. 'You need clothes. Enough to cover any situation.'

But so many at once? It would cost a fortune!

In the end he bought her two day dresses—one a gossamer white muslin with embroidery on the bodice and hem, the other a sprigged muslin with a matching green spencer—two travelling dresses—one dark blue silk with gold stripes, the other, a patterned dark green silk—and the beautiful evening dress. In addition to the essentials she'd already selected, he added slippers to match the dresses, hats, gloves, even reticules.

The clothing needed only minor alterations. 'I will send the seamstress to you at the hotel tomorrow,' the clerk said. 'Every dress will be perfect.'

Claire had entered the shop dressed as a tavern maid. To

leave, she wore the dark blue travelling dress and the new half-boots, with a lovely bonnet and gloves to match. While Lucien made the final arrangements to have the clothing packed in portmanteaux and delivered to the hotel, Claire took a final glance at her image in the mirror.

This dress and the others were probably out of fashion, having made it to the second-hand shop, but she thought every piece was exquisite.

Had she once worn such elegant clothes? If so, why did she feel so strange in them? Was it because of all the weeks dressed so comfortably as a fisherman, then as a tavern maid?

She loved the feel of the fine fabric against her skin and she'd felt beautiful when Lucien looked at her approvingly.

She could not remember feeling beautiful before.

Lucien glanced at her, looking at herself in the mirror, so pleased with these clothes that were some wealthy aristocrat's cast-offs. Surely she'd once been accustomed to the latest fashion in finery.

Her face was flushed with colour and her eyes sparkled. She even carried herself differently. More regally. She was exceptionally lovely, even more so than when he'd glimpsed her on the packet ship, when her complexion had not been brightened by the sun and when she had been so carefully coifed. And confident. Now she was unconscious of her allure. And of her status. Little did she know a woman of her station would scorn purchasing clothes at a second-hand shop rather than delight in the experience.

Her pleasure was disarming, though. As was her concern about being too extravagant. His prize money was more than he could imagine ever spending. It caused him no sacrifice to enable her to look presentable as she re-entered her former life.

Perhaps such clothing would help her remember who she was.

And that she belonged in a world that valued a title over character, where one married to improve one's status, a higher title, more lofty connections. He disdained such shallow pretensions. He would shun such a world even if its door opened to him.

Lucien completed the transactions and approached her. 'The shop will send someone to deliver the purchases.

Her eyes shone. 'Thank you, Lucien. I assume I wore pretty clothes before, but I do not remember them. Surely they could not have been as pretty. I love all you purchased for me. I am very grateful.'

'You look well in them.'

The colour heightened in her cheeks, making her look even more beautiful.

She thanked the clerks and took Lucien's arm, walking with him to the door of the shop and a waiting hackney coach.

When they reached the hotel, the same footman who had met them with such disdain earlier in the day now showed them every respect.

'He does not look at us with contempt this time,' he murmured to Rebecca. 'Because now we are dressed the part.'

'I suppose one is always judged by appearances,' she responded. 'I would like to think I would not judge so precipitously, but I suppose I am like everyone else.'

Except she wasn't like everyone else, at least not everyone else in her class. She'd accepted the fishermen, the innkeepers and the villagers just as they were.

Because she could not remember to disdain them?

They ate dinner in the hotel dining room, the first formal meal they'd eaten together. Lucien noticed that men at other tables stole admiring glances at her, perhaps a bit more subtly than the men in Molloy's inn had done. She seemed oblivious of the fact this time.

They chatted throughout the meal about the day's events and their unusual adventures.

'I wonder how our fishermen are doing,' she said, taking a sip of wine. 'I miss them all. I hope they received good money for the fish.'

They'd soon receive good money from Lucien. 'I hope so.'

She glanced away. 'Think what would have happened if they had not found us.'

The sea would have claimed them.

He did not want her to dwell on that. 'Luck was with us.'

She lifted her wine glass. 'To luck—and fishermen.'

He lifted his glass as well.

When dinner was over they walked back to their rooms.

'There will be a maid coming in to tend to you,' he told her.

She smiled. 'I promise I will not ask you to do it this time.'

The memory of that night flooded back. 'We did what we had to do. But it is over now and life should feel more like it should.'

She sighed. 'If I knew what it should feel like.'

They reached her door and she handed him the key. He unlocked the door and opened it. Better he escape to his own room. Resist temptation.

She stepped across the threshold, but turned back to him. 'Do you mind if I do something?'

He had no idea what she had in mind.

She did not wait for an answer, but stepped back to him. Her arms encircled his neck and he bent down to her.

'Thank you, Lucien,' she murmured. 'My rescuer. My modiste.'

She placed her lips on his.

Lucien's body flared into arousal. How easy it would be to lift her in his arms, carry her to her bed and make love to her.

Was that her wish? It was hardly the behaviour of a proper lady. Had she forgotten what was expected of a lady of her status?

She broke off the kiss and stepped away. 'I—I am so grateful to you. That is all. That is why—' She blinked. 'That is why I kissed you.'

He nodded slowly. It had not felt like a kiss of gratitude, but was that his fault? Was that because it aroused him?

'Will I see you in the morning?' Her tone was uncertain.

'For breakfast?' he asked. 'I rise early.'

She smiled. 'It would be nice to share breakfast, unless you have more errands.'

He ought to put more distance between them, but, at the moment, he was fighting to keep his hands off her.

'No errands,' he responded. 'Breakfast, then.'

Lucien left her, but did not go to his own room. He walked back downstairs to ask the footman attending the hall to have a bottle of brandy sent up to his room.

Claire leaned against the closed door, covering her face with her hands.

She'd done it again. Kissed him.

She'd meant the kiss as one of gratitude, just as she'd told him, but touching him, feeling his lips on hers, had enflamed her senses. She did not wish to feel this way towards Lucien. She esteemed him too greatly.

He'd been everything to her.

Was this the sort of woman she was? It must be, because

it seemed so natural to her, much more natural than donning pretty dresses.

But she must have always worn pretty dresses.

A knock at the door made her jump. Had Lucien come back? Her heart beat faster.

She opened the door to a young woman. The maid.

'You asked for a maid, my lady?' the young woman said.

'Yes. Yes. Come in.' Claire stepped aside, trying not to show her disappointment.

She'd wanted it to be Lucien.

Chapter Six

The next morning when Lucien knocked on Lady Rebecca's door, a maid answered. From behind the maid, the lady said, 'I am ready, Lucien.' She addressed the maid. 'Thank you, Ella.'

'M'lady.' The maid curtsied and stepped past Lucien out of the room.

Lady Rebecca wore another of her new dresses, a white one with dots of green all over it. Her hair was not pinned into a knot at the nape of her neck. Instead it had been piled atop her head with curling tendrils escaping and framing her face.

For a moment her expression turned sad, but she quickly seemed to school her features into the very picture of an aristocratic young lady—a beautiful one.

It was his turn to feel sad. He missed the girl in the fisherman's clothes.

Not that he would tell her. 'You look very nice today.'

She turned back to the mirror. 'Do I? The dress is pretty, but my hair looks wrong. Too fancy.'

'It looks as it should,' he responded, not much of a compliment, but she glanced away as if not even hearing him.

They ate breakfast in the dining room, where a sideboard had been set up, much as was done in aristocratic houses. Not that he'd been in many.

She continued to look preoccupied during their meal.

'Are you feeling unwell?' he asked.

'Unwell?' She glanced up in surprise. 'No. I am very well.' She smiled wanly. 'Troubled by what is ahead of me, perhaps.'

How he wished he could fix it. Bring back her memories, even though he'd lose this version of Lady Rebecca.

'It looks to be fine day,' he said. 'Would you like to take a walk? Explore Dublin a little?'

Her smile turned more genuine. 'I would love that.'

Lucien knew from his previous stay at the Castle Hotel that this part of Dublin catered to the titled and wealthy. If Lady Rebecca had ever visited Dublin—it would be odd if she had not—she likely would have walked these same streets. Perhaps something would jog her memory.

She gave no signs of recognising anything, though. Just the opposite—she reacted as if everything was new.

They stopped to look in the window of a print shop, showing cartoons, one of the Prince Regent, before and after he became Regent, another of several people trying to board a ship.

Lady Rebecca pointed to the one of the Prince Regent. 'I know that is the Regent and I understand the cartoon. It is so odd I cannot actually recall another time I saw a caricature.'

He did not call attention to the one about a ship. It made him think of the shipwreck. She had enough to cause her distress.

There were more prints of Dr. Syntax, that popular fictional character who appeared in cartoons satirising British life.

She frowned at the one of Dr Syntax trying to romance a dairy maid. 'I know of Dr Syntax, as well.'

'Perhaps that is encouraging.' He believed her memory

would return. She'd eventually remember she was an earl's daughter, a privileged lady.

She shivered. 'It is cold for summer, is it not?'

It was August.

'The whole summer has been unusually cold,' he agreed.

His uncles had worried about failed crops and rising prices. At least the money he'd given them would keep them in food and supplies until better weather returned.

They continued walking and he resisted putting his arm around her to warm her.

One of the shops showed a window display of paisley shawls and other ladies' accessories. He pulled her to the doorway. 'You need a shawl.'

She resisted. 'Lucien! You have bought me enough! You purchased one shawl.'

'You need another.' What woman did not want more than one shawl? Even his mother had loved the exotic shawls and other gifts his father had sent from faraway lands.

Almost as much as she'd valued the trinkets Viscount Waverland had purchased for her.

There were colourful shawls displayed on pegs all around the shop. She blinked at them, looking overwhelmed.

'Do you see any you like?' he asked.

Before she could answer, a female clerk approached. 'M'lady, welcome back to my shop. How may I assist you?'

Lady Rebecca blinked as if in confusion.

The clerk recognised her. Did she not realise that?

Lucien quickly spoke for her. 'The lady is looking for a shawl, something to complement this dress.' He turned to her. 'Is that not so, my lady?'

'Yes. Yes.' She cleared her throat. 'To complement this dress.'

'I have several that would look lovely with that dress.' The clerk pulled five shawls, all with designs that favoured her green spencer and the green dots on her dress.

She made a quick decision. 'This one will do.'

Its background colour was green, but the rest was embroidered with a melee of colourful flowers in pinks and purples and vivid aquas and oranges.

'An excellent choice,' the clerk said. 'This shawl is from Kashmir and is one of our finest. I believe you purchased one very like it the last time you visited. Different colours, of course.'

Lucien saw the confusion return to Lady Rebecca's eyes.

'We will take that one,' he told the clerk.

'Shall I wrap it?' the clerk asked. 'Or have it delivered?'

'She will wear it.' Lucien pulled his purse from his jacket pocket.

The clerk turned to Lady Rebecca as she waited for Lucien to pay her. 'And how did you find London, m'lady?'

'London?' Her voice rose. 'Oh…very pleasant indeed. London is very pleasant.'

Lucien handed the clerk the money.

'It was a short trip, then, was it not?' the clerk added.

'Very short,' Lucien replied for Lady Rebecca.

He wrapped the shawl over her shoulders and they walked out of the door.

'Lucien!' She stopped him a few steps from the shop. 'She recognised me. I was in that shop before. I purchased something before.'

'Was the shop familiar? Was anything familiar?'

Her expression looked anguished. 'No. Nothing. As though I'd never seen it before.'

Over the next three days, they walked as many streets of Dublin as they could and visited any sights she might have visited before.

Nothing seemed familiar to Claire. The closest she came was when they happened upon a coaching inn. She knew at a glimpse that it catered to public stagecoaches and the mail coaches, but how she should know that, they could not fathom.

'It is not the sort of inn you would visit,' Lucien told her.

'Is it not?' she asked. 'Why is it not the sort I would visit?'

'It is for more common folk.'

So perhaps she'd merely guessed that it was that sort of inn. She didn't remember it, but neither did she remember not being common folk.

Their efforts to discover something she remembered had been to no avail that day, but Claire relished the time they spent together. She was glad he did not purchase anything else for her. Goodness! The Kashmir shawl was extravagant enough.

Had he meant the shawl as a gift or had he merely felt obligated to outfit her as the lady she was supposed to be? Perhaps she would never know which, but she was certain she would treasure the shawl the rest of her days.

They explored yet one more street of shops.

This time he stopped in front of a jewellery shop. 'That is what we forgot,' he said. 'You should have jewellery.'

'No, Lucien.' She tried to pull him past the shop. He'd spent enough on her.

He resisted. 'It will look odd if you have no jewellery at all. It does not need to be extravagant.'

'Please, Lucien,' she said. 'You cannot spend so much on me.'

'I can make one more purchase.' He took her inside.

Glittering necklaces, bracelets and rings were arrayed on black velvet in glass-covered display cases.

She must have looked awed, because Lucien murmured to her, 'Surely as the daughter of an earl you wore such jewels.'

'I feel as if I wouldn't dare wear such expensive things,' she responded.

'We will select something modest, then.' He picked out a simple pearl pendant and matching earrings. They were quite the loveliest things.

Before they left the shop, he fastened the pendant around her neck, his fingers against her skin sending a thrill down her spine.

The thought of him touching her ears to help her with the earrings made her feel giddy. And she'd been so careful over the last few days to keep from overstepping her bounds with him.

'I—I think I should carry the earrings safely in my reticule,' she said.

She fingered the pearl pendant that she would treasure for ever. The pearls, gifts from the sea, would remind her of him for ever.

It was mid-afternoon when they returned to the Castle Hotel. Mr Castle was seated at his desk, but he rose when he saw them.

'Captain. M'lady.' He called them over. 'There is a gentleman waiting for you in the drawing room.'

Lucien halted. 'Who?'

'Lord Keneagle,' Mr Castle replied.

Claire's heart pounded. This was the moment she'd dreaded. This brother she did not remember had probably come to take her away to a home she could not recall. Worse than that, this meant saying goodbye to Lucien, her anchor.

Lucien walked with her to the drawing-room door, but stopped her before they entered. 'Are you ready for this?'

She drew in a long breath and nodded, although she thought she could never be ready.

A thin, russet-haired, impeccably dressed gentleman rose from a sofa.

'Lord Keneagle?' Lucien asked.

The man gave him no heed, instead strode up to Claire. 'What are you about this time, Rebecca?' he sneered.

'Sir!' Lucien's voice broke in like a hard blow.

Her brother looked stricken for a moment, but collected himself quickly. 'And you are Roper, I presume?'

'*Captain* Roper.' Lucien straightened. 'If you received my letter, you know what happened to your sister.'

'My half-sister,' Keneagle corrected.

Claire stared at this man—she was nearly his height— but she was staring at a stranger. She'd feared meeting a brother—*half*-brother—she didn't know, but she'd also yearned to know she belonged to somebody. She never expected he'd not be pleased to see her. What sort of man would not welcome his sister—even his half-sister— presumed lost at sea?

'Explain yourself, Rebecca,' he demanded.

She faced him. 'You know I cannot explain myself. I am certain Captain Roper wrote about my loss of memory in his letter. It has been a nightmare. It does have some benefits, I am newly discovering.' She looked him directly in the eye. 'I do not remember you.'

Her insult seemed to escape him. 'Do not give me that nonsense about losing your memory—'

Lucien stepped closer and Keneagle shot him a wary glance, turning back to her with a slightly more moderate tone. 'You can see how I would think it your latest ploy, can you not? To escape doing what I've obliged you to do?'

'What you've obliged me to do?' she repeated.

He shook his head. 'You pretend not to know what I speak of?'

'As I explained to you in my letter, sir, her loss of memory is genuine,' Lucien stated icily.

Keneagle swung back to him with a sneer. 'I thought you were a captain, not a *physician*.'

Lucien glared directly into his eyes. 'Captain of the HMS *Foxfire*.'

Keneagle stepped back in apparent surprise. 'The renowned *Foxfire*? From the war?'

'The same.'

Claire wished she could have remembered reading of Lucien's ship. She'd had no idea he was renowned.

Her brother recovered his nasty tone. 'Precisely what is your connection to this woman?'

Claire responded this time. 'He saved me. I would have drowned otherwise!'

Keneagle scoffed. 'I was informed you had drowned. It was vastly more convenient that way.'

Lucien made a dangerous sound. Like a growl.

Keneagle's rant continued. 'For all I know this shipwreck story is to cover up cohabiting with this man—'

'Good God, man,' Lucien broke in. 'How dare you make such an accusation? I have accompanied Lady Rebecca to see her safely to you.'

Keneagle lifted his hands in submission. 'I meant only that if her reputation is ruined, Stonecroft will never marry her.'

'Stonecroft?' Claire cried. 'Who is Stonecroft?'

She was expected to marry this Stonecroft? How could she? She remembered nothing of this. Of that man.

Her half-brother laughed drily. 'Very well. I will play your game. Baron Stonecroft of Gillford. He was awaiting you in London. I was compelled to inform him of your death. You will be very lucky if he has not married someone else.'

None of this made any sense to her. None of it. 'I agreed to marry Baron Stonecroft?'

Surely she would remember a man she had agreed to marry. Would that not be the most important decision a woman could make in her life?

Keneagle peered at her, his expression turning shrewd. 'Of course you agreed to marry Stonecroft. Why otherwise would you have been on the packet to England?' He darted Lucien a scathing look. 'If this man has ruined you, tell me now. Otherwise, I will post a letter to Stonecroft this very day and inform him you are alive. We can only hope he will still accept you after this debacle.'

How dare this man accuse Lucien when Lucien had been completely responsible for saving her life?

Her temperature rose. 'I assure you Captain Roper has been honourable. My virtue is intact.' She was the one who'd lacked propriety.

Lucien's eyes blazed at Keneagle. 'Stop these accusations. Now.'

Keneagle shrugged. 'What I believe is of no consequence. You had better hope Stonecroft believes your story.'

Lucien broke in, his voice firm. 'Enough. So you will write to Stonecroft. Will you wait in Dublin or in the country?'

Keneagle's brows rose. 'I am not waiting.' He reached into a pocket and pulled out a purse, shoving it towards Claire. 'This should pay the way to London for you and the maid.'

The maid? 'What maid?' she asked.

He rolled his eyes. 'Oh, yes. You would have *forgotten* her, as you say.' He shoved the purse at her.

She froze. 'Did—did she accompany me?' Her heart pounded again. 'What happened to her?'

Her half-brother huffed. 'Well, we never heard from her.'

'She drowned,' Claire whispered, her insides twisting in pain.

She'd had a maid who likely drowned in the packet ship and she could not even remember her.

Keneagle pulled the purse back. 'You won't need all that money, then.'

Lucien reached out and took the purse from his hand. 'She will need all of this money and more. Everything she'd packed was lost.'

Keneagle opened his mouth as if to protest, but Lucien's expression brooked no argument.

'Oh, very well,' her brother said. 'I will arrange for a money draft in her name.'

'See that you do.' Lucien glared at the man. 'What of her dowry?'

'Dowry?' she cried. She had a dowry?

She'd never thought about it, but certainly, as the daughter of an earl, she'd have a dowry.

Keneagle finally spoke. 'I will write to the solicitors. Stonecroft will expect a dowry. I'll see he gets it. Assuming you do marry him.' He glanced around the room. 'Customarily I stay at Castle Hotel when in Dublin. Much easier than opening the town house, but this time I prefer the house.'

Her family had a Dublin town house? Had they walked past it in the last couple of days?

Her brother ran a hand through his hair and turned to a table containing his hat and gloves. He picked them up.

He was leaving?

After this meeting, if she never saw him again, she'd be glad of it.

Keneagle pointed to the purse. 'You make this work with Stonecroft, because the draft I send you and this purse are all the funds you will receive from me.' He made a mocking bow to her and a more respectful one to Lucien. 'Good day.'

Claire's emotions swirled inside her. Anger at her brother's ill treatment of her and of Lucien. Shock that he so easily washed his hands of her. Anxiety at the prospect of marrying a man she could not remember.

And, worst of all, grief for the maid who had probably

died in the shipwreck. The poor maid who, if it had not been for the need to accompany her to London, would never have been on that ship.

It all was too painful to think about.

Lucien stared at the door through which her brother had departed. 'What a cursed cur.'

He tried to quiet his rage at Keneagle. The damned man showed no caring of his sister, no compassion for her situation. The man had no honour. No honour at all. He was precisely like the stories Lucien's mother told of his grandfather.

The Earls of Keneagle must be bred to be miscreants, caring for no one but themselves. Was that Lady Rebecca's true character, equally as self-centred? He descended into gloom, as if such a transformation had already come to pass.

No matter. She'd already endured much tribulation and now, thanks to her brother, her situation had become even more difficult.

'Am I to travel to London. To be married?' She said this more to herself than to him.

Still, the words *to be married* echoed in his mind.

A marriage of an Irish earl's daughter to an English baron was probably not the best match in the eyes of society. Why this man? Why not one of the highest rank?

She sighed. 'At least I will not have to share a house with the Earl of Keneagle.'

Lucien seethed at the mere thought of the man. 'He came a hair's breadth from being challenged to a duel.'

'I almost wish you had,' she murmured. She seemed to gird herself. 'So I must travel to London to this Lord Stonecroft, this man I am supposed to marry.'

At least it was an aristocratic marriage. That was as it should be for her. When she recovered her memory, an aristocratic marriage would be the sort she would desire.

Among the aristocrats, love and true regard were less necessary than status and dowries and what other aristocrats thought.

'Well, I suppose I must make arrangements.' She lifted up the purse, heavy with coin. 'At least I have funds. Perhaps even enough to repay you.'

'Keep your money,' he said too sharply.

She turned her head away.

He'd not meant to snap. God knew he needed to calm down.

He quieted his voice. 'You might need it.'

She kept her gaze averted.

Suddenly he felt her pain. She'd thought she would be taken back to a place where she belonged, one she might some day remember. Now she was facing more unknowns. Quite alone.

His heart ached for her. 'I will escort you to London. If you desire it, that is.'

She turned back to him, her eyes glistening. 'Are you certain, Lucien? I have been such a burden to you.'

He was caught for a moment in those hazel eyes. They'd turned green against her green spencer and the Kashmir shawl. And they glistened with tears. He admired her for trying to put on a brave front.

'I must travel to London anyway,' he responded. Although in that moment he would have done anything for her. 'So it is no burden to escort you. Mr Castle will take care of all the arrangements.'

She lowered her gaze. 'Lucien, you are too good to me.'

They walked out to the hall and Mr Castle called them over. 'There is someone else to see you.' He indicated a man dressed more as a merchant than a gentleman.

The man approached. 'Lady Rebecca, Captain Roper, I am from the *Dublin Journal*. Might I have a few moments of your time to interview you about your ordeal?'

Lucien frowned. What next? 'How did you hear of us?'

The man turned stoic. 'I cannot say who told me of you. He asked not to be revealed.'

Someone from the hotel? Or the second-hand shop. Or the bank. His bet was on the hotel's footman, the man who'd scorned them on their arrival because of their clothing.

Lucien turned to Lady Rebecca. 'Do you wish to speak to a reporter?'

'I already have the story,' the man told them. 'I know you were both passengers on the *Dun Aengus* and when the ship sank, you were reported lost at sea. Instead a fishing boat picked you up and you were forced to wait until the fishing was over before coming to Dublin.' He looked sly. 'The story needs embellishment. It might as well be with the truth.'

Lucien took Lady Rebecca by the arm and led her a short distance away. 'I will send him packing if you desire it.'

She shook her head. 'He will only invent something to write. The truth is better.'

Lucien walked back to the reporter. 'We will speak with you.'

They returned to the drawing room where the man pulled out a notebook and pencil. 'Tell me how you survived the shipwreck,' he began.

Lucien related the tale, ending with their arrival in Dublin.

The reporter turned to Lady Rebecca. 'How was it for a lady such as yourself, to endure such hardships?'

'I was so grateful to be alive.' She spoke fondly of the fishermen and everyone who helped them. 'I would not be alive if not for Captain Roper. You know who he is, of course. The Captain of the famous *Foxfire*.'

Lucien wished she had not mentioned that. It would only bring more attention to the story.

The reporter asked for more details about their stay on the fishing boat and they both obliged him with a more respectable version of their stay than the truth.

'And you are still together?' the reporter asked, clearly wanting more details.

'Lady Rebecca is a lady alone,' Lucien replied. 'As a gentleman I must see her to where she belongs.'

'So you will take her back to Keneagle House?' the man asked.

'To London,' Lucien responded. 'We were both headed to London before the shipwreck.'

That was enough for the reporter to know.

He didn't need to know about Lady Rebecca's amnesia. Or how despicably her half-brother had just behaved towards her. Or how close Lucien had come to doing precisely what her brother had accused him of.

Chapter Seven

Mr Castle had booked them passage on a packet ship that was leaving in two days. He'd also arranged for Ella, the maid who'd attended her at the hotel, to attend her on the trip.

How nice it was to have the services of a maid, but each time Ella untied her laces, Claire remembered when Lucien had done so.

How tender he had been. In everything.

So opposite to the thoughtlessness and cruelty of her brother.

Her brother's letter to Stonecroft would probably arrive a day or two before they reached London. Stonecroft would know she was alive and he would be told she'd show up on his doorstep. Would she be welcome?

How would it be to see this man without remembering him from before? Had she loved him? Was that the reason she'd agreed to marry him? If so, would she still love him even though she couldn't remember him?

How could she forget a man she loved?

How could she marry a man she could not remember?

What was the use of agonising over this? What other choice did she have? She must marry him.

Unless he refused her, that was.

What would she do if Stonecroft, like her half-brother,

believed her ruined merely because Lucien rescued her? What if it became known she and Lucien had shared a cabin on the fishing boat?

Her head ached with these thoughts that had swirled around her mind throughout the two days until the carriage picked them up at the hotel to take them to the packet boat.

The carriage left them off at the dock which was a jumble of sailors, passengers and wagons filled with boxes and barrels and chests.

The maid had gone ahead in another carriage and would meet them at the packet ship with their luggage.

Claire took Lucien's arm to navigate the commotion at the docks. The rough seamen they passed reminded her of the fishermen. How she wished they were both back on the fishing boat with them. She'd been happy on the fishing boat.

She gazed at the bustle on the dock to the ship they were to board. She must have been here once before, but she could not remember it.

Ella, the maid, waited at the gangplank, a young man at her side.

The young man removed his hat.

Ella curtsied.

Ella and the young man were together, Claire realised, and the exact opposite in looks. Ella was fair with almost white-blonde hair and light blue eyes. The young man was black-haired, dark-eyed and swarthy.

Ella spoke. 'M'lady, sir, your luggage is on board.' She glanced nervously at the young man. 'This is Cullen. Rory Cullen. My—my friend. We have something to ask of you. I pray you'll hear him out.'

'Cullen.' Lucien nodded kindly. 'What do you have to ask us?'

The young man straightened. 'I wish to go with Ella.' He spoke with determination. 'I offer my services as your valet, sir, for the time of the trip or as long as you will have me. I ask only for passage over and I will repay that as soon as I am able.'

'We want to stay in England,' Ella added. 'There are good jobs there and Cullen is a hard worker. He will do well.'

Claire heard the yearning in the voices of the young couple. They wished to be together, not separated by the Irish Sea. She turned to Lucien, ready to plead their case, ready to pay for the young man herself, if necessary.

'You may very well meet my needs, Cullen,' said Lucien. 'I have no valet.'

Both the maid and her young man broke into smiles.

'I have already ascertained that there is a berth for me, the cheapest, as well,' Cullen said.

'Only one thing—' Lucien said.

The young couple's smiles dropped.

'If you do work for me, then I must pay you.'

Their smiles returned.

Ella gave Cullen a worshipful look. 'It was Cullen who saw to your luggage. He knows exactly what to do in everything.'

'Then we are already indebted.' Lucien gestured with his arm. 'Shall we board?'

Claire smiled as well, infected by their happiness.

They boarded the ship and made their way to their cabins. Claire's cabin was near Lucien's. Ella and Cullen said theirs were not far.

Ella followed her into her cabin. 'Shall I unpack anything, m'lady?'

Claire shook her head. 'Not for one night.'

Her portmanteau was already in the cabin. Thanks to Lucien, she also had a small trunk with her other clothing stowed in the hold.

'I really do not need you now,' she said. 'Not until bed-time. Please do as you wish.'

Ella's eyes widened. 'Are you certain, m'lady?'

Claire stifled a smile. 'Yes. Do as you wish. I am going on deck. I like to watch the ship leave the harbour.' She felt a chill rush up her spine.

How did she know she liked to watch the ship leave the harbour? Had she remembered it?

She hurried up on deck.

Lucien stood at the railing near the stern of the ship.

She rushed over to him. 'I think I had a memory.'

He turned his entire attention on her. 'A memory? Of what?'

'Nothing of consequence.' It was a very small thing. 'I remembered that I like to watch the ship leave the dock.'

He smiled, but his eyes remained serious. 'Perhaps this is a start.'

'Yes.' But she suddenly did not feel any enthusiasm. She leaned against the railing and watched Dublin recede. 'But I do not precisely remember ever watching a ship leaving the dock.'

He gazed back at the dock, as well. It was still as busy as when they had been there.

'I remember you watching the ship sail. On the *Dun Aengus*,' he said. 'You stood at the railing, much like this. You jumped away when the sea sprayed you with water.'

She had no memory of this.

'You wore a grey cloak with a hood covering your head,' he went on. 'And I did not see your face until I met you again in the companionway.'

It warmed her that he had noticed her then.

She sighed. 'So it was almost a memory. I must have been on deck because I like to watch the ship leave the dock.'

'It very well could be,' he agreed.

Ella and Cullen emerged from the hatch and walked to the bow of the ship.

How ironic that they'd aim their sights on where the ship was headed, while she watched where it had been. They were filled with optimism for their future, whereas she could only look upon her future with dread. And she had no past at all.

Until she woke up in Lucien's arms on a raft in this very sea.

She scanned the sky. 'It looks like a clear day.'

Had the sky been clear when she'd stood on the deck of the *Dun Aengus*? she wondered. She closed her eyes and tried to remember. When had the storm started? Had she been frightened? Had all the passengers been frightened, even all those poor passengers who'd drowned?

'No storm clouds,' she added.

'This should be an easy crossing,' Lucien assured her. He had already examined the skies and the rigging and the ship's Captain and crew. He was taking no chances with this voyage.

She closed her eyes and they fell silent for a time.

She opened them again. 'I just tried to recall the other crossing. Or the storm. Or being swept overboard. I can't remember.' She shuddered. 'I only remember waking up on the water.'

That was terror enough, Lucien thought.

She turned and glanced at her maid and his new valet.

'Look at how happy they are!' She turned back to him. 'Thank you so much for agreeing to hire him.'

He shrugged. 'I had no desire to crush their hopes.'

'You saw what I saw, then?' she said. 'That they belonged to each other?'

'It was clear as a windless sea.' He even envied them a bit. A lot.

'I hope life will be kind to them,' she said wistfully.

Life had already been kind to them. They'd found each other and they had the foresight to know it would not do to be separated. 'They'll have the strength of being together.'

'But life could still be cruel to them,' she said.

'Having each other will make up for much.'

She gave him a quizzical look. 'I did not realise you possessed such romantic notions.'

He'd talked of this on the raft.

He frowned. 'I told you about my father and mother's loveless marriage and how his absence made her turn to the local lord.'

She nodded. 'I recall you telling me of your parents.'

He gestured towards Ella and Cullen. 'They are the antithesis of my parents. My father was wrong to marry my mother. He was gone most of the time and they were always like strangers. Absence is not good in a marriage.'

Her brows knitted. 'Surely navy men marry all the time.'

'I do not think they should,' he said emphatically. 'I will not marry, not as long as I have a ship to sail in.'

She spoke soberly. 'Perhaps your parents' marriage met their needs at the time. Your father wanted a son. Your mother needed security.'

'I have no doubt those needs were met.' But there was so much more to life than security and heirs. 'But they abandoned happiness.' And they abandoned him. He again directed his gaze at the maid and valet. 'Those two might achieve happiness.'

She turned quiet while she gazed back towards the shore, growing more and more distant.

It seemed a long time before she said anything. 'Different people have different needs, Lucien,' she finally said. 'You, at least, have a choice, a way to support yourself well. Most women, like your mother, do not have choices. Perhaps she did the best she could.'

He felt his cheeks heat. What choice did Lady Rebecca

have, besides going to this marriage she could not remember wanting?

She stared out at the sea. 'My choices are not good ones.' She straightened, pushing away from the railing. 'I must make the best of what fate has handed me, though. I must believe that I wanted to marry this man, so I must make the best of it.'

'You cannot love him.' He spoke his thoughts aloud.

'You would think I would remember a man I loved, do you not?' She turned to him and looked straight into his eyes. 'You are lucky, Lucien. You can choose the navy life. The sea. And I hope you never compromise on what you most desire.'

At that moment he wished he could give her what she most desired, as well—her memory.

He could easily give her a choice about her future. He could offer to marry her, like his father married his mother. He could give her a life of comfort and security. And she would not have to be bothered by him much, except the brief times he was on shore.

No. One thing he could never give her was her rightful place in society. Any regard she had for him would certainly perish when she must live on the outskirts of the aristocracy.

Besides, theirs was an attachment created out of necessity and gratitude. Not love.

One thing Lucien knew for certain. If his parents had loved each other—and him—things would have been very different.

They remained at the railing until Dublin and Ireland disappeared and the sun dropped lower in the sky. Claire's mind calmed some from the rhythms of the sea and the ship. She let go of her worries for the moment and simply enjoyed Lucien's companionship.

Ella and Cullen approached them.

'Sir?' Cullen took a respectful tone. 'They have informed us that dinner will be served soon. I will bring the food to you. In your cabins?'

Claire frowned. She'd rather not eat than eat alone in her cabin where her unhappy thoughts would certainly return.

Lucien shot her a look. 'There is a table in my cabin, if you would wish to share the meal with me.'

How did he always know what would make her most comfortable?

She released a breath. 'I would love to share a meal with you.' She turned to Ella. 'There is also a table in my cabin and you and Cullen are welcome to eat there.'

There would not be tables in their cabins.

Ella's eyes lit up. 'Truly, m'lady?'

'Yes. Truly,' she responded. 'If I dine with Captain Roper, I will not need that table. You might as well use it.'

Ella and Cullen brought them their meal and quickly fled to be private together.

Should she have made it so easy for the young maid and her young man to be private together? Perhaps she should have been more protective.

On the other hand, Cullen clearly adored Ella and Claire could not bear to separate them any more than she wished to be separated from Lucien, her anchor.

Claire sat across from Lucien. She lifted her spoon, but stopped mid-air.

How had she known there would not be a table in the servants' cabins? She'd not seen them. 'Lucien, I think I had another memory, as if I'd seen what the servants' cabins would be like. I knew they would not have tables.'

He looked up from his plate. 'Another small piece. Your memory may come back like that. A little at a time.'

She took a bite of the stew. 'I wonder. I am used to what

I remember from the raft onwards. Will everything change again when my old memories return?'

'You will be who you were, then.' His tone seemed solemn. 'You will know what you want, what you think, what your hopes are.'

Yes, but she had new hopes. Impossible ones, but she didn't know if those hopes came from fear or desire.

She wished she could stay with Lucien.

But she could not tell him that. Any obligation he felt towards her could not go that far, not so far as for him to give up the sea. Or to marry without love.

'Will I be different, I wonder,' she said instead, 'when my old memories return?'

He stared down at his food. 'Different than you are now, certainly.'

Her throat tightened. Was she to lose this fledgling sense of herself, born of all the frightening and wonderful experiences she'd had with Lucien?

He went on. 'We will dock tomorrow at Holyhead and I will engage a carriage to take us to London.'

A frisson of anxiety ran up her back. 'Very well. It should take days, should it not?'

'About four days.'

Four more days with him. Four more days to get used to having to say goodbye.

When she got her memory back, it *would* change her, Lucien knew. How could it not? She had a lifetime of memories as the daughter of an earl. A few weeks of new memories would count for little.

But did he hope her memories returned soon? No. He wished to spend these last few days with the lady he knew, not the one he feared she would become.

For the rest of the meal he tried to return to their former ease with each other. It was becoming more and more difficult. He, too, missed those days on the fishing boat. When they'd been close. When they'd touched. When he'd slept near her.

Dinner included a bottle of wine and she poured herself glass after glass.

'Tell me about the shipwreck,' she asked. 'You never spoke much about it and, I confess, I did not feel ready to hear it. Tell me what happened. There were storms?'

He'd not spoken of the shipwreck, not in any detail. He'd not wanted to cause her more distress than she'd already experienced.

On the other hand, she'd nearly remembered two things about the ship. Would talking more of it spark still more memories?

Even if remembering changed her back into a selfish, thoughtless aristocrat, how could he refuse?

So he spoke. 'We never should have sailed that day. The sky filled with storm clouds even before we left port. We should have delayed a day, but the Captain…' He paused, picturing the Captain and recalling his concerns about the man. 'Something was wrong with the Captain. He was ill. He must have been ill. At the time I thought he was merely preoccupied, but I was concerned enough to walk the deck and check on the ship and crew. All seemed well.'

'He was ill?'

Lucien nodded. 'I think he was unable to command.' His chest constricted. 'I went below—that is when I encountered you and the other woman in the companionway—I stayed below even when the storm began, but I should have remained on deck. I could have taken command. I could have sailed us out of danger.'

'Would that have been possible?' she asked.

'To sail us out of danger?' He knew he could have done so. 'Yes.'

'No,' she said. 'I meant, was it even possible for you to take over for the Captain? Are there not rules for that?'

'You are right,' he admitted. 'The Navy drove it into us. The Captain is in command. I accepted this, even in the face of danger. I've spent most of my life under this rule.'

He'd believed in the rule of command. Wholeheartedly.

But he'd turned a blind eye to the obvious. The Captain had been ill. Unfit. He should have done something.

'It was not your fault.' She reached across the table and took his hand. 'Look at me, Lucien. It was not your fault.'

But he might have been the only man on board who could have changed what happened.

His insides twisted as he remembered. 'He sailed right into the storm. When I finally went on deck, it was too late. The wind was blowing us closer and closer to the rocks. There was nothing to do but get people to the rowboats. That was when I knocked on your door and told you we had to abandon ship.'

'And I was with that other woman? The governess?' She still held his hand.

He ought to pull away, but she was the lifeline to keep him from drowning in guilt.

'I only caught a glimpse of her.' Had the other woman drowned? 'She handed you the reticule and ran off to get someone else.'

She tightened her grip.

'When we got on deck it was in shambles. The main mast had split. There was debris everywhere. I led you towards the boats, but before we reached them, a big wave washed over the side and plunged us into the sea. Something hit you on your head and knocked you out.'

'Is that why I cannot recall anything?' she asked.

'I do not know.' He looked up at her.

She took her hand away and poured herself another glass of wine.

He put his head in his hands. Sometimes remembering was filled with pain.

She left her chair and walked over to him. She placed her arms around him and her lips close to his ear, said, 'It was not your fault, Lucien.'

He rose from his chair and embraced her, holding her close, letting her comfort seep into him. She smelled of lavender and sea air and he wanted never to let go of her.

Even though he knew he must.

'Oh, Lucien,' she murmured against his chest.

She lifted her face to him. With her arms twined around his neck, she rose on tiptoe. Her lips were near. Tantalisingly near.

And he could not resist. He closed the short distance and crushed his lips against hers, so hungry for her, so needing her solace.

An urgent sound escaped her and she returned the kiss with a matching hunger. He widened his stance and pressed her against him. Every moment of wanting her seemed to explode into need. When had he ever needed a woman more? He could not remember. They were inches from the berth and no one would see them.

He backed her towards it.

'Yes,' she murmured. 'Yes, Lucien.'

His legs touched the side of the berth.

And he stopped. 'No. No, my lady. We will not do this.'

He eased her away from him, his body aching with protest and desire.

She was not some willing widow or tavern maid; she was an earl's daughter with her virtue intact. Her virtue assured her marriage to one of her kind. To lose it meant ruin.

She blinked up at him as if dazed. And wounded. 'I believe I want to, Lucien.'

He shook his head. 'No. You've had too much wine, that

is all it is. We must keep our wits about us. This would ruin you. You would regret it.'

'I do not think so. I think I will regret stopping.' She reached for him.

He eluded her embrace and grasped her arm instead. 'Come. It is time you returned to your cabin.'

She looked petulant, ready to defy him, no doubt the aristocrat coming out in her, believing she should have something merely because she wanted it.

He put his arm around her and walked her to the door of her cabin.

He reached for the latch to open it, but she stopped him. 'Wait. We should knock. Ella and Cullen.'

Perhaps their dinner had been less complicated. The rules were different for the common folk like them. Like him. Perhaps they were free to indulge in their desire for each other. If so, he envied them.

He knocked.

The door was almost immediately opened by his new valet.

'Sir.' Cullen stood stiffly, like Lucien's men had done when they toed the line.

The valet looked as put together as he'd been before the meal. Had they not taken advantage of their privacy?

'We have finished our meal,' Lucien told him.

Ella spoke from behind Cullen. 'So have we, Captain. Our dishes are stacked.'

'I will remove them,' Cullen said. 'From your cabin, as well.'

Lucien and Lady Rebecca stepped aside so the valet could pass.

'Goodnight, my lady,' Lucien said, more stiffly than he intended. He backed away from the cabin door.

She gave him an intent look, moved towards him and reached up to touch his face. 'Goodnight, Lucien.'

Chapter Eight

Claire strode into the cabin, breathing fast, her head spinning, her emotions in turmoil. He was correct. She'd consumed too much wine. It had quieted her nerves about her future—without Lucien—but had left another disorder. Of yearning.

She could not recall how it had happened, but he'd kissed her. Really kissed her. And her whole body had flared into awareness and desire. She wanted him in the most intimate way. She wanted him to touch her bare skin, as he had when he'd once undressed her. She wanted her tongue to join with his, to taste of him. She wanted—she could not even put it into words. It was too scandalous.

It was what her half-brother had accused them of. And now it was what she wished could happen.

'M'lady?' Ella looked at her with concern. 'Are you unwell?'

She put a hand to her head. 'No. I am quite well. The wine. It went to my head a little.'

'Oh.' Ella stepped towards her. 'Do you need any assistance?'

Claire waved her off. 'No. No. I will sit a moment.' She lowered herself into a chair and put her head into her hands.

'Did you have a row?' Ella asked.

Claire lifted her head quickly. 'A row?'

'A quarrel,' Ella clarified. 'Captain Roper looked very upset, and so do you.'

Weren't maids supposed to keep opinions to themselves? 'I suppose you could say we had a disagreement.'

It had been more than a disagreement. He'd stopped and she'd not wanted him to.

Ella gave her a very sympathetic look. 'Do not upset yourself. Cullen and I argue sometimes. It never lasts. It was a lovers' row, that is what it was. Or the two of you would not be so upset.'

No. She and Lucien were not lovers. Even if that was what she'd wished for. What she'd attempted.

'It is not like that,' she quickly retorted. 'He—he is my escort. Nothing more.'

The maid gave her a very sceptical look, then busied herself tidying the cabin, which needed no tidying.

Claire rested her head in her hands again.

Finally Ella asked, 'Would you like me to head on and come back later?'

And leave her alone? To her thoughts? To memories of what had transpired? The knowledge that she was probably a hoyden.

'No. Please stay.' She needed to fill her head with something else besides Lucien. 'Tell me about yourself, Ella. About you and Cullen.'

Ella stood behind the other chair, her hands resting on its back while the ship rocked gently.

Her eyes glowed. 'He is right grand, he is. My Cullen.'

Claire could not help but smile. 'Where did you meet?'

'Oh, we were just children.' Her expression sobered. 'My ma and pa were in service, but his tilled the land. I was not allowed to see him, Ma and Pa said. We were better than he was, Ma and Pa said.'

'How did you manage, then?' she asked.

'We were clever.' Her fleeting smile disappeared. 'My

ma and pa came to Dublin to work and Cullen followed. When I was hired at the hotel, he found a job there, too. A low job, but he paid attention. He learned about gentlemen. He wanted to do better, he did.'

'That is admirable.'

'It is admirable indeed. But my pa did not think so. He found out Cullen was workin' at the hotel and Pa went into a tear, he did. That was when I took the chance to travel with you and Cullen came, too.'

They were running from her parents? 'How old are you, Ella?'

The maid straightened. 'I am eighteen, I am. Old enough.'

'And Cullen?'

'He is twenty.'

They were so young! Young lovers filled with hope.

How old was she? she wondered. She felt much older, but how old could she be? She could not be more than twenty or twenty-one if she were to be married? Any older and she'd be considered a spinster.

'That is a romantic story,' Claire said. Lucien would admire their determination to stay together, but she worried about what was in store for them. Life could bring hardship—although she did not know how she knew that. 'It seems like your parents would have been wiser not to try to separate you.'

'That is the right of it.' Ella nodded vigorously. 'But my pa would say, "Once a land tiller, always a land tiller." He thought he could convince me to marry a shopkeeper or one of Mr Castle's sons.' She laughed scornfully, then sobered again. 'This is Cullen's chance. No one would hire him as a valet with no experience. Not in Ireland. Not knowing where he came from. A good letter from Captain Roper will mean everything to us. Do you think the Captain will write a letter of recommendation? Could you ask him, please?

Cullen won't ask, I fear. It was my idea to ask the Captain for this trip.'

Did she have any influence with Lucien? She was more a burden than anything else. And a coquettish fool.

'I will try,' she said.

She did not see Lucien until the next morning when Holyhead was in sight. Since Ella took charge of repacking her portmanteau, Claire went up on deck. Lucien stood at the rail.

Her heart skipped a beat.

She loved his erect, alert bearing, the easy way he wore his coat and buff-coloured pantaloons when other men looked stiff and uncomfortable in the same garments. His dark hair curled out from beneath his beaver hat, uncut since their rescue. He was a man secure in what he wanted, sure of his future and fully aware of his past.

So unlike her, with no past she could remember, a future filled with just as many unknowns and the feeling that she more belonged on a fishing boat than in such beautiful dresses and hats.

She took in a breath for courage and walked to his side, placing her hands on the rail.

He turned his head towards her. 'We'll dock within an hour, I expect.'

She nodded, unable to make herself speak.

Was he also thinking of the kiss? Her head ached from the wine of the night before and she wished she could remember more clearly.

She mentally shook her head. He would not have kissed her. Every other intimacy had been initiated by her. This must have been, as well.

'What then?' she finally managed to ask.

He did not answer right away. 'We can either engage a

carriage and begin the journey to London today or rest a night in Holyhead.'

Surely he did not expect her to make that choice. 'You must decide, Lucien.'

'I do not wish to ask too much of you,' he said.

He spoke to her as if the previous night had not happened, as if she'd never thrown herself at him and admitted she'd wanted to bed him. It made her angry.

She lifted her chin. 'Surely after three weeks on a fishing boat, you know I am not delicate. You offered me your escort. I do not assume that means I command you. On the contrary, I am in your debt.'

Lucien spoke sharply. 'My offer of being your escort did not mean you would have no say in how and when we travelled.' He regretted his tone, just the opposite of how he'd vowed to behave.

He'd vowed to act the gentleman, to make up for his decidedly ungentlemanly behaviour of the previous night.

Now, though, merely seeing her unsettled him anew. The sun shining on her face, her hazel eyes reflecting the green colour of her hat, her moist pink lips.

Was it not gentlemanly of him to give her the choice, though? And what did she do? Acted as if she were not an aristocrat, as if she were the woman who'd wished she could remain on the fishing boat. What aristocratic lady wished to live on a fishing boat?

'It is your choice, Lucien,' she insisted.

So now he must guess which was better for her. To stay the night in Holyhead or to start their journey to London, a journey he had to admit he'd like to delay?

He took time to decide, but instead of thinking of carriages and inns, he savoured the faint scent of lavender that enveloped her.

Finally he forced a decision. Of sorts. 'If we can procure a carriage under such short notice, we leave today. If not, tomorrow.'

She did not respond right away. It seemed like minutes went by before she said, 'Very well.'

'But you must tell me if you become fatigued or ill,' he insisted.

'I rarely become ill,' she shot back. Her eyes widened. 'How do I know that?'

He forgot about the night before and all his other nonsense. 'Another memory?'

She glanced away and back. 'So very strange. I cannot remember ever being ill or not being ill, but I simply know I have a strong constitution.' Her eyes widened again. 'I can almost hear myself saying those words.' She looked even more pensive. 'On a ship.'

She was getting closer and closer to retrieving her past. How long would it take, he wondered, before her memory returned in full?

He smiled, hiding his unhappiness. 'See? I'll wager this will happen more. Especially when you are in familiar surroundings.'

Perhaps being in London would do it. If she had ever been in London before.

'Close your eyes and see if more comes.'

She did as he suggested, but opened them again and shook her head. 'Nothing. Emptiness.' She waved her hand. 'But, never mind. I will simply enjoy this lovely day and the excitement of docking at Holyhead and of seeing all the sights there.'

She turned back to the railing and gazed out at the land on the horizon.

The grey and green hills of the Anglesey coast soon gave way to the wooden docks of the harbour and white-stucco buildings of Holyhead and, as they came even closer, they could see the activity on the dock awaiting their arrival.

Lucien marked it all. The harbour was much like count-less other harbours he'd sailed into. This time, though, he was a mere passenger with absolutely no role to play in reaching the dock safely. Soon he hoped to have another ship under his command. With luck he could gather most of his old crew. He'd be at home again.

As the ship eased its way to the dock, Lady Rebecca spoke. 'This was what was supposed to happen on the other ship.'

Where instead many died.

When it came time to disembark, Cullen and the maid appeared, Cullen carrying both his and Lady Rebecca's luggage.

'We are ready, sir,' Cullen said. 'I will collect the trunks as soon as they are unloaded.'

'Any memories of this?' Lucien asked Lady Rebecca as they stepped on to the dock.

'None. It is like I've never seen it before.' She sounded resigned.

His impulse was to ease her pain. 'It is possible you've never been here before.'

'I suppose,' she responded. 'But I must have travelled to England before this. Perhaps I even had a London Season. I must have met Lord Stonecroft somewhere. There must have been some sort of courtship.'

He ought to have asked that reprobate of a brother of hers more about the matter. It certainly would have helped her if he had.

He took her to a nearby inn to wait until Cullen and the maid collected the trunks. While there he enquired about hiring a carriage and managed to make the arrangements. It would take them at least four hours by carriage to travel over Four Mile Bridge on to Anglesey Island and across the island and on to the ferry to the mainland. They had enough daylight to do that.

The carriage was large enough for their trunks and other luggage and to seat all four of them inside. Ella and Cullen took the rear-facing seats and Lucien was very aware of Lady Rebecca beside him. Lucien was distracted from his jumbled emotions by the unrestrained excitement of the maid who could hardly remain in her seat at the sights that passed by the windows.

They passed by stucco houses with slate roofs gleaming white in the midday sun.

Ella exclaimed, 'Look!' as they passed a huge stone church.

Within an hour they had crossed the Four Mile Bridge connecting Holy Island to Anglesey and Ella actually moved so she could lean out of the window.

'I've never seen the like, I haven't!' she cried.

Lucien turned to Lady Rebecca with a silent question— did she have a memory of this?

She shook her head.

After several changes of horses they arrived at the Menai Strait where they waited for the ferry that would transport them to Caernarfon on the Welsh mainland. The crossing was not without its hazards, Lucien knew. The strait near Caernarfon was known for its shifting sandbars. He kept his eyes open and his mouth shut as the four of them stood on the deck of the ferry, the wind blowing cool as the sun lowered in the sky.

'Look! Look, m'lady!' Ella jumped up and down and tugged on Cullen's arm. 'A castle! A real castle!' She turned to Lucien. 'Do you know what castle it is?'

It loomed high above the town around it. Old stone with crenellated towers. The town itself looked as if it were behind the castle walls.

'Caernarfon Castle,' Lucien said. 'Built by King Edward about five hundred years ago, I think.'

'It is grand.' Ella's voice was full of awe. 'Grander than any I've seen in Ireland.'

'But you've seen hardly a castle in Ireland, wouldn't you say?' Cullen smiled.

She rolled her eyes at him. 'Cullen.'

While the two servants bickered good-naturedly, Lucien stepped over to Lady Rebecca.

'No,' she answered his silent enquiry. 'I know it is a castle. I can name the parts of it, but I do not remember seeing it.'

The ferry landed without mishap and they disembarked, the carriage taking them into the town to a posting inn. Their carriage and trunks were secured and the four of them entered the inn. At Lucien's behest, Cullen arranged for four rooms, the servants' rooms near the other two, and for a private dining room.

When the servants were about to leave them at the private room, Lady Rebecca stopped them. 'We could eat together, could we not?'

Lucien was startled at this new example of common, non-aristocratic behaviour from her.

All three sets of eyes turned to him.

'Certainly, if that is what you wish,' he responded.

During the meal Cullen kept his distance, but Ella chattered her way through each dish, detailing all the remarkable sights she'd seen that day and asking questions of what was to come.

Lucien was amused by the young maid. 'Ella, surely it

is not typical of a lady's maid to be such a chatterbox. How is it you are so?'

Ella laughed. 'My pa said I was born this way. He could never do a thing with me. Believe me, he and Ma tried.' She gave Cullen a worshipful glance. 'My friendship with Cullen made me bold, I think. It always felt right to be with him, no matter what Pa and Ma said.'

When their plates were empty and some port was served, Ella stood up. 'Cullen and I will remove the dishes and prepare your rooms for sleeping.' She seemed to be trying to suppress a smile. 'Name a time we should attend you.'

She was not only outspoken; she was taking command.

'Ten o'clock?' Lucien looked to Lady Rebecca.

'That suits me,' she replied.

When they left, Lady Rebecca said, 'I believe they wanted some time together.'

Which also left Lucien alone with her.

He poured each of them some port. 'She is a somewhat unusual maid.'

She smiled. 'I agree. I am not certain how I know that, but I do agree.'

He lifted his glass to his lips. 'Any more memories?'

She scoffed. 'I don't know if I would call them memories, but, no. Nothing further.'

He leaned forward. 'I have an idea.'

Her brows rose as she took a sip of port.

He went on. 'An idea of how you might recover some memories.'

She hesitated, then fingered the stem of her glass. 'I know I should answer you eagerly, but I am a little afraid. I should remember, but I am not certain I want to.'

Perhaps that was the impediment—not wanting to remember.

She took another sip of her port. 'Shoulders back, right, Lucien? I must face this. Do tell me what your idea is.'

The idea was forming as they spoke. 'I will ask you to talk about something and we will see if any memories come.'

Claire straightened in her chair and lifted her chin. 'Very well.'

She considered downing her glass of port and asking for more to settle her nerves, but too much wine the night before had led her into trouble. Drink too much wine. Throw herself at Lucien.

'What will you ask?'

He paused, as if thinking, then leaned towards her again. 'Tell me about school.'

'School? I do not remember school.' He knew this.

'Not your school,' he said. 'Tell me about any school. What kind is it?'

'Do you mean a girls' boarding school?' she asked.

'That will do.' He gestured for her to go on. 'Tell me anything about what a girls' boarding school would be like.'

This seemed ridiculous. 'Well, there would be girls there.'

He accepted her answer with equanimity. 'And what would they study?'

She hesitated only a few seconds. 'Music, dancing, Italian, French, literature, mathematics, needlework.' She looked up at him. 'Shall I go on?'

'What would the school look like?'

'How can I know that?' she shot back.

'Make it up,' he said.

She closed her eyes. 'Red brick, at least four floors, green park surrounding, dormitory rooms with beds, one after the other, classrooms with slate boards and wooden desks and chairs.' She opened her eyes again.

'Tell me about the teachers.' He anticipated her protest. 'Make it up.'

'Very well.' She took a breath. 'Some of them are bitter and unhappy, because they have nowhere else to go, but others seem to care about the girls and want to try to help them.'

A glimpse of a smiling woman flashed through her mind.

She looked directly at Lucien. 'A woman…'

His eyes kindled with interest. 'What does she look like?'

She shook her head. 'It was too brief.'

He reached across the table and took her hand. 'Now answer this without thinking. Where is this school?'

'Bristol.' She blinked in surprise.

He squeezed her hand. 'I believe you remember a real school, one you attended. A real teacher.'

'But it doesn't feel like a memory,' she protested. 'Not like remembering the fishing boat or Dublin.'

'It is there, though,' he insisted. 'You'll have more.' He released her hand, glancing at his own as if surprised. 'Do you want to go on?'

She pressed her fingers to her temple. 'No. My head aches. Perhaps later.'

Had she remembered a real school? A real teacher?

She felt as if she were a water-filled ewer with a tiny crack growing larger and larger, but she did not want to split open. She did not want the water to spill out.

There was a knock on the door and the innkeeper entered.

'Pardon me, sir, m'lady,' the man said nervously. 'Have a problem, I do. His lordship, Lord Provey, demands a private dining room and this is the only one.'

Claire immediately rose. 'We have no further need of it, do we, Lucien?'

He frowned. 'Perhaps not.'

The innkeeper looked wretched. 'So grateful, I'd be.'

Lucien stood as well and escorted her out.

Passing them was an expensively dressed gentleman, wafting strong scent, and his three equally well-dressed cohorts.

'It is about time,' the gentleman snarled at the innkeeper. 'I expect brandy and glasses forthwith, a clean deck of playing cards and a set of markers. Hurry, man.'

The innkeeper dashed away and the men disappeared behind the room's door.

'I detest men like that,' Lucien mumbled.

Claire was not certain she was to have heard that, but she responded. 'What sort of men? Rude, pushy ones?'

'Aristocrats.' He nearly spat out the word.

The venom in his tone struck her like a physical blow. They walked to the hall.

Claire glanced through the window. She did not wish to say goodnight, not until she understood why he'd reacted so vehemently to aristocrats.

'It is still a little light outside. Might we take some air?' she asked.

'A turn around the yard may be safe enough.'

They walked outside. The yard which had been all abustle had quieted, although there were still hostlers moving horses into the stables. The setting sun turned the sky golden, making the brown stone of the inn glow as if lit from within. A light breeze freed the air of the scent of horses.

Claire took Lucien's arm as they walked the perimeter of the yard.

'Why did you say you detest aristocrats?' she asked at last, well aware she was one.

He frowned. 'Because they believe they are entitled to whatever it is they want.'

That sentiment rang true inside her. Was it true of herself, as well?

She countered, 'Surely not all of them.'

'Too many of them in my experience,' he stated. 'Your brother for one.'

She readily agreed with that. 'He was detestable, was he not? And that lord, the one near your village, the one your mother—'

'Viscount Waverland.' His voice tensed.

'He was detestable, too?' she asked.

'Yes. Not only in how he treated my mother, expecting her to run to him whenever he fancied her, but he expected the whole village to jump to his demands.' He made a derisive sound. 'Of course, my mother was always eager to comply. Whatever he wanted.'

They walked on, covering a quarter of the distance, before she spoke again. 'And the ladies? Aristocratic ladies, are they cut from the same cloth?'

Was she? She wanted to know.

He missed a step. 'Often the same.'

Did he believe she would become demanding and entitled when she recovered her memory?

The thought sickened her.

No wonder Lucien became angry when she'd kissed him. It must have seemed to him that she expected him to comply because it was what she wanted.

But she had wanted it.

Was she nothing but a selfish aristocrat?

'Viscount Waverland was not the only reason for my antipathy,' he went on. 'I was raised to detest aristocrats.'

'By your mother?' His father was absent, she recalled.

'Yes.'

''That makes no sense. She fell in love with one.'

He cocked his head. 'We came to different conclusions. She wanted to be one. I wanted nothing to do with them.'

And she was one of *them*. 'Something must have happened, then.'

He halted and gazed down at her with an intent look she did not understand.

Finally he spoke. 'My mother's father owned land in Ireland. He was fairly prosperous, but he was tricked into losing the property by an unscrupulous lord. My mother and her brothers were suddenly impoverished and my mother never recovered from the change in her circumstances and prospects for a good marriage.'

'What a terrible occurrence.' The poor family. No wonder Lucien felt as he did.

'That is why I was in Ireland,' he explained. 'To provide some needed funds for my uncles.'

Her heart warmed towards him. Of course. It was the sort of thing he would do. Dear Lucien.

'I should tell you more.' His tone put her aback.

'More? What more?'

He faced her directly and looked down into her eyes. 'The aristocrat who impoverished my family was the Earl of Keneagle. Your grandfather.'

She felt a chill run through her. 'My grandfather? My father's father?' Had she known her grandfather?

He kept on. 'I did not tell you before, because…well… you had enough to deal with. I feel I should have told you when we met your brother.'

Her grandfather must have been as horrible as her brother. It was a wonder Lucien could even look at her.

She wrapped her arms around herself, feeling as miserable as she could remember. 'It has turned cold. We should go back in.'

Chapter Nine

Lucien felt her withdrawal. Her pain. He was instantly sorry he had spoken. Why had he?

If he was trying to separate himself from her, he'd done a fair job of it, but it brought him no ease at all.

He shook his head. 'I should not have told you all that. I fear it has only caused you pain.'

Her muscles had stiffened. 'Better for me to know—to know what sort of a family I came from.'

Had he told her because he'd been tempted to pull her into the many shadows around the yard and taste her lips again?

They re-entered the inn and climbed the stairs to their rooms. At her doorway, he reached out his hand for her key.

She placed it in his palm and avoided a direct look at him.

He turned the key in the lock and opened the door.

All he could see in the room was the bed and temptation flared through him. Enter her room. Taste her lips again and this time allow her to say yes.

'Shall I have breakfast sent up to your room?' he said instead.

'As you wish, Lucien,' she responded in a sad voice.

She held out her palm for the key and he returned it to

her. Before he could say another word, she strode into the room, closing the door behind her.

Curse me, Lucien said to himself.

He returned to the public rooms, seated himself at a table and sent the tavern maid to bring him some brandy. A whole bottle.

He poured one glass and downed it and poured another. Sipping this one more slowly, he let his gaze drift around the room, so much like any public room of a fairly respectable inn. Weary travellers. Jocular town folk. Easy women, needing to make enough to survive. Eager men willing to pay their price.

Tucked away in a booth in the corner of the room sat his new valet and the chatterbox maid, staring into each other's eyes as if no one else in the room existed. They had at least another hour before their duties would call them away.

Too bad he could never have what they possessed. Love between equals. Strong enough that nothing or no one else mattered.

But she would always be Lady Rebecca and he would always have the sea.

He must stay the course. Bring her to London. Deliver her to Lord Stonecroft.

And say goodbye.

He downed his second glass of brandy and poured a third.

He still wished he had not hurt her so this night.

Their trip the next day took them through the mountains, and the scenic views of the peaks and valleys and lakes kept them all entertained. Lucien could hardly ignore that Lady Rebecca said as little as possible to him. Though they still sat next to each other and could not fail to touch, it was as if she were in another coach altogether.

This was an odd choice of a route, Lucien thought. The

pace was slow, the horses needing to conserve strength because the few coaching inns were a greater distant apart
than on busier roads.

When they stopped at an inn at midday, Lucien asked
the coachmen about it.

'More direct, it is,' the coachman said. 'Saves time.'

But the man did not look him in the eye.

Twice that day they had to leave the carriage and walk
so the horses could make it up a steep piece of road. This
was not saving time. They should be out of this wooded,
mountainous area and on to more-travelled roads.

By late afternoon, Lucien's impatience grew, even as the
road narrowed and the pace slowed even further.

The carriage stopped one more time and the coachman
opened the window below his perch. 'Need you to walk
again.'

Lucien disembarked first and helped Lady Rebecca out.
Cullen and Ella came next.

'We might as well walk the whole way,' Ella said as her
feet hit the ground.

Lady Rebecca, however, had not uttered a word of complaint.

They walked ahead of the carriage, able to make more
speed than the horses. When they reached the crest of the
hill, they faced two horsemen aiming pistols at them.

Ella gasped.

'Your money or your life,' one growled.

The two men dismounted.

Lucien edged Lady Rebecca behind him, but kept walking towards them. 'We have little of value.'

'Stop there. Empty your pockets,' the highwayman said.

The other man's hands shook.

Lucien had faced men with pistols before when capturing enemy ships. Hesitation got men killed.

'I'll show you.' He kept approaching and made it look like he was reaching in a pocket. 'There's a pittance.'

Instead he charged the man, who stepped back in surprise, but fired his weapon. Lucien felt a sharp pain pierce his arm, but he leapt at the man, grabbing the arm with the pistol. Out of the corner of his eye, he saw Cullen grappling with the other man.

'What ho?' The coachmen jumped from the box.

'They are with them!' Lucien cried.

Lady Rebecca pulled Ella away from them and around to the other side of the road. The two coachmen rushed into the fray. Lucien held his own, but barely, and a punch to his injured arm nearly caused him to pass out. How long could he and Cullen keep this up?

He grabbed the robber by the lapels and slammed him into the coachman. Both staggered backwards, struggling to keep on their feet.

Cullen was having a worse time of it. The other robber held him while the other coachman pummelled him with his fists.

Ella let out a cry as unearthly as a proper banshee. She leapt on to the coachman's back and held on to his hair. The man swung around, trying to rid himself of her.

Lucien swung at his attacker with all his strength. His fist connected to the man's jaw with a loud crack and the man spun around and fell to the ground. The coachman charged him again and both he and Lucien tumbled over. Somehow the man's hands wrapped around his throat. Lucien tried to pry his fingers loose, but his injured arm had lost its strength.

Suddenly Lady Rebecca appeared. She threw her shawl over the man's head and jerked his head back. He lost his grip on Lucien, who rolled away, but he turned, trying to get his hands on her. Lucien came down with both fists on the back of the man's neck.

The man fell to the dirt.

Cullen freed himself and now brandished a knife, its blade gleaming as he slashed at his assailants. Ella had finally been flung off, but the man she'd leapt on took one look at the knife and yelled, 'Flee! Or we're done for.'

The man started for the horses, but Lady Rebecca ran ahead of him, waving her shawl and scaring the horses into galloping down the road.

Lucien went to the carriage. There was no way he'd allow these men to escape in the carriage and leave them stranded. He held the horses.

Lucien's assailants scrambled to their feet and stumbled off into the woods where their partners had already fled.

Lady Rebecca walked back to Lucien.

Ella had flung her arms around Cullen and was weeping loudly. 'I thought they would kill you.'

Lucien had a strong urge to hold Lady Rebecca in the same manner, but he held back.

She was breathing hard, but remained remarkably composed. 'What now, Lucien?'

'We need to leave. Right now.' He didn't want the highwaymen to regroup or return with reinforcements. 'Cullen!' he called. 'Are you able to drive the carriage?'

Ella released him.

'I can try, sir.' Cullen limped over to the carriage, climbed on to the box and took the ribbons in his hands.

Lucien turned to Lady Rebecca. 'I am going to ride on top with him. You ladies ride inside.' He opened the door and helped them in. Closing it again, he leaned in the window. 'You both did well.'

The ladies had saved them all.

Lucien climbed on the box with Cullen who flicked the ribbons. The horses started down the road.

* * *

'Are you injured?' Claire asked Ella.

The girl had not stopped weeping, but she shook her head. 'I thought they would kill Cullen. What would I do if that happened? How could I live after that?'

She put her arm around the maid. 'There, now. It is over. And you were very brave. Cullen is unharmed, is he not?'

'He was limping,' Ella whimpered.

'Well, he is a strong man. A very strong man,' she said. 'I am certain he will be right as rain in no time.'

'He is a strong man,' Ella agreed with a sigh.

Claire's heart was still pounding. The whole scene played over and over in her mind. The highwaymen pointing their pistols. Lucien rushing towards them. She'd been terrified that he'd be shot. Ella's sentiments were not unlike her own. How could she live if Lucien were killed? He was her one constant. When that man choked him, something in her snapped. She'd have killed that man if that was what it took to save Lucien.

She glanced out of the window, her senses on alert lest the attackers return. The coachmen must have set up the attack. How could they have done such a thing?

After about a half-hour they reached a road with more traffic and soon crossed an old stone bridge and entered a village that looked as if time had not touched it in a century. The carriage stayed on the main road until they came upon a coaching inn.

When the carriage turned into the inn's yard and stopped, Claire heard Cullen's voice. 'Ella, m'lady. Come quick. I need you.'

Claire opened the door and, without waiting for the steps to be put down, jumped to the ground, Ella behind her.

Cullen had already climbed off the box. Lucien, pale as chalk, was leaning heavily on him.

'He's hurt, m'lady,' Cullen said. 'We must get him inside.'

She sprang into action. 'Ella, collect his things. Cullen, help me bring him into the inn.' She came to his other side, ready to have him drape an arm around her shoulder, but his sleeve was dark with blood.

'Lucien!' she cried.

'Started bleeding,' he said. 'Not serious.'

He looked as if he would pass out at any moment.

One of the hostlers ran ahead to alert the innkeeper who met them at the door.

'What happened?' the innkeeper asked, immediately taking over for Claire.

'We were set upon by thieves,' she answered. 'Our coachmen were part of it. He's shot, I believe.'

The innkeeper directed them to a nearby room on the first floor. She and Cullen sat Lucien on the bed. Claire very gingerly removed his coat. His shirtsleeve was bright red.

'The ball hit my upper arm.' Lucien's voice was low and strained.

She looked over at the innkeeper. 'Please send for a surgeon.'

The man nodded and left.

Cullen helped him off with his waistcoat and shirt. Claire moistened a towel from a basin in the room.

'He bled something terrible,' Cullen said.

'It is still bleeding!' She pressed the towel against his wound.

He winced.

Cullen removed Lucien's boots.

'Lucien, you must lie down,' Claire insisted.

He did as she said, closing his eyes as his head rested against the pillows. 'Need to summon the magistrate.'

'We will worry about that later,' she said.

He was so pale and weak. It frightened her.

This would not have happened if not for her. He would have already been in London by now, well on his way in his new life.

'I am so sorry, Lucien,' she whispered.

'No need,' he said. 'Just a scratch…' His voice faded off.

Claire and Cullen did all they could to control the bleeding and to make Lucien as comfortable as possible, but he clearly was growing weaker and weaker. Claire was nearly wild with worry. An hour had passed and the surgeon had still not arrived.

'Cullen, go see what is happening,' she pleaded. 'Why is the surgeon not here?'

The valet nodded and immediately left the room.

A few minutes later Ella entered with some broth. 'For the Captain. The cook here said he should drink as much as possible.'

She placed the tray containing a pot of broth and a cup on the table next to the bed.

Claire poured some and put her arm around Lucien to help him sit. She lifted the cup to his lips. 'Drink this.'

She slowly poured a little of the broth down his throat. He swallowed cooperatively, but could not keep his eyes open.

His skin was hot to her touch and that worried her as much as the bleeding.

'What is going to happen to him, m'lady?' Ella asked, wringing her hands.

'He is going to recover,' she said determinedly.

Because no other option could possibly be entertained.

She could not remember attending church or saying prayers, but she prayed now that God would help him.

There was a knock on the door. It opened before they could answer and Cullen entered with a grey-haired man carrying a leather bag.

'The surgeon,' Cullen said.

'I am Mr Hughes,' the man said.

'This is Captain Roper.' Claire moved away from Lucien's bedside and the surgeon took her place. 'He's been shot in the arm. We—we haven't been able to stop the bleeding.'

Mr Hughes sat down. 'Let us see it, then.'

He removed the bloody towels Claire had wrapped around Lucien's arm, dabbed at the fresh blood and touched the wound, examining it.

Lucien roused and pulled away.

Claire went to the other side of the bed and eased him back against the pillows. 'It is all right, Lucien. It is the surgeon. Let him look at you.'

It looked as if the pistol ball had taken a slice out of Lucien's upper arm.

'Bring me some fresh water and towels,' the surgeon said. 'We'll clean the wound and stitch him up. That should do it.'

Claire held Lucien's other arm and shoulder while Cullen held his injured one. Lucien trembled in pain as the surgeon picked out pieces of cloth and small pebbles from the wound, but he did not cry out.

'It will be all right, Lucien,' Claire murmured. 'Hold fast.'

Mr Hughes poured water in the wound to wash away smaller debris. Lucien gripped Claire's hand and shook some more.

'Now we'll sew you up, young man,' Hughes said in a calm tone.

Ella stood behind Cullen, her hands covering her mouth as the surgeon stitched the wound closed. Lucien's muscles tensed and his face was pinched, as he stoically endured this last bit of pain.

Claire felt every poke of the needle, every stroke of the thread passing through his skin as if it were happening to her. Only when the surgeon had finished, giving the wound a final dab of the towel and leaning back, did she realise she'd been as tense as Lucien.

'There you are,' Mr Hughes said. 'All done. Now let us wrap it up and all will be well.'

'Thank you, sir,' Lucien mumbled as he once more relaxed against the pillows. He gestured towards his coat, flung across a table. 'Will pay you.'

Cullen retrieved the coat and lifted the purse from a pocket, taking out some coins and paying the surgeon.

Mr Hughes packed up his things. 'He should rest a day at least. More if he still seems weak.' He glanced towards Lucien. 'Do you hear that, Captain?' he said louder.

Lucien nodded.

He turned to Claire again. 'He should have the stitches taken out in a week, assuming he's healing well.'

Claire rose and walked Mr Hughes to the door. 'Is there anything I should be on watch for? Anything that could go awry?'

The older man smiled at her. 'He will do well, I believe. Only danger is fever, but he's strong. Even fever will not beat him, I expect.'

She certainly had no intention of letting Lucien out of her sight until she knew he would recover completely.

After the surgeon left, she returned to the chair next to his bed.

'I will stay with him,' she told Cullen and Ella. 'You two go and get something to eat.'

'Shall I arrange a room for you?' Cullen asked her.

She shook her head. 'I am staying here.'

'I will stay, as well, then,' he said. He turned to Ella. 'You'll have a room, though. You need your rest.'

Ella hugged him. 'You are so good to me.'

They went out of the room arm in arm.

'You should rest, too,' came a weak voice from the bed.

She took his hand. 'I am staying with you.'

'Your reputation,' he mumbled.

'Dash my reputation,' she said. 'You did not let go of me on the raft and I am not leaving this room until I know you are better.'

She sat by his side throughout the night when he thrashed in fever. She and Cullen bathed his face with cool cloths.

Somehow she knew that fever could kill, just as an illness or a pistol shot could kill. Or how the sea could kill. She could not remember, though, knowing anyone who had died. Not even the woman on the *Dun Aengus*. Not the maid sent to accompany her. No one.

If Lucien died, though, it would be as if her whole remembered life died with him.

Chapter Ten

After fitful dreams of stormy seas and highwaymen and Lady Rebecca perishing at the hands of both, Lucien opened his eyes to a room lit by dawn peeking through the window. It took him a moment to realise where he was and what had happened.

Cullen was sprawled out in two chairs, one holding his feet, the other, the rest of him. Lady Rebecca sat next to him. Though in a chair, she rested her head in her arms on the bed's mattress. Her hair had come loose and he fingered one tendril.

She'd said she'd stay the night in his room, he dimly recalled.

He smiled. She looked peaceful in sleep, youthful and unspoiled by the events she'd endured since encountering him.

His arm throbbed and he had a powerful thirst, but he did not wish to rouse his guardians. Across the room on a table was a pitcher of water and a glass. He could reach it.

Keeping his eye on Lady Rebecca, he edged his way out of the bed, taking care not to disturb her. He wore only his unmentionables, he noticed. His chest was bare and his aching arm was wrapped in a bandage. He took his first step gingerly, pausing until the dizziness passed. Bracing himself against furniture, he made it to the water, poured himself a glass, and, still watching Lady Rebecca, drank the whole amount.

She lifted her head and sat up in surprise until she spied him. 'What are you doing?'

He put a finger to his lips and pointed to Cullen, still inhaling the even breaths of sleep. Lucien poured another glass and finished it before making his way back to the bed.

'You should not be up,' she whispered.

'Thirsty,' he said.

'You should have awoken me,' she scolded. 'I would have brought you water.'

'You were sleeping.' He winced as he climbed back into bed.

She put her hand to his forehead. 'Thank God. You are finally cool.'

Her hand felt soft and warm against his skin. 'I had a fever? That explains the dreams.'

'Dreams?' she asked.

'Fever dreams,' he responded. 'They did not make much sense.' Except they were mostly about losing her.

Prophetic dreams, perhaps.

'Did you summon the magistrate?' he asked.

She pursed her lips. 'No, we were too concerned with keeping you alive.'

'From this?' He pointed to the bandage. 'Takes more than a scratch to kill me.'

'You lost a great deal of blood.'

Another ordeal for her to endure, he thought. 'I am sorry. I worried you.'

She reached over and brushed the hair from his face. 'As long as you mend.'

It seemed so natural to have her seated close to his bed, touching him, conversing together. He'd grown used to her presence over these eventful weeks. He did not want to part from her, but his duty was clear. Help her remember as much as she could. Return her to her life. Return to the sea.

Her hand rested briefly on his shoulder before she placed it in her lap. He might have had a feverish night, but his senses were still alive. Her touch roused him with desire and he was acutely aware of being bare chested in her presence.

'Is my bag nearby?' he asked.

'Yes.' She could not quite meet his eye. Had she felt that pang of desire, as well?

He sat up straighter. 'Could you bring me a shirt?'

She rose and walked over to the bag, opened it and found a clean shirt Cullen had packed. She carried it to him and helped him put it on. The rest he could do when Cullen woke up.

'Are you hungry?' she whispered.

He was. Very hungry. 'I can wait for Cullen to wake up.'

'I will happily get you something to eat.'

But it was not proper for an earl's daughter to seek out the kitchens of an inn and ask for food.

'Ask Ella to do it if she is awake.' It was a maid's job.

She stood and stretched, reminding him of the Lady Rebecca of the fishing boat. Completely at ease.

'Very well. I will ask Ella to bring the food if she is awake.'

Only after she left did he realise she had not said what she would do if Ella were sleeping.

They had only procured two rooms at the inn and Ella had slept in the other one. Claire rapped lightly on the door.

'One moment.' Ella's muffled voice came through the door. She opened it. 'Oh, m'lady. It is you.'

She was dressed and the bed was made.

Claire stepped inside the room. 'I was not certain you would be awake.'

'Me? I am used to rising early.' She gave Claire a concerned look. 'How fares the Captain?'

'He is well.' It gave Claire pleasure to say so. 'His fever is gone and he is hungry.'

'And Cullen? I expected him, not you, at the door.' Her eyes widened. 'Oh, I did not mean to sound like I would not want you to come, m'lady.'

Claire held up her hand. 'I do realise that, Ella. Cullen was sleeping when I left the room. He was up with the Captain most of the night.'

The young man had been a great help, holding Lucien down when he thrashed about in the bed. He brought fresh water and towels and made both Lucien and Claire as comfortable as possible.

Ella peered at her. 'You look like you were up most of the night, too. I think you should rest. I'll fetch the food for the Captain.'

Claire glanced in the mirror. She had circles under her eyes and her hair had escaped its pins. And there were bloodstains on her dress.

'I should change my clothes.' She waved her hand. 'But that can come later. The Captain is hungry.'

'Right.' Ella headed to the door. 'I shall go to the kitchen directly.'

After she left, Claire glanced at the bed, longing to simply lie down, but she did not wish to muss it after Ella had made it so tidy. She sat in an upholstered chair and leaned her head against its back, drifting off to sleep.

Next thing she knew Ella was leaning over her. 'M'lady? M'lady? Why don't you lie in the bed?'

She shook her head. 'I'd muss it.'

'Nonsense,' Ella said. 'I'll simply make it again. You need some sleep.'

She let herself be persuaded. The maid helped her out of her dress and she climbed under the bedcovers in her shift.

* * *

When next she woke, Ella stood over her again. 'The magistrate is here, m'lady. Captain Roper would like you to come speak with him.'

She sat up and felt her hair, now half-down on her shoulders. 'I cannot go looking like this.'

'Let us make you presentable, then. Right quick.'

Ella was true to her word. The girl helped her into her other travelling dress and put her hair in a knot as quick as could be. There was nothing to do for Claire's pale complexion and dark circles.

The magistrate was the local squire, Squire Vaughn, a man in his forties.

He bowed to her. 'My lady.'

Why did this acknowledgement of her status always feel so foreign?

'Sir.' She curtsied.

She glanced over at Lucien, who was clean shaven, seated in a chair and fully dressed, wearing a clean coat draped over his injured arm. He looked very pale.

The magistrate asked each of them to tell what happened on the road and to describe the men involved.

After they spoke and answered his questions, he said, 'I can put the word out to look for men of their description. We can check at the inn where you engaged the carriage and drivers, but, you must understand, the people may not be inclined to turn in their own. There's hardship here. Desperate people do desperate things.'

The unusually cold weather had damaged crops and led to hunger throughout the country, not to mention the unemployment and privation caused by the war.

'You do not believe the men will be caught,' Lucien said in a grim voice.

'I do not,' the magistrate admitted. 'And if I were you, I'd proceed on your trip as soon as possible. I am not saying you are in danger, but it seems to me many men must have been involved in the attempt to rob you and they all are probably worrying you'll be looking to find out who and turn them in.'

Claire could not believe this. 'But if these men are not caught, they might rob someone else. Any one of us could have been killed.' She gestured to Lucien. 'Captain Roper's injury could have killed him.'

Squire Vaughn inclined his head. 'I do understand, my lady. I am merely telling you what I think will happen.'

'But—' she started.

Lucien cut her off. 'Very well, Squire. I will take you at your word that you will try to discover who the guilty parties are. You have my direction in London. Write to me if you need me to return to press charges.'

The squire twirled his hat in his hands. 'I will do that, sir.' He turned and bowed to Claire. 'M'lady, I bid you good day.'

When the door closed behind the magistrate, Lucien rose from the chair. 'We leave today, if possible.'

'No, Lucien!' Lady Rebecca cried. 'You must rest a day. The surgeon said—'

'No matter.'

The magistrate had been very clear. By foiling the robbery attempt, they were likely in danger from the men who'd attacked them and those who aided them.

He turned to Cullen. 'Will you see if we can find drivers for the carriage or engage a new carriage and drivers to leave today?'

Cullen straightened. 'I will try, sir.' He hurried out the door.

'Ella, you can pack for us and arrange for some food to carry with us?'

She nodded and followed Cullen.

Lucien sank back into the chair.

Lady Rebecca swung around to him. 'See? You are too weak to travel.'

He rubbed his forehead. 'I am able to travel. It is nothing but sitting down.'

Once they were on Watling Street, the road well travelled since even before Roman times, the danger would be minimised. No more isolated sections of roads where they might be attacked.

She knelt down, bringing herself even with him. 'Please reconsider, Lucien. Wait one day. Will it matter so much?'

Yes. If it put her life in jeopardy one more time, it would matter a great deal.

He took her hand in his and looked into her eyes. 'Do you not realise I have been through events more treacherous than what we met on the road? I have been wounded before. I will manage, I promise you.'

She brought his hand to her lips. 'I do not wish any harm to come to you. You were so very ill during the night.'

He wished he could take her into his arms for his comfort as well as to comfort her.

'I am better,' he said in a low voice. 'It will be quite all right.'

By midday, Cullen had engaged a carriage and two coachmen who were eager for the employment.

'I'll ride above,' Cullen said. 'To watch the road.'

And to watch the coachmen.

Lady Rebecca had insisted upon purchasing several pillows and a blanket to make Lucien more comfortable and, by the time they were several miles down the road, he was glad of it. He felt every bump and rut in the road.

They travelled the whole day, stopping only to change horses and take quick refreshment. By the time they reached

Shrewsbury, it was still light, but the sun was low in the sky. Shrewsbury, a market town, was still lively even at that late hour. They passed whole streets of timbered buildings that made it appear they'd travelled back to medieval England, but the inn the coachmen turned into could have belonged in Mayfair. Four storeys of red brick, it sported a gold statue of a lion above its door.

When they entered, they were greeted by Mr Lawrence, the owner and innkeeper, who set them up in two rooms, each with a closet where Cullen and Ella could sleep. By the time they climbed the stairs to the rooms, Lucien was spent, but he pushed himself, intending to arrange a private dining room.

When they reached the door of the room that was to be shared by Lady Rebecca and Ella, he took a moment to lean against the wall.

Lady Rebecca saw him. 'Lucien!' She rushed to his side. 'You ought to be lying down. You look like death itself.'

'I'm well enough,' he said, straightening again.

'No, you are not,' she insisted. She turned to Cullen. 'Cullen, take him to his room and put him into bed. This day has been entirely too difficult for him.'

Cullen dropped the portmanteaux he carried and helped Lucien to the room next door.

Lucien heard Mr Lawrence ask, 'What is wrong with him? It is not the influenza, is it?'

'Not the influenza. He was shot by highwaymen yesterday,' Lady Rebecca replied.

He could not hear the rest.

Cullen helped him undress. Lucien climbed into the bed. 'Arrange for a meal for yourselves,' he told the valet. 'Secure a private dining room. I merely need to rest a bit.'

'As you wish, sir.'

He heard Cullen leave the room and close the door behind him.

He hated feeling so weak, but, in the end, he could not fight it. He fell asleep within minutes.

Lucien became aware of sounds, a rustling in the room, but could not force himself to wake. A moment later the scent of broth reached his nostrils, as well as another scent. Lavender.

He opened his eyes.

Lady Rebecca stood next to the bed, placing a tray on a table.

She smiled down at him. 'I thought you should eat something.'

The tray held a bowl of soup, some bread and cheese. Though eating had been the last thing on his mind as they reached Shrewsbury, his stomach now cried out in hunger.

'Thank you.' He sat up. 'What of you? Did you eat?'

She nodded and draped a napkin around his neck, her fingers touching his bare skin and waking him in ways that had nothing to do with sleep.

What did it say about him that he was at ease with her even though he was dressed only in his drawers?

He'd become too close to her, obviously, which was an intimacy of sorts. Sharing the room on the fishing boat had started it, but with each step in her difficult journey, he felt more and more connected to her. At times he had to force himself to face the fact that, once she remembered everything from her upbringing, she would become an earl's daughter again.

But tonight…tonight he was simply glad of her company.

He glanced around the room. There was a table and chairs by the window. 'I'll get up. Sit at the table.'

'Very well.' She picked up the tray again and carried it over to the table.

He climbed out of bed and quickly donned his trousers

and a shirt, wincing as he pulled his injured arm through the sleeve.

She must have been watching. 'How is your arm?'

Again it seemed perfectly natural that she witness him dressing. 'It is better.'

She looked unconvinced.

He sat at the table.

She took the chair opposite him. 'You have soup, as you can see. Turtle, I believe.'

He dipped his spoon into the bowl and tasted it, nodding his approval. 'It is good.' He gave her a half-smile. 'Of course, I am suddenly so hungry that anything would taste good.'

She cut him a slice of bread and a slice of cheese. Simple fare, but exactly what suited him right now. 'See? I was right. I knew you would be hungry.'

Their time together had attuned them to each other. In fact, he was so used to her company that he expected it would be wrenching to separate from her in London.

He looked up at her. 'How are you, my lady? The carriage ride must have been taxing for you as well.'

She smiled again. 'I have endured worse things.'

He could not help but smile back. 'Yes, we have, have we not?'

Their gazes caught and held.

She lowered her lashes and poured herself a cup of tea. 'Cullen learned something. There is a public coach, the Shrewsbury Wonder, that departs from this inn at five in the morning and reaches London the same day, although late at night. They have space for four passengers—'

He broke in. 'Do you wish to take this coach?'

Was she in a hurry to reach London? He'd not thought of how she might feel about this trip. Perhaps she wanted to pursue her true life faster than he desired.

She looked surprised. 'No. I already told him no. It is too difficult a trip for you.'

Then why mention it? 'I can endure it if it is what you wish.'

Her eyes flickered with pain. 'It is not what I wish. I wish—' This time she interrupted herself. 'Never mind what I wish. I believe it is too difficult for you, but I have delayed your arrival in London by many days and I thought you should know there was a way to reach the city faster.'

'Do not say it.' He caught her gaze again. 'A couple more days will not matter.'

He hoped.

Chapter Eleven

There was so much more Claire wished to say to him, but when she looked into his eyes, the words wouldn't come. If only she could tell him how much she loathed the idea of reaching London, how much she wished she could simply stay with him.

Even if it were on a fishing boat, she would be content. Her security. Her anchor.

But he wanted a ship, wanted to be back at sea, where he felt he most belonged. She could not stay with him. Besides, she was his family's enemy, a member of the loathed privileged class, and set to return to the world to which she was supposed to belong. More reason he did not wish to stay with her.

She hated seeing him in pain, had hated the fear he might die, the only secure part of her world. Life as she knew it—remembered it—began with him. Until his fever broke she'd been distraught with worry that he would die and her world would end with him.

And yet she knew she would soon part from him.

She reached across the table and grasped his hand. 'Have I told you how grateful I am to you, Lucien? And how sorry I am that I have put you through all this—this delay— and—and—the highwaymen and all.'

He moved a finger to stroke her skin. 'The highwaymen were not your fault, you know.'

'You would not have been in that carriage on that road if it had not been for me,' she said.

'We would not have survived the attack if it had not been for your bravery. And Ella's,' he countered.

That scene came back to her. 'Ella was so fierce and daring. She made me feel I could be, too.' She turned it around in her mind. 'I know this sounds silly, but I relish knowing I can remember what happened. Even the awful things like the highwaymen and the raft.'

And fearing him ill enough to die.

Their hands remained clasped.

'I know memories are important to you,' he said. 'And ours have been memorable.'

She felt that pull towards him, the one that made her wish to have his arms around her, his lips against hers, to have that physical intimacy that men and women desire. Those feelings that made her feel she must have been less than ladylike before the shipwreck.

If she did convince him to make love to her, she knew his sense of honour would compel him to offer marriage to her and a naval marriage was one he did not want.

She pulled her hand away. 'I am keeping you from eating and, I must confess, I am fatigued myself. I believe I should go to my room.' She stood and yawned for effect. 'Will you be all right without me?'

He picked up a piece of bread. 'I am feeling quite well, my lady. And Cullen will be here soon, I am sure.'

She walked to his side and, because she could not resist, leaned down to kiss his forehead.

'Goodnight,' she murmured.

She hurried out of the room.

Her room was right next door and she rushed inside, fearing she would burst into tears before she reached it.

They would have two more days together. Merely two.

She took a deep breath and paced the room willing herself not to weep. Weeping had never done her a bit of good—

She stopped.

That was almost a memory!

She closed her eyes and tried to imagine a time that weeping had not done her a bit of good.

Nothing came.

The door opened and Ella walked in. 'What are you doing, m'lady?'

'Trying—trying to remember something.' She wiped her eyes.

Ella came closer. 'Are you weeping, m'lady? Why are you weeping?'

'I wasn't weeping.' She'd been trying not to weep.

'Well, you look as if you were,' the maid insisted. 'Did you and the Captain have another row?'

'We did not have a row.' On the contrary. He'd been lovely with her. Tears threatened again and she blinked rapidly to force them away.

Ella put her hands on her hips. 'You had a row. But do not worry. The Captain will come around. Cullen always does and then he is sweeter than ever.'

Claire needed to correct this impression of Ella's. 'Ella, Captain Roper and I are not—not in a romantic way towards each other. I have told you before. He rescued me from the sea and has helped me ever since.'

The maid shook her head. 'You can tell me a hundred times, but I will never believe it.'

Claire had this inexplicable need to convince her, though. 'Do you not know why I am travelling to London?'

'Because that is where the Captain wishes to go,' Ella replied.

'No,' she said patiently. 'I am going to London to be married.'

Ella broke out in a huge grin. 'You and the Captain are going to be married?'

'No!' A stab of pain pierced her insides.

'Then who are you to marry?' Ella asked, looking very sceptical.

Claire turned away. 'I am to marry Lord Stonecroft.'

'You are not!' Ella's voice rose in shock. 'Who is Lord Stonecroft?'

She waved a hand. 'Some baron.'

'Some baron?' Ella repeated.

Claire turned her back to the maid. 'Here. Help me dress for bed.'

Ella untied her laces and helped her out of the dress.

'This Baron Stonecroft,' the maid went on. 'Is he as nice as the Captain?'

'I—I do not know.'

Ella untied Claire's corset. 'Well, is he as handsome?'

Claire wriggled out of her corset. 'I do not know.'

'What do you mean, you do not know?' Ella cried. 'Have you not met him?'

'I do not know if I have met him.'

'You must know!' Ella turned her around and peered into her eyes. 'Are you ill, m'lady? You are talking nonsense.'

Claire had a sudden empathy for Ella's parents. Ella's outspokenness was unrelenting.

'It may sound like nonsense,' Claire said, 'but it is true. I know very little about Lord Stonecroft except that I was betrothed to him. I do not remember him. I learned about him in Dublin when my brother called upon me. I did not remember my brother either.'

Ella shook her head. 'I do not understand you.'

'Let us have some tea.' Claire wanted to tell Ella everything. She needed a friend right now.

There was a kettle in the fireplace, a pot, cups and milk on the table and tins of tea and sugar. Ella, still looking baffled, set about making the tea while Claire changed into her nightdress. She wrapped her Kashmir shawl around her shoulders and lowered herself into a chair at the table.

'Sit with me,' she told Ella.

Ella, a wary gleam in her eye, sat opposite her.

Claire poured tea for both of them.

'Something happened to me because of the shipwreck.' She handed Ella one of the cups. 'Captain Roper said he was taking me to one of the rowboats when a wave washed over us and swept us into the sea. I was hit on the head.' She took a sip of her tea. 'But I do not remember this. When I woke up, we were on a raft—a door from the ship, really. And I remembered nothing about myself before that moment.'

'You lost your memory?' Ella asked.

'Yes,' Claire replied.

'Because of being hit on the head?'

'I do not know about that,' Claire said. 'I remember some things. Everyday things. How to care for myself. I know things, like about the war or about London or Dublin. I don't remember anything about myself, though. I don't remember being in London or Dublin. I don't remember reading about the war or learning anything that I simply know.'

'But-but…' Ella stammered, 'you seem like an ordinary lady.' She put her hand to her mouth. 'Beg pardon. That sounded wrong. I don't mean you are ordinary. I mean, it doesn't show.' She peered at Claire. 'You really don't remember about yourself?'

Claire sipped more tea. 'No. I know my name because Captain Roper told me my name. It never sounds right when I'm called Lady Rebecca, though.'

'G'way.' Ella's eyes grew big.

'When my brother—my half-brother—came to Dublin, he looked like a stranger to me. When he told me I was to

marry Lord Stonecroft, it was as if that was the first time
I'd heard it. The only people I remember are the Captain
and the people I've met since the shipwreck, the fishermen
who saved us, the innkeepers where we stayed, the clerks
in the shops we visited.' She smiled at Ella. 'And you and
Cullen, of course.'

'My poor lady!'

The young woman's sympathy touched her and tears
stung her eyes again. She took another sip of tea to regain
her composure.

Ella did the same, looking very thoughtful.

'So,' the maid finally said. 'You are going to London to
marry this lord you don't remember?'

Claire nodded.

Ella slammed her hand on the table. 'How can you? You
don't know him!'

'I don't know what else to do,' Claire admitted.

'Stay with the Captain!' Ella cried. 'Marry him!'

Her heart ached in her chest. 'He does not wish to marry
me, Ella. He is going to London so that he can get a new
ship.'

'No,' she said.

'He wants to go back to the sea.' Claire knew this without question. 'And even if he did not, his family and mine
were enemies two generations ago. My grandfather caused
his grandfather to lose his fortune and property. He would
not wish to marry an enemy.'

'That is nothing,' Ella insisted. 'Cullen's family and
mine have been enemies for longer than that, but what is
that to us?'

'I—I became upset tonight, because we will likely reach
London in two days and what will I do when I must say
goodbye to the Captain? He is the only one who knows
about my loss of memory.' She quickly added, 'And now
you, of course.'

'I won't tell anyone,' Ella promised.

Her loyalty made Claire wish to weep all over again.

Ella set down her teacup and stood. 'I think we will be rising quite early tomorrow, so I think you should go to bed.'

Claire smiled inwardly. Her servant, a girl younger than herself—probably—was telling her what to do. 'Very well, Ella.'

'And tomorrow we'll start trying to get your memory back.'

The next morning Claire rose early, hearing Ella already moving about the room. They washed and dressed and met Lucien and Cullen for breakfast. They were on the road by eight o'clock.

Cullen again rode on the outside, but he'd already decided that the coachmen seemed like honest, hardworking men. This road would be well travelled and their coach never out of sight of some other horseman or vehicle. The possibility of another attack seemed remote.

Claire was heartened that Lucien's colour had improved. He reported feeling well, but, then, he would say that, so she watched him closely.

'I sent a messenger ahead,' Lucien told her. 'To let Lord Stonecroft know you will arrive tomorrow.'

Claire's stomach plummeted. 'I suppose that was wise.'

Parting from him was becoming more real.

When they were well on the road, Ella spoke up. 'Captain, m'lady told me about losing her memory.'

Lucien responded to her in a careful, non-committal tone. 'She did?'

'I think it must be a hardship not to remember anything about yourself,' Ella went on. 'I think we should help m'lady remember.'

He looked as if he were stifling a smile. 'I agree. How do you think we should do that?'

Ella appeared lost in thought for a moment. 'We should ask her questions.'

Claire felt her stomach clench in anxiety.

Lucien must have noticed. 'Are you willing, my lady?'

She took a couple of long breaths. 'I am willing to try.'

He turned to Ella. 'So what questions?'

Ella tapped her cheek with her finger. 'I don't know,' she finally said.

'I tried something before,' Lucien went on. 'Asking general questions. Nothing about an actual memory, just questions about life.'

Ella blinked. 'I don't understand.'

Claire's hand shook, but she wove her fingers together to disguise that fact. 'The Captain told me to talk about a school.'

The maid brightened. 'Did you remember anything?'

Claire shook her head. But she'd almost remembered.

'So,' Lucien said, 'we should ask about something different. Like...' He paused. 'Like, tell us about a house.'

'A house?' Claire felt her skin heat. She wished she had a fan.

'Yes,' Lucien said mildly, as if it was the most inconsequential of subjects.

'Do you mean like a country house?' she asked.

'Yes.' He sat up straighter. 'A country house. Describe it.'

'I don't remember a country house.' Her heart pounded.

'Imagine one. Any one,' he said. 'Remember. Do not think about it too much. Just respond.'

She released a shuddering breath. 'Like one of stucco?'

'What colour stucco?' he pressed.

She waved a hand. 'White.'

'What style?'

'Style?' She stalled.

He nodded. 'Jacobin? Tudor? Palladian?'

'Palladian,' she said. 'Tudor or Jacobin would not be stucco, would they?'

One corner of his mouth lifted. 'I would not know. Very well, we have a white Palladian country house. What does the hall look like? Remember, you are merely inventing this.'

'It is long and narrow with a wide staircase at the end and plasterwork cornices and ceiling.' She blinked. That seemed so specific.

'Very well,' he went on. 'Now imagine a room. Any room.'

A vision of a room flashed through her mind. A schoolroom. She heard a child's laughter. Her heart raced. 'A—a schoolroom. Tables, slates, books.'

Ella broke in. 'You are remembering something, m'lady!'

The vision vanished. 'But it does not feel like remembering. I cannot place myself there.'

'Try imagining another room,' Lucien suggested.

She saw a small sitting room and a man. More like the shadow of a man. Her anxiety rose until she wished she could jump out of the carriage.

'I—I cannot!' She wrapped her arms around herself.

He reached across the carriage and touched her arm. 'No matter,' he murmured. 'We will leave it now.'

'M'lady!' Ella cried. 'Do not fret so. We did not mean to upset you.'

She took a deep breath. 'I am quite restored. I do not know what happened.'

Lucien thought he knew what happened. Something she almost remembered frightened her. Perhaps it was not the blow to her head; perhaps it was fear that made her lose her memory. What else could have happened to her besides the shipwreck?

And how did he know he was not delivering her to the lion's den by taking her to London?

'I have an idea.' Ella leaned forward. 'Let us sing a song. Maybe you will remember music.'

Lady Rebecca still looked strained, but she seemed to force a smile. 'We can try.'

The maid began singing.

Yonder stands a pretty maiden,
Who she is I do not know,
I'll go court her for her beauty,
Let her answer yes or no.

Her voice was a crystalline soprano. She turned to Lady Rebecca. 'Do you know this one?

Lady Rebecca shook her head.

'Are you sure?' Ella sang more.

Pretty maid, I've come to court you,
If your favour I do gain
And you make me hearty welcome,
I will call this way again.

Ella looked at Lady Rebecca. 'No?'

'I do not remember it.' She looked distressed.

Ella sighed. 'How about this one?'

As we marched down to Fenario
As we marched down to Fenario
Our captain fell in love with a lady like a dove
And the name she was called was pretty Peggy-o

'I do not know that one either,' Lady Rebecca said quickly.

Lucien was glad she interrupted. That song was about a captain.

'Sing a song you know,' Lucien suggested to Lady Rebecca.

She gave him an annoyed face. 'You sing a song first.'

Before Lucien rose in rank, he'd loved singing along with the seamen as they did their work. He hadn't sung much since then.

And most of those songs the seamen sang were not fit for ladies.

He thought a moment, then remembered one that was not too scandalous.

Beauing, belleing, dancing, drinking,
Breaking windows, cursing, sinking,
Ever raking, never thinking,
Live the Rakes of Mallow—

Ella laughed with delight and he even made Lady Rebecca smile.

He finished to the end where the Rakes of Mallow married and raked no more. They married and he remembered he was taking Lady Rebecca to be married.

'Now it is your turn,' he told her, hoping she had not made that same connection.

She closed her eyes and he feared she would not find one she remembered.

But she began in a halting but rich contralto that warmed inside him like a good glass of brandy.

The hours sad I left a maid
A lingering farewell taking
Whose sighs and tears my steps delayed
I thought her heart was breaking...

'I cannot finish it.' Her eyes glistened.

With tears? he wondered. *Sighs and tears.*

'I don't remember.' Her voice cracked.

Ella put an arm around her. 'But you remembered a little!'

Ella continued to ask Lady Rebecca questions, but all that resulted in was more distress in her eyes.

'I think we should give Lady Rebecca a rest,' he told Ella. 'She'll have a headache soon enough if we persist.'

He would not be surprised if her head ached right now.

'But her memory must come back before tomorrow,' Ella cried. 'I cannot bear to leave her if it does not.'

Yes. The closer they came to London, the worse Lucien felt. He would be leaving her adrift without any tether connecting her to her past. He was in her memory longer than anyone else and everything they'd been through since the shipwreck had bound them together even more.

How was he to leave her?

Chapter Twelve

Later in the day the weather turned even colder and rain poured down, making it hard going for the horses. They were forced to stop for the day at the next coaching inn. With luck they could still make London the next day.

Cullen was soaked to the skin, not having the same coats and hats the coachmen wore. Lucien let Ella tend to him, to see he changed into dry clothes and to care for the wet ones. That left Lucien alone with Lady Rebecca in a private dining room he'd engaged.

He lowered himself into a chair. His arm ached like the devil.

'You are in pain,' Lady Rebecca said, approaching him.

He looked up at her. 'The last of the ride was a bit rough. It'll pass.'

She crouched down. 'Let me see it.'

Her face was even with his and their eyes met briefly. Hers were filled with determination and concern. She'd fight him over this.

'Help me off with my coat, then.'

He turned in the chair and she gingerly pulled his coat over his shoulders and off his arms, taking care to avoid his wound.

His shirtsleeve was dotted with blood.

She frowned and drew the sleeve over his shoulder. Her

fingers on his bare skin made him flare with desire as she exposed the bandage, red where blood seeped out of the wound.

'It is bleeding,' she said. 'I am going to take the bandage off.'

She untied the knot and unwound the bandage. Although she was gentle, it felt as if she were pounding on his arm instead of barely touching it.

He much preferred the desire over the pain.

When the bandage was off, Lucien could see that some of the stitches had been pulled apart, causing the bleeding.

She looked closely at the wound. She rose and walked over to an ewer and basin on a table in the corner of the room. She poured some water in the basin, put a towel around her arm and brought them both back to Lucien.

'Let me clean it a little so we can see how serious this is.' She moistened the towel and dabbed at the wound.

It throbbed. Lucien talked through the pain. 'I thought ladies became squeamish at the sight of blood.'

She darted a glance at him. 'I lost that sensibility when your blood soaked your coat and would not stop flowing.'

She'd been valiant at that time. 'That was a lot, I admit.'

She focused on cleaning his wound. 'This hardly signifies.' She leaned back. 'I think the bleeding is stopping. We should bandage it and you should rest that arm.'

They had been in such intimate situations these last weeks that this felt entirely normal to him, he in his shirtsleeves, his arm bared, so she could tend to him.

Tomorrow they would part.

How would he stand never seeing her morning, noon and night? He'd become so used to her.

She stood. 'I am going to find some clean bandages. I am sure the innkeeper has some.'

She walked out of the room and it seemed devoid of light without her.

* * *

It appeared as if they'd both decided to treat this last night together as if their parting was not imminent. They spent a comfortable dinner with Ella and Cullen. Ella, ever the one to spur everyone on, got Lucien to tell of some of his exploits at sea. He shared the ones fit for ladies to hear. Cullen talked of events on the farm and of coming to Dublin after knowing nothing but the farm. Ella was a gratifying audience and even Lady Rebecca seemed to relax and enjoy herself. But, then, the memories others experienced seemed to comfort her.

In the morning of their last day, the messenger Lucien had sent to Lord Stonecroft knocked at the door of the dining room where Lucien sat with Lady Rebecca, Ella and Cullen.

'I have news for you,' the man said.

'How did you find me?' Lucien asked. There must have been dozens of inns along the route he might have stopped in.

'Just stopped at every inn I could see.' He held out the envelope that Lucien had given him the previous day. 'Lord Stonecroft is not in London. He is spending the summer in Bath.'

'Bath?' Lady Rebecca exclaimed.

Bath was one of those places naval officers retired to after leaving their ships. Once most fashionable to the titled elite, it now had been replaced by Brighton where the Prince Regent preferred to spend his time.

'I thought it best to come back to find you,' the man said. 'If you want me to deliver the letter to the gentleman in Bath, I'll be off straight away.'

Lucien handed the man some coins. 'Yes. By all means deliver the letter to Bath.'

The man looked happily at the money in his hand, bowed and rushed off.

'So we go to Bath, apparently,' Lucien said.

'No, Lucien,' Lady Rebecca cried. 'You cannot go to Bath. You need to be at the Admiralty to be assigned a new ship.'

'I will escort you to Bath,' he said quietly. 'I will see you safely to where you must go. What kind of man would I be if I left you now?'

'But what will happen if you do not appear at the Admiralty?' she asked.

He did not know what would happen. He'd been absent for weeks. He wished he'd asked the messenger to wait. He'd not even informed the Admiralty that he was alive.

'It will be a longer trip than to London,' Cullen spoke up. 'Shall I go speak to the coachmen?'

'Thank you, Cullen. And if they are in agreement to transport us, see if they can be ready in half an hour.' Lucien would write to the Admiralty from Bath.

Bath echoed in Claire's mind. Golden buildings. Hills. A towering cathedral.

She held her breath. Was that a memory?

She glanced from Lucien to Ella and decided not to say anything. They would only press her and she'd disappoint them again by not remembering as they wished her to.

And likely she'd wind up with a raging headache, as well.

When they were on the road again, Claire paid close attention to the scenery outside. Would something look familiar?

Nothing did.

The weather outside was dismal and damp with a steady drizzle. It matched Claire's mood. She must still say goodbye to Lucien, if not today, tomorrow.

She tried to think of how she might feel to meet Lord Stonecroft, but her insides twisted with anxiety at that thought. Instead, she pushed herself to remember everything about her time with Lucien, from waking in his arms in the middle of the Irish Sea to tending his wound the night before.

The coachmen drove the carriage at a daring clip, jostling its passengers as it made good time on the often muddy roads. Claire worried about Lucien's wound, but he insisted it was fine. Since Cullen rode with them and sat on the backward-facing seat with Ella, Claire, next to Lucien, could not easily see Lucien's face.

They reached Bath as the sun dipped below the horizon turning everything a sombre grey. They pulled into a coaching inn called the West Gate. A letter for Lucien awaited them. The messenger had delivered Lucien's letter to Lord Stonecroft and he agreed they could call upon him the next day.

Too soon, thought Claire. But Lucien had altered his plans more than once for her sake. She must think of him.

They procured two rooms, and all were so exhausted that they retired for the night without dinner.

'Tomorrow you might meet Lord Stonecroft,' Ella remarked as she helped Claire ready herself for bed. 'I wonder what he will be like.'

Claire's anxiety about Stonecroft had settled like a hard rock inside her stomach. 'I wonder, too.'

'Do you think you fell in love with him?' Her eyes turned starry for a moment. 'You'd think you would remember someone you fell in love with. I could certainly never forget Cullen.'

'I wish I did remember.' Then she would know, too. Did she love him?

Ella helped her into her nightdress. 'What time will you call upon him?'

'I believe Lucien said eleven, by Lord Stonecroft's request.' Perhaps she would have most of the morning with Lucien.

Claire rose early and dressed in the same travelling dress she'd worn the day before, the patterned dark green one. In their fatigue last night, they'd made no plans for breakfast or for the rest of the morning. Claire wanted to spend that time with Lucien. She hoped he would knock on the door and invite her to dine with him.

Ella was busy straightening the room while Claire paced up and down, waiting to hear more bells marking the hour.

'Shall I go to his room and see what is what?' Ella asked.

'His room?' She knew precisely who Ella meant.

'The Captain,' Ella said.

'No,' she replied. 'The Captain may have other plans. I will wait until the next bells and then you may see about breakfast for us both.'

Ella folded Claire's Kashmir shawl and placed it on a chair by the door. 'I'm going to see what their plans are.'

Before Claire could protest, Ella dashed out of the room. Claire paced faster. Now he would feel obliged to spend the morning with her. She walked to the window and looked out over the street.

The buildings in their golden Bath stone felt comfortable. Familiar.

Had she been here before?

A knock sounded at the door. She crossed the room to open it.

Lucien stood in the doorway. 'Would you like to have breakfast?' he asked.

She peered at him. 'Did Ella put you up to this?'

He looked puzzled. 'Ella? No. I was simply waiting until I knew you were awake.'

She smiled.

'I am ready.' She put on her hat and picked up her Kashmir shawl and gloves.

He glanced at the shawl. 'Did you not want to eat in the public rooms here?'

'No. I—I—I assumed we would walk around the city first and see what else is here.' Although why she assumed that, she did not know.

He bowed. 'Whatever your pleasure.'

They walked down the stairs to the hall and out the main door that opened on to the street.

'I have not been in Bath before,' Lucien said.

Claire did not know why she knew, but she knew they should turn left. 'Let us go this way.'

They crossed the street and walked past the Pump Room. She knew this was where one could drink from a fountain the metallic-tasting waters that made Bath a place where people came to cure whatever ailed them. They turned again when in front of Bath Abbey and crossed another street to an area of shops.

She stopped in front of one establishment. 'We could eat here,' she said.

'You know this place?' His eyes widened.

She should have realised he would guess that she had not been simply wandering. 'It is where they sell Sally Lunn's buns.'

They went inside and ordered the sweet spongy rolls that had been served there for decades.

'How much did you remember?' he asked, tearing off a piece of roll.

'Only the places,' she responded. 'I know Bath, but I do not know why. I believe I could walk the whole of it and know each notable place, but I cannot remember ever being here.'

'None the less, it is more than you've remembered before.' His tone was encouraging.

'Why should I have been here, though?' she added. 'Did I live here? I cannot close my eyes and picture a place I could call home, but I can close my eyes and see the Crescent.'

'You remember it.' He took a sip of a mug of coffee.

'I must have been here.' She nibbled on her bun.

He leaned forward. 'Perhaps you also remembered a school in Bristol. Bristol is not far from here. It would make sense that you might have had many opportunities to visit Bath.'

How she would love to travel to Bristol and find that school. Maybe someone there could help fill in some of the blanks in her mind.

How she wished she could travel there with Lucien.

After they finished breakfast, they stepped outside again into a day that was chilly and grey, but at least not raining. Claire wrapped her Kashmir shawl around her, closing her eyes for a moment and remembering the shop where Lucien had purchased it for her. She remembered the display of all the colourful shawls and the clerk who seemed to know who she was, the scent of the fabric, the expression of approval on Lucien's face when she selected this shawl.

She still felt it was too extravagant.

But, then, it had also helped save Lucien's life.

She made herself remember that terrible day, as well. All memories, even that horrible one, were precious to her.

And it seemed all her memories involved Lucien.

If today was to be the last chance to build memories with him, she was determined to do so.

'Would you like to see the Royal Crescent and the Circus?' she asked him.

He looked directly into her eyes before answering. 'Yes. Certainly.'

She smiled, so glad he was willing to spend more time together. 'Then, come! I know the way there.'

She led him back to Westgate Street, walking to the end and turning to walk past the Theatre Royal to Queen Square. Claire was able to name each notable spot they passed.

She paused before the square, staring at the obelisk in its centre. 'The square is different,' she said. 'The obelisk—I think it used to be surrounded by a pool of water.'

Lucien touched her hand. 'You are remembering things in more and more detail.'

But what use was it if she could not put herself in those memories?

They continued to the Circus, a circle of terrace houses built in the Palladian style fifty years before and one of the most admired sites in Bath.

They walked the entire circle.

'Is it not beautiful?' she asked Lucien.

'Quite grand,' he admitted.

An older gentleman approached them. 'Roper? Is that you? As I live and breathe.'

Lucien's face lit with pleasure. 'Sir Richard!'

The two men shook hands, holding on longer than was typical.

'What the devil?' his friend asked. 'I'd heard that you'd drowned. But here you are in Bath.'

'I am indeed alive.' Lucien glanced at Claire. 'Let me present you to Lady Rebecca Pierce. My lady, this is Admiral Sir Richard Bickerton. I served on his ship in my younger days.'

'And a fine young midshipman he was.' Sir Richard grinned. He turned to Claire and bowed. 'Lady Rebecca.'

Bowing to her never felt right.

She curtsied. 'A pleasure, sir.'

Lucien and the Admiral must be full of memories of their days together.

The Admiral gave Lucien an approving look. 'Will you be in Bath long?'

Claire was eager to hear that answer.

'I am uncertain at this time,' Lucien responded.

'Tomorrow?' Sir Richard persisted. 'Would you call upon me tomorrow?' He pointed to one of the terrace houses in the Circus. 'I reside at Number Fifteen.'

'I will come, sir,' Lucien said.

The two men arranged a time and shook hands again. Sir Richard turned and bowed to Claire. 'You must come, too, my lady.'

'I—I may not be at liberty, sir, but thank you.' She did not know what tomorrow would bring.

He bowed again and went on his way.

Claire and Lucien walked on to the Royal Crescent.

'This is also very grand,' Lucien said as the buildings came into view.

'It is one of Bath's greatest attractions,' she said, although her enthusiasm had waned.

They walked on to the lawn in front of the Crescent and took in the whole expanse of terrace houses with identical front façades, built on a curve.

'My lady,' Lucien said quietly.

She turned her attention to him.

'The direction I was given to Lord Stonecroft's residence was Number Five Royal Crescent.'

Lucien watched her face fall as if disappointed at this news.

He thought she would be glad that Lord Stonecroft resided in such a desirable location.

The Royal Crescent was an imposing sight. What lady would not want to live in such a beautiful location?

She set her chin. 'I suppose this is a very good address.'

What could he say when every part of his body wanted to keep her with him longer? He was used to protecting her, that was it. But he'd posted a letter to the Admiralty, telling them he would be in London in a few days.

She smiled wanly. 'I am a bit apprehensive.'

For that brief moment she looked very apprehensive.

'I will call upon him with you,' he said impulsively.

She looked relieved. 'Will you? I was not certain.'

He had not been certain either.

She smiled again, this time bravely. 'I am sure all will be well. I only wish I could remember. I must have wanted to marry him, do you not think? Otherwise why would I have agreed?'

What was the likelihood of it being a love match? Lucien thought. Members of the *ton* married for advantage, did they not? On the other hand, what if she did love Stonecroft, and he, her? Is that not what Lucien would most wish for her?

So why did that thought bring Lucien no comfort?

'It is very hard not to know,' he finally said, but he was not sure if he was speaking about himself or about her.

'How long before we must call upon Lord Stonecroft?' Anxious lines creased her forehead again.

He pulled out his watch. 'Two hours.'

She averted her head, almost as if the words had slapped her on the cheek.

'Do you wish to return to the inn?' he asked. Perhaps she wished to freshen up before meeting the man to whom she was betrothed.

'Only if you wish it,' she replied.

'I am content to walk,' he said.

She nodded and they turned and retraced their steps, making their way back towards the Abbey.

When they walked past one building, she said, 'This is the Pump Room. You must try the waters before you leave Bath.'

'Would you like to go in now?' he asked, wanting in these last moments together to please her.

She shook her head. 'It is always full of people and I do not wish to be around people right now.'

They walked instead to the river and watched the boats travel on its water.

'We have been through much together, Lucien,' she remarked, not looking at him. 'I must, while I have this opportunity, thank you for all you have done for me.'

He felt his throat tighten. 'You saved me, as well, remember.'

She turned and looked up at him. 'You did more than save me, Lucien.'

It was Lucien's turn to avert his gaze. 'It was my pleasure.'

Emotions he was not quite sure how to name churned inside him. Parting from her would be more difficult than he imagined.

She looked up at the sky. 'We are lucky it is not raining.'

Although rain would suit his mood.

They looked out on the River Avon again. Its expanse was so narrow in comparison to oceans, he felt as if he could jump it.

He stole a glance at her, looking lovely in her green dress and colourful shawl. The green of her hat framed her face and those changeable eyes of hers matched her clothes.

A memory of her lips against his returned to him and desire stirred inside him. He should not desire this woman of all women. Because of her status. Because of her family. Because he was delivering her to the man she was supposed to marry.

Because he needed to get back to the sea.

He pulled out his watch again. 'We should walk back.'

Chapter Thirteen

They did not speak much on the walk back to the Crescent. Claire held Lucien's arm, very aware that this might be the last time she could touch him. She again recounted her memories of him in her mind, determined not to forget a single detail.

Too soon they stood at the doorway of Number Five.

Lucien sounded the knocker and the door was opened by a footman in livery.

'Lady Rebecca Pierce and Captain Roper,' Lucien told the man. 'Lord Stonecroft is expecting us.'

The footman stood aside, holding open the door. They entered the hall with its white and black marbled floor. Straight ahead was a staircase with an arch above it. All the doorways on this floor were also arched.

It did not look like a place she had ever seen before.

'I will announce you,' the footman said.

They followed him up the stairs to the drawing room.

Claire's heart was pounding in her chest and she found it hard to breathe.

The footman knocked on the door. A voice on the other side answered and the footman opened the door. 'Lady Rebecca Pierce and Captain Roper.'

Claire stepped inside first.

Seated on a sofa was a grey-haired gentleman. He rose

and gestured with his hand. 'Come in. Come in, my dear,' he said.

Could this be Lord Stonecroft?

He looked to be in his fifties. Not unpleasant in countenance, but so much older than she'd imagined.

Claire took only a step forward.

On a chair nearby was a woman near to his age.

The woman rose and crossed the room to her. 'Lady Rebecca, how delighted we are to see you. Goodness! We thought you had drowned.'

Claire turned to Lucien, grasping for a lifeline. 'This is Captain Roper. My rescuer.'

The woman smiled at Lucien. 'Captain Roper? How nice that you have brought Lady Rebecca to us.'

Lucien tilted his head. 'Forgive me. You are?'

The woman laughed. 'I am Miss Attwood. Stonecroft's sister.' She glanced to the man.

He must be Stonecroft.

'Lady Rebecca, come to me.' Stonecroft patted the back of the sofa.

She gave what must have been a panicked look to Lucien. She did not move.

'How much do you know about what happened to Lady Rebecca?' Lucien asked.

Lord Stonecroft shrugged. 'Keneagle wrote that she had not drowned and would be travelling to London. Of course, I was not in London, but the letter reached me here. Then your message came that you would be in Bath today.'

'You need to know what happened to her.' Lucien told a shortened version, glossing over the sleeping accommodations on the fishing boat. And the kisses.

'My goodness!' Miss Attwood exclaimed. 'How very dreadful.' She gestured to the chairs and sofa. 'But do let us sit. We should be getting tea.'

Claire wanted to sit with Lucien, but Lord Stonecroft

patted the space beside him on the sofa. 'Sit next to me, my dear.'

She lowered herself there.

'There is one more thing you should know,' Lucien said.

'What is that, Captain?' Miss Attwood responded.

'Lady Rebecca has lost her memory.' He glanced at her, his gaze giving her strength to endure this interview. 'When we were swept out to sea, some debris struck her head, rendering her unconscious. When she woke up on the raft, she remembered nothing from before that moment.'

'Unbelievable!' Miss Attwood exclaimed.

'You remember nothing?' Stonecroft asked her.

'I know things. Like about the war. About how things work,' she explained. 'I remember places, but I cannot remember myself being in them.'

Stonecroft looked annoyed. 'You remembered we are betrothed.'

'No, my lord.' She lowered her voice. 'I did not remember. My brother told me. I do not remember anything about you.'

'Pffft!' Miss Attwood made a dismissive gesture with her hand. 'Surely this loss of memory is temporary.'

The footman brought in tea.

'Would you like to pour, dear?' Miss Attwood asked her, then looked worried. 'Do you remember how to pour tea?'

'Yes, I remember those sorts of things.' Claire reached for the teapot. 'How do you take your tea?'

They told her and she busied herself pouring the tea.

'Where are you staying, dear?' Miss Attwood asked.

'The West Gate Inn,' Lucien replied as Claire handed them each a teacup.

Lord Stonecroft's brows rose. 'West Gate, you say? No. Not the best place. All sorts stay there.'

It seemed to Claire like a fairly normal coaching inn, like many where they'd stopped on this trip.

'Stonecroft.' Miss Attwood's expression brightened. 'We should have Lady Rebecca stay here. It would be entirely respectable, because I am here to chaperon. And you are to be married anyway.'

'Yes, that would do.' Stonecroft nodded. He turned to Lucien. 'You will have her things sent here.'

Lucien stiffened. 'Only if Lady Rebecca wishes it.'

What other choice did she have? If she moved in with Lord Stonecroft, Lucien would be free to go to London.

'It is the perfect solution, dear,' Miss Attwood went on. 'Where else would you stay? Unless you have a relation here.'

Lucien replied in a taut voice, 'She cannot remember if she has a relation here. Her brother did not speak of any relations.'

Stonecroft waved his hand. 'Well, she cannot stay at West Gate Inn.'

Miss Attwood put down her teacup. 'Really, dear, you must stay with us. We have a lovely room that will be perfect for you until the nuptials take place.'

Claire's stomach clenched.

She was supposed to marry this man. She'd never expected him to be old enough to be her father. Or to seem so much of a stranger, but marrying him had been already arranged and she'd already agreed to it.

It was just so difficult to think of moving into this gentleman's house.

And being apart from Lucien.

Lucien turned to her with a troubled expression. 'Do you wish to stay here?'

She took a sip of her tea and could barely meet his gaze. 'It appears to be the best solution.'

She had to release Lucien; she knew that.

'Excellent!' Miss Attwood said. 'I will show you your room and the house as soon as we finish tea.'

Claire quickly added, 'I must have my maid with me. I insist upon that.'

'You have a maid?' Miss Attwood said. 'Was she in the shipwreck, too?'

Claire felt the pain of that poor maid lost in the shipwreck. 'No. This maid is new, but I must have her.'

Immediately she felt guilty. She'd be separating Ella from Cullen, but Lucien might not need Cullen to go to London with him. Perhaps she could also insist Cullen be employed.

'Her maid is at the inn,' Lucien said.

Stonecroft rose and walked over to a bell pull. He addressed Lucien. 'I will arrange for my carriage to take you back to that inn. You will arrange for Lady Rebecca's things to be sent back with the carriage. And this maid, of course.'

Claire felt her face heat. How dare this man command Lucien as if he were a servant!

Lucien stood. 'No, sir. I will walk back to the inn. And I dare say I will reach it before your carriage can be ready.'

Stonecroft shrugged.

All Claire could think was Lucien was leaving! She panicked inside. 'I will walk you out.'

She rose, as did Miss Attwood and Stonecroft.

No! She did not want them anywhere near her when she had to say goodbye.

'Please.' Her voice rose. 'I would like to say goodbye to the Captain alone.'

Stonecroft glanced away.

His sister said, 'Of course you would, dear. We will wait here. Come back when you are finished.'

'Good day.' Lucien bowed to them both.

She followed him out the door and closed it behind her.

They were private for that moment in the hallway at the top of the stairs.

He turned to her. 'Are you certain you wish to stay here?'

No! she wanted to cry. 'It seems a good solution, does it not? It is what I was bound to do before—before the shipwreck.'

He nodded and turned to the stairs.

She caught his arm. 'I—I do not wish to say goodbye, Lucien. After all this time—' The whole of her memory. Her only anchor.

He wrapped his arms around her and held her close and she luxuriated in the familiarity of his warmth and strength. She felt safe in his arms, as he'd kept her safe on the open sea.

He eventually released her. 'You will be able to reach me through the Admiralty. If you need me, you have merely to ask.'

If she asked him to stay with her longer, she knew he would do so. He would never abandon her. But she cared about him too much to ask that of him. The sooner he returned to London, the sooner he could be back in command of a ship, where he most wanted to be.

He descended the stairs and retrieved his hat and gloves from the footman attending the hall. The footman opened the door.

Before he crossed the threshold, he turned and looked up at her standing at the top of the stairs. Their gazes caught and Claire thought her heart would stop.

He walked out the door.

A fine mist of rain met Lucien as he stepped on to the pavement in front of the Royal Crescent terrace house. He filled his lungs with the cool air, wanting it to refresh him. But nothing eased the turmoil inside him.

He detested Lord Stonecroft.

The man was everything he despised about aristocrats. And it was not merely because he had commanded Lucien to do what he expected. He detested that Stonecroft exhibited no sympathy for Lady Rebecca having endured a shipwreck and the loss of her memory. Lucien imagined the man would have shrugged off learning of the attack by the highwaymen had Lucien told him about it.

Plus he was old. An old nobleman coveting a young, vital woman.

Stonecroft would touch her, bed her.

It made Lucien churn with rage.

But he had no right to feel such emotions. She'd made her decision to marry the man before Lucien had ever known her. It was what ladies of her status aspired to and better than to marry a man whose first love was the navy and the sea.

He and Lady Rebecca were merely attached to each other through what they'd endured together. He could admit that he'd admired her. Desired her. But they belonged in two different worlds. Once her memory returned, she would realise that.

He strode down the pavement, past the Circus where Sir Richard lived. He'd promised to call upon the man the next day. So he would not start for London this day.

He'd been pleased to see his former Captain, who had been so instrumental in making him the navy man he was. Who knew when he would ever see Sir Richard again?

One more day's delay could not matter.

He walked swiftly, and when he reached the West Gate Inn, he searched for Cullen and Ella and found them in the public rooms having refreshment.

'Have you need of me, sir?' Cullen jumped to his feet as soon as he spied Lucien.

Lucien gestured for him to sit. 'Let me join you for a moment.' He pulled up a chair and signalled for the tavern maid to bring him a tankard of ale. 'Lady Rebecca is at Lord Stonecroft's.'

'At Lord Stonecroft's? What time will she be returning?' Ella asked.

'She will not be returning. She will be staying in Lord Stonecroft's house.'

Ella's face fell. 'No!'

'She would like you to come to her,' he told Ella. 'To be her lady's maid.'

Ella frowned and looked over at Cullen. 'What about Cullen?'

Lucien had forgotten about Cullen.

Cullen's face shone with disappointment. 'I will miss serving you, sir.'

Lucien felt the impending loss harder than he expected. 'I will miss you, too, Cullen. You are a good man.'

The tavern maid brought Lucien's ale and he took a long sip of it.

He placed the tankard on the table and turned to Cullen. 'You are welcome to come with me to London, if you prefer. I can use your services until I go to sea.'

Ella gave Cullen a pained look. 'I do not want us to be separated.'

And Lucien hated the idea of separating them.

'I am not leaving yet,' he told them. 'Tomorrow I call upon my old navy commander. Perhaps he can assist in finding a position here for Cullen.'

Ella and Cullen exchanged uncertain glances.

Lucien added, 'And I intend to stay until I am certain Lady Rebecca is settled.' Where had that decision come from? He turned to Ella. 'Lord Stonecroft is sending a carriage for you and for Lady Rebecca's things. If you wish to go to her, that is.'

Lucien could not bear the thought of Lady Rebecca not having Ella with her, but it had to be Ella's choice.

She nodded. 'I do want to stay with Lady Rebecca. Not remembering things is hard on her. Someone must help her.'

Lucien felt as if he was making Ella do his duty. 'She wants you. And I would like you to be her lady's maid. You will be able to tell me if she does well there.'

Ella brightened. 'I could be a spy for you!'

Essentially, yes.

She shot up from her chair. 'I had better pack her things, then.'

Cullen stood. 'May I have your leave to assist her?'

They were facing a parting of their own of sorts, except, if Cullen found a position in Bath, they'd have opportunities to be together. 'Of course you have my leave. I'll be in my room after I finish my ale.'

Although Lucien had the feeling he would be consuming stronger spirits before the day was over.

Lord Stonecroft quickly excused himself for an engagement with some other gentlemen at the Pump Room, leaving Miss Attwood to show Claire the house. She began by assembling the servants so that Claire could meet them all.

'My dear brother spares no expense with servants,' Miss Attwood boasted. 'He hires as many as he likes and tries to select footmen who are pleasant of face and all of a similar height and build.'

Perhaps he would hire Cullen, too, then. Except he already had three footmen, a butler, a valet, two housemaids, a housekeeper, cook and two kitchen maids, as well as Miss Attwood's lady's maid. Where did they all sleep?

Would there be room for Ella? If Ella agreed to come, that is.

Miss Attwood began the tour of the house on the ground floor where Stonecroft had a respectable library and a fine dining room, as well as a sitting room and closets. The first floor had the impressive drawing room and bedrooms for Lord Stonecroft and his wife.

'You will move into this bedchamber after you and Stonecroft are wed,' Miss Attwood said, showing her the Lady's room connected by a door to Lord Stonecroft's.

The second floor consisted of two other bedrooms, one for Miss Attwood and the other, the bedchamber where Claire would stay. Behind these two bedrooms were two rooms that were sparsely decorated.

'These will be for the nursery and the governess,' Miss Attwood told her.

Claire had a flash of a table and three little girls seated around it, but the image disappeared before she could tell if it were memory or imagination. Of all of the rooms in the house, though, these two back rooms were the two in which she felt the greatest degree of comfort.

After the tour, Miss Attwood drank tea with Claire in the less formal sitting room on the ground floor.

'Have I been in this house before?' asked Claire. That might explain her reaction to the back rooms.

'No, dear.' Miss Attwood looked askance. 'Do you really not remember where you have been?'

Why would she feign what was so difficult for her?

She tamped down her irritation. She must accept these people as they were if she was going to live here. 'I remember places. Or I think I do. I knew Bath, but I have no memory of my ever having been in Bath.'

'How very strange.' Miss Attwood took a sip of her tea.

'Will you tell me, please, a little of how I met Lord Stonecroft?' Perhaps it would help spark some memory.

'You do not remember?'

Claire gritted her teeth. 'No. I do not remember.'

The older lady took another sip of her tea. 'I do not know the details. He travelled to Ireland—Stonecroft has some property there. I believe your brother arranged the introduction. He met you at your brother's country house. I was very happy to hear he'd decided to marry.'

It simply was not possible that Claire had fallen in love with Stonecroft. He held absolutely no attraction for her. And she did not seem to interest him greatly either.

How was she to marry this man?

She must find some reason to marry him, because at this moment all she wanted to do was run out the door and return to Lucien.

She felt her eyes sting and sipped her tea, blinking away tears.

She placed her teacup down. 'Tell me something of Lord Stonecroft. Why he wished to marry me.'

Miss Attwood's lips pursed. 'Well, I believe he found you suitable.'

She did not wish to set this lady against her. 'I meant, why did he wish to marry at this time?' This advanced age, she meant.

Miss Attwood hid behind her teacup again, but when she put it down, she leaned forward. 'I will tell you, only because it would pain my brother to have you ask him questions like this. I beg you will not ever speak to him about it.'

Claire nodded.

Miss Attwood spoke in a hushed tone. 'My brother was married when he was quite young. In his twenties. Our parents were against the match because she had no fortune at all and brought no status to the union. They were able to keep the couple apart, but our father died unexpectedly. My brother was free to do as he wished and he married the girl. She was a sweet thing and he was totally besotted with her.'

He'd married before. For love.

Miss Attwood went on. 'They tried to have children,

but his wife could not carry babies. She lost several. Then finally she was able to carry one to term, but the birth was a terrible affair. Lasted two days and finally the baby was born, but did not live. And she died as well.' Miss Attwood's voice caught on these last words and she quickly took another sip of tea. 'As you can imagine, Stonecroft was desolate.' She cleared her throat. 'That was nearly twenty-five years ago.'

'How very sad,' Claire said.

'Yes,' Miss Attwood agreed. 'Very sad. Poor Stonecroft has never recovered, really, which is why you must never speak to him about this.' Her voice turned severe.

Because it made him remember? Some memories can be unbearable, Claire thought. But it was so much worse to have no memory at all.

'You want to know why Stonecroft wishes to marry now?' the older lady challenged.

Claire stared at her.

Miss Attwood did not wait for her reply. 'He needs an heir. I convinced him so.' She finished her tea and poured another cup. 'Otherwise everything will go to his cousin's son, who is a perfectly responsible young man, but much too distant a relation and Stonecroft's cousin married an actress, you know, so the family is less than respectable.'

So Stonecroft's parents were not the only ones who considered one's birth important.

'But why did he choose me?' she asked. 'Surely there are many English ladies who would be honoured to be his wife.'

'Indeed so,' agreed Miss Attwood. 'But he wanted someone whose family had no connection to his wife, nor any knowledge of her.'

Nor any memory of her?

The older lady leaned closer to Claire. 'I hope you do not have any romantic notions, dear. Stonecroft will be good to you, but his heart will never be engaged. He's made that perfectly clear.'

Because he loved his wife so much, he has no more love to give to another?

'I do not have romantic notions,' None she could remember, that was.

None except one unattainable one.

Chapter Fourteen

Claire finished her tea. 'Might I retire to my room? I would love a rest.' She had not done anything exerting, but she desperately wished to be alone.

With her memories.

'As you wish.' Miss Attwood stood wearily and started to escort her to the door.

Claire stopped her. 'Please do not feel you have to accompany me if you would rather stay. I can find the room myself.'

The older lady sat down again. 'Thank you, dear.'

Claire walked back to the hall and climbed the two flights of stairs to the bedchamber she must call hers.

At least until she must move to the room next to Lord Stonecroft.

She opened the door and a surprised Ella gave out a cry. 'Oh, m'lady. You startled me so.'

Claire rushed over to her, taking both Ella's hands in hers and squeezing them. 'I am so happy to see you, Ella! No one told me you had arrived.'

'Yes, a little while ago.' Ella smiled. 'The housekeeper said I was to unpack your trunk.'

Claire released her. 'Did you meet the other servants?'

'I think so. I suppose I will find out if I met all of them when I appear for a meal.' Ella turned to the dressing room with its clothes press and cupboard. 'I was putting everything in here. Will that do?'

'Certainly.' Claire watched her unpack the trunk with its lovely clothes purchased by Lucien. Her heart ached.

'So,' the outspoken Ella started asking as she lifted another dress from the trunk, 'what is this Lord Stonecroft like?'

Claire's ache intensified. 'He is older. Old enough to be my father, easily. But there is nothing to object to in him.' Those last words seemed to echo as she spoke them, as if she'd heard them from someone else's mouth.

'Old enough to be your father?' Ella cried. 'He must be ancient. Fifty? As old as fifty?'

She shook the strange sensation away. 'Quite as old as fifty.'

'Did you remember him at all?' Ella asked.

'Not at all.' The cold Bath stone with which the Crescent and the Circus were built was more familiar to her.

'Are you going to marry him?' the maid pressed.

Claire's hands rose in a futile gesture. 'It is what I am supposed to do.'

'Yes,' mumbled Ella. 'And I was supposed to marry some well-to-do merchant.'

There was a knock on the door and it opened before Claire could acknowledge it.

Miss Attwood walked in. 'I was informed your maid had arrived.'

Claire swallowed a retort about respecting her privacy. 'Miss Attwood, may I present Miss Ella Kiley, my lady's maid.'

'Kiley?' Miss Attwood's brows rose. 'You are Irish, then?'

Ella curtsied respectfully. 'I am Irish, ma'am.'

'Miss Attwood is Lord Stonecroft's sister,' Claire explained to Ella. 'She runs his house for him.'

Ella curtsied again. 'Ma'am.'

'She is very young for a lady's maid,' Miss Attwood said in disapproving tones.

'Perhaps,' Claire responded. 'But I am well satisfied with her.'

'Have you been told where you will sleep, girl?' Miss Attwood asked.

'In the attic, ma'am,' Ella replied.

'No!' Claire broke in. 'I want her to sleep in the dressing room here. There is plenty of room for a cot.'

It jarred Claire to order anything to be as she wished it to be, but she could not allow Ella to be squeezed into the attic with all the other female servants.

Miss Attwood's brows rose. 'If you insist, dear.'

'I do.' Claire nodded. 'It is what I wish.'

'Very well.' Miss Attwood turned to leave, but stopped. 'Dinner will be served at six. Stonecroft prefers country hours. And he prefers to dress for dinner.'

'I understand.'

After Miss Attwood left, Ella expelled a breath. 'Whew! She makes me quake in my shoes.'

'I have not yet taken her measure,' Claire said. 'She seems very kind one minute and somewhat intolerant the next.'

Ella's eyes widened. 'I will watch out for her. And for the housekeeper. She is a dragon.'

Ella's forthrightness made Claire want to hug her, but she suspected an unguarded tongue could cause the girl trouble in this house.

'Remember, you answer to me, not to the housekeeper,' Claire told her. 'You must tell me if you have any problems at all.'

Ella laughed. 'Do not fear, m'lady! I'll tell you.'

Claire smiled in return, so happy she was no longer alone.

* * *

Claire went down to the drawing room before six o'clock to await dinner being announced. Both Lord Stonecroft and Miss Attwood were already there.

Stonecroft rose as she entered. 'Lady Rebecca,' he said cordially. 'May I offer you a glass of claret?'

'Thank you, sir,' she said.

She sat on the sofa where she'd sat before when she and Lucien had been in this room. Stonecroft handed her the claret and sat next to her, as she'd expected.

'I hope you have settled in.' His words were polite, but his tone flat.

'Yes, my lord,' she responded.

'And is all to your liking?' he asked.

'I am quite comfortable.' Although she'd rather be dressed in men's clothing mopping fish guts off the deck of a fishing boat.

He turned to his sister and talked of the people he'd met with that day. The names meant nothing to Claire. The conversation swept over her.

Dinner was announced and he escorted her to the dining room. Its formal table was set with three places. Stonecroft sat at the end and Claire and Miss Attwood adjacent to him. Miss Attwood asked him more about his afternoon meeting. Claire sat quietly and relived the meals she'd shared with Lucien, Cullen and Ella.

Eventually Stonecroft noticed her. 'There is an Assembly two days hence. Would you care to attend?'

'If you desire me to,' she responded.

'You had only one trunk delivered,' Miss Attwood said. 'Was your ball gown among the dresses in that trunk?'

'I have no ball gown.' Claire gestured to her clothes. 'This is my best dress. Will it do?'

Miss Attwood's brows shot up. 'No, it will not do.'

Stonecroft looked annoyed. 'For God's sake, get her what she needs, Honora. Have the bills sent to me.'

'We cannot have a ball gown sewn in a day,' his sister shot back.

'Pay whatever they wish, but she should have decent clothes.'

Claire glanced down at the beautiful dress she wore, the dress Lucien bought for her, the most beautiful dress she could remember ever wearing. She loved this dress.

She straightened in her chair and glanced from one to the other. 'You do realise that all my possessions, all my clothes, were lost in the shipwreck, do you not?'

Stonecroft merely looked down at his food.

Miss Attwood appeared contrite. 'Of course, dear. We had not taken that into consideration.'

They all ate in silence for a while until Stonecroft spoke again. 'I have an engagement tonight. I will be home late.'

Miss Attwood asked who he would see and the two of them again spoke about people Claire did not know. Or, rather, people she might have once known, but could not remember. Claire contented herself with remembering the second-hand shop and trying on dress after dress and seeing which met Lucien's approval. What a lovely memory.

When dinner was done, Stonecroft excused himself and left the room. Claire and Miss Attwood sat for a time in the small sitting room for yet another cup of tea.

The next morning Claire rose early, but Ella was already awake and full of information.

'Breakfast is served in the small drawing room at eight o'clock,' Ella told her. 'But apparently Miss Attwood doesn't rise until ten and then she eats in her room.'

'Do you think I am expected to eat at eight?' she asked.

'Oh, I think you might do as you wish, but the servants are all trying to figure out if you are going to create lots more work for them or not,' she responded. 'I've told them how agreeable you are, but they don't believe a word I say, because I am Irish.'

Claire bit her lip. 'I hope they will not be unkind to you.'

Ella smiled. 'I'll manage it.'

'I suppose I should appear at breakfast at the appointed time.' Claire had already washed and donned her shift.

Ella helped her with her corset, petticoat and her sprigged-muslin day dress.

'Just dress my hair plainly,' Claire said.

'Not too plain,' Ella insisted.

So she wound up with curls around her face.

She wore the pearl pendant Lucien had purchased for her, fingering the cool smoothness of the pearl and remembering when he insisted upon buying it for her.

When Ella declared her ready, she stood and eyed the Kashmir shawl, wanting to wrap herself in it and the memories it evoked, but instead she chose a lighter one they'd purchased at the second-hand shop.

She walked out of the room, but instead of heading for the stairs, she paused, looking at the doors to the two unused rooms. She stepped to the one that would be the nursery and opened the door. She could almost hear little girls laughing.

There would be a table and chairs and children seated at the table writing on slates or reading books. Had she dreamed this? It did not seem any more real than an invented story, but the image had come a second time.

She closed her eyes and tried to see herself in the vision, but nothing came.

She turned and walked back to the hallway and down the two flights of stairs.

'Good morning,' she said to the footman attending the hall.

He bowed. 'Good morning, m'lady.'

Would she ever feel right about being bowed to?

'Breakfast will be in the back sitting room,' he added helpfully.

As she had known from Ella. 'Thank you.'

When she reached the sitting room another footman bowed and opened the door for her.

A table had been set up in the middle of the room and a sideboard was filled with food. Lord Stonecroft glanced up from his newspaper. He stood, watching her every move as she approached the table as if to check she was all in one piece.

'Good morning, sir,' she said.

'You are up early,' he responded.

'I tend to rise early.'

He gestured to the sideboard. 'Shall I prepare you a plate?' His tone was unenthusiastic.

'Please sit and continue reading your paper.' She went to the sideboard. 'I will serve myself.'

The footman who had attended the door now stood at the ready to place the food on her plate for her.

She chose some toasted bread and slices of ham and cheese and sat opposite Lord Stonecroft. The footman poured her some tea.

Stonecroft was still watching her.

It made her heart race in anxiety, but she did not wish her nerves to show.

She lifted her chin. 'Am I not dressed properly, my lord? You keep staring.'

He quickly looked down at his food, but his gaze rose again. 'Your dress is out of fashion, but you look well in it.'

'I thank you for the compliment.' Such as it was. She spread some butter on her bread.

She'd told Stonecroft and his sister that she'd lost everything in the shipwreck. Had he no interest in how she had any clothes at all to wear?

She'd tell him anyway. 'I cannot remember the clothes I lost or what is in fashion. When we reached Ireland, I had to wear a dress the innkeeper's wife provided. It was very generous of her. It was also very generous of Captain Roper to buy me my present clothing at a second-hand shop in Dublin.'

She loved every item Lucien purchased for her.

He glanced up. 'A second-hand shop? Clothing discarded by its owners?' His gaze assessed her anew. 'Second-hand clothes will not do. Order whatever you need from the modiste and when we go to London, you will be able to fill your wardrobe with the latest fashions.'

The food tasted like dust in her mouth. She did not need sympathy for what she'd been through, but she certainly wished to see some semblance of feeling from him.

She had to force herself to keep eating.

Had this man been understanding with his beloved wife? Had he seen her sorrows? Soothed her disappointments? Comforted her in her losses?

She had promised not to ask.

He appeared to be reading his newspaper, but he spoke again. 'Shall I stop by the Abbey and arrange to have the banns read?

Her head snapped up. That would mean marrying in three or four weeks. 'So soon?'

He gave her a severe look. 'You were supposed to arrive two months ago.'

It became difficult for her to breathe. 'My lord, the delay was not my fault. I was in a shipwreck. And I cannot remember anything but these last two months. I do not remember you. I did not remember my brother. I did not know my name. Everything but these last two months is like an empty slate—' An image of a little girl writing on a slate flashed through her mind. Again. And it was gone so quickly she did not know if she'd really experienced it.

'Oh, come. You must remember something,' he said.

'Nothing connected to me. I have been in Bath before. I know this, because I knew of the Circus and the Crescent and how to walk here, but I cannot remember ever being here.'

'That does not make sense to me,' he said.

'It does not make sense to me either!' she cried. 'I want time to recover. I want to have my memory back. I do not want to have the banns read until my memory returns.' She surprised herself by speaking so forcefully. It seemed out of character.

He frowned. 'Very well. We will wait. But I do hope you will not announce to the whole of society that you have lost your memory.'

'I have no wish to speak of it to anyone,' she said. But she would expect to receive more sympathy from others than Lord Stonecroft showed.

He wiped his mouth with a napkin and rose. 'If you will excuse me, I must leave. My sister will see what can be done about your wardrobe.'

He bowed and walked out.

That morning Lucien walked to the Circus and knocked at Number Fifteen. His head ached and his mood was foul. Not the best way to meet an old friend.

The door opened and he followed a footman to Sir Richard's study. The Admiral shot to his feet upon seeing Lucien.

'Prompt as ever, eh, boy?' Sir Richard grinned and pumped Lucien's hand.

He invited Lucien to sit and poured them both a brandy, although the hour was early and Lucien had consumed enough brandy from the night before.

'Now let me know all about how you are alive and about

that lovely lady you were with yesterday,' Sir Richard insisted. 'I am disappointed she is not with you.'

How was Lucien to tell of Lady Rebecca? 'First tell me how is your wife? In good health, I hope.'

'Very good health, thank you. She is visiting her sister in Brighton. Taking part in all that Brighton frivolity. Not for me at all.' He seemed unconcerned about his wife's absence. 'Now about the Lady Rebecca…' He lifted his glass to his lips.

Lucien told him about the shipwreck, about saving Lady Rebecca and himself from drowning. He told of their rescue by the fishing boat and about escorting her back to England.

'Remarkable story,' Sir Richard said. 'Remarkable.'

'There is more.' Lucien decided to tell Sir Richard about Lady Rebecca's amnesia. He could trust this man. 'But I must have your word that you will not speak to anyone about this.'

Sir Richard's brows rose. 'You have my word.'

'Lady Rebecca was knocked unconscious from debris from the shipwreck. When she woke, she had no memory. She remembers nothing of her life before waking on the raft. I thought it would be temporary, but so far she has not recovered it.'

'Nothing?' the Admiral asked.

'Nothing. She did not remember her brother. She does not remember being betrothed.'

'Betrothed?' Sir Richard frowned. 'To whom?'

'Lord Stonecroft.'

'Stonecroft?' Sir Richard's voice rose. 'Why, he is as old as I am.'

'You are acquainted with him?' Lucien asked.

'Acquainted. Yes.'

Lucien leaned forward. 'Then tell me what you think of him.'

The Admiral shrugged. 'He is a decent sort. Pays his

gambling debts. Not one to chase skirts. A bit…' He looked as if he was searching for words. 'A bit standoffish, if you know what I mean.'

If he meant an autocratic stiff-neck, Lucien knew precisely what he meant.

Lucien took a sip of his brandy. 'I—I feel a duty to Lady Rebecca.'

'A duty, you say.' Sir Richard looked amused.

'A duty,' Lucien insisted. 'Because of her amnesia. Because of the shipwreck. I feel a responsibility to make certain she is where she belongs. I delivered her to Lord Stonecroft. She is residing there, but I find I cannot leave until I know she is well settled.'

'Leave? For where?' the man asked.

'For London. To the Admiralty,' he responded. 'I was promised a ship.'

'A ship?' Sir Richard's brows knitted. 'That would have been months ago. You realise they would believe you dead?'

'I wrote to them.' Only recently, however.

'My dear boy, the navy is ridding itself of ships. Like your *Foxfire*.'

There would not be many commands to be given, he meant. 'I know. But I cannot leave now. Not until I know how Lady Rebecca fares.'

Sir Richard gave him a knowing glance. 'This lady has become important to you.'

'We have endured much together,' Lucien admitted. 'But she is the daughter of an earl and eventually she will remember how that matters to her. And I am determined to have another ship.'

'Even if all you can get is a merchant ship?' his friend asked.

Lucien lifted a shoulder. 'I want the navy.'

Sir Richard poured Lucien and himself more brandy as their conversation turned to their experiences in the war.

Finally a clock chimed. They'd been talking for three hours.

Lucien stood. 'I should leave. I am overstaying my welcome.'

Sir Richard rose as well. 'It has been my delight to converse with you.'

He walked Lucien to the hall where Lucien retrieved his hat and gloves. Lucien then remembered Cullen. He'd forgotten to ask Sir Richard about finding a position for Cullen.

It felt too late to do so now.

They shook hands once more and Lucien turned to leave.

Sir Richard stopped him with a hand on Lucien's shoulder. 'Wait, my boy. I have an idea. Come stay with me. I am rattling around in this house alone; I would welcome the company.'

He started to tell Sir Richard that it would be too much of an imposition, but then he realised it was the perfect way to show Cullen's worth. 'I have my valet with me.'

'A valet?' Sir Richard laughed. 'We can accommodate a valet. You would do me a favour to be my guest.'

'Perhaps…' Lucien said.

Sir Richard gave his shoulder a fatherly pat. 'I have always thought of you as the son I wished God had given me. I would delight in having more of your company.' He lifted a finger. 'Consider this. There is to be an Assembly in tomorrow night. It is the sort of event Stonecroft attends. I would wager he will be there with your Lady Rebecca. You may come as my guest. It will provide you the chance to see for yourself how she gets on.'

Lucien nodded. 'Then I am grateful to accept your kind invitation.'

'Excellent!' Sir Richard beamed. 'Come to me with your valet before the day is out. I have no plans. I will tell Cook to prepare a meal for two and to expect another servant at the servants' table.'

'I will make the arrangements as soon as I return to the inn.'

This might be the very way he could see the three people newly in his life settled. Their welfare—especially Lady Rebecca's—had become important to him.

Chapter Fifteen

The night of the Assembly arrived and Claire wore a blue silk dress with a gauze overdress trimmed in lace. It was lovely, but, because Miss Attwood directed everything about its creation, Claire felt as if it was more hers than Claire's. The seamstresses were putting the final touches on the gown while Ella arranged her hair under the watchful eyes of Miss Attwood. When she finally donned the dress and put her pearl earrings in her ears, Miss Attwood declared her ready.

She and Miss Attwood walked into the drawing room where Stonecroft waited for her. He again gave an assessing scan of her from top to toe, but this time his eyes revealed an admiration she found equally disturbing.

'I am pleased you are prompt,' he said, looking over her again. 'Of course your jewels are lacking.'

'I only possess the pearl pendant and earrings,' she said.

Miss Attwood wrung her hands. 'Oh, dear. I did not give jewellery a thought. Shall I run upstairs and select some of mine?'

'No time,' Lord Stonecroft said. 'The sedan chairs are waiting.'

'Sedan chairs?' Claire could not imagine making men carry her such a short distance. The Upper Assembly Rooms were right behind the Circus.

Stonecroft escorted her to the hall where two footmen stood ready to help them on with their outer garments. Claire wore the cloak Lucien had purchased for her.

Lord Stonecroft eyed it disapprovingly. 'Is that from the second-hand shop?'

It was a perfectly serviceable red cloak made of a good quality wool. 'All my clothing was once worn by someone else, my lord. Except this gown, of course.' And her Kashmir shawl.

One of the footmen held open the door.

'We should not need such outer garments in the summer.' Lord Stonecroft gestured for her to walk out first. 'It is unseasonably cold.'

The footmen followed them out.

In the street were two sedan chairs, white with gold embellishments and a crest on each side. She assumed the crest was Stonecroft's. Four burly men stood next to the chairs. One of the footmen helped her climb into the second chair.

She hated the trip to the Upper Assembly Rooms. So silly to be carried a few streets away.

When the chairmen put down the chair in front of the Assembly Rooms, Claire opened the door and exited herself, so eager was she to be out. She waited at Lord Stonecroft's sedan chair until he emerged.

'What sort of event is this?' she asked as she took his arm and they walked to the door.

'A private party,' he responded.

They entered and walked through the ballroom, a huge room lit by five magnificent crystal chandeliers. At one end was a balcony where musicians would play for a ball. Here and there in the room groups of people stood in conversation or sat in the chairs that lined the walls.

Claire could almost imagine music and lines of dancers, but she could not remember ever being there.

In the Octagon Room tables were set up and men and

women were intent on their card play. Only a few looked up as they passed.

The Tea Room was the actual setting for the party and the hostess stood near the entrance receiving greetings from the guests. She was of an age with Lord Stonecroft.

He brought Claire over to her. 'Lady Milliforte, may I present Lady Rebecca Pierce, daughter of the Earl of Keneagle.'

Claire curtsied.

'Earl of Keneagle, you say?' Lady Milliforte asked.

'An Irish peer,' Stonecroft explained.

'Delighted to meet you, Lady Rebecca,' the woman said kindly.

'Thank you, ma'am,' Claire said.

Stonecroft leaned towards Lady Milliforte. 'No formal announcement has been made, but Lady Rebecca has consented to be my wife.'

'Oh?' Lady Milliforte looked at her with more interest. She turned back to Stonecroft. 'Well, Jonas, I am glad you have at last come to your senses.'

'I am telling only my dearest friends,' he said to her.

'I do understand.' She smiled from Stonecroft to Claire. 'I am gratified to be so considered.' She patted his hand. 'Is Honora with you?'

'Not tonight,' he responded. 'You know how my sister abhors crowds.'

'This is not a crowd,' she exclaimed.

Claire thought there were plenty of people there to make it a crowd, but she did not listen to the rest of their conversation. Obviously they were close friends to be using given names, but she could tell no more than that.

Lady Milliforte took Claire's arm. 'Let me present you to my husband, Lord Milliforte.'

The Baron was conversing with two other gentlemen

who stepped away. He and Stonecroft exchanged pleasantries. Another old friend, Claire surmised.

She felt quite separate from the people surrounding her. Perhaps if she had her memory she would recognise the names and titles of these people. Most seemed to be contemporaries of Lord Stonecroft. There were very few guests who looked to be around Claire's age. It seemed odd to her to be around so many older people.

Was that a memory of sorts?

Lady Milliforte tapped Stonecroft on the shoulder. 'Jonas, introduce Lady Rebecca around. She must not know a soul.'

But she did know someone.

A gentleman in naval uniform strode over to her. 'Good evening, Lady Rebecca,' he said cheerfully.

'Sir Richard, how lovely to see you again.' He was connected to Lucien and that made her feel less alone.

Stonecroft turned, then, and stepped away from the host and hostess. 'Sir Richard.' He nodded in greeting.

Sir Richard laughed. 'You are wondering how I know this young lady, are you not, sir? Captain Roper introduced us the other day.'

Claire's insides fluttered at the mention of Lucien. She wanted to ask the Admiral if Lucien had called upon him, as they'd arranged. Did he know if Lucien had left for London?

He must have done, she thought depressingly.

Stonecroft took her by the elbow. 'If you will pardon us, Sir Richard. I wish to introduce Lady Rebecca to my friends.'

'I do not mind at all,' Sir Richard said, although Claire thought Stonecroft's words were rude. Sir Richard winked at Claire. 'I trust we will meet again, my lady.'

'I do hope so,' she responded.

Stonecroft took her around the room and introduced her

to many people. She tried to remember each one, but he pulled her to another group before she could fix the names in her memory.

He brought her to yet another older lady, whose costume was more colourful than most with a turban that she wore slightly askew.

'Lady Rebecca Pierce?' the lady cried. 'Not *the* Lady Rebecca Pierce?'

'I—I am not certain what you mean,' Claire responded.

'I was just reading about you!' Her voice rose. She turned to those people standing near her. 'Everyone! She is here. This is Lady Rebecca Pierce who was thought drowned in the *Dun Aengus* shipwreck!'

It seemed as if all eyes turned to her.

Stonecroft frowned. 'How do you know this, my lady?'

'It was in the *Morning Chronicle*. From London,' the lady said. 'Did you not receive the *Chronicle*?'

'I read the *Post*,' he said.

'What did the article say?' another lady asked.

'That she was swept out to sea and rescued by a fishing boat. Everyone thought her dead and then she appeared in Dublin.' The lady's eyes grew larger. 'But her rescuer is here! I met him not a few moments ago.' She stood on tiptoe and called, 'Captain Roper? Captain Roper?'

Claire felt the breath knocked out of her.

He was here. He had not left.

'Someone calls me?' The crowd parted and Lucien appeared.

The lady took his arm. 'This is the man who rescued her! Captain Roper is also a war hero. Captain of the *Foxfire*. Is that not grand?'

'Lucien,' Claire murmured.

His gaze was on her. He smiled.

'Do tell us of the shipwreck!' one of the ladies cried. 'What happened?'

Half the room was attending. Lucien described being swept out to sea and finding the door to use as a raft.

'Were you not terrified?' another lady asked Claire.

'It was very frightening,' she admitted, leaving out the extra terror of not knowing who she was or how she came to be in the middle of the sea. 'The Captain kept me calm.'

They asked more questions about the fishing boat. 'It must have been horrible to be stuck with all those fishermen for all that time.'

Claire answered. 'Not at all. They were the kindest, most generous people I have ever met.' Or could remember. 'I adored each one of them.'

Some of the faces looked approving, but others, including Lord Stonecroft, looked horrified.

When Lord Stonecroft had walked her around the room introducing her, most of the guests showed polite interest, but learning she was rescued from drowning in a shipwreck by the handsome young Captain made her and Lucien objects of great interest.

The few younger ladies present and some of the older ones flocked around Lucien, as well they should. He was a true hero. None of them could comprehend just how heroic he had been; saving her in so many ways. Her heart felt full to bursting at the mere sight of him, but it was excruciating not to be in his company, sharing everything with him.

Lord Stonecroft approached her with a petulant look. 'If I might have your leave, I will retire to the card room.'

'You must do as you like,' she responded.

It did not take long after that for people to drift away, attracted by other conversations. Claire found herself alone. With a glance to where Lucien still was surrounded by admirers, she walked to one of the chairs set against the wall.

And forced herself not to look at Lucien.

* * *

Lucien noticed the minute Lord Stonecroft left her side. He watched her walk to the chairs and sit by herself.

What sort of gentleman would leave a lady alone?

Lady Rebecca certainly looked the part of an earl's daughter at this entertainment. The gown was obviously new and looked lovely on her. The pale blue under the sheer overdress shimmered in the candlelight from the chandelier. She looked composed as Stonecroft walked her around the room and gracious when he introduced her to someone. And only slightly uncomfortable when she was questioned about the shipwreck.

He'd never expected the story they gave to the Dublin reporter would reach London and Bath. Or that it would have been greeted with such interest by these people.

Lucien had been proud of her praise of the fishermen, even though she might have answered differently if she had remembered her life before the shipwreck when fishermen would have been a class way below hers.

Had she been worried they would question her about before the shipwreck? All that she did not remember? Although she looked so poised, perhaps she knew she could handle those questions even about what she did not remember. She looked as if she'd settled in quite well.

As soon as he could, he extricated himself from the ladies who were much too enthralled by something any man would have done in the same situation.

He made his way over to Lady Rebecca. 'May I sit with you?'

She looked up in surprise, but her eyes turned warm when she saw it was him. 'Please do.'

He sat next to her. He'd become so used to being at her side over these last weeks that he'd felt out of kilter since leaving her at Stonecroft's.

'How is your shoulder?' she asked.

He touched his wound and winced. 'It is healing.'

Her expression became concerned. 'I hope you are taking care of it.'

'Cullen makes certain of that,' he said.

She smiled at that.

'I thought you would be off to London by now,' she said after a pause.

He would travel to London as soon as he knew she would do well.

But he said, 'Sir Richard has made a house guest of me. I believe I'll keep him company for a while. I hope Sir Richard will help Cullen get a position here in Bath.'

'Ella will be pleased.' She smiled. 'We will be practically neighbours, will we not?'

He'd missed her smiles these last two days.

'But what of getting a ship?' she asked.

'I've written to the Admiralty.' He changed the subject. 'How are you faring?'

'Well enough.' She took a deep breath. 'Although I cannot shake the feeling that I am out of place.'

He gazed at her. 'You look like you were born and bred to be right here, in this sort of company.'

Her cheeks flushed with colour. 'Miss Attwood would have it no other way, I am certain.' She added, 'Neither would Stonecroft for that matter.'

'Has he been good to you?' Lucien had intended to be less direct.

'I should have no complaints.'

Which made him suspect she did have complaints. 'What complaints should you not have?'

She glanced away as if considering how to answer. 'He is a bit too concerned about what I wear. Apparently I am to have an entire new wardrobe.'

'Is that not what any woman would desire?' he asked.

She tilted her head. 'It seems so extravagant. There is

nothing wrong with the beautiful dresses you bought me in Dublin.'

'They are out of fashion, I suspect,' he said. 'Otherwise why would anyone give them away?'

She waved a hand as if saying that was a trifle.

'Other than that complaint?' he persisted.

'It is just strange.' She turned her gaze on him. 'I suppose because we have spent so much time in very humble places—except the hotel in Dublin, of course. The only rooms in which I feel comfortable are unfurnished ones, the ones meant to become a nursery or a schoolroom.' Her gaze turned intent. 'I have this strange thought of little girls at a table in a schoolroom. Do you suppose that is a memory?'

He sat up straighter. 'It might be. Do you think you are remembering a part of your life?'

She shook her head. 'It feels like I am simply imagining it.'

A violin began playing Haydn in the balcony, joined by another violin, a viola and a cello.

'Do they dance at these affairs, I wonder?' she asked.

He certainly did not know. 'I am less accustomed to events like this than you must be.'

Lucien had no great fondness for dancing, but this night he wished he might dance with her.

'How—how long might you stay in Bath?' she asked.

It depended on her. 'I do not know. A few days perhaps.'

'Look at the two of you.' The lady who had first recognised him as the rescuer from the shipwreck in the newspaper stood in front of them. She sat down. 'What a bond must be formed between you when you survive such danger!'

Yes. A bond. Lucien agreed.

'Captain Roper will always be important to me,' Lady Rebecca told her. 'I wish his happiness above all things.'

The lady patted her hands. 'That is so dear.' She clutched one hand and squeezed. 'Now you must tell me the reason you are in the company of Stonecroft, though. There are quite a few of us who are pining to know.'

Lady Rebecca did not answer right away. 'I suppose you could say Lord Stonecroft is courting me.'

The woman grinned. 'We thought so! About time. He's been a widower for over twenty years. He is a good catch, my dear. Doesn't gamble much. Doesn't carouse. Has a respectable fortune.'

'So I understand,' Lady Rebecca responded.

He also seemed to think anyone below him in status was his to command, Lucien thought. And he lacked empathy about her loss of memory. Would he ever care what Lady Rebecca endured?

Lucien hoped she would have the courage to stand up to Stonecroft if he ignored her wishes or her needs. This Lady Rebecca had not seen in many men. Lucien hoped she would not lose that courage when her memory returned.

Which he thought could be imminent. Lady Rebecca's thoughts of a schoolroom could mean cracks had formed in the wall around her memory.

Other guests walked over and joined the conversation with them. The chance to be alone with her had disappeared.

Servants began setting up the room for supper and when the supper was called Lord Stonecroft emerged from the card room and found Claire sitting with Lucien.

He acknowledged Lucien with a slight nod and extended his hand to her. 'Come, Lady Rebecca. Let us be seated for the supper.'

She rose, but turned back to Lucien. 'Take care, Captain.'

He nodded. 'And you, as well.'

After Stonecroft led her a few steps away, he said in a snappish tone, 'Did you keep company with Captain Roper all this time?'

'Not all the time,' she replied. 'He joined me where I was seated.'

'With that newspaper piece, you must be careful. Respectable ladies are not written about in newspapers. It is only a matter of time before someone suggests something more scandalous between you and this Captain.'

She bristled. 'Do not speak ill of the man who saved my life.'

'I am not speaking ill,' he retorted, his voice low. 'I am saying that people gossip.'

'I cannot stop people from gossiping.' Really. What did he think?

A footman held the chair for Claire and they sat down. They were seated at the hostess's table.

'I am not happy that you were written of in a newspaper like the *Chronicle*,' Stonecroft went on.

She shot back, 'When we told the story to the reporter from the Dublin paper, how were we supposed to know it would appear in the *Chronicle*?'

He looked aghast. 'You spoke to a reporter?'

'Better he know the real story than to have one he made up.'

He was annoying her greatly.

If she looked at Lord Stonecroft through his sister's eyes, she could see something to admire about him. The warmth between him and Lady Milliforte lent credence to that impression. But with her he seemed condescending and overbearing. Perhaps if she recovered her memory, she would remember something she had liked about him. So far, the only redeeming quality she knew he possessed was the love he'd had towards his first wife.

She tried to keep that in mind as she ate the supper and answered more questions about the shipwreck, this time from the gentlemen seated at the table.

Stonecroft frowned through the whole conversation.

* * *

After the supper was done, Stonecroft turned to Lady Milliforte. 'Iona, may we have your leave? I am quite fatigued.'

They were leaving? It seemed early. She'd hoped for another chance to speak with Lucien.

'Of course, Jonas,' Lady Milliforte responded. 'So lovely of you to come and to bring your Lady Rebecca with you.' She turned to Claire. 'I hope we see more of you, my dear.'

Claire put down her glass of wine. 'Thank you, my lady.'

She rose and Stonecroft led her out of the room. There was no chance to even say goodbye to Lucien, although her gaze caught his as she passed by.

They walked through the Octagon Room and the magnificent ballroom to the entrance of the Assembly Rooms where she retrieved her red cloak, the one that was not good enough for Stonecroft. They again climbed into the detestable sedan chairs and she was carried the short distance to the Royal Crescent.

When they entered the house, Lord Stonecroft looked shrunken and even older than before.

He turned to her. 'May I escort you to your room?' He sounded weary.

She took his arm.

As they ascended the steps, he said, 'I should not have taken you away from the party so early. I was not thinking you might want to stay longer.'

This was close to an apology. It helped.

When they reached the first floor she said, 'If you are fatigued, you need not take me to my room. I can leave you here.' No need for him to climb another flight of stairs.

'Very well, I will say goodnight to you here.' But rather than walk to his room, he took her hand and leaned towards her, placing his lips on to hers.

The only kisses she remembered were Lucien's. Lucien's

lips lit a fire inside her that made her wish to abandon all propriety. Lord Stonecroft's kiss left her cold. As soon as she could, she drew away from him.

'Goodnight, sir,' she said. She turned to the stairs and hurried up them before he had a chance to kiss her again.

She walked swiftly to her bedchamber door and opened it.

Ella stood up from one of the chairs. She rubbed her eyes. 'You are back?'

Claire untied her cloak and handed it to Ella. 'Early, I know.'

Ella took the cloak from her hands. 'I'll fold it and put it away.'

'I have something else to tell you,' Claire said. 'Lucien did not leave Bath. He is staying in the Circus with a naval admiral he once served with. At least for a few days.'

'The Circus?' Ella asked from the dressing room.

'The buildings built in a circle,' she explained.

'Oh! I remember it! That is close by.' Ella skipped back to the bedchamber. 'The Captain said he might ask a friend to help Cullen find a position.'

This made Claire happy. She had no wish to separate the two lovers. 'This means Cullen will be nearby. We must devise a way to let him know that you can see him whenever you wish.'

'Whenever I wish? Thank you, m'lady.' She danced over and hugged her, but let go quickly. 'What about the Captain? Will you see him again?'

How she hoped. 'I suppose, if he attends the same functions as Lord Stonecroft, I might.'

Ella untied the laces of the net overdress and carefully lifted it over Claire's shoulders. She draped it over a chair while she helped Claire out of the silk ball gown.

'Perhaps I might see Cullen tomorrow,' the girl said excitedly.

'I have no idea what tomorrow brings,' Claire said. 'But any time I have no need of you, you are free to see Cullen.'

When in her nightdress, Claire climbed beneath the covers of this bed that felt stranger to her than the berth in the fishing boat. She did indeed not know what tomorrow would bring. When she was with Lucien, she could at least know he would be with her. But now, not only was her past a *tabula rasa*, so was her future. Her future seemed empty of anything worth anticipating.

Chapter Sixteen

A week went by and Claire's life settled into a routine of stultifying boredom. Because of her newfound notoriety Lord Stonecroft received more invitations than he was accustomed to, although at that time of year the entertainments were all very like Lady Milliforte's party, with all the same people.

That meant she often saw Lucien and watched him become a sought-after bachelor among the younger unattached ladies.

Stonecroft often took the waters for his health, so he frequently bathed in the waters, leaving Claire and his sister to promenade in the Pump Room where his sister met her friends and liked to pass much of the day.

This day Miss Attwood was in a tête-à-tête with Lady Milliforte. Claire wandered over to the fountain where a server filled glasses with the medicinal water of the hot springs. She accepted a small glass of the water and put it to her lips. It smelled of rotten eggs and tasted like liquid metal.

As unpleasant as the taste and smell were, they were familiar. She'd tasted the waters before, she realised. She closed her eyes and an image of herself laughing with other young ladies flashed through her mind.

A memory!

It had no context, no attachment to anything but the taste and smell of the waters, but it made her heart beat faster. She'd experienced a memory!

'Lady Rebecca, surely you do not need the waters. You are the very picture of health.'

She opened her eyes to see Sir Richard, Lucien's Admiral friend.

'I tasted it for a lark,' she said. 'How are you today, Sir Richard? Are you here for the waters?'

He smiled. 'I am here in hopes of meeting a lovely young lady and, look! I have done so.'

'You flatter me,' she said.

His expression turned serious. 'And how do you fare, my lady?'

She had the sense he was asking about more than the state of her health. And, perhaps, asking for his friend.

'Oh.' She sighed. 'I shall do well enough.'

The truth was, she was ever more clear that marriage to Lord Stonecroft would not do. The life he offered her was as desolate as the blankness of her mind. She felt more like a piece of furniture in his presence than a betrothed woman. And when he did look upon her as a person, it was merely to point out some way he disapproved of her.

She had the money her brother had given her. It provided her some means to do something else besides marry Lord Stonecroft.

She still had the recurring image of children in a schoolroom. She'd dreamt of it the night before and it gave her the notion that she could support herself as a teacher in a school or as a governess. All she needed was to find someone who would recommend her. Lucien had been convinced that she'd remembered a real school in Bristol when he'd questioned her. Perhaps she could find it and they would remember her.

'Yes,' she repeated to Sir Richard. 'I shall do well enough.'

The Admiral looked sympathetic, but he changed the subject. 'I suspect you are wondering where our mutual friend is right now.'

She felt her cheeks turn warm, but she tried to cover up by smiling. 'I suspect you might tell me whether I wondered or not.'

'He is at the West Gate Inn,' Sir Richard responded. 'He is speaking with yet another newspaper man, this time from a newspaper here in Bath.'

'Oh, dear, I do hope the reporter will not wish to interview me,' she said. 'Lord Stonecroft finds it unacceptable for a lady to be written of in a newspaper.'

Sir Richard turned to the door. 'Ah. Here he is.' He waved a hand to get Lucien's attention.

Lucien walked towards him and Claire saw his gait falter for a step when he spied her next to his friend. Was he disappointed to see her? Her spirits sank.

'Sir Richard.' He nodded to his friend and turned his gaze on Claire. 'Lady Rebecca.'

She made herself smile. 'Hello, Lucien.'

'So,' Sir Richard said, 'was the reporter satisfied with your interview?'

Lucien rolled his eyes. 'I hope so. I believe he was disappointed there was little to tell that had not appeared in the London paper.'

'Will he try to interview me, as well?' she asked.

'I discouraged him from doing so.' His gaze rested softly on her. 'How are you, my lady?'

'I—I am well, Lucien.' She wanted to tell him of her memory, but how could she? 'All is well.'

Miss Attwood strode over. 'There you are, dear. Last I saw, you were at my side.'

'I had a fancy to drink the waters, ma'am. And then I met my friends.'

No doubt Miss Attwood would tell her brother that she had been speaking with Lucien in a public place. Stonecroft had taken to warning her that people would talk if she and Lucien were too often seen together.

'Well, we should go,' Miss Attwood said. 'Stonecroft sent me a message that he has some business to attend to. He will meet us back at the Crescent.' She nodded to Lucien and Sir Richard. 'Good day, gentlemen.'

Claire felt her anger kindle. Both Miss Attwood and her brother expected she do whatever they wished when they wished it. But, at this moment, defying Miss Attwood would serve no purpose and would only risk a scene.

Still, she wished for more time with Lucien.

'Good day,' she said, hoping her tone was not too resentful.

They started to walk towards the door when a man approached. The reporter, perhaps?

He broke into a smile and opened his arms. 'My dear! I have found you at last!'

An inexplicable sense of dread engulfed her. Was this someone she should know?

He went on. 'Ever since I learned you were in Bath I have frequented the Pump Room and other places hoping to locate you.'

She drew back. 'I fear you mistake me for someone else, sir.'

'No, it is you, I know that now!' He gave her an entreating look. 'Are you not happy to see me?'

He spoke with a hint of an Irish accent. Was he someone she knew in Ireland?

Her knees shook and she did not know what to do or say. She did not remember this man, but should she? Would this encounter expose what she'd hidden so successfully from all but a few, that her mind was disordered, that she had amnesia? How long before that on dit reached the newspapers?

Lucien saw the red-haired man approach Lady Rebecca. He watched her recoil and immediately strode over to her.

'Do you need assistance, Lady Rebecca?' he asked.

'She is not Lady Rebecca,' the man protested. 'She is—'

Lady Rebecca broke in. 'He has mistaken me for someone else. I tried to tell him he was wrong.'

'He has been quite rude,' added Miss Attwood. 'Speaking to us without an introduction.'

Lucien placed himself between the man and the ladies. 'Perhaps you should leave, sir.'

'But I need to speak to her,' the man argued, trying to move around him. 'It is what I have come all this way to do.'

Lucien blocked his way and used his greater height to loom over the man. 'You are distressing these ladies. You need to leave them. Now!' He kept his voice low, but commanding.

The man backed up. 'Very well.' He bowed. 'I see I cannot speak with you here, *Lady Rebecca*.' He put a strange emphasis on her name.

He strode off.

Sir Richard joined them. 'Are you all right, Miss Attwood?'

'What a strange creature,' she said.

While Sir Richard engaged Miss Attwood, Lucien stepped aside with Lady Rebecca. 'He alarmed you.'

'I was afraid he was someone I should remember,' she whispered. 'I did not want all of Bath society to know about—about—me.'

Lucien nodded. 'I understand.'

She took a breath and pressed a hand to her chest. 'I am relieved, though. He thought I was someone else. That was clear.'

Sir Richard interrupted. 'I do not think these ladies should walk home alone, do you, Captain?'

'No, he may be waiting for them outside.' He looked at Lady Rebecca. 'We will see you home safely.'

Sir Richard offered Miss Attwood his arm, leaving Lucien just where he wished to be. With Lady Rebecca. They left the Pump Room and started up Barton Street.

Lady Rebecca slowed her step so that they lagged enough behind Sir Richard and Miss Attwood that their conversation could be private. 'Lucien, I had a memory.'

'A memory?' Perhaps this was the start.

'In the Pump Room. Just a little while ago. I drank the waters and I distinctly remembered the smell and taste. I knew I'd tasted it before.' Her voice was quiet but excited. 'And then the memory came. I remembered laughing with other girls and I knew them. Or I had the sense that I knew them. It was very fleeting, but I remembered being in the Pump Room.'

He squeezed her hand. 'I told you that you'd get your memory back.'

'It is a little thing, though.'

'You probably came to Bath as a schoolgirl,' he said. 'Makes sense if you were at a school in Bristol. It is not that far.'

'I wonder if I would have more memories if I travelled to Bristol and found that school.'

It was on the tip of his tongue to offer to take her there, but he'd be delayed even longer from getting a ship.

Besides, Stonecroft should be taking her to Bristol and helping her regain her memory.

'Where is Stonecroft today?' he asked.

She waved her hand. 'He was taking the waters. It helps his arthritic knees, he said.'

They walked without talking for a while and were quiet enough to hear Sir Richard regaling Miss Attwood with some tale. Lucien glanced around, making certain the man who'd bothered her was not in sight.

Lady Rebecca broke their silence. 'That man alarmed me, Lucien.'

'You must let me know if he bothers you again.'

She turned to him with a wan smile. 'So you can rescue me once more?'

He ought to remain in Bath until he was certain that man would not distress her further.

'When do you go to London?' she asked.

'Soon,' he replied. 'I should go soon.'

'Will you let me know when you plan to leave?' she asked. 'I would like to say goodbye.'

'I will.'

They reached Queen Square.

Miss Attwood turned around and called to Lady Rebecca, 'Do not lag so! Come up here.'

They could no longer be alone. From then they said little to each other.

When they reached the door to Number Five Royal Crescent, Lucien faced her. She extended her hand and he clasped it. They held on for a moment longer than was needed to say goodbye.

'Thank you again, Captain.' He missed hearing her call him Lucien.

'I am at your disposal.' He released her hand.

The footman opened the door and the ladies went inside.

Sir Richard clapped Lucien on the shoulder. 'I do not comprehend why you fail to simply tell that lady of your regard for her.'

'It is very difficult to explain,' Lucien said as they walked to the Circus.

He did have a great regard for her, he admitted to himself. He was concerned for her happiness, but knew it could not be achieved with him.

'She is recovering her memory,' he told his friend. 'Being among people of her class may have been the catalyst. She will not want a mere captain when she remembers who she is.'

'Falderal,' Sir Richard said. 'You overrate status and titles and such.'

'Overrate them?' Lucien shot back. 'I despise what status and titles do to people. You've met them. They believe they deserve whatever they want merely because they want it. It is inconsequential what more humble people need. They think nothing of moving villages so the view from their estate is more picturesque. Or they ruin a life for a moment of pleasure—' He stopped, realising he was ranting.

'Might I remind you, boy, that I have a title?' Sir Richard's tone was kind.

'That is another matter entirely,' Lucien said defensively.

Sir Richard laughed.

As they reached the door to Sir Richard's house, Lucien said, 'Yours is not a very elevated title, Sir Richard.' He slanted his friend a glance and smiled.

Sir Richard clapped him on the back. 'You are a hopeless prig.'

Sir Richard's point was not lost on Lucien, though. Was it possible he put too much importance on titles and status? Sir Richard was the opposite of what Lucien abhorred. He was generous and accepting of all kinds of people from all walks of life. Was he merely a rare exception? Or was Lucien wrong to cut all aristocrats from the same cloth?

None of this mattered, though. Because Lucien wanted to be back at sea where he belonged. He missed the rhythm of navy life, the way every man mattered and everyone depended on each other. He missed the scent of the sea air and the rocking of the ship. He missed knowing his duty to his ship, his crew and his King.

* * *

All that afternoon Claire had flashes of the man who had approached her at the Pump Room. She did not know why he returned to her thoughts or why the instances were so fleeting that she could not hold on to them to make sense of it.

She told Ella about the man. And about Lucien once again coming to her aid.

'You must watch out for that fellow,' Ella said. 'I have a premonition he will not be good for you.'

'You have a premonition?' This was the first Claire heard of Ella having premonitions.

'I have premonitions, I do,' insisted Ella. 'My grandmother had the sight, too.'

Then Claire wished Ella could tell her when she would get her memory back and when she should make her break from Stonecroft.

Ella had helped Claire dress for dinner. There was a concert at the Upper Assembly Rooms this night so she wore yet another dress that the modiste in Bath had made for her, another dress chosen and approved by Miss Attwood.

It was pretty enough, a lilac satin with silver embroidery along the hem and neckline. Miss Attwood lent her amethyst earrings and a matching necklace.

When she entered the drawing room before dinner, Lord Stonecroft's gaze swept over her as a man might look over a horse he wished to purchase.

He turned to his sister. 'The dress is very fitting. You did well.'

His sister smiled. 'Thank you. The modiste did wonders to work so quickly.'

Stonecroft never complimented Claire directly. He seemed determined not to do anything that would endear him to her.

Dinner was announced and they went to the dining room.

As they began the first course, Stonecroft said, 'Honora tells me that you engaged with a strange man at the Pump Room today and nearly made a spectacle of yourself.'

Claire glanced at Miss Attwood before responding.

The woman's brows knitted and Claire was fairly certain Lord Stonecroft was distorting what he'd been told.

'Are you certain you understood what happened, sir?' she finally said.

She thought she saw a guilty look flit across his face before his expression turned bland again. 'Suppose you tell me what happened.'

'A man came up to me and professed to know me, but I did not know him.' That was the gist of it.

Stonecroft gave her a steady look. 'You did not know him or you did not remember him?'

A wave of anxiety washed through her. He'd homed in on precisely what she'd feared. 'I did not know him. He mistook me for someone else.'

'I do not like this. Strange men speaking with you.' He took a loud sip of his soup. 'It does not look seemly.'

'The contact was quite brief,' she said, trying not to let her irritation show. 'Captain Roper intervened and sent the man away.'

He pointed to her with his spoon. 'That is another thing. You and Roper. You spoke privately together.'

'In the Pump Room surrounded by everyone else who was there,' she retorted.

'And on the walk home?' His brows rose.

She had spoken privately to Lucien. She lifted her chin. 'Yes. I did engage in conversation with Captain Roper as he and Sir Richard escorted us home in case the stranger reappeared.'

The next course was served. The food at Stonecroft's dinner table was bland in taste and unimaginative. Boiled fish, stewed chicken, boiled vegetables, small tarts for dessert.

That she observed that fact meant she must have eaten finer food elsewhere. Of course, the food on the fishing boat had been nearly the same every night and she'd found no fault in that.

'Honora believes you spend entirely too much time with that Captain Roper,' Stonecroft went on.

She glanced at Miss Attwood again. This time it seemed that had been what the woman had told her brother.

Claire straightened in her chair. 'If I see Captain Roper at the Pump Room or at an Assembly or a concert, or on the street in Bath, I will speak to him. I will never snub him or avoid him. And you well know why, my lord.'

Because he had saved her life and was once her life and now deserved a life of his own.

Lucien was not in the habit of attending concerts. Concerts usually were more about the elite wanting to see and be seen. However, Sir Richard had learned from Miss Attwood that she, Stonecroft and Lady Rebecca would attend this night and Lucien was concerned that the stranger would be there, too, and would try again to approach her.

The tea room was set up for the concert, but the Octagon Room was filled as well, its tables filled with card players, another aristocratic pastime which Lucien disdained. Sir Richard joined some friends who sat near the middle of the room, but Lucien stood in the back where he could watch who entered and left.

Lord Stonecroft entered with Lady Rebecca on his arm and his sister following close behind. The Baron looked as arrogant as the other times Lucien had seen him. Miss Attwood greeted her friends with a tight smile. Lady Rebecca looked remote, as if her thoughts were anywhere but on the concert and the people attending.

She did not appear content and that worried him.

Stonecroft chose seats near the front of the room.

Lucien was reasonably certain they had not seen him. From Miss Attwood's eagerness to separate them earlier, that was probably a good thing.

Gradually the seats filled and the din of the many voices sounded in his ears. Lucien scanned the crowd many times to be certain the stranger had not arrived unseen by him.

Soon the musicians entered and took their places. The soloist, a soprano, was introduced, and a tenor who'd been trained by Rauzzini, the Italian castrato who'd made much of his fortune singing in Bath.

The soloist sang the 'Exsultate, jubilate' which Mozart was supposed to have composed for Rauzzini—or so the introduction said.

The music and soloist's voice were pleasant, but Lucien's attention remained on the door. Finally he saw a man slip in. The stranger. He watched the man look through the crowd. He walked part way up the side of the room. Lucien knew the moment the man spotted her. He paused and his posture tensed. He smiled and returned to the back of the room. Lucien watched him from the opposite side. He would probably approach her during the intermission when refreshments would be served.

When the soloist finished and the applause ended, the audience stood and some left their seats, Stonecroft and Miss Attwood among them. Lady Rebecca remained where she was, sitting alone.

The stranger started to walk towards her. Lucien quickly crossed the room, intending to intercept him and escort him out. But the stranger spied him and turned back, mixing in with the crowd. Lucien could not reach him. He saw the man leave the room and he quickly followed. When he reached the door the man was already across the Octagon

Room. By the time he made his way across that room, the stranger had quickened his step and was nearly at the other end of the ballroom. Lucien sprinted to catch up. Outside a cold drizzle darkened the streets. Lucien quickened his pace and caught the stranger by the collar.

'Wait!' he ordered. 'I want to know who you are and what business you have with Lady Rebecca.'

The man squirmed under his grip. 'Let me go!'

'Answer me first.'

The man struggled. He and Lucien spun around as he tried to escape. Lucien's injured shoulder ached with the strain of holding on to the man.

One of the Assembly Rooms attendants emerged from the building. 'What goes here?' he shouted.

The stranger cried, 'He is trying to rob me!'

The attendant hurried towards them.

'I am not robbing him,' Lucien said.

'Help me!' the stranger wailed.

The attendant reached them.

Lucien said, 'I want to question him.'

The attendant was close enough to see his face. 'Captain Roper?' He turned to the stranger. 'This is Captain Roper. He is not a robber, sir. He is the Captain of the *Fox-fire*. What is this?'

Lucien's notoriety came to his assistance, apparently.

The stranger stopped struggling. 'Very well. I will tell you. Make him let me go.'

Lucien loosened his grip, but did not release him. The man took advantage, though, and pushed against him, knocking Lucien off balance. The stranger wrenched away and fled down the street. Both the attendant and Lucien dashed after him, but he disappeared in the dark streets behind the Assembly Rooms.

Lucien uttered a low curse.

The attendant breathed hard. 'What—who was he?'

'That is what I wanted to discover.' Lucien also needed to catch his breath. 'I believed he means to do harm to a lady.'

'Which lady?' the man asked.

'Lady Rebecca.'

'Ah,' the attendant said knowingly. He must have been aware of the connection between Lucien and Lady Rebecca.

They walked back to the Assembly Rooms.

When they reached the door, Lucien stopped him. 'Let us not speak of this. I do not wish to alarm anyone unnecessarily.'

'Very well, sir.'

Lucien returned to the tea room where the concert had resumed, but he remained in the back, avoiding encountering Lady Rebecca. When the concert was over, he followed Lady Rebecca and her party in their sedan chairs back to the Royal Crescent, just to make certain that the stranger did not accost her.

When the chairmen dropped them off in front of Lord Stonecroft's door and Lady Rebecca was safe inside, Lucien walked back to Sir Richard's.

One thing he knew—he would not leave Bath until he was certain Lady Rebecca was safe from this strange man's interest in her.

Chapter Seventeen

The next morning Claire had planned to sleep late and miss breakfast, the time of day she was almost certain to be alone with Lord Stonecroft, but she woke even earlier than usual.

From the nightmare that plagued her over and over during the night.

She'd dreamed about the red-haired stranger who'd approached her at the Pump Room, disturbing dreams mixed with the vision of the little girls at a schoolroom table. He loomed over her in the dream and the sense of danger woke her each time.

The sun was up, though, and leaving her bed was less undesirable than risking one more nightmare. She padded over to the dressing-room door to peek in on Ella, but the girl's cot was empty and neatly made. The maid must rise before the sun.

She walked back to the bureau and poured water from the pitcher into the basin. With a nice piece of scented soap—soap Lucien had purchased for her—she removed her nightdress and washed herself.

She'd donned her shift and was brushing her hair at the dressing table when Ella walked in.

'Oh, you are awake early, m'lady!' Ella carried a pail of coal over to the fireplace. 'And looks like you are half-dressed, as well.'

'I could not sleep more.' No need to tell Ella of her nightmares. She'd only hear more about premonitions. And she did not wish to worry the girl.

'What dress would you like to wear today?' Ella asked, crossing over to the dressing room.

She'd like to wear the sprigged muslin that Lucien had bought her, but did not wish to hear Stonecroft's complaints. 'Any one of the new walking dresses.'

Ella chose a blue printed cotton that the modiste had delivered the day before. 'You might as well wear this new one.'

After Ella helped her into the dress, she again sat at the dressing table. 'Arrange my hair simply today, Ella. I do not feel up to a fussy do.'

'Whatever you say, m'lady.'

She put Claire's hair into a knot atop her head, but could not resist pulling a few curls out to frame her face.

Claire went down to the sitting room where breakfast was served and was not surprised to see Stonecroft already seated there.

'Good morning, sir,' she said.

He stood and gave her an assessing scan. 'Good morning.'

'Please sit,' she said.

Each day started the same.

She chose her food from the sideboard and sat opposite him as she had every day of the past week. She was no closer to knowing this man—or he, her—than she had that first day.

Was this what the loss of love did to a man?

She wanted to feel something for Stonecroft, but it became more and more evident that his guard would never be lowered. As she nibbled on her toasted bread, she again ran through her plan to run away to Bristol where, if she could not find herself there, she could at least find someone who knew her and could perhaps help her find employment.

'It is time to announce the banns,' he said behind his newspaper.

She glanced up at him. 'My lord, I have asked—'

'I know what you have asked.' He lowered his paper. 'But I fail to see what recovering your memory will do to alter the matter. At present there is entirely too much talk about you and your rescue. Perhaps your Captain Roper will leave Bath if you are a married woman. Then the talk will cease.'

So that was it. 'Captain Roper is not your rival, sir, I assure you.'

'I believe he has aspirations.'

Her brows rose. 'Aspirations?'

'To wed into the aristocracy,' he said.

She almost laughed. 'Oh, no, my lord. I can assure you he has no wish to marry into the aristocracy. His attachment to me is merely one of duty.'

He gave her a sceptical and patronising look. 'He is everywhere you are,' he said. 'Even at the concert last night. A man of his background certainly would not come for such elevated music.'

He'd been there? She'd had no idea. 'I did not see him.'

Stonecroft lifted his paper again. 'Nevertheless I will have the banns announced next Sunday.'

That left her three days to make her decision and take action.

She stood. 'If I may have your leave, sir.'

'As you wish.' He did not stop reading his paper.

She rushed out of the room, past the stony-faced footman who'd heard the whole exchange. In the hall she looked around, feeling as if the walls would close in on her. She hurried up the stairs to her bedchamber.

Ella was straightening the room. 'M'lady. That was a quick breakfast.'

'Where is my Kashmir shawl?' She opened the bureau drawer. 'I am going to take a walk before I turn mad.'

Ella stepped into the dressing room and emerged carrying the shawl. 'Are you walking with Lord Stonecroft?'

'No.' She wrapped herself in her favourite possession. 'No one. I just need some air.'

'Wait a moment, then,' Ella said. 'You should not go alone. I will go with you.'

They put on hats and gloves and walked down to the hall.

'If Lord Stonecroft or Miss Attwood should ask for me, I am taking a walk,' she told the footman in attendance.

'Yes, m'lady.' He opened the door for her.

Like all days of that summer, the air was chilly. The sky was grey, but it did not look like rain was imminent.

'Do you want to walk through the fields?' Ella asked.

'Not with the cows grazing there.' The green fields in front of the Royal Crescent were a piece of the country in that city, but Claire did not want to view the Crescent. She wanted to escape it. 'Let us wander the streets.'

They walked to Church Street towards Cottles Lane, away from the Crescent.

'So, what is this about, m'lady?' Ella asked.

'Nothing.' She knew Ella did not want her to marry Stonecroft, but her emotions were too raw to discuss. 'I am restless, is all.'

As they turned on Cottles Lane, Ella gripped Claire's hand. 'M'lady! I think a man is following us.'

Claire immediately thought of the stranger, the man in her dreams. Though an occasional carriage or sedan chair passed them, there was no one else on the street. They quickened their pace and when Claire had an opportunity, she turned and saw the man, who stopped abruptly.

It was the red-haired man from her dreams.

'He is the man who approached me at the Pump Room,' she told Ella.

'Oh, I do not feel easy about this.' The girl shuddered.

They came to an alleyway connecting Cottles Lane to Rivers Street.

'Come with me!' Ella cried.

They raced down the alley and ran to Rivers Street, ducked down another alley and another until they reached the mews to the Circus. Ella guided them through the mews to the back entrances of the terrace houses.

She knocked on one of them. 'This is Sir Richard's house. The servants know me because of Cullen.'

One of the kitchen maids answered the door and saw it was Ella. 'Oh, it is you.' The girl then spied Claire and looked puzzled.

Ella pushed them both past the girl and entered the house. 'We were out for a walk, Lady Rebecca and I, and a man was following us. Is Sir Richard here? Or Captain Roper?'

The kitchen maid curtsied. 'I am sure I do not know, miss, but best you take her ladyship above stairs and ask there.'

'Come on, m'lady,' Ella said. 'I know the way.'

She took her up the servants' stairs to the hall where a surprised footman rose to his feet from the chair where he ought not to have been seated.

'Miss Kiley? You'll be wanting to see Cullen?' He also noticed Claire. 'Beg pardon, ma'am.'

'We need Sir Richard or Captain Roper. Tell them it is Lady Rebecca and Ella.'

'Sir Richard went out,' the man said.

'Then Captain Roper,' Ella demanded.

The footman nodded and hurried up the stairs. A few

moments later he returned with Cullen in tow. 'Captain says he will meet you in the drawing room directly.'

Cullen looked concerned. 'What is it, Ella? What has happened?' He glanced at Claire. 'Lady Rebecca, I forget myself.' He bowed to her.

They no sooner entered the drawing room than Lucien appeared. He walked straight to Claire. 'What has happened?'

She wished she could fall into his arms.

'I am sorry for the intrusion, Lucien. Ella brought us here,' she said. 'We were on a walk and that stranger from the Pump Room started following us.' She did not wish to show him how shaken she was.

'That stranger.' His voice dipped. He turned to Cullen. 'Would you and Ella arrange for some refreshments to be brought to us? And find some refreshments for Ella, too.'

Cullen nodded and he and Ella left the room.

He led Claire to a sofa and sat next to her. 'I do not comprehend this. You told him at the Pump Room that you were Lady Rebecca, not the woman for whom he searched. Why is he persisting?'

'Could he be in my memory?' she asked him. 'I dreamed about him.' Frightening dreams. 'If he was in my memory, it would make sense.'

He stood and rubbed his forehead. 'I need to find him. Talk to him. I almost had him—' He broke off.

'What do you mean, you almost had him?' What had he done?

He paced. 'I attended the concert last night. He was there, but noticed me approaching and ran out. I chased him. Had him in my grip, but he managed to get away.'

So he had been at the concert, like Stonecroft said. 'Lucien, did you attend that concert because of that man?'

He shrugged. 'It occurred to me he might seek you there.'

'You were watching over me, then.' As he'd done since she'd woken up on the raft.

He did not respond, but his expression told her yes.

She stood and faced him. 'Are you staying in Bath because of me?'

He glanced away.

She put her hand on his arm. 'You are delaying your trip to the Admiralty because of me.'

He met her gaze, but still did not answer.

More than anything she wanted him to stay with her. More than anything but his happiness, that was. And his happiness was being at sea. Suddenly she could see how selfish she'd been to want him to stay.

'You must not remain in Bath for me, Lucien.' Her guilt cut into her. 'I have burdened you enough.'

He frowned. 'A few more days will not matter. I want to find this man first. Make certain he is no threat to you.' He glanced towards the door. 'Wait here a moment.'

Before she could say another word, he strode out of the room.

Lucien went in search of Cullen and Ella, finding them below stairs in the servants' room.

Cullen rose at his entrance. 'Sir?'

'I want you both to go out, wander around and look for that man,' Lucien told him. 'If you can, bring him to me. If not, find out where he is staying. It is time we discovered what his business with Lady Rebecca is.' He turned to Ella. 'Will you be comfortable doing that?'

'Yes, sir!' She smiled and gazed up at Cullen.

He nodded.

As he left the room, he encountered the footman carrying a tea tray with biscuits. 'I'll take that,' he said.

He carried the tray to the drawing room and placed it on the table in front of Lady Rebecca. 'I've sent Cullen and Ella out to look for the stranger. My guess is he is still wandering around in hopes of discovering where you are.'

She poured the tea for him, not needing to ask him how he liked it, after all the time they'd spent together.

She took a biscuit. 'I did not have much breakfast.' After eating it, she said, 'Perhaps he is simply mistaking me for someone else. Maybe he is not a threat at all.'

She sounded as if she were trying to convince herself not to worry.

'Let us hope Cullen can find him and we'll discover for sure.'

She took another biscuit.

Sitting here with her felt comfortable. They had spent so much time together since the shipwreck that it felt strange not to be in her company.

'How are you faring?' he asked after a time. 'Besides this matter with the stranger. The truth, please.'

She placed the biscuit on her saucer. 'I am trying to accustom myself to my situation.'

'That is no answer,' he said.

She stared into her tea for a time before speaking. 'Stonecroft is not cruel. Neither is Miss Attwood. No one is unkind. I do wish for more time, though.'

'More time?'

She released a breath. 'Lord Stonecroft says he will have the banns announced beginning this Sunday, but I am not ready for it.'

Lucien stiffened. 'Then you should stop him.'

'Yes, I should do that,' she said without conviction.

Meaning she would not stop him, he thought. Meaning she intended to go along with the plans made for her.

She glanced around the room. 'I should return to Lord Stonecroft's house.'

He did not want her to go, but he extended his hand. 'I will escort you.'

She picked up her shawl and allowed him to help her up. Theirs gazes locked for a moment and he kept hold of her hand. But he released it as soon as she stepped away from the sofa. When they reached the hall he told the footman, 'I am walking Lady Rebecca home. If Cullen returns, tell him to wait for me. I'll be back shortly.'

When they left the house, Lucien scanned the area. There were a few people about, but none looked like the stranger. Some of the people they passed, people he'd met at the various entertainments he'd attended, greeted them.

'I suppose we will be gossiped about,' she said, glancing back at them.

'Will that distress you?' he asked.

'No.' She slanted him a look. 'I know you have always behaved honourably towards me. You've proved it over and over.'

He, on the other hand, remembered almost taking her to bed and almost giving in to his desire for her.

They reached Stonecroft's house.

'Do I knock?' he asked.

'Yes,' she responded. 'I am not really a member of the household.'

He sounded the knocker and stepped away.

A footman answered and seeing it was Lady Rebecca, opened the door wide for her.

She turned back to Lucien. 'Thank you once again, Lucien.'

'Promise me you will not venture out alone,' he said.

'I won't.'

He started to turn away, but turned back. 'I will let you know what we discover.'

She nodded and disappeared inside the house.

As Lucien turned towards Church Street, he spied a man who quickly ducked behind some buildings. The stranger. And now he knew where Lady Rebecca lived.

He ran to the spot where he saw the stranger disappear, but there was no sign of him.

'Blast!' Lucien swore.

When Claire walked inside Stonecroft stood in the hall.

'Do you mind telling me what you are about?' His voice was stern, but his eyes showed no more interest or emotion than any other time.

She would not tolerate being scolded like a child. She removed her hat. 'I took a walk with my lady's maid and we saw the man who approached me at the Pump Room following us. We were near the Circus so we knocked upon Sir Richard's door.'

He raised his brows. 'And where is your lady's maid?'

'She is with the Captain's valet. Captain Roper asked them to try to search for the man and discover who he is and where he is staying.' She started to climb the stairs.

'So, you were with Captain Roper.' He followed her on her heels up the stairway.

Had he not heard the most important part? That this stranger was following her?

She could not keep the annoyance from her voice. 'Captain Roper escorted me so I would not have to walk alone when there is a stranger who might threaten me.' She turned to face him. 'What else would you have had me do?'

He pursed his lips. 'I merely want the talk about you and Captain Roper to end.'

She continued up the stairs. 'And what of this man who is following me?'

Did that not matter to him?

He responded, 'You said he believes you are someone else. There is no reason to think he wishes you harm.'

How could he be certain of this?

When they reached the first floor, he said, 'Come to the drawing room. I wish to speak with you.'

She gritted her teeth as she followed him to the drawing room. He gestured for her to sit.

She chose a chair. 'Well?'

He remained standing. 'As you know, I expect you to produce an heir. That is the reason for our marriage. That is why I want the banns.'

Had she agreed to that?

'If you discussed that with me before, I do not remember it.' She drew an irritated breath. 'You have said nothing to me since. You want the banns, but I believe you do not understand how difficult it is for me not to have any memory of those agreements we made about marriage. I want to remember those things before posting the banns.'

'It is ridiculous to wait.' He paced in front of her. 'You do not need a memory to get with child. It is not as if you have other choices. How many offers do you expect to receive at your age?'

She disliked having to look up at him. 'You see, sir, I do not know my age. That is what I am trying to make you understand—'

He waved an impatient hand. 'You are twenty-three, if your brother told the truth about it.'

Twenty-three was old enough to be considered a spinster.

'I have no idea what my brother told you.'

'I suppose your birthdate is in the documents your brother sent to me when we reached a settlement.' He stopped pacing and leaned down to her. 'If you are planning to cry off, or if you are the sort to engage in affairs, I beg you tell me now. I have wasted enough time.'

A wave of guilt washed through her. Should she simply tell him now that she would not marry him? She did not know what to do.

She stood and faced him. 'Sir, I have no idea if I am the sort who has affairs.' She certainly had experienced wanton impulses with Lucien. 'I do not know at all what sort of person I am.'

He took a step back. 'Well, you can show me by staying away from Roper.'

Her face warmed with anger. This man failed to hear or consider anything she had to say. She'd had enough of being at the mercy of men who expected her to do what they wanted and did not listen to her.

Where had that thought come from?

Once in her room, she could not sit still.

She'd promised Lucien she would not walk out alone, but staying inside would drive her mad. The streets would be busier at this time of day. It should be safe enough.

She needed to discover how to reach Bristol. Once in Bristol she could find the school she had attended and from there beg them to find her work. Her recurrent dream about little girls seated at a school table must mean something. If it was school that could crack open her memory, she must find that school.

She put on her hat again and, before she could change her mind, walked out of the room, down the stairs and to the hall.

'I am going out again,' she said to the footman in the hall.

'Going out?' He sounded surprised.

'Yes. To the shops.' She walked to the door.

He stepped quickly to open it and she hurried into the street.

Chapter Eighteen

Lucien had tried to follow the stranger, but by the time he reached the buildings where he'd seen the man, he'd disappeared. He walked the streets around there, but did not see him again.

He started back to Sir Richard's, hoping Cullen and Ella had had better luck.

As he neared Brock Street from Church, he saw Lady Rebecca walking swiftly towards the Circus. Alone.

What the devil was she doing? She'd promised not to venture out.

He took a breath, but didn't hesitate. He followed her at some distance.

She walked past the Circus on to Gay Street, but paused and glanced around. When she spied him, she looked alarmed at first, but then stood her ground and waited for him to catch up to her.

'Lady Rebecca—' He was vexed with her.

'I know. I know,' she responded. 'I promised not to go out alone.'

'Then why are you?'

She averted her gaze. 'I have errands…'

He crossed his arms over his chest. 'You will have to do better than that.'

She returned an obstinate look.

'Tell me.' He softened his voice. 'What would make you take a chance like this? It must be something important. Because I know you are not a fool.'

She lifted her eyes to him briefly, then looked away. 'I want to find out how to go to Bristol. I'm convinced if I can find my school, my memory will come back.'

'Can you not ask Stonecroft to take you?' he asked. 'He would want your memory restored, would he not?'

Her gaze met his again. 'He thinks my memory loss a trifling matter.'

Lucien fell silent for a time as they walked down Gay Street together.

Finally he said, 'I will take you to Bristol. There are coaches to Bristol from the West Gate Inn.'

Her step faltered. 'Oh, Lucien. No. You need to go to London, not Bristol. It might take me several days to locate the right school.'

Yes. He should go to London, but how could he? He could not leave until he knew she was safe.

The sky that had been grey for days darkened even more and fat drops of rain pattered the pavement.

Lucien glanced up at the clouds. 'Quick. Let us find some shelter. It will be pouring in a moment.'

They dashed behind the buildings on Trim Street and found a garden doorway that provided a semblance of shelter.

The shower grew thicker and Lucien put his arms around her to help keep her out of the rain in the small space they occupied. Their bodies were pressed together.

'Lucien.' She sighed and rested her head against his chest.

'Like on the raft,' he murmured. 'I must hold you to keep you safe.'

He savoured the feel of her in his arms, one more moment in so many they had shared together.

She touched his shoulder. 'How is your wound? I have not asked these several days. Does it still pain you?'

'Very little,' he told her. 'Sir Richard's surgeon examined it and removed the stitches. It is healed over.'

He'd missed the warmth of her, the scent of her. Something shifted inside him about her. Could he be happy without her? He was no longer convinced that she could be content with Stonecroft, who was so indifferent to her needs.

They did not speak, but clung to each other like they had on the raft. Perhaps that was the way to get through life, he thought. Clinging together.

The rain shower stopped as abruptly as it had begun and Lucien reluctantly released her.

'I—I believe I should return to Lord Stonecroft's,' she said. 'You have told me how to find a coach to Bristol, so I do not need to go further.'

'I mean it, that I will take you to Bristol, if you wish it,' he repeated.

She looked up at him and brushed the raindrops from his shoulders. 'I will think about it.'

He offered his arm once more. 'I will walk you back.'

They stepped around puddles behind the buildings and returned to Gay Street.

'You know you took a risk leaving the house by yourself,' he told her. 'I saw the stranger when last I left you. That is why I was still out. I searched for him to no avail.'

'I thought there would be enough people out to keep me safe,' she said.

'Do not take another chance like that, my lady. Not until we know more about this man and his interest in you.'

They walked several steps before she answered, 'I will be cautious.'

It was not precisely a promise to do as he said. He must try to discover this man some other way. He'd check the inns in Bath and see if a man of his description was staying there.

They continued past the Circus until eventually they reached the Crescent.

He sounded the knocker. 'Again I say goodbye to you, my lady.'

She took his hand in hers and smiled. 'Again I say thank you, Lucien.'

The door opened and Lord Stonecroft stepped out. 'Captain Roper, I would speak with you.' He stepped aside so Lucien could enter.

Lady Rebecca gave Lucien a distressed look. He tried to return her a reassuring one, but certainly nothing good could come from this meeting. 'Very well, sir.'

'Lady Rebecca,' Stonecroft said in a stern voice. 'You may go upstairs and change into dry clothing. I will speak with you later.'

With one more glance at Lucien, she did what Lord Stonecroft ordered.

Lucien followed the man into a library right off the hall. The books on the shelves looked as if they'd not been removed in a decade and the chairs and sofa were arranged in perfect symmetry. Only one chair looked inviting, a large leather chair that sat behind a desk embellished with gilt.

Stonecroft turned and faced him. 'What are your intentions towards Lady Rebecca?'

At least the man was forthright. 'Intentions? As from the beginning, to see her safe and well.'

Stonecroft walked to a cabinet and took out a decanter and two glasses. He poured brown liquid into both and handed one to Lucien.

Stonecroft took a sip of his before speaking again. 'You being so frequently in her company causes talk. That whole shipwreck story just adds fuel to the flame. It was bad enough you were written of in the newspapers.'

'The shipwreck happened,' Lucien said. 'Our rescue was news.'

'Having one's name in the newspaper makes people talk.' Stonecroft grimaced. 'I find it distasteful.'

Lucien's spine stiffened. 'You, sir, are more concerned with how people talk than the traumas Lady Rebecca endured. Even now she suffers from her loss of memory. It affects her greatly.'

Stonecroft sneered. 'You talk like a lover, Roper. I took you at your word that nothing improper occurred between you and my fiancée—'

Lucien raised his voice. 'Heed me, Stonecroft. Lady Rebecca needs consideration. That is more important than newspapers and gossip.'

Stonecroft lifted his chin like a petulant child. 'Do take note of who you are speaking to, Roper.'

'I know precisely who I am speaking to,' Lucien shot back.

Stonecroft sputtered. 'You are disrespectful, sir!'

'Show some respect for Lady Rebecca,' Lucien countered.

Stonecroft's face turned haughty. 'Your association makes people speculate about impropriety over dinner and cards. Still, I am willing to marry her, but I dislike scandal above all things. I demand you honour my wishes in this matter.'

Lucien's voice rose again. 'You demand?'

'Yes. I demand you stay away,' the man said. 'Leave Bath. You cause me nothing but trouble here.'

Stonecroft was still missing the point.

'What of this stranger stalking Lady Rebecca?' Lucien asked. 'What will you do to protect her?'

Stonecroft shook his shoulders. 'I will marry her. When she is my wife no man will dare trifle with her.'

That was a ridiculous statement.

Lucien set down his glass, untouched, next to Stone-croft's. 'I find your lack of concern for the lady who is to be your wife reprehensible, sir. You care nothing for the danger that may lurk out there for her. Or for the ordeal she has endured. Or for her loss of memory.'

Stonecroft's face turned red. 'You dare to lecture me?'

Lucien countered, 'I merely state what should be obvious to anyone who has a regard for her.'

Stonecroft fumed. 'I believe I know what is best for her and for the children I will beget with her.'

Lucien directed a steely glance at the man. 'If Lady Rebecca needs my assistance, I will always come to her aid. If I see her at an entertainment or on the street, I will greet her and speak with her. I will also decide when I leave Bath and it will never be because you commanded me to leave.'

He turned away from the man and walked out the door.

Claire had delayed going upstairs, wanting to know what Lord Stonecroft had said to Lucien.

As she waited on the first floor, looking down on the hall, Miss Attwood came down from the floor above.

'Lady Rebecca, what on earth has been happening this morning? First I am told you and your maid go out, then you come back without her—and in the company of Captain Roper—then you leave again, alone this time and again return with the Captain. What is all this?'

She had half a mind to tell Miss Attwood everything. About how her brother was pressuring her to have the banns read before she was ready. How he was discounting the difficulty she experienced over the loss of her memory. How unconcerned he was about the stranger who'd approached them.

'I desired a walk after breakfast and Ella went with me,' she said instead. 'We noticed that the stranger who bothered us yesterday was following us and we fled to Sir Richard's house. Captain Roper was the only one at home. He walked me back.'

'And your maid?' Miss Attwood asked.

'She and Captain Roper's valet went in search of the stranger.'

She frowned. 'The other servants tell me that maid of yours is always running off to Sir Richard's. Did you know there was some carnal attachment between her and that valet? You'd best be wary. That girl will be increasing in no time and, I tell you, Stonecroft will not tolerate a servant in his household with low morals.'

Now they were casting aspersions on Ella?

'Miss Attwood, Ella is a fine young woman.'

'I believe at my age I may know more about servants and what can happen than you. I am simply warning you. If you want her to stay as your lady's maid, you ought to sever these goings on right now. Nip them in the bud.' She made a gesture with her fingers as if she were doing that very thing.

On the contrary, Claire thought. She should encourage Ella to go after as much happiness as she could, because in a moment everything could be washed away.

Claire climbed one step of the stairs leading to the second floor. 'If you will excuse me, I must change out of these wet clothes.'

She fled to her bedchamber and was surprised to find Ella there.

'Oh, m'lady.' Ella removed her hat and eyed Claire's wet clothes. 'I just came in. Where were you?'

'Captain Roper and I got caught in the rain.'

Ella seemed to accept that explanation.

What was Claire to do about Ella? She could not take her along to Bristol. Claire would be lucky to find a way to support herself; she certainly did not want to spoil Ella's chances of good employment. And she did not want to separate Ella from Cullen. At least one of them should be happy. She would leave an excellent reference for her and trust that Lucien would help her find a position.

She pulled the hat off her head. 'You can help me change into dry clothes.'

'Of course, m'lady.' She took the shawl and draped it over a chair and came back to undo Claire's laces. 'Cullen and I almost caught up to that strange man, m'lady.'

'You did?' Her heart pounded faster.

'We saw him standing on the field in front of these houses. Cullen ran after him and almost caught up to him, but he disappeared into the shrubbery.'

The stranger must know where she lived. Was he watching the house at this very moment? She shivered at the thought.

She was trapped in this house with Lord Stonecroft and Miss Attwood, who both considered her a mere means to an end—the means by which Stonecroft's heir would be born. Neither cared much for her beyond that and beyond how she appeared to their society.

Well, if she could endure a day and night on a raft at sea, three weeks on a fishing boat and the loss of all her possessions—and her memory—she could endure three more days with these people.

Because she was determined to make her escape before Lord Stonecroft had the banns read.

Lucien spent the rest of the morning and half the afternoon asking at inns in Bath to discover the identity of man who'd accosted Lady Rebecca. The only possibility he'd found so far was the White Hart. No one remembered the red-haired man, but the inn was large enough that the stranger could be staying there without anyone's notice.

He visited the West Gate Inn last.

The innkeeper remembered him. 'Captain Roper, a letter just arrived for you from London. You save me sending a man to bring it to you. Wait a moment.'

The man disappeared into another room and returned with the envelope.

'Thank you.' It was from the Admiralty, but Lucien had to put it in a pocket. 'I am searching for a man,' he said and described the stranger.

The innkeeper said, 'I do not recall such a man, but ask the hostlers and in the public room. Someone else might have seen him.'

While Lucien queried every inn worker he could find—to no avail—the letter burned in his pocket. He sat at a table in the public room, a tankard of ale in front of him when he finally opened it and read.

> *Dear Captain Roper,*
> *The Admiralty is delighted to hear of your survival and rescue and we are eager to have the hero of the Mediterranean return to service.*
> *Most ship assignments were of necessity made in your absence due to important action in Algiers. There is one more opportunity.*
> *The* HMS Gaius *is ready to sail to the Baltic Sea, but its Captain must be on board by September the tenth. If you can reach our offices by September eighth and be ready to sail by September tenth, the ship is yours.*
> *Yours respectfully,*
> *Melville*
> *First Lord of the Admiralty*

Lucien folded the letter and put it back in his pocket. September the eighth. Two days away.

If he could get passage on the mail coach, he might reach London in a day. There was time. He could do it.

If he left the next day.

Lucien walked slowly back to the Circus. The weather had turned to drizzle, but he did not heed it.

If he left for London tomorrow, it would be without making certain that red-haired stranger did not endanger Lady Rebecca and without taking her to Bristol.

He'd be abandoning her in a time of need, the way his parents had abandoned him.

But it might be his only chance to get a ship.

He reached Number Fifteen in the Circus. Sir Richard was at home.

Sir Richard encountered him on the stairs. 'Good God, Roper! You've been caught in the rain, have you not? You'll catch your death.'

Lucien forced a smile. 'After the weather we've both endured on our ships, I doubt a little dampness will hurt me.'

Sir Richard smiled. 'Well, change into some dry clothes and come have a brandy with me. I'll be in the library.'

Lucien continued up the stairs to the guest room he'd been given. Cullen was there, brushing one of Lucien's coats.

Cullen. What was he to do about Cullen?

'Sir! I am glad you are back at last,' the valet said.

Lucien started to take off his jacket. Cullen hurried over to assist him.

'I went to some of the inns in Bath. Trying to find the stranger.' Lucien felt his waistcoat. It seemed dry enough. He sat and took off his boots.

'Ella and I saw the man when we were out,' Cullen said. 'He knows where Lady Rebecca lives. He was watching the house from the field in front of the Crescent.

'I saw him, too. Just for a second. He ran off before I could reach him.'

'Do you think he means Lady Rebecca harm?' Cullen asked.

Lucien lifted a shoulder. 'There is a big risk assuming he does not.'

'That is what I thought, too, sir.'

The young man helped Lucien into a dry coat. He put on a dry pair of shoes and walked down to the library.

'Ah, just in time,' Sir Richard said. 'I was about to pour the brandy.'

This room was a huge contrast to Lord Stonecroft's library. Books were stacked on tables and laid sideways on the shelves. The furniture was aimed more at comfort than symmetry. Sir Richard spent a great deal of time in this room and it showed.

'So your valet said our red-haired gentleman has been seen around Lord Stonecroft's residence.' Sir Richard handed Lucien a glass of brandy. 'You have let Lord Stonecroft know?'

'He knows,' Lucien said in a tight voice.

Sir Richard's brows rose. 'What does that tone mean?'

'He is more concerned with gossip and reputations than whether some stranger poses a threat.'

The older man nodded. 'It is you he wants away from her, then.'

'Because people talk if we are seen together.' Lucien imitated Stonecroft's speech.

Sir Richard lifted his glass to his mouth. 'I am sure people do talk.'

Lucien's eyes flashed. 'I cannot control what people think or say.'

Sir Richard leaned back in his chair. 'You handed her off to him, my boy. You say that is for the best. You have to let go of her, then. She is the responsibility of another man now. Not you.'

Lucien had run out of time to help her.

'There is nothing you can do except cause her more

trouble as long as she is with Lord Stonecroft,' Sir Richard went on.

Lucien downed his brandy in one gulp. 'It is a moot point. I had a letter from the Admiralty. I can be given a ship, but I must appear at the Admiralty by September the eighth.'

'September the eighth!' his friend cried. 'That is two days' time.'

'I can make it if I catch the mail coach tomorrow.' Lucien frowned. 'So Stonecroft will have what he wishes. I will be gone.'

Sir Richard poured Lucien a second brandy.

'I have one favour to ask of you,' Lucien said.

'Ask it and I will comply if I can,' his friend replied.

'Cullen. He needs work. I'll write a good recommendation and leave him enough money to tide him over for a while, but will you help him?'

Sir Richard sipped his brandy. 'I'll do all I can. I may even hire him myself, I'm that fond of him. In any event, he may live here until the matter is settled.'

'I am very grateful.' At least Cullen would be off his conscience.

He and Sir Richard lapsed into an uncomfortable silence, during which Lucien mulled over his worries about Lady Rebecca. After a time spent staring into his glass, Lucien looked over at his friend.

Sir Richard was sound asleep.

Lucien drank the rest of his brandy and set the glass on the table. He rose quietly and left the library. Once in the hall, he hurried up to his room.

He flung open the door. 'Cullen! I have a favour to ask of you.'

Chapter Nineteen

Claire sat in front of her bedchamber window, staring out at the sunless day. She wondered if she could beg off from attending dinner and so avoid being in Lord Stonecroft's company or that of his sister.

There was so much to think about. The stranger. Lord Stonecroft. Ella.

Lucien.

Much less painful to plan her escape.

She did not know the departure time for the coach to Bristol, so the best she could hope for was to be at the West Gate Inn early in the day. Perhaps no one would think to look for her there until she was safely on her way.

She had ink, pen and paper in her bedchamber so she could write her letters without having to ask for those supplies. She'd write to Lord Stonecroft and to Ella, also leaving her a favourable letter of recommendation and instructions of what to do with her belongings. She'd leave Ella money, too, of course.

She must pack. Only what Lucien had purchased for her, though. She wanted none of the dresses Lord Stonecroft wanted her to wear. She would pack a portmanteau for the trip to Bristol and fill her trunk with the rest of her clothes and hope Sir Richard would agree to keep it until she knew where it could be sent.

Her disappearance would cause more talk among Bath society, a situation that would likely upset Stonecroft more than her crying off. Well, Lord Stonecroft and Miss Attwood would merely have to weather that small storm.

She must write to Lucien.

What would she say to him? Thank him one more time. Release him from any further obligation to her. Tell him she hoped he'd get his ship. That she hoped he could again be free and happy once he was back at sea. Be in a place he felt he belonged.

Ella entered the room, interrupting Claire's thoughts.

The girl looked distressed. 'M'lady, Cullen is below stairs. He says the Captain wants to see you right now!'

Claire rose from her chair. 'Has something happened?'

'I do not know,' Ella cried. 'I only know that Cullen said the Captain can't simply call on you, because of his lordship, so he wants you to come with Cullen and meet him outside in the garden.'

Claire had never been in the garden, had never seen the back door to the house, nor accessed the garden from the outside.

'I cannot leave by the front without the footman knowing.' And risking the stranger seeing her if he was watching the house. 'How am I to reach the garden unseen?'

'I do not know,' Ella admitted. 'Cullen is waiting at the bottom of the servants' stairs, but if you go out that way, you have to pass the servants' hall and the kitchen. That is the way I leave the house when I am to visit Cullen and where he comes to visit me.'

'Then if you go out with Cullen, no one will remark on it?'

'Oh, they will remark on it,' Ella said with feeling. 'But what good will it do for me to go to the Captain?'

'Not you. Me. We will exchange clothes and they will think I am you.' Where had this idea come from? 'I'll wear your shawl and cap. I'll hide my face some way. They will think I am you. They know you have my permission to see Cullen whenever you want.'

'That is why they remark upon it,' Ella said, but she was already untying Claire's laces.

They hurriedly changed into each other's clothes. Claire covered her hair with Ella's cap and draped the shawl around her head.

'Cullen is waiting at the bottom of the stairs?' she asked. Ella nodded.

Claire had never been below stairs where the servants' rooms and the kitchen were, but she descended the servants' narrow and steep stairway until she reached its lowest level.

Cullen turned at her approach. 'Ella?' He sounded surprised.

Claire revealed her face.

'Oh, m'lady.' He bowed. 'You fooled me. That is good. I was puzzling how to get you to the Captain.'

'If I fooled you, we should fool the servants.' She looked up at him. 'Do you know what has happened? Ella made it sound urgent.'

'I don't know.' He looked sheepish. 'I'll have to be askin' you to take my arm, m'lady. I hope you don't mind.'

She smiled at him. 'I do not mind at all.'

She wrapped her arm though his and walked close to him, as Ella usually did. He led them down the hallway to the back door.

When they passed the kitchen, he called out, 'I'll be having her back in time for dinner.'

'You had better,' the housekeeper shot back. 'Or she'll not eat.'

When they reached the outside he stepped away from her.

'The Captain will be by the outbuildings back here.'

She and Cullen crossed the garden to where the outbuildings stood and where Lucien could be seen pacing back and forth. When he spied her he strode over to her.

'Lucien, what has happened?'

He took her hand and led her to a relatively private spot between two small storage sheds. Cullen waited a short distance away.

All her senses were on alert. 'Tell me, Lucien, what is wrong?'

His expression was as serious as she'd ever seen it.

'I could not call at the house, not after that encounter with Stonecroft.' He was unsettled.

Her Lucien was never unsettled.

'Was he dreadful to you?' she asked.

'I care nothing for that.' His face filled with anger. 'He is an abominable man. Everything I abhor in an aristocrat.'

'I know,' she said quietly.

'But never mind that. I am—' He faced her, holding her upper arms. 'I am leaving. Tomorrow. I heard from the Admiralty. I will get a ship if I can reach London in two days' time.'

This was what he'd counted upon.

This was really and truly goodbye.

'That is wonderful, Lucien,' she managed to reply. 'I am so happy for you.'

Inside her heart was breaking. She might never see him again.

He released her. 'I promised I would say goodbye.'

She reached up and touched his face. 'I appreciate that.'

'If you need me, though—'

She placed her fingers on his lips. 'Do not say it. You must have your ship.'

'But there is the red-haired stranger.' His brow furrowed. 'And you need to go to Bristol.'

'I'll go to Bristol. Perhaps I'll hire Cullen to come with

me.' Although she wouldn't. Because when she went to Bristol she wasn't coming back.

'There will be other ships,' he went on. 'I will stay if you need me.'

Oh, how she needed him! But even more she needed him to be happy.

'I will do well enough,' she said. 'You must go.'

'You will marry Stonecroft?' He spoke the name with scorn.

She skirted around the truth. 'That is the plan.'

'But earlier you seemed distressed by the idea,' he protested. 'You did not want him to have the banns read.'

She still did not.

'That was because I want to wait until my memory comes back.'

'He cares nothing for that.' He raised his voice.

'I know.' She fought to keep her emotions under tight control. 'He does not understand.'

His expression turned earnest. 'Lady Rebecca, he cares nothing for you.'

'And I care nothing for him, but at least I'll gain a home of my own to manage. Children. Comfort and security. Status—' She stopped herself. It felt like she'd spoken such words before.

He looked as if she'd struck him across the face.

'What about the stranger?' he asked stiffly.

'I'll be careful, Lucien. No more running out alone.' Except when she made her escape.

'Then this is goodbye,' he said.

She put her arms around him and hugged him close to her. For the last time. 'Goodbye, Lucien,' she murmured.

His muscles were taut, as if he were anticipating an attack, but he relaxed and hugged her back. They remained in that embrace for a long time, reluctant to let go.

But let go they must. Claire released him first.

He stepped back. 'I have not told Cullen yet. You are first.'

'I will not say anything.' Her throat constricted. And her heart was shattering.

'Cullen!' he called.

The valet hurried over to them.

'You can return Lady Rebecca to the house.'

'I'll do that, sir,' Cullen said. 'Come, m'lady.'

Claire let Cullen lead her to the door, but she turned for one last glimpse of Lucien.

He opened the door for her. 'Thank you, Cullen,' she said.

Cullen looked confused and concerned, but he did not ask her what had happened. 'Tell—tell Ella I'll see her when I can.'

Would her decisions and Lucien's separate those two? She prayed not.

'I will.' She touched his arm. 'You are a good man, Cullen.'

Before breaking down completely, she covered her face with Ella's shawl and entered the house, hurrying by the kitchen and the other rooms.

The housekeeper's voice trailed after her. 'You had better not be late for dinner!'

Lucien waited for Cullen to walk back to him. 'You are at liberty, Cullen. I am going into town. Tell Sir Richard I'll miss dinner. I'll be back late.'

'I will tell him, sir.' Cullen's expression was questioning, but Lucien was in no mood to explain.

He walked off, his pace brisk. He should have told Cullen he was leaving on the morrow. Given the young man some warning. Too late now. He'd speak with him when he returned to Sir Richard's.

Why was he feeling so desolate? He wanted a ship

and he would get one. This was always what should have happened.

He passed several of the people he'd met at the Pump Room and at various entertainments. They all greeted him warmly. Decently.

Perhaps not all aristocrats were like Stonecroft or Lady Rebecca's brother or his mother's viscount lover.

The lady who had first recognised him as the Captain rescued from the shipwreck spied him and crossed the street to speak with him.

'Captain!' she called. 'Are you all on your own tonight? Come with us. We are having a few friends for dinner and would love to have you come.'

She was on the arm of her husband, who nodded his agreement. 'Should have sent an invitation. Have Sir Richard come, as well. Nine o'clock.'

It was kind of them.

'I cannot tonight,' he responded. 'But I am honoured you would invite me.' He meant that.

'Another time!' the lady called as they proceeded on their way.

Lucien wanted to find the most humble tavern in Bath, a place where no one would know him. He planned to drink until this ache inside him disappeared.

Saying goodbye to her, leaving her to marry Stonecroft, had ripped him to pieces.

Claire had run up the servants' staircase, but stopped before reaching the second floor, her emotions finally over-taking her. She'd taken deep breaths and fanned her face to keep the tears from flowing. Her insides felt as if they'd broken into sharp shards, the pain was so great.

The pain of saying goodbye to the man you loved.

Because she loved him, she had no other choice. To ask him to stay would have been the height of selfishness.

With a fragile sense of control she climbed the rest of the stairs and returned to her bedchamber.

Ella, who had been standing at the window overlooking the garden, swivelled around. 'I was watching, but I couldn't see anything. What did he want, m'lady?'

Claire forced a smile. 'He is leaving tomorrow. He came to say goodbye.'

Ella's eyes widened. 'No. He cannot leave.'

Claire put down the shawl and took off Ella's cap. 'He must. He is a captain in the navy. He belongs on a ship at sea.'

Ella looked distraught. 'Did Cullen know that?'

'No,' Claire said. 'The Captain wanted to tell me first.'

Claire presented her back to Ella so that she could untie her laces and also so Ella would not see her blink away tears. Claire turned around and did the same for Ella.

'I suppose you could dress me for dinner,' Claire said. Although how she would manage to sit through dinner with Lord Stonecroft and Miss Attwood she did not know.

'I do not see how you can be remaining so unaffected!' Ella cried.

Claire met her eyes. 'I am affected. But I've known from the beginning that I would have to say goodbye.'

'I think you could have made him stay,' the girl grumbled.

'Yes. If I did not care for him so much,' Claire responded.

She held her emotions in check while Ella helped her into a dinner dress and rearranged her hair.

With that complete, she said, 'You may do as you please, Ella. I will not need you until time for bed. Say ten o'clock?'

Ella pursed her lips before speaking. 'As you wish, m'lady.'

When the girl left the room, Claire allowed her tears to flow.

* * *

That night at dinner Lord Stonecroft never mentioned the red-haired stranger or his conversation with Lucien. Instead he and Miss Attwood discussed the people they had seen that day and what they were planning to do the next day. Claire was glad they paid no attention to her, but she attended to the times they planned to be gone the next day.

'You are very quiet tonight, Lady Rebecca,' Miss Attwood said in a kind tone. 'Are you not feeling well?'

'Perhaps a little unwell,' she replied. 'I was caught in the rain.'

She glanced over at Stonecroft to see his reaction. He merely kept eating.

Miss Attwood peered at her from across the table. 'I do believe you look a bit pale. You should take care. Do not exert yourself.'

Claire had no doubt she was pale.

Miss Attwood gave her a concerned look. 'I would ask you to accompany me to the Pump Room tomorrow, but if you are unwell…'

Claire's spirits rose a slight fraction. Tomorrow would be her chance to leave.

A pain stabbed her heart. Her whole life was about to change again. She hoped she could hold on to the memories. The memories of being with Lucien.

Perhaps she would glimpse him tomorrow at the West Gate Inn. Perhaps she'd see him board the coach to London.

It was something to hope for.

Chapter Twenty

The next morning Claire did not have any difficulty convincing anyone that she was unwell. She'd hardly slept and her eyes were red from weeping into her pillow so Ella would not hear.

'Should I ask Miss Attwood if we should send for a physician?' Ella asked her worriedly.

'No. No.' Claire managed a wan smile. 'I have no fever. I am certain the stress from yesterday has merely left me fatigued. I intend to spend the day in this room.'

'Do you wish to stay abed?' the girl asked.

'I am not so ill!' she insisted. 'I'll simply have you put me in one of my old dresses in case I wish to see if the library has a book worth reading.'

She chose one of the travelling dresses, hoping Ella did not think it an odd choice.

As Ella finished arranging her hair, Claire told her, 'I will not need you here today. Not at all. Spend the day with Cullen, if you can.'

Cullen's future was uncertain now. Ella would soon learn hers was as well.

'But if you are not feeling well, I should stay here,' Ella protested.

Claire took the girl's hands in her own. 'I tell you, I am

not ill. I just need rest. Go. Be with Cullen. He will need your support.'

Ella looked uncertain. 'If you think so.'

'I do.' She shook her hands in emphasis.

Ella stepped back. 'I could go now, I suppose.'

'Yes. Go now.'

'I'll just put some of your things away.' She started to tidy the room.

Claire rose from her chair. 'I'll do that. It will give me something to do. You could ask Cook to send breakfast up to my room. That would be very nice.'

'I'll do that, m'lady.' She skipped into the dressing room and picked up her hat and shawl. She hurried to the door. 'Is there anything else?' she asked before leaving.

Claire took one long look at her, committing her image to memory. 'Only one more thing,' she murmured.

'What, m'lady?'

Claire smiled. 'Enjoy your time with Cullen.'

Ella grinned. 'I will!'

As soon as Ella left, Claire went over to the desk and took out paper and ink. She began writing a letter of recommendation for Ella.

Before she finished a footman brought up a breakfast tray. Though she had no appetite, she made herself eat. She did not know when she would have another chance.

Then she returned to her letters. The one to Stonecroft was by far the easiest, because she was certain he did not care about her, nor she, him. She wondered what he would have been like if his wife and child had lived. Whatever part of him that had died with them was a part for which she might have developed a fondness.

Ella's letter was difficult. She was saying goodbye to her only woman friend.

It turned out she did not need to write Lucien at all. That was almost harder than putting pen to paper for him. She wrote a letter to Sir Richard instead, begging him to look out for Cullen and Ella.

When she finished she was in tears again. This time she let herself weep openly, because she was alone on this floor and no one would hear. She'd heard Miss Attwood leave a while ago and peeked out her door to see that she'd taken her lady's maid with her. Lord Stonecroft was to have left very early. Both would be out until late afternoon.

When her letters were completed and her tears dried, she opened the desk drawer and placed the letters inside for safe keeping until she was ready to leave. Nothing else left to do but pack her trunk and portmanteau.

She went into the dressing room and found the small bag Lucien had purchased for her that first day in Ireland. As she packed one other dress, one nightdress and the brush, comb, hairpins and other essentials Lucien had bought her, she had the sense of packing like this once before. Not while with Lucien. Some other time, a time of packing with a sense of urgency. It was not quite a memory, but almost one and she had an inexplicable feeling of dread.

A knock on the door made her jump.

She walked into the bedroom. 'Yes?' she called through the door.

'M'lady?' It was one of the footmen.

She opened the door.

'A Lord and Lady Brookmore here to call on you,' he said.

Who? 'Did they say what they wanted?'

Was she supposed to know a Lord and Lady Brookmore? She'd not met them in Bath, she was certain. She'd worked very hard to remember all the names of people she'd met.

'They did not say, m'lady,' he responded. 'But they said it was very important they speak with you. They will wait all day to speak with you if necessary.'

'Very well. I'll be down directly.' Was this someone from her past? 'Are they waiting in the drawing room?'

'They are.' He bowed and left.

She took a deep breath and started down the stairs.

The footman announced her.

'I will not need you,' she told him.

He bowed again and continued downstairs to attend the hall.

She stepped into the room.

A lady and gentleman, more her age than the Stone-crofts, stood.

'You wished to speak with me?' she asked.

The lady's face was obscured by a veil over her hat. Neither she nor the gentleman said anything. The lady walked towards her.

And lifted her veil.

Lucien had time to kill before the mail coach left. He woke early and took a long walk, turning in his mind everything that had transpired between him and Lady Rebecca. Everything on the walk reminded him of her, of when she'd led him through the streets of Bath, knowing all the buildings, but not knowing why. Even the passersby reminded him of her.

A gentleman and lady passed him on his way back to the Circus. The lady reminded him of Lady Rebecca. Not her face, because it was obscured by a veil, but otherwise she had the look of Lady Rebecca.

So had another woman, though, who did not look anything like Lady Rebecca, but her laugh reminded him of Lady Rebecca's laugh, the first thing that had attracted him to her.

He'd been drawn to her from the start, from the moment of hearing that laugh. She was unlike any other woman he'd known with her courage and her vulnerability.

He'd told himself what he admired was caused by her amnesia. He'd convinced himself she'd turn into a haughty aristocrat as soon as she remembered who she was. Now he was not so sure. There was an essence of her that could be genuine.

He'd done a lot of thinking since the day before. Turned out he was not able to drink away his emotions. Instead he'd nursed his second tankard of ale for several hours. A man had to be a very sorry sort, if he lost even the solace of drink.

He kept telling himself how glad he was to be getting another ship, but inside he only felt loss.

He returned to Sir Richard's house and handed the footman his hat and gloves. 'Do you know where Cullen is?'

'Believe he and his Ella are visiting below stairs, sir,' the man replied. 'Shall I send him to you?'

'No.' Lucien might as well speak to Ella, as well. 'I'll go down to them.'

He found them in the servants' hall eating biscuits and drinking tea.

Cullen jumped to his feet. 'Sir! Do you have need of me?' He wore a wounded expression.

'Sit, Cullen,' he said. 'I want to talk to you both.'

Ella piped up. 'He already knows, Captain. I told him.'

Lucien felt a stab of guilt. 'Forgive me, Cullen. I meant to tell you last night.'

'Do not fret, sir,' Cullen said in a stoic tone. 'I knew you would be leaving sooner or later. I've packed for you.' He looked like he'd lost his best friend.

Which was rather like Lucien felt when he thought about the young man.

'Are you sure you must leave?' Ella asked.

Was he sure? 'Yes. I need to leave today or lose the chance to get a ship.'

'Because I am worried about Lady Rebecca,' Ella went on. 'She says she's not ill, but she looks so pale and her eyes are all red. I think she is sick, but she doesn't want a physician and I do not know what to do.'

Sick? Lucien felt an immediate impulse to run to her, send for a doctor. Something. Anything.

Cullen spoke up. 'I told Ella Lady Rebecca is probably just upset. Red eyes usually means a fit of weeping. Or, at least, that's what it always meant on my sisters.'

She'd seemed composed the day before when he'd said goodbye. Had something else happened?

'Did she say how she felt?' he asked.

'Unwell, is all.' Ella toyed with her teacup.

'I do not know what to say.' He sat in one of the chairs and picked up a biscuit from the plate.

Ella rose this time. 'Shall I find you a cup, Captain? Would you like some tea?'

'No, stay here a moment. I want you both to know I am leaving Cullen a year's wage, just to help tide him over until he gets a new position.'

'That is kind of you, sir.' Cullen's voice thickened.

Ella sat down again. 'I do not think you should leave. Not with my lady sick and that mad man out to harm her and all.'

'She's to marry Stonecroft, Ella,' he said in a patient tone he did not feel. 'It is not up to me to help any more.'

'She can't marry that old man!' Ella cried. 'He is as cold as stone. You have to stop it.'

His insides twisted in pain. 'It is what she wants, Ella. She told me.'

'Well, she doesn't mean it!' She lowered her head into her hands. 'She simply can't.'

Cullen put his arm around Ella. 'Now, do not you become upset.'

Lucien stood again. 'I should speak with Sir Richard.'

'Yes, sir,' Cullen said in depressed tones.

Lucien walked away with Ella's voice echoing in his mind.

She doesn't mean it.

Claire stared into a face that looked exactly like her own, so alike the lady could have stepped through a looking glass.

'You look like me,' she whispered.

'Claire! It is me! Yes, I look like you. I am so sorry. So sorry. I thought you had drowned. I saw you get washed overboard! I thought you were dead!'

Claire's head started to pound. 'You were on the *Dun Aengus*?'

'You know I was!' the lady cried.

Claire held up a hand. 'Wait. Are you my sister?' She didn't know she had a sister, especially not a twin sister.

'What sort of question is that?' the lady cried. 'Of course I am not your sister.'

The gentleman spoke. Lord Brookmore. Was that name familiar? 'Something is wrong, Becca. Let her speak.'

Becca? Did he mean Rebecca? Who was he talking to? Let who speak?

She lowered herself into a chair. 'Forgive me. I cannot stand.'

The woman who looked like her—Lady Brookmore—pulled a chair close to hers, with an expectant look on her face.

Her husband chose another chair nearby. 'We read about you in the newspaper. About your rescue after the shipwreck. I assure you, we have not come to cause you any trouble. None at all. But there is something you must know—'

Claire pressed her fingers against her temple. This was

like waking up on the raft all over again. In a world she did not know. With people she did not recognise.

'I—I don't remember,' she said.

'You don't remember?' Lady Brookmore cried. 'How can you not remember?'

Claire lifted her gaze to the face so like her own. 'When I woke up. After the shipwreck. I—I did not remember anything.'

'You forgot the shipwreck?' Lord Brookmore turned to his wife. 'I have seen that before. Soldiers injured in battle. Afterwards they can't remember it.'

Claire pressed her temples harder. 'You do not understand. I remember nothing from before waking up on the raft.' In Lucien's arms. 'Not who I am. Not my family. Or my home. Not you. Or what I had done the day before or the month before or ever before.'

Understanding dawned on the woman's face. 'Then you think you are—' She broke off and turned to her husband. 'She thinks she is—'

He leaned towards Claire. 'You did not know your name?' he asked gently.

Claire shook her head. 'No.'

'Someone told you that you were Lady Rebecca?'

'Lucien.' Her head pounded. 'I mean, Captain Roper.'

'The man who rescued you,' he stated.

She nodded.

'Oh, Claire! You don't remember?' Lady Brookmore cried.

'I know how to do things. I remember facts. I could even lead Lucien all around Bath, but I have had only one memory and that was fleeting. I remembered drinking the waters here in Bath, but nothing else.'

Except that sinister figure in her dreams. And the little girls doing their schoolwork.

She turned to Lady Brookmore. 'Why do you call me Claire?'

'Because that is your name,' Lady Brookmore said in a low voice full of sympathy. 'You are Miss Claire Tilson.'

The name did not surprise her, but neither did it feel real.

Lady Brookmore continued. 'And I am Lady Rebecca Pierce.'

Chapter Twenty-One

Claire thought her head would burst. Lady Brookmore's words echoed over and over in her mind, *I am Lady Rebecca Pierce.*

The lady continued, 'We met by happenstance on the packet boat. Like this, suddenly seeing each other's faces. It was remarkable and we spent time together to try to understand it all.'

'Are we related?' Claire asked.

'We never found any connection,' Lady Brookmore went on. 'We are not related. It is merely a fantastic coincidence, but it was a little like finding a long-lost sister. We spent most of the voyage together, talking as if we were sisters. I was headed to London to marry Lord Stonecroft and you— you were travelling to the Lake District to be governess to Lord Brookmore's nieces—'

'No. No,' Claire broke in. 'I was not dressed as a governess.'

Lady Brookmore blushed and she lowered her head. 'We swapped clothing. To fool people. I dressed you in my clothes and everyone thought you were me. Even—even Nolan, the maid sent with me.' Her voice cracked. 'The maid who drowned.'

A maid! The maid her brother—Lady Rebecca's brother—spoke of.

Could this be the truth?

'Then I am this Claire Tilson? A governess?'

'You are the daughter of a vicar. Your mother died when you were young, or when you were born. I don't remember. Your father sent you to school. When he died, you became a governess.'

She pressed her temples again. 'Was this school in Bristol?'

'Yes,' her likeness said. 'Yes, it was.'

She started to believe this. Even though she did not remember, these facts did not unsettle her. The name did not alarm her. She'd been more alarmed to think she was Lady Rebecca.

'Everyone thinks I am Lady Rebecca.'

'And you can stay Lady Rebecca for all I care.' The lady's voice thickened with emotion again. 'I pretended to be you. I woke up after a fever and—and Garret—' She glanced over at her husband. 'Garret was there. He thought I was you. And, because I did not want to be me, on my way to marry a man who cared nothing for me, I let him and everyone think I was you. I am so sorry, Claire. I thought you were dead.'

Claire turned to Lord Brookmore. 'I was supposed to be your governess?'

'To my nieces. Yes,' he responded.

She looked from Lady Brookmore to Lord Brookmore. 'You pretended to be the governess, but now you are married?'

They shot each other adoring looks. 'Yes,' they said in unison.

How lovely for them.

So unlike a marriage with Stonecroft would be, a marriage that would never occur.

She held a hand against her forehead. 'Forgive me. I do not remember any of this, but it makes a certain sense.'

She gazed from one to the other. 'Am I truly Claire Tilson, a governess?'

They both nodded.

'Then what do we do now?' she asked.

'You have not married Lord Stonecroft,' Brookmore said. 'I assume the footman would have addressed you as such if you had.'

'No, I have not married him.'

'Do you want to?' Lady Brookmore—Rebecca—asked. 'Because I remember you thought marriage to him would bring me security. A house of my own to manage. A place in society. Children. It is all right with me if you want to.'

She'd said almost those exact words to Lucien.

'How can I marry him?' Not that she still intended to. 'I cannot sign the register as Lady Rebecca if I am not she. Did you marry as Claire Tilson?'

'We went to Scotland to marry,' Lady Brookmore responded. 'I married as myself. We're going to make up some story about why Garret will call me Rebecca, but otherwise we'll simply let people think what they will.'

'How did you know about me? That I'd be here?' Claire asked.

'We read about it in the *Morning Chronicle*,' Brookmore said. 'We knew it must be you, because, of course...' He inclined his head towards his wife.

'Honestly, I would never have pretended to be you if I'd had any idea you could be alive.' Lady Brookmore looked distressed again.

Claire had no feelings at all about this woman impersonating her. She certainly could not have assumed that governess position. 'It hardly matters.'

'If you wish to marry Lord Stonecroft and remain Rebecca Pierce, you are welcome to. I will not cause you any trouble over it. I do not need to be Rebecca Pierce any more, now that I am Lady Brookmore.' She cast another loving gaze at her husband.

'I will not marry Lord Stonecroft,' Claire admitted.

'There is another matter we must tell you about,' Lord Brookmore broke in. 'Warn you about. It is the reason we sought you out.'

That sense of dread that hovered in her dreams returned. 'Warn me?'

He leaned forward to explain. 'Before you became governess to my nieces you were a governess in Ireland. That is why you were sailing from Ireland to England on that packet boat.'

She was not from Ireland?

'You were governess to the young daughters of Sir Orin Foley, a baronet, and his wife,' he went on.

The little girls at the school table, the ones who appeared in her dreams?

His wife took up the tale. 'Sir Orin apparently developed a romantic attachment to you.'

'A romantic attachment?' Had she been wanton after all?

Lady Brookmore quickly added, 'Oh, we do not think you returned his sentiments. We believe you were running away from him.'

'How do you know all this? Did I tell you all of it?' That seemed unlikely. Surely she was more private than that.

'No. He came for you at Brookmore House,' Lord Brookmore explained.

'He thought I was you,' his wife said.

'We have reason to believe he is a danger to you,' he added.

'He tried to kidnap me!' Lady Brookmore told her.

'And he said that his wife died,' Lord Brookmore went on, 'which we thought was very convenient. He came to take you away with him because he was now free to marry you.'

'We think he may have killed his wife!' Lady Brookmore cried.

Then that sinister figure in her dreams might have been real? And that figure might be the man who was probably watching the house this very moment?

No. It could not be. 'But if he thought you were me, why would I be in danger here?'

'We feared he would find out as we found out. From the newspaper,' Lord Brookmore said.

'I had to tell him I was not you. I told him my real name.' Lady Brookmore looked distressed again. 'If he reads that newspaper, he'll realise that the Lady Rebecca in the article is probably you. If we found you, he could find you.'

Claire stared at the room's window, facing the green field across from the Crescent. 'Tell me. Does this Sir Orin have red hair?'

'Yes!' Lady Brookmore said.

'Then he has already found me.'

Claire explained her encounters with the red-haired stranger and the Brookmores were convinced it was Sir Orin.

What these people told her about herself settled comfortably inside her, but she still did not remember any of it. Worse, it made her feel that what happened to her while she'd thought herself Lady Rebecca had been nothing more than a fantasy. Would it become so unreal she would lose her memories of the fishermen, the innkeepers, the store clerks in Dublin? Ella and Cullen?

Lucien.

She was more determined than ever to find her school in Bristol. The Brookmores offered to accompany her, but she declined. Being with them distressed her. More people telling her who she was and what she did not remember.

Lord Brookmore insisted upon hiring a carriage for her and that offer she accepted.

They also devised a way for her to leave the house without Sir Orin knowing it. She and Lady Brookmore would exchange clothing and Claire would leave looking exactly like the woman who called upon her. When she was safely on her way to Bristol, he'd come back for his wife.

Claire brought Lady Brookmore up to her bedchamber.

'I am nearly ready to leave,' she told her.

She glanced in the full-length mirror in the room and saw them both reflected in it.

Lady Brookmore stood at her side. 'We compared our images in a mirror on the ship.'

Claire could not remember.

As they helped each other change dresses, Lady Brookmore said, 'It must have been terribly difficult for you to not remember your past.'

'It has been a challenge,' she responded. 'Tell me about what happened to you, though.'

While they arranged their hair, Lady Brookmore told about her experiences as Claire, about Brookmore's dear nieces, about the house and estate and its people there.

'I learned I am a terrible governess,' the lady added.

They looked in the mirror again, this time dressed as each other.

Lady Brookmore put an arm around Claire's shoulders. 'If not for this remarkable resemblance and for meeting you on that ship, I would never have met Garret. Because of you, I have the greatest happiness I can imagine, being his wife.' She leaned her head on Claire's. 'Thank you, Claire.'

Without this remarkable resemblance Claire would have never met Lucien and though she now experienced a great sadness, she would never regret knowing him.

Claire finished packing the portmanteau and walked over to the desk.

'I have letters. One for my maid. One for Stonecroft. And one for Admiral Sir Richard Bickerton.' She took them from the desk drawer and put them on top of the desk where Ella would be sure to find them.

Claire picked up Lady Brookmore's hat and placed it on her head. Lady Brookmore arranged the veil.

'Wait a moment.' Claire realised she'd almost left her Kashmir shawl behind. She draped it over her arm. 'I am ready now.'

They returned to the drawing room where Lord Brookmore waited.

He looked at them side by side. 'Remarkable.'

He kissed his wife goodbye and picked up Claire's portmanteau. 'I'll arrange her a coach to Bristol and I'll come back for you.'

His wife smiled. 'In the meantime I'll pretend again to be Claire.' She turned to Claire. 'You must write to us at Brookmore House. Tell us how you are doing. Let us know if you ever need anything. Anything.'

She hugged Claire.

Claire left the house with Lord Brookmore, for the last time, playing Lady Rebecca.

Lucien paced the floor of his bedchamber.

She doesn't mean it.

Ella's words echoed in his mind, repeating over and over.

He'd not even thought of speaking to Sir Richard like he'd said. Instead he left the house and walked down Gay Street towards Queen Square, turning on Back Lane and entering the Gravel Walk. The Gravel Walk ran behind one section of the Circus and at its top opened up into the field facing the Royal Crescent.

Lucien stood and stared at that magnificent example of Bath architecture, but he was not admiring buildings. He was hearing Ella's words.

She doesn't mean it.

Could it be that she, Lady Rebecca, was lying to him about planning to marry Stonecroft? Was she weeping because Lucien was leaving her with no other choice?

The footman attending the hall went in search of Lady Rebecca.

When he returned, he said, 'Her ladyship is resting and does not wish to receive callers.'

'She'll see me.' He straightened and used his Captain's voice. 'Tell her I will search this whole house until I find her and she listens to me.'

His message landed firmly. The footman's eyes grew large and he hurried up the stairs again.

He returned shortly. 'She will see you in the drawing room.'

Lucien climbed the stairs and entered the room where he'd developed that first instant dislike of Lord Stonecroft.

She was alone in the room and turned at his entrance. 'Captain Roper?'

Captain Roper? Something was off. 'You become formal now, my lady? You've used my given name almost since you've met me.'

'Well,' she said uncertainly, 'tell me what is so urgent you had to interrupt my rest.'

Good God. She sounded like an aristocrat.

'Something's wrong…' He could not place it.

A nervous look crossed her face, but she steeled it into something haughty. 'I am still waiting to hear the reason for this visit.'

He came closer. The light from the window illuminated her face. He could not place his finger on it, but something was wrong.

But he went on. 'I came to urge you to reconsider your decision.'

That distressed expression returned. 'What decision?'

He changed tack. 'Ella said you were ill. I came to see for myself.'

The lines in her forehead smoothed. 'Oh, I am quite recovered. Not ill at all. There is no cause at all to be concerned.'

She started to show him the door, but as she passed him, he took her arm and stared directly into her face.

'Release me this instant!' she cried.

He did not release her. 'You are not…' No, it was impossible.

He let go in confusion.

She sank down in a chair. 'Sit, Captain Roper. I have something to say to you.'

'That you are not her,' he said. 'You are not her.'

It was impossible, but that was the only conclusion he could make.

'That is correct,' she admitted. 'I am not her, but I am Lady Rebecca. And I will explain it all.'

Chapter Twenty-Two

Claire stood in the hall of the White Hart, waiting until the coach that Lord Brookmore had hired was ready to pick her up. The coachman had said it would be only minute, but she waited a great deal longer. She held the Kashmir shawl in her arms like a blanket.

She was Claire Tilson, a governess, a woman without relations, alone in the world. She certainly felt alone at this moment. She must become used to this new identity, though. It must be the true one. All the bits and pieces flitting through her mind, her dreams, what Lord and Lady Brookmore told her about herself, were like pieces completing a puzzle. Everything fit.

Everything was there except her memory.

And Lucien, of course. He'd become a part of her—a part of a fictitious Lady Rebecca. He never knew her at all. And now he was gone.

The pain of losing him stabbed at her heart once more. She closed her eyes, trying to bear it.

'Claire Tilson?' a man's voice spoke.

Expecting word of her coach, she lifted her head and opened her eyes.

But it was not a coachman. It was the red-haired stranger. Sir Orin Foley.

He smiled. 'It *is* you.'

Before she could rise to flee, he sat down next to her and pressed something sharp against her ribs.

'This is a knife,' he explained in an eerily calm voice. 'Make a sound and I will push it through your skin.'

She clutched her shawl.

'I thought that was you,' he went on in that mild tone. 'Not the other one. She would not have walked back from the Royal Crescent with a portmanteau, now, would she? And she wouldn't have answered to your name.'

He had been watching her, both at the house and here.

'I was quite surprised to see the other one show up here. In the same inn as I, no less. Then imagine my surprise when they walked precisely where I was bound.' He laughed. 'It did not take me long to surmise what was afoot. An attempt to fool me again.'

The hall of the inn was not without other people about, but everyone seemed preoccupied with their own affairs. No one noticed the look of alarm on her face, her silent pleas for help.

'Now.' He became firm. 'You will stand when I stand and come with me. We will go to my room until I figure out how to take you back to Ireland where you belong.'

He walked her to a deserted staircase and together they climbed to the third floor. When they reached it, Claire attempted to pull away.

The knife cut through her dress and pierced her skin. She ceased her struggle.

They walked down a long hallway.

'How fortuitous it is that they provided me with such a secluded room,' he remarked.

The hallway was empty and quiet.

He painfully gripped her arm while he worked the key in the door. The room was sparsely furnished. One bed. One chair. A bureau. He shoved her on to the bed and walked towards her, like the sinister figure of her dream.

Her head pounded and she closed her eyes.

And the memories came.

First of him trapping her in rooms of his country house, trying to seduce her, forcing her to kiss him, fearing that he would force more on her. Then other memories. It was like starting a book at the end and flipping the pages back to the beginning, to her childhood, her father smiling at her, her playing in the churchyard.

She doubled over with the onslaught. How ironic that she would be given back her memory at a time when her life could very well end.

But not if she could help it. She'd endured too much to let this man rob her of life.

'You have gone to a great deal of trouble to find me, Sir Orin.' She kept her voice calm.

He laughed again, a crazed look in his eyes. 'You must know I would do anything for you, my dear Claire.'

'Then let me go.'

He looked wounded. 'I can never let you go. I need you. My children need you. Their mother died, you see.' He made a smirk, then a sad face.

'I am so sorry to hear of your wife's death,' she said. 'Such a dear lady. Had she been ill?'

He smirked again. 'Not ill.'

A shiver went up her spine. Perhaps he had killed her.

This man was inhuman. 'How could you have left your children after they lost their poor mother?'

He had never paid the children much mind. She remembered—she *remembered*!—he was far more interested in her, the governess, than his own daughters.

He waved her words away as if they were inconsequential. 'Oh, my two sisters came to take care of them. They are spinsters, poor as church mice, and quite devoted to the girls. And to my son, though he is at school most of the time. They will be happy to live off my wealth and I am delighted for it, because it freed me to search for you. We can be married quickly, my dear Claire. In Scotland, perhaps.'

She would escape long before Scotland, she vowed. 'But I have had a better offer, Sir Orin. Yours does not signify.'

His expression darkened. 'That Captain? What can he offer you that I cannot?'

He thought she meant Lucien? If he were here, Sir Orin's life would be in danger.

But Lucien was not here, so she must fend for herself.

'Not the Captain,' she said scornfully. 'He has no title, after all. I meant Lord Stonecroft. He is a baron and that would make me a baroness. And he would marry me properly. In church.'

Sir Orin looked wounded. 'I am a baronet. That is almost as high. Besides, I have better things to offer you than some old man.'

His eyes raked her and she remembered when she'd first seen that look on his face. After that narrow escape she had confided in his wife and they hatched a plan for her to leave in secret.

His poor wife.

She lifted her arm and felt where the knife had cut her. Blood had seeped from the wound.

'I think you should release me, Sir Orin, and court me properly. After your period of mourning is up, that is.' She stood.

He pushed her back down. 'And have you marry that feeble Baron first? Never!'

She clutched her shawl and thought of Lucien. Her rescuer. She was alone now, though. She remembered now just how alone she was. But she also was not the same defeated person as that governess who'd first stepped on the deck of the *Dun Aengus*. She'd gained strength and courage. Lucien had taught her both.

* * *

Lucien listened to this unbelievable tale Lady Rebecca told him and he believed it. She fit the picture of the Lady Rebecca he imagined would emerge if his Lady Rebecca—Claire Tilson—regained her memory.

Although Lucien rather liked this version as well, aristocratic or not.

When she finished, he said, 'I believe you.'

She looked relieved.

'There is something I should tell you, though.' This time he would not hold back. 'We have a connection, you and I, and it is not a happy one?'

'A connection besides Claire?' she asked.

'Yes.' He took a breath. 'Your grandfather tricked my grandfather out of his property in Ireland. He impoverished my mother's family.'

She averted her gaze. 'That horrible man. I detested my grandfather. He was vindictive and cruel.' She looked back. 'Rather like my half-brother, as a matter of fact.'

He went on, 'That is why I travelled to Ireland and was returning on that packet boat. I went to provide financial assistance to my uncles. They'd struggled for many years and this year has been the hardest.'

Her expression turned sympathetic. 'I am so sorry for it. You must let me know if there is anything I can do to help them. My Garret would certainly understand.'

He was greatly surprised at her reaction. 'I am actually in a good position to help them.'

She sighed. 'You should have known my father, though. He was the dearest man.' She regarded him quizzically. 'And why are you here, Captain? Why did you call on Claire today?'

'Because I realised I wanted her more than I wanted a ship.'

She looked puzzled.

'I love her more than the sea.' It was that simple. 'The sea has been my life heretofore, but today I had a choice to make. Return to the sea and probably never see her again, or return here and convince her not to marry Stonecroft.' He turned serious. 'To marry me instead.'

'Did she tell you she would marry Stonecroft?' she asked.

'Yes.' And he'd hated her saying it. 'Last night when I thought I needed to say goodbye.'

She leaned forward and touched his arm, much as her likeness would have done. But her touch did not set his senses on fire.

'She is not marrying Stonecroft,' the lady said. 'She is leaving today by private coach to Bristol, to find her old school and see if they will help her procure another governess position.'

'Leaving?' He must stop her. Or join her.

A footman interrupted to announce Lord Brookmore.

Lucien and Lady Brookmore both stood.

Brookmore walked directly to his wife and kissed her. Then he noticed Lucien. 'I beg pardon. I did not know you had a caller.' He looked at his wife with a question in his eyes.

'Do not worry, Garret,' she said. 'He knows. Garret, this is Captain Roper. You know. The Captain who rescued Claire? I have just told him everything.'

'Lord Brookmore.' Lucien nodded.

'Garret.' She grasped his arm. 'The Captain is in love with Claire. Please tell us she has not left yet. He must see her.'

'I left her waiting for the coach to be ready,' he responded. 'There won't be much time.'

She pushed him. 'Go, then. You and the Captain. I will follow as soon as I find a hat and gloves.'

'What about Sir Orin?' her husband asked. 'He will think you are Claire.'

Lucien broke in. 'Tell me where she is. Follow later if you must.'

'I left her waiting in the hall of the White Hart. The hall attendant will know if the coach left or not.'

Lucien started for the door, but it opened again and Lord Stonecroft stood in the doorway.

'See here, Roper. I told you to stay away!' His face was puffed and red. He noticed Lord Brookmore and turned to Lady Rebecca—Lady Brookmore. 'Who the devil is this?'

Brookmore stepped forward. 'You do not remember me, sir? I am Brookmore. We were introduced in Lords.'

Stonecroft looked him up and down. 'What the devil are you doing here?'

Lucien refused to wait. 'I've had enough of you, Stonecroft. Step aside and let me by.'

Stonecroft sputtered. Lady Brookmore laughed and Lucien pushed the man aside.

He rushed out of the house and ran all the way to the White Hart. At this late morning hour, there were many people on the streets, especially near the inn which was right across from the Pump Room. He did not care who saw him.

He slowed only when he reached the door of the White Hart. He strode in, looking around. He did not see her, but beside an empty sofa sat her portmanteau, the one he'd purchased for her. He scanned the hall frantically.

A footman approached him, one of the men he'd spoken to the day before when he'd enquired about the stranger— Sir Orin Foley. 'Captain Roper? Remember that man you were asking about? I believe I saw him today. Right here, actually. A little while ago. With a lady.'

'I know his name now.' Lucien's heart pounded. 'Can we find his room?'

'We will ask the attendant.'

* * *

Claire frantically looked for some means of achieving her escape, especially as he came to sit next to her on the bed. She spread her shawl across her lap.

'Let me show you why you cannot marry that old man. Why you must marry me instead.' He face came nearer, until his lips touched hers.

She forced herself to remain still, but she gathered her shawl in each of her hands and pulled it taut. When she did not flinch from his kiss, Sir Orin became bolder. His hands moved to her breasts and she tolerated his fingers kneading into her flesh. Pretending she found it pleasurable she slid her hands, still holding her shawl, up his chest. When she reached his neck, she threw the shawl over his head and pulled him to the side. He tumbled on to the floor. She scrambled off the bed and ran for the door.

He had forgotten to lock it.

She threw open the door and ran down the hallway. He'd regained his feet, though, and was right on her heels.

He caught up with her at the top of the stairs. Remembering Ella's wild fight with the highwayman, Claire pulled Sir Orin's hair and pushed her fingers into his eyes.

'Stop this! Claire!' he yelled.

She kneed him in his groin and he let go momentarily. 'I'll kill you!' he growled.

He charged her.

Using the banister to assist her, she flung herself against the balustrade just as he reached the top step. He tried desperately to grab her, but she pressed herself against the balustrade and his hands slipped off her body.

With a cry of rage and fear, he tumbled down the long flight of stairs. Claire pressed her hands against her ears at the horrible sound.

She collapsed on to the step, clutching a baluster and afraid to move, but also afraid he'd rise up and come after her again. Other voices sounded. Someone bounded up the stairs. She closed her eyes, fearing another attack.

'Claire?'

Not his voice.

She opened her eyes.

Lucien crouched down beside her. 'It is all over,' he murmured, taking her into his arms. 'He won't hurt you again.'

Within an hour Claire was seated with Lucien, and Lord and Lady Brookmore, in the innkeeper's office at the White Hart Inn. Also present were the magistrate and coroner who had sought their testimony. By mutual agreement, they held nothing back, telling the two men the whole story. No more secrets, even though they knew their story would likely become public.

The magistrate was dumbfounded. 'By God, this sounds like one of the novels my wife and daughters rave about.'

No, too unbelievable to be a novel. Claire would not have believed it had she not lived it.

The coroner placed both hands on the desk. 'The man's death was obviously accidental. We should not need any more from you about this.'

'Those poor little children, both parents gone.' Claire remembered the darling little girls and their brother. Perhaps they were better off with devoted aunts to care for them instead of an insane murderer for a father.

She wrapped her shawl tighter around her. Her lovely Kashmir shawl. She'd insisted on returning to Sir Orin's room to get it, this shawl that had saved Lucien from the highwayman and her from Sir Orin.

She glanced at Lucien. 'I remember the children now. I think I remember everything.'

He took her hand and held it in his.

They were all dismissed and when they came out of the

office, Sir Richard, Ella and Cullen were waiting for them in the hall.

Ella ran up to Claire and hugged her. 'Oh, m'lady!' she cried.

Cullen had Claire's portmanteau.

Introductions were made and Sir Richard invited everyone to his house where they could dine in some privacy. They walked together as a group.

When they reached Sir Richard's house, Claire said, 'I should call upon Lord Stonecroft and Miss Attwood. I believe I owe them some explanation.'

'I'll go with you,' Lucien said.

'We have already told him the whole story,' the real Lady Rebecca said.

Would it do any good to tell him to open his heart to some lady who would appreciate him? Perhaps not today. She was still reeling from learning the truth.

And finally having her memory restored.

Lucien took her arm. 'If you all do not mind, I would like to walk with Lady—I mean—Claire on the Gravel Walk.

Ella and Lady Brookmore grinned.

'We do not mind at all,' the lady said.

Lucien led Claire away from their companions and they were soon rewarded with the privacy for which the Walk was known.

Claire smiled. 'I remember walking here when I was a girl.'

He put his arm around her. 'Your memory is back. You are whole again.'

'I wish it had been returned to me differently.' Not because of an attack by a mad man.

They walked in silence for a few steps, before Claire stopped. 'Lucien, are you certain you will not regret giving up this ship?'

He faced her. 'I know I will not regret it. When it came

down to it, losing you was more intolerable than losing a ship.' He smiled. 'I have become too used to you, I suppose, and I cannot imagine my life without the woman I fell in love with.'

She put her arms around his neck. 'When do you think that happened?'

He cocked his head. 'When you were mopping up fish guts, I think.'

She rose on tiptoe. 'I thought I merely depended on you. It took saying goodbye to you to show me I loved you.'

He lifted her closer so that her lips were inches from his. 'It took the fish guts for me.'

He closed the short distance between them and kissed her.

Epilogue

December 1816

Captain and Mrs Lucien Roper came in the back entrance of their country house laden with evergreens, holly and mistletoe to decorate the house for their first Christmas together.

They had settled where Lucien had begun life, in a property near the Lancashire village where he'd spent his lonely boyhood. It had been Claire's idea for them to settle there so he could reconcile with the parents who had so overlooked his needs as a boy. The end of the war had forced his father, the Admiral, to retire. Lucien's parents were truly together for the first time. It was not without its rough waters, but it helped that Viscount Waverland had abandoned Lucien's mother, now that she was older.

To Lucien's surprise, there were villagers who remembered him and who welcomed him home. So even if his parents did not pass muster, Lucien had the sense he belonged.

Claire was more optimistic about having his parents near. She, who'd never known her mother and, with her memory restored, newly grieved the loss of her father, considered any family connections as precious.

Their property was a modest farm with sea views that helped Lucien feel connected to where he'd spent most of his life. His prize money provided them a comfortable living and enabled him to employ servants and other workers who would have faced unemployment and hardship if he'd not hired them. The farm was a new challenge to Lucien, but he also had his eye on other ventures. Their proximity to Liverpool piqued his interest in investing in shipping or shipbuilding or even radical new ideas such as ships run by steam engines.

But that was all for another day. Today he was content to remain at home with Claire.

They left their snow-caked boots and outerwear in the entryway, dropped off their cuttings in the still room and walked up to the warmth of a fire in their drawing room.

Cullen walked in. 'We brought the mail from the village.' He handed the tray holding several envelopes to Lucien.

Lucien sorted through them.

Cullen and Ella were still with them, biding their time until Ella reached twenty-one so they could marry. Lucien could not imagine life without them. He was as attached to them as he'd been to his crew. Claire loved them like the siblings she'd never had.

'A letter for you from Lady Brookmore.' Lucien handed the envelope to Claire.

She took it excitedly. 'I am so glad to hear from her! She must have received my letter.'

Lord and Lady Brookmore had returned to Brookmore's estate in the Lake District and the nieces he adored. Lucien counted Brookmore and Rebecca among the few aristocrats he truly esteemed.

He glanced over at Claire.

Her lovely face glowed with pleasure as she opened her mail.

Lucien settled into a chair and read his own letter from Sir Richard who was in good health and spending Christmas in Bath.

'This is marvellous!' Claire cried.

She jumped up from her sofa and climbed into Lucien's lap so he could read over her shoulder.

She told him what was in the letter anyway. 'Rebecca writes that she and Garret are expecting a baby, too.'

She pressed a hand over her only slightly rounded belly and gave Lucien a contented smile.

'Listen to this!' She snuggled closer as she read on. 'She thinks she is due in June, too!' She put down the letter and put her arms around his neck. 'Would it not be a lark if we both have girls and if they both look alike?'

He kissed her on the cheek. 'I think it would be like lightning striking twice.'

And he silently said a prayer of thanks for being given what he thought he could never have. A home. A woman to love and to love him back. A family. A place to belong.

He would never take this for granted.

He kissed her again and held her close. 'Who would believe that so much happiness could result for so many when a governess and a lady swap places?'

* * * * *